C

The Five  Book Four

Toby Neighbors

Published by Mythic Adventure Publishing
2483 Partridge Loop, Post Falls, ID, 83854 USA

ISBN-13: 978-1497340763
ISBN-10: 1497340764

Copyeditor Jodie Young, Rooftop Copy
www.rooftopcopy.com

Cover design by Camille Denae

Find out more about Toby Neighbors and join the mailing list to receive an email whenever new titles become available at
www.tobyneighbors.com

Other Books By Toby Neighbors
Third Prince
Royal Destiny
The Other Side
Wizard Rising
Magic Awakening
Hidden Fire
Fierce Loyalty
Evil Tide
Wizard Falling
Lorik
Lorik The Protector
The New World

Dedication:
To Bella Story Neighbors
We can't wait for you to join our family

And to my forever love, Camille

Cry 'havoc!' kings; back to the stained field,
You equal-potents, fiery-kindled spirits!
Then let confusion of one part confirm
The other's peace; till then, blows, blood, and death!

- <u>The Life and Death of King John</u>
Act II, Scene I
William Shakespeare

Prologue

Brianna shook Zollin, but he didn't stir. He was breathing, but just barely. She looked up at the dragon, which was roaring in pain on the mountaintop. It was using its tail to try to pull her arrow from its chest. The thought that she had wounded the beast gave her a sense of satisfaction she had never known before. She only wished she still had her bow and could finish the job, but at that moment she knew she had to find a way to get Zollin off the mountain or he would die. The air was too thin, and he needed food, wine, and rest.

She had a length of rope that she kept slung over one shoulder. It wasn't enough to lower Zollin down the mountain, but it would come in handy. She still had her quiver of arrows attached to her belt. And she had a few odds and ends in her pockets. She looked around and realized that they were on a part of the mountain that would be impossible to descend, and going back into the cave was not an option. Their only chance would be to climb over the mountain and hopefully find a way down.

"Zollin," she said loudly, slapping him in the face. "You have to wake up!"

His eyes fluttered and then closed again. She tried to lift him, but she couldn't. Tears stung her eyes. She had to save him, but she didn't know how. Then she heard the sound she had been dreading, the *whoosh, whoosh, whoosh* of the dragon's wings.

She looked up and saw the beast taking flight. She knew she had to do something. There was still snow on the sides of the mountain, and she grabbed a handful and dropped it on Zollin's face. He sputtered, and she rubbed his cheeks with the snow. His skin turned bright red and he opened his eyes.

"What are you doing?" he said in a weak voice.

"We have to get off this mountain, or we're going to die," she told him.

"Can't," he whispered. "Leave me here."

"I will not," she said. "I'm jumping off the ledge, Zollin. I'm going to pull you to the edge, and we're falling off together. Are you listening to me?" she said, slapping him hard in the face when his eyes started to close. They snapped back open and she told him her plan.

"There was an avalanche," she said. "The valley is full of snow. All you have to do is slow us down enough that we aren't killed. Can you do it?"

"No," he said. "I'm too weak."

"Then we'll die together," she said. She pushed him to the edge of the ledge. Looking down at the drop was terrifying, but she could see the snow far below. Her hope was that the snow would soften their landing.

"Stay with me, Zollin!" she shouted.

She glanced up and saw the dragon wheel toward them. She lifted Zollin's head and shoulders so she could wrap the rope around him. Then she lay on top of him and wrapped the rope around her back as well. The sounds of the dragon were growing louder. She could hear the deep growl in its voice and the flapping of its wings as the beast swooped down toward them.

"We're going to die if you don't help me, Zollin!" she screamed as she tightened the rope.

"I love you," she whispered. And then she rolled them both off the ledge.

* * *

A power too great for the eyes and minds of mortal men erupted in the far north. It sent a shock wave roaring through the Five Kingdoms. It was like thunder that shakes a house and cows all inside. Offendorl, Master of the Torr, was knocked off his feet. His brittle bones, centuries old, snapped as he fell, but even though the pain was agony, his mind was consumed by the shock of power.

Zollin, the wizard in the north, the bright flame of power that Offendorl had felt blossom years ago, was back and brighter than ever before. For months now, the young wizard had been able to hide his power. Now suddenly, it was back, and it had grown, more than even Offendorl had thought possible. It was as if the boy were a roaring fountain of raw power. It took a huge effort for Offendorl to pull his mind away from the radiance that he felt from the boy. They were separated by hundreds of miles, and yet the ancient wizard felt like he was standing in the sunlight after a long, cold winter.

He was in the tower of the Torr, a massive, round structure that stood like a silent sentinel over the Grand City of Osla. Armies were massing along the coast, marching toward Brimington Bay, from which they would sail north under Offendorl's command. The Master of the Torr was over three centuries old. His mind was sharp and his magic strong, but his body was like an antique, still functional, but brittle. The floor of his chamber was polished stone, worn smooth by the master's constant pacing, and his body had broken against it. He closed his eyes and focused on healing himself. It was difficult with the distraction of Zollin's power. It was like trying to sleep in bright sunlight that floods through closed eyelids. The shine of power seemed to invade his mind and draw his attention away from the matters at hand.

The pain didn't help. He was used to pain: it was always with him, and although his magic allowed his mind to bypass the pain, his body was in shock. It took a long time to heal the many fractures and bruises. Only then did he rise up off the floor. He moved slowly, careful not to hurry; he didn't want to have another accident. He sank into a thickly padded chair and rested his hands on the smooth finish of the massive desktop in front of him. Without moving he levitated a crystal decanter that was filled with a mixture of spirits, many of which were decades old. The decanter rose up and floated across the space between the bar and the desk. It was followed by a goblet with jewels and gold decorating the outside. The drink seemed to pour itself.

Offendorl drank and then settled further into his chair. He loathed the thought of the journey before him. He didn't like to leave the Torr. It was too inconvenient. He had spent centuries gathering everything he might need around him, but now he needed the boy in the north—the young wizard named Zollin. Offendorl had sent three of his most capable wizards to bring the boy into their fold, but Zollin had defeated all of them. Then he had sent the twins, but with so many wizards spread far across the Five Kingdoms, his strength had waned, and he had lost control of the witch. It was just one more problem he would have to deal with, but first he needed Zollin to shift the balance of power back to him alone.

So now Offendorl would go with the armies of Osla and Felxis, sailing up the coast to attack Yelsia from the west, while the armies of Ortis and Baskla invaded Yelsia from the east. The two-prong attack would crush the Yelsian army and force Zollin to join the Torr. The young wizard had defied Offendorl, an act no one had even attempted before. Even Offendorl's master had died without a fight when Offendorl had usurped his mentor's place as head of the Torr. Zollin was like a dream, alluring but untouchable and totally out of his control, but that would change, the ancient wizard thought.

He smiled, a rare sight, for the Master of the Torr rarely felt amused or excited. Most things in life held no more pleasure for the wizard, but power still made him giddy, and once he controlled Zollin his own powers would increase exponentially. Offendorl strengthened his resolve to capture the boy and add Zollin's bright, billowing power to his own.

Chapter 1

It felt like a dream. He was falling and he couldn't stop it. Icy wind was whipping around him, and his arms wrapped around Brianna instinctively. He opened his eyes and saw the blur of gray granite, white snow, and blue ice as they hurtled toward the canyon floor. He knew the only way they would survive was if he used his magic, but he was afraid. Saving himself from the dragon had taken all his magical strength, and it felt as if his power was merely a white-hot spark deep inside him. His skin and face were stinging with cold, but inside he was roasting, as if the tiny spark were radiating such intense heat he could hardly stand it. He was afraid that tapping into his magic would kill him, but then he realized that if he didn't do something he would die anyway, and Brianna with him.

Brianna was in his arms, and if he had to choose how to die, this would be the way. They were tied together with rope that Brianna had carried since they had left Brighton's Gate. They hadn't needed it to scale the steep mountains because Zollin had levitated them with his magic, but after the dragon had almost crushed Zollin in its cave, Brianna had used the rope to tie them together, and then she had pushed them off the ledge. Brianna had been so brave, Zollin thought. She had saved him, if only for a moment longer. He knew that no matter what it cost or how badly he was hurt, he had to save Brianna. His love for her fed the flame of his power, and although it was like reaching his bare hands into a blacksmith's forge, he took hold of his magic and slowed their descent.

He had wanted them to land softly on the ice and snow below, but there wasn't enough time. He managed to slow their descent only marginally and rotated himself so that he landed on the bottom. The impact with the snow, which had filled the canyon after an avalanche caused by the battle Zollin had fought with the dragon in the beast's lair deep inside the mountain, was much softer than the boulder-strewn canyon floor, but to Zollin it felt as if he had slammed into solid bedrock. He felt a terrible, rending snap, and then everything went black.

* * *

Brianna remembered rolling off the ledge with Zollin in her arms. After that she had shut her eyes and held her breath. The fall took less than three seconds, but it felt much longer. She had felt Zollin holding her tight, then suddenly they hit the snow and the jarring impact was terrible. Brianna felt as if she had been kicked by a giant horse, but she was alive.

She raised her head and opened her eyes. They were surrounded by snow. The force of their fall had plunged them deep into the snow, ice, and debris from the avalanche. The light was dim, but she could make out Zollin's face. He looked peaceful, like he was sleeping. Brianna pushed her aching body off Zollin, causing snow to fall on top of them. She took a deep breath and looked at Zollin again. Something was wrong with him somehow. She wasn't sure what it was, but she knew she needed to get him up and out of the snow.

"Zollin," she said out loud, her voice sounding strange in their snowy hole. "Zollin, wake up."

She patted his face, but there was no response. She leaned close, placing her ear next to his nose and listened. He wasn't breathing. Terror of a magnitude Brianna had never experienced struck like lightning. Zollin wasn't breathing. He was dead or dying and she didn't know what to do.

"No, Zollin!" she screamed. "Don't you die! Don't you leave me! Zollin?"

She slapped him hard in the face. She knew that if he died she would die, but fear of her own mortality wasn't what scared her the most. She loved him, and more than anything in the world, she wanted to spend her life with Zollin. She had no more doubts, no second thoughts or contingency plans. He was her life, and without him she was lost.

"Wake up!" she screamed again, this time slamming her fist down on his chest like a hammer blow. "You wake up and talk to me Zollin! You aren't allowed to die!"

She hit him again and then again. For some reason it felt good to hammer away at Zollin, to fully embrace the fear and terror she was feeling and act it out, even if it meant hurting him. She hit him again and screamed at the top of her lungs. This time there was an answering cry, but not from Zollin. The dragon roared in reply, its terrible scream echoing off the mountains and sending more snow toppling down on Zollin and Brianna.

She grabbed snow and rubbed it over Zollin's face until his skin was bright red, then she leaned forward, her hands on his stomach, and kissed him. Then she lifted herself back up, hoping for some subtle sign of life. She hit him again, and tears rolled down her checks.

"No, Zollin!" she cried. "Don't leave me! I love you, Zollin. Please, don't leave me."

She leaned forward again, and this time she saw his lips move. It was a tiny movement, but she saw it. More importantly, she felt his breath as it gushed out from between his lips. She sat up again, and then she understood. She had pushed the air out of his lungs when she lay down on him.

"Breathe, Zollin!" she ordered him sternly. "Breathe!"

She leaned forward again, this time blowing air into his face. She sat up and watched his chest. It wasn't inflating the way it should if he were breathing, she realized. She needed to get air into his lungs. She leaned forward again, this time pulling his chin down to open his mouth and placing her lips over his and blowing air into his mouth. She felt the air rush in and then come back out of his nose. She pinched his nose and tried again. This time she could feel his chest inflate with air. She let go and sat up again, pressing on his stomach as she did. Again the air whooshed out of his mouth. She leaned forward and repeated the process. Over and over she breathed for Zollin, telling him not to give up and letting hot tears drip onto his face.

* * *

Zollin saw light. It was bright and warm, and he felt himself moving toward it. He wasn't walking; he felt weightless and still, but he could sense that he was moving, that he was in control of the movement. The light felt good. It was more than simple warmth, it was as if the light were love. He felt loved and accepted and welcomed. He wanted to go to the light and stay there forever. He could feel every inch of his body and every part of him felt good. It was an ecstasy like nothing he had ever felt or even imagined that he could feel. He was so happy that he felt like laughing for joy.

Then he heard a voice. It wasn't coming from the light, but from somewhere else, a dark place that was cold and hard and frightening.

Don't leave me, the voice said. *Don't you dare leave me.*

Zollin was conflicted. He wanted to drift away, into the light, but for some reason the voice made him hesitate. He knew

17

he didn't want to move back into the dark, but there was a note of desperation in the voice that made him pause. He couldn't remember what had happened or how he had gotten to the this place, where the light was calling to him. He didn't associate the voice with anyone or anything. He knew that he had lived a different life, but it was so dim and distant from the light that he didn't want to remember it.

Wake up! the voice said. But Zollin didn't think he was dreaming. In fact he had never felt so alive before in his life. He decided to ignore the voice and go into the light, but then pain racked his body. It was a sharp pain that started in his chest and drove out the ecstasy. Over and over the pain shot through him.

I love you, Zollin, he heard, even though his ears were ringing so loudly now that it was hard to make out the words. *Please don't leave me.*

Then he remembered Brianna. She was calling to him from the dark place of pain. She was desperate for him. He could see her in his mind, jet black hair surrounding her beautiful face. Her high, proud check bones and fierce, intelligent eyes were as tangible in his mind as the light. He didn't notice that he was moving away from the light now. He was simply thinking of Brianna, remembering her long, shapely fingers, the graceful way she moved, the beautiful sound of her laugh.

Then the pain came again, and this time it was hot like fire. His magic seemed to be cooking him from the inside out. He knew he had to embrace the pain to see Brianna again. He had to give himself to the pain and let it take him wherever it wanted. He was afraid and not sure what to do, but then he heard the voice again.

Breathe, she told him.

Yes, he realized. He needed to breathe. He focused on breathing, on pulling the air into his lungs and blowing it back out. It was difficult. In fact it was the hardest thing he had ever tried to do. His body ached with the effort, but he didn't give up, and the more he breathed the easier it became. Then, there was a snap. It felt almost like popping his fingers, but with the snap came a deeper awareness. He could remember everything. The dragon, the mountains, falling with Brianna in his arms and the dreadful crash at the bottom of the canyon. His arms, neck, and shoulders were stiff, and his head ached dreadfully. He could hear Brianna crying, but opening his eyes was difficult.

"Oh, Zollin," she said, bowing down so that he couldn't see her anymore.

Her cries were muffled, and Zollin felt confused. He could see the gray walls of snow above him and a bright patch of blue sky high above. But he couldn't see Brianna. He tried lifting his head, but the pain was too intense. It shot sharp stabs down his neck and into his arms and chest.

"Brianna," he said weakly.

"Zollin," she said, and he felt his body shift. It was like being nudged by an invisible hand.

"I can't see you," he said.

She raised herself up and looked at him with a worried expression.

"You can't see?"

"No, I can see you now. I just couldn't see you when you were bent over."

"I'm sorry," she said, wiping at something. "I've gotten your shirt all wet."

"No, it's okay. I can't even feel it," he said.

"You can't feel that?" she said.

"No," he said.

"What about this?"

"I don't feel anything," he said.

Brianna looked at him and there was something in her face that Zollin knew he should recognize, but he didn't know what it was. Why did she look so afraid? They were alive, they were together, what could possibly be wrong?

"Zollin," she said in a trembling voice. "You can't feel your legs?"

"Of course I can," he said. But then he realized he couldn't.

He was hurting everywhere from his chest up, but below that, he felt nothing at all. No pain, not the cold snow, not Brianna's tears, not even his magic.

* * *

The boat was rocking, and Quinn was leaning against the ship's railing. His stomach seemed to clench and lurch with every movement the ship made. His lips were chapped and every muscle ached. He knew he was dehydrated, but even the thought of water made him nauseous. Still, his mind focused on his duty. He had been sent to get Zollin and bring him back to Gwendolyn. His heart seemed to soar whenever he thought of her. She was stunningly beautiful, although he couldn't remember exactly what she looked like, and his desire for her was like a wild fire. Being with her, pleasing her, doing whatever she wanted him to do: that was his life's ambition. There were other things in the back of his mind, important things, but he resolutely ignored them.

The ship he and Mansel had been ordered to take north was sailing smoothly. The wind was propelling them along, and the

Great Sea of Kings was not like sailing across the ocean. The waves were smaller, and the Great Sea was not saltwater so there was no briny smell to further sicken his stomach. Still, it always took Quinn several days to overcome seasickness. He couldn't do anything until the nausea passed except huddle down against the railing and wait.

Mansel had been sick too, but his own sea legs had returned much more quickly than during his first time at sea. Quinn and Mansel had been sent to Osla to protect Prince Wilam, who was serving in the Grand City as Yelsia's ambassador. They had sailed south, and Mansel had been sick for two whole days before the debilitating nausea had finally passed. They had survived an attack by pirates, but then Quinn had left Mansel behind in Cape Sumar. It was merely a stroke of good fortune that their paths had crossed again as Quinn led the Prince north through Falxis, and although Mansel had not brought up the incident, he had not forgotten it. Now, he let his anger against his mentor burn, and he used that anger to strengthen his resolve. He couldn't let Quinn steal the credit for bringing Zollin back to Gwendolyn. Just one look at the Lady of the Sea, as he had come to think of her, was all it took for him to know that he would do anything to be near her. Quinn was in Mansel's way, and although he owed Quinn everything he knew about swordsmanship and fighting, he couldn't let the older man steal Gwendolyn's affections.

He unbuckled his sword belt and left all his weapons in a neat pile on the deck. The ship was small and they didn't have private quarters, but he doubted that any of the seamen would bother his things. He walked toward Quinn, hardening his resolve.

"Still sick?" he asked.

"Aye," Quinn said through gritted teeth.

21

"Here, let me help you up. I think you'll fare better near the rear of the ship."

"What?" Quinn asked.

Mansel didn't try to explain. He just took hold of Quinn's arm and hoisted the man up. Quinn was too weak to resist. His legs were too shaky to support his own weight, and he leaned into Mansel.

"Sorry," Mansel said, and then he shoved Quinn hard.

Quinn felt the hard railing of the deck dig into his lower back, and then his feet flew up into the air. That terrifying moment seemed to last ages. He could feel his center of gravity shifting out over the water. His legs kicked but they touched nothing. His hands scratched at the railing, trying desperately to find something to hold onto, something that would stop his plunge into the water below. Even though his muscles were galvanized with adrenaline, he couldn't hold himself up. He saw the ship's rail and Mansel's face as he fell. Then the water covered him in cold darkness.

Mansel saw Quinn splash into the water, but the ship was moving swiftly along, and his mentor was soon swept away. Some of the sailors witnessed Mansel's treachery, but the warrior merely turned and glared at the sailors. None of the seamen wanted to follow Quinn overboard, so they went on with their work without saying a word. One of the sailors in the rear of the ship tossed a wooden bucket overboard, but no one took notice. Mansel strapped on his weapons and settled down on the deck with his back to the mast.

Quinn was not a strong swimmer, but he was able to get his head above water in time to see the ship sailing away. Around him he could see nothing but dark, cold water. The water wasn't cold enough to be life-threatening, but it was a shock to Quinn's body, which was still weak from sea sickness. Then he saw the bucket. It came flying over the rear of the ship and splashed into the water not far from Quinn. He swam to it and found it bobbing in the water. He wrapped his arms around the bucket and felt the tiny vessel's buoyancy hold him up in the water. His shivering body relaxed and let the bucket take his weight.

He couldn't believe what was happening. He had been shoved overboard by Mansel. He couldn't imagine why, and in fact his mind was struggling just to comprehend the situation. All he knew for certain was that he had to hang onto the bucket. His stomach churned, but there was nothing left to vomit. He dry-heaved, his body shivering from cold, his mind struggling to understand.

Then he remembered... everything. He and Mansel had been sent on a mission to bring Prince Wilam safely back to Yelsia. Then they had met the witch in Lodenhime. When Quinn thought of Gwendolyn he felt an emotional tug, but he was no longer bewitched by her. He felt anger rise up inside him, stronger than the seasickness that had plagued him. He couldn't believe that a woman had somehow pulled him away from his duty. He had never experienced anything like the witch's power before. He could remember what he did and even why he did it, but he couldn't isolate why he was so enthralled with the woman. She was beautiful, he knew that, even though he couldn't remember exactly what she looked like. Still, he didn't feel affection for her, it was more like animal passion.

He knew two things for certain as he clung to the bucket. First, Prince Wilam was being used by the witch. It didn't take a master strategist to understand the benefit of having the Crown Prince of Yelsia in the witch's service. He knew that somehow he needed to get to the Prince and rescue him from the witch's power, but he had no idea how he could do that without falling under her spell again.   Secondly, Quinn knew that Mansel was going to Yelsia to fetch Zollin back to the witch. He couldn't believe how stupid he had been. He remembered that he had planned to leave Mansel behind as well. He remembered how he had felt in his zeal to please Gwendolyn. He shook his head angrily. He should have been on his guard, but he had been consumed with his seasickness since the ship had set sail. Now, he was in trouble. He couldn't see land in any direction. He knew the ship had been sailing north, but he had no idea how far they had come or even how long they had been at sea.

He kicked his feet and tried to look for any signs of land, but all he could see was water in every direction. He was lost at sea, and that prospect filled him with dread. His son needed him, but he was completely helpless and dependent on a wooden bucket just to stay alive.

Chapter 2

"Oh, no," Zollin said softly.

He was trying to move his legs but nothing was happening. He tried to delve into his magic but he couldn't. He felt completely helpless.

"I'm hurt," he said, his voice shaking slightly.

"Okay," Brianna said. "It's going to be okay."

"No, I think my back is broken."

"Okay," Brianna said again, her face a mask of restrained panic. "You just need to heal yourself, that's all."

"I can't," Zollin said, fighting the tears that were stinging his eyes. "I can't feel my magic."

"What do you mean?"

"I mean it's not there. I'm helpless."

The tears couldn't be contained. He was in pain and he was afraid that he was going to die, but what shook him the most was the realization that he couldn't feel his magic. He was a wizard with no powers.

"You mean you lost your magical powers? How?"

"I don't know," he said, his breath coming in ragged sobs. "I don't know if I lost it or used it all up or if I just can't feel it."

"Okay," Brianna said, as she stroked his face and wiped the tears away. "It's going to be okay. I promise it will. We just need to figure out what to do next."

She looked around. There wasn't much to see. They were at least ten feet below the surface of the snow in what amounted to a small crater formed by the impact of their falling bodies.

"We need food and a way to stay warm," she said. "Maybe if you have some wine and some rest you could get your power back."

"Maybe," Zollin said, but he didn't really believe it.

He had been exhausted by his magical powers before. Once, when Kelvich, the old sorcerer who had taken Zollin under his tutelage, had first started helping Zollin discover and control his power, he had been tied to a post for hours in the freezing cold. He had been exhausted and unable to free himself, but he could still feel his magic then. Now, however, he felt nothing. It was as if the lower half of his body was gone.

"Okay, so we've got to get out of this hole," Brianna said, trying to remain positive and productive. "I can climb out. Then I'll find our supplies and get you some food. Are you okay to stay here?"

"I don't really have a choice," Zollin said bitterly.

"All right," Brianna said. Then she leaned over him again and stared fiercely into his eyes. "We're together," she said. "We're both alive and we can make it through this. Don't you dare give up on me, Zollin."

"I won't," he said, though his voice, quivering and cracking, was unconvincing.

"You stick with me. It won't be easy, but one way or another we're getting out of this mess. I love you, and you promised you'd never give up on me, remember?"

Zollin nodded. He did remember. He remembered being on the road with Brianna, happy and carefree, when she suddenly withdrew her affections. She had been afraid that Zollin was using his magic to influence her feelings. Zollin had been afraid that she would never trust him again, but after weeks of struggling as they pursued and fought the dragon, she finally came back to him. He had her heart now, and even though he was hurting and scared, he resolutely fixed his mind on doing whatever it took to get Brianna out of the Northern Highland Mountains.

"Okay, try to stay awake," she told him.

Then she stood up. It was difficult at first because there was so little room around his legs. She was afraid she might step on him and hurt him without realizing it. But once she got her feet set, she was able to stand up. The top of the snow was much higher than she was, but she had her dagger, and she went to work chiseling out a place right at knee height that she could use as a place to put her feet. She stepped up and braced herself with her arms on either side of the snow cave. She repeated the process again, but this time she was almost tall enough to reach the top of the snow, and when she tried to brace herself her arms sank into the snow where it was not as compacted. After a moment's struggle to get her balance and make sure she wasn't going to fall onto Zollin, she made another small hole and then put her dagger back in its sheath on her belt.

When she stepped up to the third hole she was more careful. She could see above the snow now. It was a weird feeling to see what looked like the ground right at eye level. She began digging in the snow with her hands, careful to toss the snow so that it didn't fall back down into the hole. It was hard work. Soon her back and legs were aching with fatigue and her hands were burning from the cold, but she was able to crawl from the larger hole into the smaller one she had created. From there she was able to get on top of the snow.

Her feet sank down in the loose snow, so that her leg was buried almost up to her knee. She took a few clumsy steps and then looked back. The hole seemed dark and foreboding, like and open grave. She looked up and saw that the sun was sinking behind the mountains. What little warmth the sun gave to the northern range of mountains would soon be gone, and Zollin would freeze to death if she didn't do something to save him.

"I made it," she shouted. "I made it to the top, Zollin. Can you hear me?"

"Yes, good job," he replied, but his voice was frail and weak.

"I'm going to find our supplies and come right back. Do you hear?"

"Yes," he said.

"Good. You stay awake."

She didn't wait for a response. She knew it would take all of her strength just to get across the snow field. But just after she had begun moving, she suddenly stopped to think. She knew right where they had left their supplies, but she had no idea how much snow now covered them. What if she struggled to get to the supplies only to realize that she couldn't dig them out? Fear felt like it was dragging her down deeper into the snow. She had no bow, no food, and no other way to get food. Their supplies were all they had to survive on. They were the only hope.

She struggled through the snow for almost an hour before finding what she was looking for. They had left their supplies near the foot of a cliff that had a twisted tree growing from it. The tree was unmistakable, but she had trouble spotting it again. She could tell the snow was angling down when she finally spotted the gnarled trunk. It had been hit by the snow and ice, and the limbs had been broken off. She hurried as fast as she could to the tree and began digging. At first the snow was easy to move. She

28

shoveled it aside with her hands. But then the snow became packed and frozen. She had to use her dagger to break up the packed snow and then shovel out the chunks she had broken free. It was exhausting work, but she knew she needed to find their supplies or Zollin might die.

It took over an hour, and the shadows were so deep that she could hardly see when her hand finally felt something other than snow. She renewed her furious digging and uncovered one of their packs. It had food inside, but no wine. She was thirsty and tired, but she kept digging. It took only a few more minutes to locate the other pack. Then she had to find their canteens and the bottle of wine. It was completely dark by the time she had all their supplies. The stars twinkled in the night sky but cast almost no light in the dark canyon. She had to make her way back slowly, following the trail of broken snow she had made earlier mostly by feel. She only hoped that she wasn't too late to help Zollin.

* * *

Zollin lay on the snow and tried not to think about the pain in his upper body or the absence of pain in his legs. He was frightened and felt absolutely helpless. Even raising his head brought a searing pain to his neck and shoulders that made his vision go dim. He knew that if he could work his magic he could heal his body, but he felt so weak and tired that all he wanted to do was sleep. The fact that he couldn't feel his magic scared him more than anything. He knew that without it he would die. There was simply no way that Brianna could carry him back over the mountains. A healthy man would spend a month, perhaps even longer, traversing the jagged cliffs and treacherous canyons that Zollin had levitated them over using his power. If that power was gone, he would die.

He had faced death before, but never in such a helpless state. In most cases, he hadn't had time to think about what he was doing or how close to death he really was. Even when he had gone down into the cave, which had been frightening, he was at least armed with his magic. Now he was completely helpless, and with every minute the snow towering over him looked more like the walls of a grave.

He fought sleep, knowing that if Brianna returned and he was unconscious, there was nothing she could do to save him. She had to get back with food, and he had to be awake when she got there. As darkness began to fall a new fear gripped him. What if Brianna didn't return? What if she had abandoned him or gotten hurt herself? The dragon may have returned and devoured her. If so, he would die all alone.

He was shivering uncontrollably as the stars came out. One by one they lit the night sky, twinkling far above him. He focused on the stars as he struggled to keep his eyes open. He tried to see patterns in the stars but it was too difficult. His mind seemed to be in a fog, and just forming coherent thoughts was difficult. He wanted to sleep so badly he was on the verge giving in when he heard Brianna calling his name.

"Zollin?" she said. "I'm coming! Can you hear me?"

She had been calling for a while, hoping that he might answer and help her find him in the dark.

"I hear you," he said, but his voice was soft and slurred. She didn't hear him.

"Zollin!" she called out again.

"I'm here," he said as loudly as he could.

* * *

Brianna finally reached the hole and was at least relieved that it seemed darker than the landscape around her. She had been afraid that she would fall into the hole and make their predicament worse.

"Oh, Zollin, I can't believe I found you," she said. "It's so dark I could hardly see anything."

"You did good," he said, but his voice was so weak she could hardly make out the words.

She had the strap from the wine bottle around her neck, and she made sure she had one canteen and as much food as she could get in one of the packs. The extra weight made the harrowing decent into the dark hole even more frightening, but she was careful, and even though it took several more minutes, she climbed safely down to Zollin.

"You stay with me!" she told him. "I've got food and wine."

There was no room in the hole to stand or sit so that she wasn't on top of Zollin, but she couldn't help that now. She uncorked the wine and raised his head slightly. Zollin grimaced in pain. She let the wine, cold and sharply flavored, run slowly into his mouth. He swallowed like a baby bird and then opened his mouth for more.

She spent the next half hour feeding him. He grew stronger, the pain less severe, but his magic didn't return.

"I still don't feel anything," Zollin said. "I can't even feel your weight."

"What about your magic? Can you do anything?"

He concentrated on kindling a flame. It was one of the most simple spells he knew, a trick he had done since he had first discovered his magical abilities, but nothing happened. It was like trying to raise his leg. The effort seemed familiar, but there was absolutely no movement.

"I can't," he said, panting from exertion. "It's no use. I'm going to die in this hole."

"Don't say that," Brianna said.

"We'll freeze," Zollin said.

"No, I'll keep you warm."

She laid down on top of him, adjusting her weight so that he could breath easily. The snow was cold around them, but it also acted to insulate their meager body heat. Zollin closed his eyes and fell asleep almost immediately. His mind was troubled, but he was too weak to resist the frightening dreams. He saw dragons and terrible wizards. There was lightning and thunder, billowing flames, and the hideous screams of people he could not save.

When the sun rose, casting a dull gray light into the mountains, Brianna found Zollin fast asleep. His skin was bluish and his eyes were darting back and forth under his thin eyelids. She sat up, her body aching and sore. Then she woke Zollin up. His eyes fluttered open.

"How are you feeling?" she asked.

"Like I fell off a cliff," he said in a whispery voice.

"Can you feel your magic?"

"No," he said after searching for it. He was numb all over. Brianna had put the empty pack under his head and covered them with blankets, but he was laying on the snow and the cold was slowly taking over his body. He couldn't feel the hypothermia, but it was only a matter of time before the freezing temperatures ruined the skin and the tissue in his back and legs.

"Well, we need a plan," Brianna said. "We can't stay here."

"You should go," he told her. "Just leave me here. There's no way I can make it out of the mountains now."

"I'm not leaving you," she said.

"I'm dying, Brianna . . ." he paused as the reality of his admission sank in. He was dying; he had finally admitted it. Now, fear gave way to relief. There would be no more fighting the inevitable. "We both know it. If you stay, it will hurt your chances of getting out of the mountains alive."

Brianna laughed. She couldn't believe what she was hearing. Zollin seemed invincible. He had fought mercenaries, assassins, wizards, and a dragon. But now he was giving up, and for some reason Brianna found that funny.

"What are you laughing at?" Zollin asked.

"You think I can survive in the mountains without you?" she said. "I don't have any way to make a fire. We're almost out of rations. I lost my bow so I can't hunt, even if I could somehow get lucky enough to find game without you. Even if I had food and could build a fire, I know there is simply no way I can climb back through the mountains alone. Do you hear what I'm saying, Zollin? If you give up, we'll both die."

Anger, fear and resentment crowded Zollin's mind, each struggling to hold his attention. He had been all right thinking only about his own death, but he hadn't realized what going back alone really meant for Brianna.

"I can't help you," Zollin said in an exasperated tone. "I can't even move."

"You can think, though, so think of something."

He racked his brain for some glimmer of hope, but there was none. He could feel the cold seeping into his body from the snow all around him. He wanted to close his eyes and sleep. It was such a struggle to keep them open that he felt if he couldn't sleep he would die.

"Don't you dare go to sleep on me, Zollin," Brianna said angrily. "You have to fight this. You have to help me."

"I want to help you but I can't think of any way to do anything for you. I can't feel my magic. I'm crippled. There isn't even a sliver of hope."

Before the words were out of his mouth he realized he was wrong. There was something: it was a long shot, but it was possible.

"What?" Brianna said, noticing the look on Zollin's face as he pondered the idea.

"I can't feel my magic," he explained. "But I might still be able to control the magic in my staff."

"Oh, Zollin. I didn't even think to look for it when I found our supplies."

"It's okay. It was near the packs. Can you look for it?"

"Of course. I'll go right now," she said as she struggled to her feet.

"Hurry, I don't know how much longer I've got."

"I will," she promised.

Then she was leaning down to kiss him. His lips felt rough and dry, almost like empty husks, and he was already closing his eyes when she pulled back to look at him. Fear sank icy claws into her stomach and made her shiver as she realized just how little time she actually had.

Chapter 3

Offendorl was on the road to Brimington Bay. He hated traveling, even though he was attended by his tongueless, eunuch servants and rode in a lavish wagon pulled by eight draft horses. His carriage was padded and had high windows that allowed air to flow through. The air was hot, of course, dry and sandy. Osla was the wealthiest of the Five Kingdoms, but it was miserably hot almost year-round. High in his tower, the air was much cleaner and cooler than at ground level, but traveling on the dusty road was irksome. Offendorl had to hold his anger in check to keep from destroying every living creature in the immediate vicinity.

He was being escorted by a squad of soldiers, even though their protection was completely unnecessary. Offendorl had crafted the plan to invade Yelsia. He wasn't interested in conquest, at least not at the moment. What he wanted was Zollin. The young wizard was hiding in the north, and Offendorl planned on using the combined might of the other kingdoms to bring the boy under his control. He had left the logistics of mobilizing their armies to the individual kings. King Belphan should have his troops mustered at Brimington Bay and enough ships requisitioned to carry them all north. They would join forces with King Zorlan of Falxis at Lixon Bay, and together the two armies would then invade Yelsia from the west. It was a good plan, simple enough that the kings could understand it, even if they weren't fully convinced that it was the right course of action. Zorlan had been easy enough to win over. Once he saw that King Belphan and King Oveer of Ortis were committed to Offendorl's plan, he joined them. King Ricard of Baskla was a different matter entirely. He was a shrewd man who had no interest in war, but he couldn't deny the rumors that a dragon was loose in Yelsia and that King Felix was harboring a wizard. This was a breech of a centuries-old treaty, and not even King Ricard could deny that. Offendorl doubted that Baskla would contribute many resources to the invasion, but the stubborn King's time would come.

The master wizard gazed out the small window that was near his padded, bed-like seat in the carriage. Most of the people on the road were stopping to stare at his procession. He had no feelings for the people; they meant nothing to him. He no longer felt a desire for human companionship, or any need for other people. They were simply resources to him, no different than chickens. Women were no longer alluring, and friendship was mere sentimentality in his mind. Food brought him no pleasure, and though wine and food helped restore his physical and magical strength, he no longer had an appetite. After three hundred years, there was nothing new or exciting in the world. His only desires were to expand his power and to control everything around him.

In the tower he was the absolute master. In the Council of Kings the leaders of the Five Kingdoms feared him. They bowed under his influence, even if they didn't literally bow before him. He ruled as surely as any king, yet he did not want to be bothered with details or mortal concerns. That was what the other wizards in the Torr had not understood, Branock in particular. They wanted to sit on thrones and be seen as rulers, but Offendorl had no need for the trappings of royalty. He preferred to keep his strength hidden until it was needed. That was how he had held his position as Master of the Torr for over two hundred years.

Zollin wasn't a person to Offendorl. He didn't want the young wizard to join his order; he merely wanted the boy's power. Zollin was merely a vessel, a tool for Offendorl to use or perhaps a weapon to wield. He would have the boy, that was certain. He would use whatever means were necessary to bring the wizard under his control. The fact that Zollin had bested three of Offendorl's best wizards did not concern the ancient Master of the Torr. Offendorl's power was unmatchable and his knowledge so vast that he was certain no one could defeat him. His mentor had always tried to foster the gifts of the wizards around him, which was one reason why Offendorl had been able to rise up and usurp his place as Master of the Torr. Offendorl had taken a different approach than his mentor. He allowed the other wizards only so much growth. He alone controlled the vast library of ancient lore at the Torr. He had set out early in his rule of the Torr to find all the greatest books and scrolls from each of the Five Kingdoms. What he didn't need he destroyed. No wizard could possibly learn as much as he had in three hundred years.

He opened the ancient book that he carried with him. It was the only book he had brought on the trip. It was so old that the writing inside was difficult to decipher even for him, but he dared not translate the text. He didn't want to give anyone a chance to steal the knowledge that only he possessed. He struggled over the text, but he was patient and had nothing better to do on the long journey to the coast. The book was about dragon lore, and he continued to call out to the beast night and day. He didn't know the dragon's name, but he had learned to sense the dragon, even though it was far to the north. He closed his eyes and sent his magic out in search of the beast. It had taken weeks before he had been able to recognize the dragon. The creature's magical powers were vastly different than that of wizards or sorcerers. Still, he found the dragon and could sense its mood. He knew from the book that the dragon could hear him and understand the thoughts he sent to the beast. He needed the dragon's name to control it completely, but for now he needed it nearer. Then he would bend the beast to his will and everyone in the Five Kingdoms would know fear unlike anything they had ever dreamed in their worst nightmares. When he possessed the dragon and had brought Zollin into the Torr, he would have all the power he needed.

* * *

The dragon didn't want to come out of its lair. The wounds in its shoulder and leg ached terribly. The arrows the human female had shot hadn't touched any of the beast's vital organs, but still the dragon felt miserable. The voice in his head was constant now.

Come south. Come to me. Join me.

The dragon wanted to hibernate, but it couldn't sleep knowing that its gold was out in the canyon. It needed to go and retrieve its precious metal, then rebuild its lair, but going out in the open wasn't something the dragon relished. The wizard had invaded the beast's sanctuary and now it felt threats all around. No place seemed safe, and leaving the rocky confines of its lair scared the dragon. It had underestimated the humans. It had destroyed villages and scattered soldiers who had been hunting it, but the wizard seemed to get the upper hand at every turn. After the disastrous raid on the stone city, it had returned to its lair once again. It had been a place of solace and safety, but the wizard had followed. The magical human had entered its den and sent shards of iron flying into its open mouth. It was a devious trick that had hurt the dragon. It had come charging out of the caverns and caught the wizard in the tunnel, crushing the pathetic human with all its strength, even cracking the rock in the cave. Then, just when the beast thought it had the upper hand, the female had pierced its scales with her arrows.

The thought of how close the dragon had come to death made it shiver. It didn't want to leave the lair, but it needed all the gold it could get. Gold, the rarest of all metals, beautiful and soft, had a healing effect on the dragon. The creature thrived on magic and chaos, and only gold had the power to bring it under any sort of control. The wizards of long ago had used gold to subjugate dragons. A golden crown inscribed with the dragon's name would give a magic-user control over the beast. Bartoom was the dragon's name, and it had been certain that no magic-user would ever control it again. Its quest had been to gather gold from all the kingdoms of the south lands, but now it lay huddled in the dark, wounded, with almost half of its gold tossed carelessly down the mountain.

It squirmed forward, its forked tongue tasting the air. It could still sense the wizard's presence. The human hadn't gone far. Bartoom had been diving for the two humans when they toppled off the ledge and fell into the snow heaped at the bottom of the canyon. It had decided then to retreat back inside its lair, hoping that it could fall into a healing sleep. Now it would have to go out and look for its missing gold.

As the dragon crawled through the tunnel toward the bright morning sunlight, it growled in pain. Every step hurt, and the beast had no idea what spreading its wings would feel like. Still, the gold was too precious to risk. The dragon crawled out onto the ledge and looked down. There was a trail in the snow and the human female was following it. The gold was nowhere in sight. The dragon would have to melt the snow with its fiery breath so that it could get to the buried gold, but first, it meant to exact revenge on the human who had wounded it.

* * *

Brianna was moving steadily across the snow field. She had made a decent trail in the soft, powdery snow the day before. Now she stayed on the trail, letting it lead her back to the place where she had uncovered their supplies. She had seen the staff. It was plain wood, easily as tall as she was, with a knobby end. Zollin carried the staff everywhere, but had left it with their supplies when he went up the mountain to search for the dragon.

She was breathing hard as her legs churned through the snow. She was making much better time than the day before, but she still felt she was moving too slowly. Then she heard a sound that made her heart almost stop.

Whoosh, whoosh, whoosh.

She looked up and saw the dragon dropping straight for her. She threw herself onto the snow, biting back a scream of terror. The dragon was trying desperately to slow its descent, but each stroke of its wing pulled the wounded muscles where Brianna's first arrow had hit the beast. The dragon overshot its target and crashed into the snow. Brianna heard the crash and the accompanying roar from the dragon. She looked up, but the dragon had plummeted deep into the snow just as she and Zollin had.

She got quickly back to her feet and scrambled forward. Suddenly a plume of steam and smoke billowed up in front of her. From inside the snowy hole where it had crashed, the dragon was shooting flames from its mouth, and the heat was beginning to melt the snow. She would have to circle around the dragon to get to where Zollin had left his staff. She plunged into the fresh, untrodden snow, sinking up to her knees.

Her heart was still pounding and she was gasping for breath as she slogged through the snow field. The dragon was thrashing and roaring and spouting flames from the hole the beast had fallen into. Brianna hoped that she could get to the staff and back to Zollin before the dragon cut off her path back to where Zollin lay. She tried to concentrate on the task of getting to the staff, but she couldn't help looking over to where the dragon was. She had almost reached her destination when the beast jumped out of the hole and settled on top of the snow. It swung its massive head on its long, snakelike neck. She saw the beast's eyes narrow, and she dove down into the snow. Flames shot over her. She felt heat and cold water soaking into her clothes. She crawled forward, staying low.

The dragon tried to walk toward Brianna, but the snow wouldn't support the creature's massive weight. It soon bogged down again. Brianna crawled down into the hole she had dug to get to their supplies the day before. She searched for the staff without taking her eyes off the dragon. She was sweating from exertion and shivering from the cold. Her hands ached terribly as they pawed through the snow. Finally her hand brushed the hard wood of the staff. She tugged it free of the snow and was surprised by the way it felt. It was much lighter than she had expected. She decided to spare a glance at the staff and was horrified when she realized it had been snapped in two.

Fear hit her like a physical blow. Zollin had searched for plants with magical properties all along their trip and had found nothing of significance. If the broken staff had lost its power, they were both doomed. She scrabbled in the snow for the other half of the staff, finding it almost immediately and pulling it free. She had only one last thing to do. She had to get back to Zollin, but than meant passing by the dragon. She no longer cringed at the sight of the beast. Having shot and wounded it high up on the mountain had given her confidence, and even though she didn't have her bow, she thought she might be able to sneak past the beast if she stayed close to the mountainside.

She used her quiver, which was still full of arrows tipped with broad arrowheads made of dwarfish steel, to secure the two pieces of the staff. The quiver had its own leather belt and, after a little work, she had the staff and quiver tied securely to her back using the quiver's belt. She was cold and tired, and her breath made thick clouds of steam as she breathed, but she didn't have time to worry about how she felt. The dragon was busy melting the snow with its fiery breath, but it was in the middle of the canyon while she was near the side of the mountain. She moved as quickly as she could through the thick snow. Her legs were soon burning from the exertion, and the cold air felt as though it was searing her lungs, but she didn't stop.

At one point the dragon managed to see her, but it only gave her a passing glance. The beast was obviously in pain and unable to fly, but its strength was enormous and there seemed to be no end to the fire it was able to spew from its gaping maw. Great clouds of steam rose around it from the melting snow, and the dragon's shining scales were now covered with mud and filth.

It took Brianna an hour to get back to where Zollin lay. Her quivering legs and shaking hands could barely support her as she crawled back down into the hole. Zollin was asleep. His skin was ashen and his breathing shallow. She settled on top of him, trying her best not to hurt him, but there was no way to make more room in the hole. She could have used her knife to dig into the snow, but it would fallen onto Zollin. She had no way to get it out of the hole. So she arranged herself as best she could and then tried to gently wake him up.

Zollin had been dreaming. He was deep in the dream, so deep that leaving the dream world was painful. He had seen a castle on a shining sea and heard a melodic voice calling to him. Inside the castle he had found a woman with a gown that seemed to glow as if it were made of pure light. She had been calling to him, and he wanted nothing more than to stay with her, but then he heard another voice, a familiar voice. It too called his name; it called him out of the castle and back into the cold, painful world. He didn't want to go, but the voice made the dream grow dim and even though he refused to leave, the dream moved further and further away. The woman in the glowing gown receded, and soon his eyes were flickering open.

Brianna was looking down at him, her face bright red from cold and exertion. Her dark hair seemed like the exact opposite of the woman in his dream, and at first he resented her. Why had she been so insistent that he wake? Why couldn't she just let him go?

"Oh, thank God," she said. "I wasn't sure if you were going to wake up. I got the staff . . ." She hesitated. "But it's broken, Zollin. I don't know if it's going to work."

She pulled the pieces of the broken staff from over her shoulder, like Mansel drawing his sword. Zollin reached up, and his arms felt so heavy it took all his strength just to reach for the staff, but he managed it. He could feel the magic inside the wood. If felt small, but it was there.

"I can feel it," he said.

"You can feel the magic?" Brianna asked.

"Yes. It's there. Do we have any more wine?"

"Only a little."

"I need it," he said.

She lifted his head and let the last of the wine dribble into his open mouth. The entire process was painful. Zollin's head hurt, not just an aching pain, but it was sore to the touch, especially the back of his head. His neck was stiff too, and every muscle in his shoulders and neck seemed to cramp as he moved. He swallowed the wine and let the liquid warm him. Normally he felt the heat from the wine spread through his body, but this time it disappeared as it slid down his throat and into his stomach. He knew it was there, but he couldn't feel it.

Then, clutching both pieces of the staff, he closed his eyes. He let the magic from the staff carry him. It was like floating on water. He let his mind dive deep inside his body. It was hard; the magic seemed weak, and Zollin didn't know if that was because the staff had been broken or if it was simply because he had grown so accustomed to his own power, which had dwarfed that of the staff. Still, he was able to use the magic of the staff to feel his way through the muscle and bone and find the fractures in his back. He healed the bones and cartilage easily enough, but the damage to the delicate nerves in his spinal cord also needed to be healed. He had to sort through hundreds of hair-like tendrils, identifying each one and checking to see if it was broken or severed. If it was, he healed it only after finding the right pieces. It was slow and exhausting work, but eventually his spine was completely healed. His pain had increased with each connection he made, but finally he felt his own magic again. It felt like the only warm thing in his body.

He took his time making sure nothing else was broken or seriously damaged, but he found nothing else wrong. He was bruised all along his back and down his legs. He knew his skin was black and blue, and the muscles were stiff from lying on the ice for so long. But fortunately, the cold had kept the swelling down. He took a few moments to heal the spots where frostbite had set in. His toes were beginning to freeze, but with a touch of magic they warmed, the wasted flesh returning to life as his magic passed through them. All that was left to do now was to loosen the aching muscles, which he could do either using his magic or the old-fashioned way. But the sound of the dragon roaring and thrashing in the ice and snow not far away was all the motivation he needed to get moving.

"I think I can get up now," he said to Brianna.

She had been watching him nervously. Time had seemed to pass so slowly as he lay perfectly still, each hand clutching a piece of his broken staff. When his eyes fluttered open she felt a huge weight lift off her shoulders. Hope appeared like the sun after a long, terrifying night.

"Oh, let me get up," she said.

Zollin waited while Brianna propped herself up on the icy walls. Her face was red with cold, and her eyes watched him nervously.

"I think I'm okay," he assured her. "Just really stiff. My back was broken, but I healed it. You saved my life."

"Of course I did," she said jokingly. "What did you expect?"

"I don't know," he said through gritted teeth as he raised his knees. "I sort of thought I was going to die."

"I would never let that happen," she teased.

"Can you give me a hand?"

She stepped carefully down where his feet had been. It was the first time she had been in the hole and not directly on top of him. She held out both hands and he took them, letting the staff fall to either side of his body as she pulled him up. Every muscle screamed in pain. Bones popped in their sockets, and blood rushed to his head. Zollin swayed dizzily, shutting his eyes and holding onto Brianna until the waves of dizziness and nausea passed. Then he flexed each muscle, bending his legs and rising up on his toes. The muscles were sore, but still strong enough. His stomach burned with hunger and his mouth was dry.

"We need to get out of here," he said.

"Can you climb?

"No, but I can get myself out of this hole."

"The surface is all loose snow. It's hard to move through," she told him.

"Well, we can't stay here."

"I know, I just wanted you to be sure. I'll go first and then you can follow me. That way you won't have to break a trail. Where are we going?"

"Away from the dragon," Zollin said. "I'm not strong enough for another fight."

"Okay, that sounds like a good plan to me," she agreed.

Brianna climbed to the top of their hole and peered out. She could see the billowing clouds of steam where the dragon was thrashing. It was a good distance from them, but she still felt a sense of urgency. She climbed out of the hole and began trudging through the snow. Zollin watched her go, then picked up their supplies. Just bending over was painful and reminded Zollin of how sore he used to get after spending days hauling wood with his father in Tranaugh Shire. Although they got most of their wood from a mill, there were times when Quinn needed a certain type of wood. They would go into the forest and spend hours felling a tree and then cutting off branches so that the trunk could be hauled to the mill. He would go to bed on those nights and then wake up feeling as if every muscle were in revolt.

Zollin picked up the two pieces of his staff. He felt the familiar crackle of magic as the power from the staff joined with his own. Then an idea formed, and he knew exactly what he would do with the staff. He tucked the pieces under one arm and slowly lifted himself using his magic. He felt heavy and his heart raced at the exertion, but he was soon out of the hole. The sun was up now, and as Zollin looked around he could see that there wasn't much in the way of shelter in the canyon now that it was filled with snow and debris from the avalanche.

"This way," Brianna said.

Zollin nodded and followed her.

Chapter 4

It was only moments before Zollin was gasping for breath. His body ached from fighting his way through the snow. He could hear the dragon behind him, but the beast's frantic efforts were sounding farther away. Brianna set a very demanding pace even though she was breaking a trail through the snow that was sometimes waist deep. Zollin soon lost track of time and direction, his chest ached, and there was a sharp pain in his side. His legs burned, and he had to use the broken pieces of his staff to help him keep his balance on the uneven trail.

Zollin could feel a strange desire that was unlike anything he had ever experienced before. Somewhere, deep inside his magic, he could feel an enticement drawing him. It was like the smell of cooking food to a starving man. He knew it was out of reach, and yet he couldn't help but want to go. He felt like running to the source of the mysterious desire. He knew he needed to raise his internal defenses, but all he could think about was keeping up with Brianna.

"There!" she called excitedly.

She was pointing toward a place on the nearest mountain that looked like a small cave. It was several hundred feet above where they were, and the mountainside was nearly vertical. There was no way that Zollin could make the climb.

"Can you get us up there?" Brianna asked.

Zollin had to swallow several times before he could speak.

"I'm not sure," he said.

"What's wrong?"

"I'm just so tired."

"Do you need something to eat? We don't have much left."

"No, just give me a few minutes to catch my breath."

Zollin slumped down in the snow. He was hot and cold at the same time. His arms and legs felt like stone. His back ached and his head felt dizzy. He wondered if perhaps he had missed something when he was trying to heal himself. It was hard to concentrate; his mind kept wandering to the alluring magical power that continued to beckon him south.

Finally, after almost five full minutes of rest, Zollin thought he could lift Brianna up to the cave. He closed his eyes and let his magic flow out. The broken pieces of his staff crackled and hissed, and then Brianna was rising up the mountainside. The effort took all of Zollin's strength but he finally managed to set her down gently. Then he slumped back down in the snow.

The cave was little more than an indentation in the solid rock of the mountain, but it was big enough that they could take shelter and perhaps even have a fire if they could find something to burn. The rock was cold, but at least they were out of the snow. Brianna had been carrying both packs, and she dropped them at her feet before peering over the edge. Far below her, Zollin seemed very small.

"Are you coming?" she shouted.

He waved and held up a finger as if to say *just a minute.* He knew lifting himself would be hard, but he also felt confident that he could do it. The power was there, but his physical body was having trouble keeping up with the demand. He was starving but felt nauseous. His mouth was dry and his head was pounding. All he wanted to do was lie down and sleep. Finally, he looked up and decided there was no more sense delaying.

He let his magic flow around him, and it was like being in the middle of a raging river. It took all his concentration to stay focused, as if he were fighting to keep his head above the turbulent waters. Halfway to his destination he began to feel as if something inside him was tearing. Whenever he used magic he felt a hot wind blowing through him, and sometimes that wind got so hot he felt as if he could spontaneously burst into flames. But now the magic felt sharp as if it were shredding his insides. His concentration wavered and he started to fall, but he forced himself to ignore the pain and finish levitating himself up. By the time he reached the cave all he could think about was the pain. He collapsed onto the floor and passed out.

Brianna felt a wave of panic flood over her. She hadn't meant to push Zollin too hard; she was just trying to get them to a place of safety. He had always been the strong one, pushing their pace as they searched the Northern Highlands for the dragon, but now he seemed frail.

She bent over him and checked to make sure he was breathing. He was, but his skin was pale and there were dark circles around his eyes. She pulled what food they had out of their packs and then arranged the packs, along with their blankets, to make a pallet for Zollin. She pulled him across the cave floor and onto the pallet. She propped his head up and then felt his forehead. His temperature was high and he was shivering from cold. There was nothing left for her to do for him. She brought their rations and canteens close, then took the last blanket and snuggled in close to Zollin. Finally, she covered them both and held him. It was only about midday, but they both slept. Brianna had not rested well the night before and so she dozed beside Zollin, who didn't move.

When she finally woke up it was getting late. The sun was hidden behind the mountains and although the sky was still bright, the long shadows in the mountains made everything look gloomy. She checked on Zollin, who was resting better. His fever was still high, but he wasn't chilled. She tucked the blanket around him and began going through their rations. They had some dried meat, but no vegetables or bread. One canteen was full, the other only half filled. She drank some of the water and wondered if she would be able to get down from their shelter to search for food. There was no more wine left and Brianna had left the empty bottle behind.

She sat on the cave floor, waiting and watching for signs of life in the mountains. She couldn't see or hear the dragon, which was a relief. She felt a small sense of pride that she had wounded the beast, but she had no desire to find and fight the dragon again. All she wanted was to get Zollin out of the mountains. She loved the rugged beauty of the Northern Highlands, but she didn't like feeling helpless. She had thought that Zollin had healed himself and would be back to normal soon. She hadn't counted on the fever.

She watched as the sky grew dark. When the first stars appeared, she moved back to check on Zollin. She shook him and called his name. It took a moment, but then his eyes fluttered open.

"What's wrong?" he asked.

"You've got a fever," she told him. "Is that something you can fix?"

"I don't know, I feel so weak. I'm hurting all over."

"Do you need some food? I've got some meat and water."

"No, I don't think I can stomach anything."

"What can I do?"

"Just stay close. I would would give anything for a soft bed right now."

"We've got to get you well, Zollin," Brianna said. She was trying hide the sound of fear that wanted to creep into her voice. "I don't think I can get down the mountain on my own."

"I just want to sleep some more," he said. "Then I'll try to heal my body."

"Okay," she said.

She lay down beside him again, but this time she wasn't sleepy. She could feel the cold, hard floor of the cave beneath their thin blankets. It was hard to lie still and she didn't want to disturb Zollin, but he was asleep again almost immediately. His breathing was deep and regular. Brianna ate a bit of the dried meat. It was so tough it made her jaws ache to chew on it, but she was hungry. She could see stars glinting through the mouth of their cave. The wind was blowing, but it didn't reach back into the small shelter.

Zollin mumbled occasionally, obviously suffering from bad dreams. Brianna tried her best to soothe him. She struggled to stay warm and finally nodded off herself. The sky was just turning a pearl gray color when she woke up. She was tired but too cold and uncomfortable to sleep. She sat up and drank some water.

"I could use some of that," Zollin said, his voice croaking.

She turned and poured a little into his open mouth. He swirled it around before swallowing it down and opening his mouth for more.

"How are you feeling?" Brianna asked as she gave him another sip.

"Terrible," he said. "My whole body hurts."

"Is there anything you can do?"

"I think so. I just need a little time. Have we got any food?"

They both ate a little of the dried meat. It was bland and tough, but by breaking off small pieces and sucking on the meat they coaxed a little flavor out and softened the meat enough to chew it. Neither spoke. They sipped water and Zollin sat up. Brianna offered to rub his back, but the bruises made it too painful.

"Couldn't you heal the bruises?" she asked.

"No, I didn't have the time. I was afraid the dragon would find us."

She felt his head. He was still feverish, but he seemed more coherent. He rolled onto his stomach and stretched a little. Brianna stood up and walked the kinks out of her own sore muscles.

Zollin let his magic flow. He had been plagued with the desire to go south all through the night. He knew he needed to deal with it, to raise his defenses, but he hadn't had the strength. He didn't have much energy, but he thought it would be enough to deal with whatever was making him ill. He let his mind move slowly through his body, which had been making antibodies to deal with his broken back. The over-production of fluids was causing both soreness and the fever. Zollin moved as much of the excess fluid through his liver as he could. It didn't take long for his body to adjust. After lying in the snow with a broken back all night long, it was no surprise that his body was in shock. He felt the familiar heat as he worked his magic and, after he did all he could for his body, he set about replacing his defenses.

"I think I'm okay now," he told Brianna.

"Good, because we need to get moving. There's a storm coming and we need to replenish our supplies."

Zollin got up and walked over to where Brianna was standing and watching the dark clouds building up to the north. He bit off a mouthful of the elk meat and picked up the broken pieces of his staff. While he didn't need to rely on magical objects any longer, he felt a pang of sadness at the thought of giving up his staff. He settled back onto the floor and sent his magic into the pale, white wood. It was stiff, but the magic that coursed through it was like lightning, crackling as it darted back and forth through the wood. He focused his mind, moving beyond the wood grain down into the tiniest molecules. Because he could perceive matter at its most basic level, he could also manipulate it. He began to use his magic to reshape the wood. The magic from the staff linked to his own magic, so that it seemed the the staff was reshaping itself.

It took only moments to complete. He opened his eyes and saw the bow he had made. It was light and elegant, with a sturdy riser and long, shapely recurve limbs. The bowstring matched the color of the bow, which was still a pale white. Zollin could feel the magic inside the bow, although it was as if the magic was concentrated in the limbs of the bow.

"Here," Zollin said, slowly getting back to his feet. "This should help."

"Zollin, that's amazing," Brianna said.

"Try it out. You've still got arrows. But I think you should take off the white alzerstone ring."

"Why?" she asked.

"Just trust me," he said, smiling.

Brianna pulled off her ring and took the bow and held it up. She was amazed at how balanced it felt. Her old bow, another gift from Zollin, had been fashioned in Baskla by a master bowsmith. She had always thought that it felt perfect, but the bow Zollin made felt like it was a part of her. Her hand fit perfectly on the smooth grip, and there was a slight tingle that made her feel powerful just holding the weapon.

Brianna picked up an arrow from her quiver, which was leaning against the wall. She nocked an arrow and drew it back. The resistance was so minimal she had to look at the bow to be sure she had it drawn all the way back. The limbs were bent and the arrow was the perfect length, but it took almost no effort to draw and hold the string. Then she took aim. As soon as her thumb touched her cheek, something magical happened. Her sight narrowed, almost as if she were looking through a long tunnel. She hadn't known what to aim at, but as her vision zoomed in she could see a small tree with a contorted trunk growing from the side of the mountain. It was more than just something she saw, it was as if her mind had linked to the tree. She released the arrow, and it shot across the expanse between the mountains so fast it was impossible to see.

Brianna's vision was still zoomed in on her target and she saw the arrow slam into the thick and knotty tree trunk. The arrow burrowed completely through the tree and came poking out the other side. Then, Brianna's vision returned to normal. She could barely see the tree now. It was so far away she shouldn't have been able to hit the tree even with a large longbow with a very heavy draw weight.

"Did you see that?" she exclaimed.

"I did," Zollin said, though a mouthful of dried meat.

"Zollin, this bow is like. . ." she wasn't sure how to describe it.

"Like magic."

"Exactly," she said loudly. "It draws as if there is nothing there. And then, I could see the target as if I were standing right in front of it. You know I shouldn't have been able to make that shot. No one could shoot an arrow that far."

"Kelvich said that some objects made with materials imbued with magic have extraordinary qualities. All the great legendary swords and weapons were magic-made. I didn't need the staff for myself anymore. This seems like a better fit. That's why I asked you to take off the ring. Do you like it?"

"Oh, it is incredible! I love it."

Then she threw her arms around his neck and kissed him. At first the kiss was merely exuberant, but after a moment it changed and became more passionate. Zollin felt desire stirring in him and he pulled away, frowning.

"What's wrong?" Brianna asked.

"I'm not sure," he said. "When Kelvich and I first started training, I didn't like using my full range of magic because it made me feel. . . ," he searched for the right words, "too powerful. I had strange impulses to destroy things. So Kelvich helped me develop a sort of defense so that other sorcerers couldn't manipulate my magic or control me. But when I first healed my back, I felt something. It wasn't malicious like before, it was . . . ," again he struggled to find the words.

"What?" Brianna asked.

"Lustful," he said.

He watched her expression, unsure how she would respond to such a revelation. They had never broached the subject of physical intimacy. There had been temptations in the past, but since they were planning on marriage, Zollin had wanted to wait. His sense of honor wouldn't allow him to taint their relationship by giving in to his physical desires. Whenever he had thought of it he was reminded of his old friend Todrek, who had been Brianna's husband for one night, before being killed while helping Zollin flee their small village when the Torr had pursed him.

"That's weird," she said.

"I know, but that's the best way I know to describe it. It's like this deep desire, and I know it is coming from my magic, but it's as real as any emotion I've ever felt."

"It can't be good," Brianna said. Her face was blushing pink.

"It isn't, and I need to get my defenses back in place, but to be honest, working magic at this point is painful."

"What do you mean?"

"Normally, when I use my power, I get tired. But ever since the accident, it's as if using magic is hurting me."

"Oh, Zollin, that can't be good."

"I've checked and there's no damage being done. Maybe I just need more rest, I don't know."

"If you can build defenses to keep other wizards from doing stuff to you, can you build some kind of defense to keep the magic from hurting you?"

"I don't know," Zollin said, very intrigued at the idea. "It will probably take some time."

"Well, that's the one thing we don't have. We need to leave as soon as possible if we're going to find food and shelter before this storm hits."

"Okay, let's load everything up and get moving."

"We can circle around the mountain to avoid the avalanche. It should be easier than trudging through the snow."

"That sounds good," Zollin said, but he couldn't help feeling a sense of foreboding. He knew that he would have to levitate himself and Brianna up and around the canyons and cliffs.

The thought of using his magic scared him a little. He really did need some sort of containment for his inner reservoir of magic. If he could block out others, why couldn't he isolate and guard his own power so that it didn't affect him physically? He was tired of being weak and dependent on food and wine to regain his strength. He needed to master his power, rather than being so strongly affected every time he cast a spell.

They gathered their supplies, and then Zollin lowered Brianna back down into the canyon. He angled her descent so that she was well down the valley where the avalanche hadn't been as severe. He followed her down, using his magic to direct and slow his fall. It was much easier than levitating them up, but the effort still sent sharp pains shooting through his body, making it difficult to concentrate on the spell.

It was still early morning when they set out. The air was frigid, and soon their feet were cold from the snow. It wasn't as deep as it had been further up the mountainside, and they made good time, but not without a great amount of effort. Zollin was breathing hard just trying to keep up with Brianna. When he had to levitate them it made his head spin with dizziness. He managed to raise his defenses enough so that the constant yearning to move south didn't bother him, but he was ravenously hungry and would have eaten all their rations if the dried meat hadn't been so difficult to consume.

It was late afternoon before Zollin sensed any animals large enough to hunt. The storm was getting closer and the air felt heavy and warmer than normal.

"I think there's a bighorn sheep up on that mountain," Zollin said.

"I can't see it," Brianna said, and then she drew the bow.

Once again her vision narrowed and zoomed across the expanse. She could see the ram now, slowly making its way across the steep mountainside. She took a deep breath and then held it for a moment before making her shot. The arrow flew like a bolt of lighting and hit the ram right behind the shoulder. The big sheep jumped and then fell to the ground dead.

"I got it," Brianna said triumphantly.

"Really? That's great."

"Yeah, but how do we get up there?"

"We don't," Zollin said.

He closed his eyes and sent his magic out again. He located the ram and levitated it off the mountain and down into the valley where they waited. The ram weighed more than Zollin and Brianna combined, and the effort left him exhausted. He sat on a rock with his head between his legs, waiting for his head to stop spinning. Brianna began dressing out the ram. It was dirty work, but at least it meant they would have food to eat. They would have to leave large portions of the animal behind; they couldn't take the hide or the head, and they had no use for the internal organs. She butchered the carcass as best she could and loaded the raw meat into their packs. They would both have to carry as much as possible.

They were just about to set off again when the wind kicked up above them in a strange gust that made an odd sound, almost like a person sighing. Zollin turned around and looked up, then toppled over. Brianna screamed and they both scrambled backward.

A giant was standing up behind them. It had gray skin that looked almost exactly like the hard rock that formed the mountains. It was easily five times taller than a full-grown man. It wore scrub brush around its waist, and its hair was gray and wiry. It looked at them with large eyes that blinked slowly.

"It's a giant," Brianna said, her voice pitched high with fear.

The creature moved slowly forward, taking one careful step and then another, until it was right where they had been a moment ago. It bent down and looked at the remains of the sheep they had butchered.

"Are you going to eat this?" the giant asked in a low-pitched, rumbling voice.

"No," Zollin said loudly. He tried to keep his voice from shaking but failed.

"Can I have it?"

"Yes."

"Oh, thank you. I'm very hungry."

The giant picked up the remains of the sheep and popped them into his mouth. He chewed the bones and horns effortlessly.

"My name's Rup," said the giant, slowly and deliberately. "You are a wizard."

Zollin mustered his courage. Rup wasn't frightening in his appearance; it was just his massive size that had startled Zollin and Brianna. He had large, round shoulders and thick arms and legs. His stomach was round, and his face was somewhat flat. He had a broad nose but no lips. His eyes were intelligent but cloudy, as if they were very dry.

"That's right," Zollin said. "My name is Zollin, and this is Brianna."

"It's very nice to meet you both. I've been sleeping here a very long time."

Rup stretched his arms and yawned.

"We're heading south," Zollin said. "There's a storm coming."

"Oh, that's good. I like storms."

"We need to find shelter," Brianna added.

"Like a cave?" Rup suggested.

"Yes," Zollin said. "Somewhere we can rest and stay dry."

"I know a place," said Rup. "It's this way."

He stepped over them both and up onto a low ridge. Brianna held onto Zollin tightly, her whole body trembling as the giant passed over them.

"I didn't know giants were real," said Brianna.

"Me neither."

"What are we going to do?"

"I think we should follow him."

"What if he wants to eat us? He could be leading us to some sort of trap so he can catch us. Did you see the way he crunched the ram's horns between his teeth?"

"Yes, but he seems nice enough."

"Zollin, he's a giant! How do you know if he's nice?"

"We might offend him if we don't follow him."

"This is insane," Brianna said. "First dragons and now giants."

"Come on," Zollin said. "I'll go first."

He levitated himself up to the top of the ridge. They probably could have scrambled up the small rise, but Zollin didn't want to fall too far behind Rup. It took nearly half an hour to reach the cave that Rup led them to. Zollin and Brianna didn't have time to worry, as it took all their energy just to keep pace. Rup could climb the mountains as easily as a child scaling a tree. It was only

Zollin's ability to levitate himself and Brianna up and down the steep trail that allowed them to keep up.

"Look," Rup said happily. "It's a nice cave. Too small for me, but just right for a wizard."

"How did you know I was a wizard?" Zollin asked.

"Because you woke me up," Rup said, as if it were the most obvious fact. "Would you like me to lift you up?"

"No," Brianna said. "We'll manage."

"Okay," said Rup. "Thanks for waking me. I'm going to find a drink."

The giant moved away slowly but gracefully. Zollin and Brianna watched him go, still in shock at what they had seen.

"I guess giants are nice," Zollin said.

"Maybe," Brianna admitted. "He didn't try to eat us."

"Why would you think that he might?" Zollin asked.

"Don't you remember the stories about the giants who steal children and stew them in giant kettles?"

"That's just a children's story."

"Yes, but we thought the same thing about dragons not long ago."

"Well, at least we have food and place to stay."

"Sure, we can just cozy up in that cave until Rup gets hungry again. Then he'll know right where to find us."

Chapter 5

Prince Wilam walked across the small drilling area, where a squad of fifty men was practicing with weapons. He looked at them, frowned, and began shouting.

"You look like a band of trollops! Don't let your shields droop, you'll be killed. Or worse yet, the man beside you will be killed."

He pushed one of the men aside, snatching away the soldier's shield. He took the man's place in line and demonstrated.

"Your shield must be locked against the next man's shield. It creates a barrier that can't be penetrated. Do you understand? Your job on the front line is to hold the enemy at bay. You'll have plenty of chances to slide your weapon into the gap, but you have to hold the line. Your shield wall cannot falter. A breakdown at any one point will spell disaster for the entire line. Do you understand?"

"Yes sir!" the men shouted.

They were a ragtag group of men. Most were farmers or merchants who had fallen under the sorcerer Gwendolyn's spell. She had an alluring quality that made men forget everything else. They left their wives and families, ignored their farms or businesses, and thought only about the witch whom they called a queen. She was living in the Castle on the Sea in Lodenhime, on the southern shore of the Great Sea of Kings. It wasn't actually a castle, but rather a large stone manor, built by a wealthy merchant. All men who came into the city eventually fell under the witch's spell, including Wilam, the Crown Prince of Yelsia. Gwendolyn had made him her general and given him the task of building her an army. He was determined not to fail her.

"The men in the second line will strike over your head and support you. In this way you form an impenetrable line. Put your shoulder into your shield, hold it up any way you can. If you drop your shield, even a little, you'll die."

"Yes sir!" the men shouted.

"Good," Wilam said as he handed the soldier back his shield. "Do it again."

The men continued to drill. There were three hundred men in his small army. Not nearly enough to go into battle, but it was a start. He had separated those with any kind of training from the rabble. Gwendolyn's charms were not reserved for the wealthy or useful; any and every man who saw her was smitten. She left it to Wilam to make something of the ragtag troops. He had made the men with military experience officers and assigned those with archery skills as castle guards.

Men with building experience were busy reinforcing the wall that surrounded the Castle on the Sea. The main structure was built on a rocky peninsula, but the compound's walls were made of stone and built ten feet high. The wall wound from the shore on one side, around the stables and work sheds, and ended at the shore on the far side. Wilam had his builders extending the walls out into the water. He didn't intend to leave any gaps in the castle's defenses. He was also building a wooden walkway that would allow the castle guards to see over the wall and patrol the perimeter without leaving the castle grounds. The walkway was six feet high and built right against the wall. The guards could fire their arrows over the wall if they were attacked and fend off anyone trying to climb inside.

Bringing order and productivity to the masses around the Castle brought Wilam a sense of pride. He had forgotten about

Yelsia and his duty as the Crown Prince. His only thoughts now were of Gwendolyn and how he could please her. She had given him a task and he worked tirelessly to see it through.

It took all his mental strength not to go in search of the witch. He wanted to see her and, more importantly, for her to see what he was accomplishing. He thought that if she could just see all he was doing for her then perhaps she would finally return his affection. But he knew that she was busy in the library and wouldn't want to be interrupted, although he couldn't imagine why she was wasting her time among the old dusty books and scrolls. She was creating an empire and Wilam was going to make sure that it was as strong as possible.

"Sir, we've finished reinforcing the section of wall on the south side of the compound," said a short man with thinning hair and a large, round belly.

"Good. Go and help with the new construction."

"You mean where they're extending the wall out into the sea?"

"That's right," Wilam said, not trying to hide his annoyance.

"I thought that perhaps Her Ladyship might want to come out and inspect our work first."

"Don't be a fool," Wilam said angrily. "Queen Gwendolyn doesn't want to be disturbed. Get back to work."

The man bowed and hurried off. Wilam watched him go. He didn't know why a man like that would hold out hope of wooing Gwendolyn. Then a thought struck him. If they were going to build an army, they needed to recruit more troops. He went into the stables and made sure there were enough horses. Then he sent word to the most experienced riders. He would send them out to bring conscripts back to their camp and bolster their numbers. The riders could also serve as scouts and bring back any news from the surrounding kingdoms.

* * *

Gwendolyn rolled over on the bed she had been lounging on. She sat up and scowled in frustration.

"He's gone again, Mina."

The witch's sister did not respond. She sat in a chair in the corner, neither moving or speaking. Her eyes stared blankly ahead.

"Why does he keep doing that?" Gwendolyn asked. "I want him to come here and join us."

Gwendolyn stretched luxuriously before standing up and walking to the large windows that looked out over the sea. The breeze from the water was cool, and it made the silky gown she was wearing flutter against her body. Her hair was a tangled mess, but still it waved softly in the breeze.

"Another glorious day of freedom, Mina," Gwendolyn said. "I like this place much better than the tower. It was so dark and tedious. We mustn't let the master come and take us away again."

She moved to an elegantly carved chair that sat before a small table with a large mirror propped against the wall on top of it. She looked at her reflection and sighed. Then she picked up a brush and began running it through her long hair.

"The wizard in the north might be a perfect match for you," Gwendolyn told her sister. "He's grown more powerful, but he isn't unsusceptible to our charms. I can sense that, even at this distance. If the men we sent north can bring him to us, I think we'll be able to defeat even Offendorl. We'll have all five kingdoms at our feet. Won't that be something?"

She spoke in a sweet, conversational voice, but it was as if her words were falling on deaf ears. Andomina was a powerful warlock but had no control over her own power. Gwendolyn controlled it for her, and in fact controlled Mina's entire life. It had been that way since they were little girls and Offendorl had taken them to the Torr as children. They had lived in the massive tower for over a hundred years, with Gwendolyn under careful guard. Offendorl knew the power of a sorceress over men. Few could resist her charms, and even the Master of the Torr restricted his contact with them. He had eventually sent Gwendolyn and her sister to capture Zollin and bring him back to the Torr, but when the young wizard had learned to shield himself from her, Gwendolyn had brought her sister to Lodenhime instead of returning to their master.

Offendorl was afraid of Zollin, a fact which had not been lost on Gwendolyn. She had sent Zollin's father and friend to bring him back to her. If she couldn't use her magic, she would use the men under her spell. It was, after all, the only thing she wanted them for. Men were weak-willed, pathetic creatures to Gwendolyn. She had always seen them give in to their most basic urges. They would surround her, throw themselves into any task to earn her favor. Eventually they would fight and kill each other, and the process would begin all over. It was wearisome to Gwendolyn, but she would use them as long as they served a purpose.

A knock on the door broke her concentration. She had been brushing her hair, mindlessly combing through the glistening strands as she thought about Zollin. He was the key to her freedom after all. The army Wilam was building was little more than a war band. She knew that a strong noble could easily defeat her rabble of farmers and tradesmen, but leaving her adoring horde idle would only hasten the day when they fell to killing each other. And she had to admit she liked order. Wilam was a natural leader and he did, in fact, know about soldiering. It only made sense to put his skills to good use.

The knock sounded again, this time louder and more urgent.

"Oh, all right, just a minute," she said loudly. "The demands of men never cease, Mina," she said as pulled on a more modest robe. The weather was warm, but she preferred to remain fully dressed.

She pushed the large metal bolt that was used to secure the door and then pulled the heavy slab of oak open. Wilam was waiting, a look of worry in his eyes that quickly passed once he saw her.

"I thought you might be ill, my lady," he said, wringing his hands nervously. "I searched for you at the library."

"There's nothing there but genealogies and herb lore. Someone," she said, knowing full well it was the Torr, "has removed all the useful books. The library was not what I hoped it might be."

"I am sorry, my Queen. But I have news, or at least an idea that I thought you might approve of."

"Go ahead, I'm listening," she said as she fell into an overstuffed chair near her sister.

"Well, I had the idea that perhaps we should send out riders. They could conscript more men for our army and perhaps bring us news of the Five Kingdoms."

"That's not a bad idea," Gwendolyn said, doing nothing to hide the boredom in her voice. "Go ahead."

"Thank you, my lady," Prince Wilam said. "Work is going well on the Castle. Would you care to see it?"

"No, it's too hot outside. I think I'll take a bath."

She watched as Wilam struggled to speak. She knew his imagination was running wild. She of course had no intention of inviting him into her bed, much less her bath, but it wouldn't do to let him know that. Toying with the men under her power was one of her favorite things, whether it was a crown prince or a pauper.

"Well, go," she said. "Send in Keevy with fresh water and towels."

"As you wish, my Queen," Wilam said, bowing low.

He had never bowed to anyone, but he was completely under the witch's spell. Each teasing suggestion bound him more closely to her. He left her rooms and hurried to find the steward of the Castle. Keevy had served at the Castle for years. He was fat and his hair was falling out, yet he oversaw every aspect of life at the Castle with the energy of a much younger man. Though he was as sly as a fox, Keevy was just as infatuated with Gwendolyn as the Prince.

"She wants fresh water sent up for a bath," he told the man, almost choking with jealousy as he said it. "And fresh towels. Be sure they're clean and neatly folded. And don't let any of your vile staff near her. They'll be eunuchs if they step out of line. I'll see to the gelding myself."

"Yes, my lord," Keevy said in a nasally voice.

Prince Wilam stormed out of the Castle. He was so angry he hit the first man who approached him. Then he gave the new assignments to the riders he had selected and took a position on the wall to watch them ride away. The town of Lodenhime had once been a busy place. Now it seemed almost haunted with emptiness.

There were still women and small children in the city, but they stayed away from the Castle.

Wilam considered his options. He wasn't sure how long he could hold himself in check. He had never dishonored himself by forcing his affections onto a woman, but every time he was near Gwendolyn his desire raged like a fire out of control. He made up his mind to try harder to win her affection. It was all he could think of to do.

Chapter 6

Quinn spent three days in the water. His body ached from cold and lack of sleep. The Great Sea of Kings was a freshwater lake that was as large as an entire kingdom. Savage storms were common, and waves could tower as high as twenty feet. Fortunately for Quinn, the weather did not turn bad. Instead he baked under hours of direct sunlight and shivered through cold, wet nights. Time became a blur. The bucket he was clinging to had a rough, rope handle and Quinn snaked his arm through it. He couldn't sleep, too afraid of losing the bucket. Whenever he dozed off he would jerk awake in terror.

Eventually he grew delirious. He saw Zollin walking toward him across the water, heard voices, and carried on conversations with people he knew were dead. When he heard the sailors on a small fishing boat calling out to him, he didn't think they were real. He ignored the voices, his mind lost in a mental fog where delusion and reality were one and the same. He felt himself grabbed by rough hands and heaved up out of the water. He felt his sodden clothes cut away and felt warm blankets cover him. Then, at long last, he slept. When he woke up he was warm and dry. He looked around and realized he was on a boat. It wasn't a great vessel, just a small boat with a canvas awning and a small sail. He could smell raw fish and heard voices. He struggled to sit up, his head spinning a little from the effort.

"Hey look, he's waking up," said a young man about Zollin's age.

There were three of them, obviously a father and his two sons. The father was guiding the ship, the boys were mending nets. Quinn saw a pile of fish between himself and the fishermen.

"He'll need water," said the father, "and food."

The boys both dipped their hands into the water by leaning over the edge of the boat. Then they each held a bucket, much like the one he had been clinging to, back toward Quinn.

"I'm Niils," said the first and clearly the youngest.

Quinn thought the boy was probably fourteen or fifteen years old. He had shaggy hair that was bleached blonde by long hours exposed to sunlight. He had a bright, cheerful face and offered Quinn a tin cup from his bucket.

"It's just water," Niils said.

"I've got food," said the older boy. "Some hard bread, and apples."

"Thank you," Quinn said, with a froggy voice.

"I'm Azel, and our father is Olton."

"Thank you for rescuing me," Quinn said after sipping the water.

"What were you doing in the water?" Niils asked. "Did your boat sink?"

"No, I was attacked and thrown overboard," Quinn said.

"By who?" asked the boy in awed surprise.

"By a friend," Quinn said. "He wasn't thinking clearly. I need to get to Yelsia. Where are we going?"

"Not to Yelsia," said Azel. "The Great Sea isn't anywhere near Yelsia."

"We can take you as far north as the Walheta Mountains," said Olton, speaking to Quinn for the first time. "We've got to get these fish to market first, though."

"Not in Lodenhime, I hope," Quinn said.

"No, we live in a small village south of the Walheta."

"Okay, thank you. Thank you for saving my life."

"No decent seaman would have left you for dead. How long were you in the water?"

"I'm not sure," Quinn said bitterly. "Too long. I've got to return to Yelsia as quickly as possible. It's a matter of life or death."

"Really?" said Niils in astonishment.

"I suppose you've heard rumors of a dragon in Yelsia," Quinn asked the boy.

"Of course. They say it's destroying whole villages and demanding gold."

"That's true," Quinn said. "My son is a wizard. He was sent to slay the beast."

"Wizards and witches and dragons," Olton scoffed. "We'll be hearing tales of sea creatures and mermaids next."

"They aren't just stories," Quinn said. "I was sent on a mission by King Felix. I was returning with my companions when we came to Lodenhime. There is a woman there who bewitched us. I can't remember much about her, but I do remember feeling like being with her was more important than anything else in the world. I was under some kind of spell, until my friend cast me overboard. The cold water must have shocked me back to my senses."

"It sounds more like they robbed you of them," Olton said.

"It's the truth. The witch sent us to bring back my son. I have to get to him before Mansel does. He can't fall under the witch's spell."

"You tell a good story, stranger," said Olton. "But I'd prefer for you not to fill my children's heads with such nonsense."

"I swear on my life it's true. Tell me, have you seen any of the merchant trading ships on the sea?"

Olton looked hard at Quinn before speaking.

"No," he said at last.

"That's because they are all at anchor in Lodenhime. The crews are bewitched by a woman with strange powers."

"Well, if that's true, it's no concern of ours."

"No, I guess not," Quinn said.

"Let our guest rest, boys. Back to the nets."

The boys left the buckets of food and water and returned to their places in the boat near their father. They worked with quiet efficiency. Quinn watched them as he ate. They seemed content, and he envied them. He wished more than anything that he could ignore the larger world and live in peace. His whole life he had tried to do the right thing, but it only seemed to bring him heartache and pain. He had lived for a long time in Tranaugh Shire, but that time was forever marred by the death of his wife and the difficulties of raising Zollin on his own. Now, after battles and travels across the five kingdoms, he wanted only to rest. To be done with strife. He thought of Miriam, the animal healer in Felson. They had met only once, but she still captivated his thoughts like no other woman ever had.

He ate only a little of the food and soon grew tired again. He lay back on the deck, thankful for the canvas that kept the afternoon sunlight off his burned and peeling skin. His head was sore and hot. It also itched, but even touching his scalp was painful. He laid his head down gingerly, using his arms as pillows, and dozed.

He heard the town before he saw it. Then he could smell cooking fires, and he decided to sit up. Olton and Azel had lowered the sail and were now working long oars to guide the boat into harbor. Niils steered the ship. He looked like a younger version of his father, standing at the steering oar. Quinn turned and saw the village they were approaching. The sun was in his eyes, but he could see the busy quay and the other fishing boats. Quinn was still naked. He had no clothes, and no coin to buy new ones.

"Olton," he said tentatively. "I don't suppose you have some clothes for me to put on?"

"The boys have mended your clothes," the fisherman said. "It's not pretty, but it'll do."

He tossed the shirt and pants to Quinn. His boots had filled with water when he was thrown overboard, and Quinn had kicked them off rather than be weighed down with them. His purse too, had been discarded, along with his sword belt. All he had was his tattered pants and shirt. The reality of his dire predicament hit him hard. He needed to do more than catch up with Mansel; he had to somehow get to Zollin first and warn him. But he was days behind the young warrior, with no money and no resources. He was in trouble and he knew it.

The ship glided into a spot along the quay where they could quickly and easily unload their catch. The boys loaded the fish into wooden boxes, which they carried to a stall in the market to lay out their catch. Most of the fish was taken to a smokehouse where they were cleaned and hung, so that they could smoke overnight; the rest was sold to the villagers who flocked to the stall to get the best of the early catch. While the boys were busy in the market, Olton scrubbed the small deck where the fish had lain and then made preparations to set sail again. He left Quinn on the boat while he checked on his sons and soon was back, this time with a bottle of wine and more food.

He handed a small sack to Quinn that was filled with fresh baked bread and smoked fish. There was also a bit of cheese.

Quinn's appetite returned, but he decided to see if he could help Olton with the boat, since the man was graciously taking him farther north.

"You've been very generous," Quinn said. "How can I help?"

"Have you ever manned an oar?" Olton asked.

"No, I'm sorry."

"That's okay. I'll teach you. We only need to row out of the harbor, then we can raise the sail and head north. We should make it north of the Walheta mountains by sunrise."

"What about your sons?" Quinn asked.

"They'll take care of themselves."

"I feel like I'm asking too much of you."

"Nonsense, I'll fish on the way south. I haven't been in the northern waters for some time. I'll probably have a good catch and get you a little closer to home. Kill two birds with one stone so to speak."

"Thank you," Quinn said.

"Don't thank me yet. Wait till you've worked the oars and helped with the fishing nets. You may decide I'm not that kind."

Quinn smiled. He wasn't afraid of hard work. They cast off from the harbor and Quinn took his place at one of the long, heavy oars. It took a little time for Quinn to find his rhythm. He braced his feet and used his entire body to pull the oar through the water. At first it felt good to stretch and use his muscles again, but soon those muscles were burning with fatigue. He was still exhausted after spending three days floating in the open water of the Great Sea. Quinn didn't complain though, and soon they were far enough from the harbor that Olton ordered the oars struck and set the sail. Quinn sat near the rear of the ship and ate his supper.

The food was good and there was a breeze. For the first time in his life Quinn thought that perhaps being on a ship wasn't a bad thing. He could see the stars above him, so vast in number and so far away. The moon gave them enough light to see the dark shore to their left as they sailed north.

Quinn was soon sleeping again. He rested well for several hours until Olton woke him.

"It's time to cast the nets," he said, as Quinn stood up and rubbed the sleep from his eyes. "You take the rudder. Just hold it steady. Keep us pointed at that bright star near the horizon. See it?"

"The reddish one?" Quinn asked.

"Yes, that's it. You shouldn't have any problems. It's a calm night."

The calm night didn't last long. To Quinn, it seemed like one moment all was well, but in the next moment the sky poured fury down on them. It wasn't unusual for violent storms to strike near the Walheta Mountains. Cold air poured down off the mountains and mixed with the warm, humid air above the Great Sea and caused vicious storms that no one could predict. There was no light around them, only the stars that were mere pin pricks in the sky. Quinn felt a cool breeze waft across his skin, and he thought it was refreshing. Then suddenly the small fishing boat dipped into the trough of a wave; it was as if the water had disappeared beneath the boat. Olton was leaning over the bow of the ship where his net had snagged. The bow was driven into the bottom of the next wave like an arrow into a target.

Water flooded across the small boat, but the little craft was now rising high into the air. Quinn held the rudder fast, fear locking him in place so that he was like a statue. The ship topped the crest of the wave and shot down the other side, slamming her nose once again into the water.

"Storm!" Olton cried from the bow of the ship. He struggling to get back to where Quinn was holding the rudder but the waves knocked him off his feet.

"What do I do?" Quinn shouted.

"We've got to get the sail down!"

Quinn couldn't see the sail, but he could hear it. It was groaning and straining in the wind, which was now whipping all around him. He was afraid to let go of the rudder and stood paralyzed. He hated sailing because it always made him seasick. When Mansel had thrown him overboard he had been afraid he would drown, but the fear of this storm was much worse than anything he had ever felt before. He had always enjoyed storms before. He didn't like being caught out in one and didn't like to be kept from working, but he had enjoyed watching a good storm while sitting in his house or in an inn where he was warm and safe. He had always thought the lightning was beautiful as it arced through the sky, and the sense of security that came from having shelter made him feel cozy. But now, caught in a violent storm on the open sea, he knew a terror that was even greater than facing the dragon in Brighton's Gate.

Being exposed to a storm was frightening, but being tossed around on the sea during a storm gave Quinn a new sense of helplessness that he had never known before. The boat creaked and popped as if the strain was going to break it apart. The rudder was starting to buck and fight as if it were alive.

Olton had gotten to his feet and was trying to untie the rope that held their sail in place. Quinn could only see his shadowy outline and only then when they were on top of a wave. When they fell into the trough of the wave the world was completely black. Cold water sprayed up and Quinn was quickly drenched. The ship had small scuppers that allowed most of the water to flow back into the sea, but some of it found a place on the small vessel. Quinn noticed that there was water sloshing over his feet.

"Should we bail this water out?" he screamed.

"No!" Olton shouted back. "All we can do is ride it out."

The sailor had finally gotten the sail untied. It was whipping wildly in the wind, snapping and popping as it was blown out across the deck. Once Olton had it wadded up he stuffed it down in between the railing and a bulkhead. Then he staggered back to Quinn. He took hold of the rudder but motioned for Quinn to stay with him. He had to shout to be heard over the wind and waves.

"We need to try and steer her so that we're running with the waves, not against them."

Now that the sail was down, the rudder seemed less inclined to fight against them, but helping Olton hold the steering oar gave Quinn something to focus on.

Olton steered on instinct. He had been on the water his whole life and could sense the direction they needed to go just by feeling the movement of the ship. Quinn followed the sailor's lead, and occasionally lightning would give him a glimpse of what was happening. They were being blown out to sea, which was fortunate. The coast along the Walheta Mountains was rocky and dangerous. The waves grew larger and larger. When Quinn could see them during a flash of lighting he thought they looked as tall as trees.

Quinn soon found himself shaking from cold and fear. He was drenched in cold sea water and driving rain, his muscles tensed, and adrenaline coursed through his body. His teeth chattered and his eyes burned from the water, which he didn't wipe away because he refused to let go of the rudder. The boat was alternately thrust up by the force of heaving water and then pulled down by gravity as they rose and fell over the huge waves. Quinn's stomach flopped as they fell off the top of one wave, then his knees tried to buckle as they slammed into the next.

Eventually, the rain stopped. The waves were still large, although they didn't seem as ferocious as before. The wind waned, the clouds broke apart, and the stars reappeared.

"Well, that was a close one," Olton said.

"What do we do now?"

"There's only one thing we can do. We wait for morning and try to figure out where we are."

Chapter 7

Zollin and Brianna considered moving on, but they were both tired. The storm was closing in on them, so they took refuge in the cave that Rup had shown them. The space was small, but once their belongings were arranged they were both comfortable. Zollin missed the merry feeling of having a fire, but there simply wasn't enough fuel to support one. Zollin used magic to warm the cave floor and also to cook the meat from the ram Brianna had brought down with her new bow. Soon after working his magic, he fell asleep.

Brianna watched as the rain fell and the temperature dropped. The dim afternoon turned into a dark night, and the rain turned to sleet and then snow. She was propped on her pack and shared a blanket with Zollin. She was tired but sleep was elusive. The night wore on as the wind whistled outside the cave. Brianna finally nodded off just before dawn, and, when she finally woke up, it was almost noon. The world outside the cave looked gray. The sky was filled with thick clouds, and the light that filtered through them seemed weak.

"Hey, good morning," Zollin said.

"I didn't mean to sleep so late," Brianna replied.

"Well, it's still miserable out there," Zollin pointed out of the cave. "The snow has turned to sleet and I didn't feel like hiking in wet clothes. I thought we were just as well off staying here."

"Aren't you tired of these mountains?" Brianna asked.

"Well, I miss having a fire at night, but to be honest, I kind of like the solitude."

"Well, I don't. I miss a lot of things, but mostly, I miss a soft mattress."

"Me too," Zollin said.

"You must be feeling better."

"I am. I finally feel like I got enough rest. And I've been working on building a barrier around my magic. I think it's working. I can still feel my magic, still control it, but it doesn't seem to affect me as much as before."

"That's good," Brianna said.

"You don't seem very happy about it. I thought you would be, since it was your idea and all."

"I never doubted you for a second," Brianna said with a smile, but Zollin could tell she wasn't sincere.

"What's wrong?" he asked.

"Nothing."

"Come on, I know you better than that. I can tell something is bothering you."

"I'm tired," she admitted. "Not just physically, but I'm mentally exhausted. It seems like I'm bouncing between mind-numbing fear and paralyzing worry over you. I want things to get back to normal."

"You mean hiding out somewhere and hoping the bad guys don't find us."

"Well, it seems better than hunting down a dragon."

They both laughed.

"You know," he said as he sat down next to Brianna, "we don't have to hurry back. We can take our time. Rest. Just be together."

"You didn't slay the dragon," Brianna said.

"No, but we wounded it. We know we can hurt it again. We just haven't figured out how to kill the wretched beast."

"I have an idea about that. I was thinking last night when I couldn't sleep that maybe with my new bow I could hit it from far enough away that we would be safe. I mean, if we could ambush it somehow, maybe we could put enough arrows in it to bring it down."

"It would have to be in a place where it couldn't escape," Zollin said contemplatively.

"Exactly, but it isn't flying now. At least, it wasn't flying yesterday. It was hurt. If it can't fly away and we can stay ahead of it, perhaps we can find a place to ambush it."

"That's not a bad plan. I'm sure we could kill it if we just knew where to shoot it."

"I was thinking about that, too. I hit it just beneath the wing. I was thinking that its wings were like forelegs and perhaps the heart was just under them. I also hit it in the leg. The arrows are penetrating, I'm just not sure if we're hitting the right places or sinking the arrows in deep enough."

"Well, the new bow should allow your arrows to penetrate deeper. That's a good thing. We'll just need to find the dragon again and stay ahead of it."

They spent the rest of the day watching the sky outside and talking through their plans. The storm finally passed late in the afternoon, but they stayed in their cave. The terrain was covered in sleet, which wasn't melting very fast, and neither of them were anxious to get back out into the damp cold. Brianna slept better that night, and the next morning they were greeted with sunshine.

"I feel better knowing we have a plan," Zollin said. "You have a very strategic mind."

"I do?" Brianna said, surprised at Zollin's pronouncement.

"Yes. You made a very calculated decision about where to shoot the dragon. Now, you've come up with a plan to kill it. It's much better than my plan. I was just hoping to find it and somehow expose it."

"Well, I'll take that compliment," Brianna said cheerily.

They spent the day loafing in their small cave. The time passed quickly and both fell asleep soon after dark. The next day they were up early and ready to get moving. They had a light breakfast of even more mutton. They couldn't make themselves eat very much. They choked down enough to curb their hunger and drank cold water from their canteens.

They both hefted their heavy packs. They were filled with dried mutton that Zollin had made from what they couldn't eat of the ram. It wasn't salted and had very little flavor, but at least they had food. Their canteens had been refilled with sleet the day before, which had melted overnight. They were ready to head south, but first Zollin needed to use his magic to see if he could sense the dragon anywhere nearby.

He let the magic flow out of him and felt the familiar hot wind blowing through him. His inner reservoir of magic churned as always, like the inner workings of a blacksmith's forge, incredibly powerful but also dangerous. He had done a fairly good job of building a magical barrier around the source of his power so that while he could feel it at work, he could also feel that it was affecting him physically to a much smaller degree than before. He had a wall of defense against others, and now he had a wall of containment to protect himself.

The magic moved out of him like a mist, rolling through the mountains. It was like a sixth sense, allowing him to feel the presence of other beings. He felt small animals and a young elk that was moving slowly through the mountains. Then he came across something strange. It was unlike any animal he had ever seen or heard of. He felt the beast waking up, as if from a long sleep. Then the animal roared, and the sound was like a cross between a hawk's piercing cry and a bull's bellow.

"What was that?" Brianna asked.

"I'm not sure," Zollin said. "I sensed it; in fact, I may have woken it up. But it was weird."

"What do you mean?"

"I mean, it was like several different animals put together. It had legs like a ram, with hoofs. The body was thick, much bigger than a goat or even an elk. It had a head that was like an eagle, with a sharp beak. And its tail was long and thick."

"You're kidding, right?"

"No, I'm completely serious. I don't think we should hang out here any longer than we have to."

"Okay, so where do we go?"

"Southwest, away from that creature."

Zollin used his magic to lower them down the mountainside. Then they spent several hours hiking through a long canyon. They stopped to rest and eat around noon. The sun was finally high enough to shine directly down on them. Although they were warm from their long hike, the sun still felt good. Zollin reached out with his magic again before they set out. The creature he had felt earlier was closer than before.

"What is it?" Brianna asked. She had been watching Zollin and saw his face go white.

"That creature is following us."

"What do we do?"

"I don't know. It may not be wild. Rup didn't try to hurt us."

"Can we really take that chance?"

"I guess there's only one way to find out. You take cover, higher up on the mountain. I'll stay here and wait for it. I should be able to protect myself well enough and, if it attacks, you can shoot it."

They spent the next few minutes trying to find a place where Brianna could keep an eye on the canyon but stay hidden herself. They identified a suitable rocky outcropping, and Zollin levitated her there. There wasn't much room, and the sleet from the day before had not fully melted behind the rocks, leaving the perch slippery and uncomfortable.

Zollin waited, sipping water from his canteen. He could feel his magic churning; it was agitated by his worry. The creature he had felt reminded him of the dragon. Both creatures radiated a type of magic that was foreign to Zollin. The dragon wasn't a magic user and although it seemed almost invincible, it wasn't immune to his power. He only hoped the creature approaching him was the same.

The roots of the mountains were jagged and steep. There were no trails, no passes through the Northern Range. The valleys between the mountains were steep canyons, filled with rocky debris. Just walking through the canyons was difficult and dangerous. Zollin let his magic flow out again. He knew that if the creature could feel his magic he was essentially giving his position away. Still, he didn't like waiting. He was impatient and he didn't want to be caught off guard.

The levy he had built around his magic seemed to channel his power and give it more potency. He felt stronger than ever. He could use his magic without being stricken with physical weakness. He let the power build, and as his senses spread along the canyon he felt as if he were growing larger. He felt Brianna, like a raging bonfire on the mountainside, which surprised him. She wasn't wearing the white alzerstone ring anymore, and he thought that perhaps he just wasn't used to sensing her with his magic. Still, the more he thought about it he realized he'd never sensed such tangible power in anyone else. He chalked it up to the magical bow, which he assumed was radiating a sense of magical power. He could sense her worry, but also her sense of resolve. She had no intentions of losing him again.

Then he felt the creature. It was close. Just around a bend in the canyon and out of his sight. Unlike Brianna he couldn't sense the creature's intentions. He waited as the minutes slowly crept by. He would have thought that the creature had no intention of getting any closer, but it had gotten closer throughout the day. Perhaps it was more afraid of him than he was of it. In fact, he had no reason to fear the beast, but there was something so unnatural about it that he couldn't help but feel that it posed a danger.

Suddenly the creature was moving, rushing toward him. Zollin saw the beast, running sure-footed across the canyon floor so fast it was a blur. He barely had time to raise a shield around himself before the creature's thick tail whipped around and struck him. The tail didn't pass his shield, but the blow knocked Zollin off his feet and the creature raced by. Zollin was bruised from falling onto the rocky ground. He felt as if he had been pushed by a much larger man, shoved unexpectedly and knocked back. He scrambled to his feet, wishing he still had his staff. The creature roared, and the sound echoed off the mountainsides until it was almost too loud to bear. Zollin was busy holding his hands over his ears, and he almost got caught by the beast, but he dove to the side and felt the wind swoosh by as the tail whipped past him. He didn't hesitate but gave the creature a magical shove of his own. It toppled onto its side and Zollin jumped up, pressing his magic down on the creature to hold it in place. But the beast was too powerful and bucked him off, then scrambled away.

Brianna was frustrated by the creature's speed. It simply didn't stay still long enough for her to have a shot. The beast sprinted forward again, but this time Zollin sent a bolt of sizzling blue energy crackling toward the beast. It saw the attack and veered up the side of the mountain. It seemed to dance across the almost vertical cliff face effortlessly and was soon out of range. Zollin readied himself for the next attack, but Brianna was ready, too. She anticipated the creature's charge and, as soon as she saw it move out of her peripheral vision, she fired her arrow. It arced down and slammed into the creature's rear leg, causing the beast to stumble and slide through the rocks toward Zollin.

Zollin felt a twinge of magic when the arrow was fired, but all of his concentration was on the creature. As soon as the beast stumbled from Brianna's arrow, Zollin pounced. He used his magic to hold down the tail that was swinging wildly in all directions. He held it down as the creature struggled to rise. It was hissing like a snake, its hoofed forelegs scrabbling among the loose rocks in an effort to rise.

"Stay down!" Zollin shouted.

It had been a verbal expression of his will. He had not intended to say it out loud, it was merely what he was thinking as he worked to hold the thick, knobby tail in place. But the creature responded instantly. It became still, the hissing stopped, the tail laying down on the canyon floor.

Zollin was sure that it was some kind of trick. The creature had heard him, had understood him even, which was a surprise. He didn't trust it, but he had to try and communicate with it.

"What are you?" he asked.

"I am an Aberration," the creature said. It's voice was high pitched and loud. It was hard to understand.

"A what?"

"An Aberration. A magical freak. Don't pretend not to know me, wizard."

Zollin was shocked. Magical creatures seemed drawn to him. They often knew he was a wizard and some even implied that his presence had an effect on them, but he was still shocked.

"Why did you try to kill me?"

"You enslaved me," it hissed.

"No, I didn't," Zollin said angrily. "I've never even heard of you or anything like you."

"Your kind made me. I will not obey. I will die before I obey."

"What do you mean?"

The creature shrieked angrily.

"Tell me what you mean!" Zollin shouted.

"I was made by a wizard. Formed and shaped long ago. Far in the south. A wizard made me. I hate all wizards. They are vile and cruel."

"I'm not. It seems to me you were the one trying to kill me."

"Yet, I am wounded, you are not."

"That was self defense."

The creature didn't answer, it was still lying on the ground, still breathing heavily. Zollin waited, but the creature didn't speak.

"What's your name?"

The creature still didn't speak.

"Tell me your name," Zollin said firmly.

"Aberration."

"Aberration is your name?"

The creature didn't speak.

"You have to do what I say, don't you?"

The only response was the creature closing its eye. It was an agonizing gesture, a look of total resignation and despair from the beast's intelligent face.

"You have to do what I say," Zollin said again. "Sit up."

The creature rose slowly and painfully lowered itself onto its haunches. It was beautiful in a strange way. Its legs were covered in shaggy hair, its body with dark, glossy fur. At the neck the creature's fur turned to dark feathers which covered the beast's round head. It had bright, intelligent eyes. The beak was large and bone white, curing down into a sharp peak. The creature's tail had no hair, but rather a tough, leathery hide. Zollin could see the muscles flexing just beneath the thick skin.

"I'm not going to hurt you," Zollin said. "And my only command is that you do not hurt me or Brianna."

The creature called Aberration didn't move.

Zollin walked slowly backwards, so that he was out of range of the beast's tail. Then he turned to Brianna, who was standing tall at her perch. She had a arrow nocked and drawn. She was aiming it at the beast.

Zollin called out to her.

"Brianna. It's all right now. I'm going to lower you down."

Brianna nodded, but didn't relax the bow or her aim. Even as she rose into the air and floated softly down beside Zollin she kept her bow trained on the creature.

"I think we're okay," Zollin told her.

"What do you mean?"

"It was made by a wizard. It has to obey me."

"How do you know that?"

"It did everything I told it to do."

"It could be a trick. How do you even know it understands you?"

"It can talk," Zollin said.

"If it's that smart it's probably playing a trick. You can't trust a wild creature like that."

Brianna's voice was strong, but her eyes were wide. She couldn't believe what she was seeing and Zollin understood how she felt. He could hardly believe his eyes either, but there was something in the creature's voice that told him it was telling the truth. He used his magic to pull the arrow out of the beast's hind leg. It roared in pain.

"I'm sorry," Zollin said, raising both hands. "I'm sorry. I'm just trying to help you."

The creature hissed at them both, but didn't come any closer. Zollin let his magic flow into the wound. The arrow had torn through muscle but didn't sever any major arteries or pierce the bone. He knit the muscle fibers back together and then healed the shaggy hide.

"There, I healed you," Zollin said. "We don't want to hurt you."

The creature stretched its leg but didn't speak.

"Aberration, please tell us where you come from."

The creature only hissed.

"Tell us now!" Zollin demanded.

"I was formed by the wizard Iccalis to fight against the Torr. But my master was defeated and I fled here."

"Your master fought the Torr?" Zollin said in surprise. "I didn't know. I didn't know that anyone had ever resisted the wizards of the Torr. But that should make us allies. I too have fought the wizards of the Torr."

"I have no allies," the creature said. "I have no kind. I am an aberration. A magical freak."

"You mean you're all alone?" Brianna said. "Aren't there other . . . ," she searched for the right word to describe the creature, "animals like you?"

"No, I am not a beast of nature, but of magic."

"What do you want?" Brianna asked.

"To survive," it hissed.

Chapter 8

Zollin and Brianna were quiet for a moment. Zollin was surprised at how much compassion he felt for the creature. It was aptly named, a true aberration. He couldn't imagine the effort it must have taken to transform the different animal parts into one, fully functioning creature. And there was also an element of magic that was totally foreign to Zollin. It reminded him that he still had so much to learn.

"I may be asking too much," Zollin said softly, stepping closer to Aberration. "But I'd like to be your friend. I don't need anything from you. And I won't command you to do anything against your will."

Aberration hissed. It was an eerie sound, one Zollin had heard frightened animals make before in an effort to scare away their attackers. It took all of Zollin's courage to stand still.

"Prove it," said Aberration. "Release me."

"Zollin," Brianna said quietly, "are we sure this is a good idea?"

"No," Zollin replied. "I'm not sure, but I'm sincere." He turned his full attention to Aberration. "I release you," he said.

The creature stood up and shook its body, like a wet dog trying to get dry. Its tail curled up over its back, ready to strike. It looked at Brianna and said, "Tell her to lower the weapon."

"Brianna," Zollin said.

"I don't think this is a good idea."

"It's a show of good faith," he implored her. "We've got to show some trust if we want some in return."

Brianna bit her lower lip. She was scared. Zollin had magical defenses. She had seen him attacked by the dragon and come through unscathed. She had no illusions that she could do the same. If Aberration attacked Zollin she wasn't sure if she could anything to save him, or herself for that matter. But she trusted Zollin. He wouldn't risk her life, or at least she didn't think he would. She took a deep breath and then lowered her bow, letting the string come back to its resting position, but she kept the arrow nocked and both of her hands on the weapon.

"I didn't think it was possible," said Aberration. The creature's voice was high pitched and hard to understand, but it lowered its tail and everyone relaxed a little. "I don't have friends, but I will leave you in peace wizard."

"May I ask one favor of you?" Zollin said.

When the beast eyed him wearily, the intelligence in the avian eyes was almost startling to Brianna.

"What do you want?"

"I have a dragon to find and kill," Zollin said. "That is why we have come so far into the mountains. And I'm not sure what the future holds after that. The Torr still wants me, I suppose. But I would like to come back someday. I would like to learn more of you, of your history. Would that be acceptable?"

"If you come in peace," Aberration said. "I will answer your questions."

The creature gave a slight bow of its head and then it raced away, the wind from its passing making Zollin and Brianna tense up. It was hard to believe that any creature could move so rapidly.

"Well, we learned one thing," Zollin said. "Your strategy for the dragon just might work. That was one amazing shot you made. I've never seen an animal move that fast."

"It was a lucky shot, really. I just guessed and took a chance."

Brianna had moved over to where her arrow lay. She picked it up and inspected it. It was stained with blood but still straight and in good shape. She put it back in her quiver.

"Lucky?" Zollin said. "Are you kidding? I think you could shoot the moon with that bow."

"It is a good weapon."

"You're a great archer. You've really got a knack for shooting."

"You think so?" she asked in genuine surprise.

"Absolutely. I'm very proud of you."

She blushed. She was surprised at how good it made her feel for Zollin to praise her so highly. He could do practically anything, yet he saw her meager talents and valued them.

She stepped close and kissed him, hard on the lips. His eyes went wide with surprise and then she was off, pushing forward up the canyon, leaving him in a daze.

Zollin had to levitate them over a high ridge and down the steep cliff on the other side. They followed what appeared to be a game trail and came upon a small pool of water. A spring, high up on the mountain, fed the pool. It ran down the mountain and ended in a short waterfall that fell with a bubbling splash into the pool. There was obviously a channel that let the water flow away underground because the pool, although being constantly filled, maintained a steady level. There were bushes growing around the pool, and nearby was a natural alcove in the mountain. There were signs that the site had been used by others, Skellmarians most likely.

"This looks like a good place to camp for the night," Zollin said. He lowered his pack and began gathering sticks for a fire.

"Are you planning on building a fire?" Brianna asked.

"Yes."

"Good, I'm going to take a bath then."

"That water is probably freezing cold," he said.

"I'm not jumping into the pool," she said. "I'll use the spring water and just wash up. I'll need a good hot fire to warm up with, and a little privacy."

Zollin went to work. He found a large pile of wood. The sticks weren't very thick, but he had enough of them to give Brianna a good warm blaze and then keep a fire going through the night. Once he had the fire going he made himself scarce by levitating up on the mountain. He was amazed how strong he felt. He was tired from the long day, and using his magic still took a toll, but he was much stronger. The internal levy he had constructed around his magic gave him focus, and because it blocked the magic's drain on his physical strength and stamina, he felt his body responding to the weeks of hard work. He had spent time exercising through the winter with Kelvich. And over the last two weeks he had spent almost every day on long, grueling hikes through the mountains. His body had gained strength, and Zollin thought it felt good. He stretched his legs and back before sitting down on the ridge. He was high enough that he could see for miles in almost every direction. Only the mountain peaks rose higher than where he sat. All around him was a gorgeous vista, and he realized it was a sight very few people had ever seen. He took a moment to enjoy how fortunate he was, then he got down to business.

He needed to find the dragon, and so he let his magic flow. He pushed his mind out and let the mist of his magic filter down into the valleys and canyons far below. He didn't try to touch everything. The dragon was a large creature and a magical one.

All he needed was a hint of the beast, and he would know where to go. It took a while, and as twilight filled the sky and stars emerged so bright he felt like he could reach up and touch them, he finally found what he was looking for. The dragon was miles away, but heading south. It had taken as direct a course as it could, but it wasn't flying. He concentrated on the dragon and could sense the beast's pain. The wounds weren't life-threatening, but they had left the dragon too weak and sore to fly. Walking and hopping on the ground had caused further pain. The beast was tired and weak, but also angry. Zollin didn't know if he and Brianna could move fast enough to get ahead of the dragon, but they would have to try.

He stood up and stretched again, feeling the muscles in his shoulders and arms flex. He wasn't large like Mansel. He would never have the thick, bulbous muscles his friend possessed. But he was strong, his muscles firm along his long arms and legs. He jumped off the ridge and let himself free fall for a moment. It was exhilarating and terrifying at the same time. Then he let his magic guide his fall, gradually slowing his descent. The effort superheated the writhing magic inside him, but the heat felt good, as his body had grown almost numb from the cold wind and dropping temperature on the ridge. His eyes stung from the cold wind, but he forced them open and looked for Brianna. She had built up the fire and was wrapped in a blanket near the blaze.

He floated down near the waterfall. Then he stripped off his own clothes and plunged them into the water. His hands burned from the cold but he scrubbed the clothes until they were clean. Then he used his magic and dried them. Next, he cupped his hands under the frigid flow and splashed the water on his body. The cold water was painful, but he worked hard, scrubbing his body of its accumulated filth. Dust, dirt, and grime had built up on his skin, especially around his neck. Finally he took a deep breath and stuck his head under the water fall. The water was so cold he struggled not to shout at the shock of it. He ran his fingers vigorously through his hair, which had grown shaggy. Then he shook his head and let the drops of water fly everywhere. It was hard to push the hair back over his head because the water rain down his back in icy drops that were painful. He pulled his pants and boots back on and used his shirt to dry his hair and shoulders. Then he hurried over to the fire.

"Where have you been?" Brianna asked.

"I needed a bath, too."

"I knew that, but you weren't around here. I've been looking for you."

He squatted close to the fire, luxuriating in its warmth for a moment before answering.

"I went up on the ridge to see if I could find the dragon."

"Any luck?"

"Actually, yes. It's making better time than we are, but I think if we push ourselves we can catch it."

"Is it flying?"

"No, I don't think it can. It's still pretty sore from what I could tell. Your arrows did some damage."

"Well, maybe if we can get close enough, I can do more than wound it."

"I hope so."

They spent the rest of the evening talking and eating. They boiled some of their dried meat in a pot that Zollin quickly fashioned out of sand. Then they took turns sleeping. The fire was nice, the warmth very welcome, and the bright flames a comforting sight after days of freezing cold nights, but they were afraid it might attract unwelcome attention. Fortunately the night passed without incident, and they set out early the following morning.

They had traveled for two hours when Zollin noticed a strange, yet familiar, chanting music that he remembered from being near the mountain dwarves at the foot of the southern range of mountains in Peddingar Forrest.

"Do you hear that?" he asked Brianna.

"What? I don't hear anything."

"I think it's dwarves. I can hear them singing."

He let his ears lead them. He followed the sound and eventually came to a small cave. Zollin lowered his head and could clearly hear the sound booming from far below.

"Hello," he said in a loud voice. "Can anyone hear me?"

The music stopped, and there was a long pause before a small voice answered.

"Who's there?"

"I'm Zollin. I'm a wizard."

"And who's that with you, wizard?"

"This is Brianna, my friend."

"Well, this is as bold as anything I've seen. A wizard in the highlands, come looking for dwarfs."

"Actually," Zollin said, still speaking into the cave. "We're tracking a dragon."

"You don't say," said the voice. "Well, what are you doing out there in the cold air, wizard? You're welcome in the warm earth."

"All right," Zollin said. "We're coming in."

He took Brianna's hand and led her into the dark cave. They both had to walk bent over. The light behind them faded, and they took a few unsteady steps in total darkness. Then a warm, orange glow appeared ahead of them. The cave led down, deeper and deeper into the earth, and finally opened into a large cavern, lit by roaring forges and glowing moss that grew on the ceiling of the cavern.

"Oh, this is beautiful," Brianna said.

"You must have dwarfish blood, missy," said a stout-looking dwarf.

Unlike Jute and the dwarves Zollin had met in the southern range of mountain highlands, these dwarves had swarthy-looking skin and dark, curly beards. A group of men, most with hammers and tongs in their hands, had gathered in the center of the cavern. Zollin caught glimpses of dwarf children peeking from the small doorways and windows carved into the solid rock.

"I'm Bahbaz," said the dwarf, "Head man of the Oliad clan. What brings a wizard this far north? Dragon hunting is dangerous business."

"Yes, it is," Zollin agreed. "We're from Yelsia, south of the highlands. A dragon has been preying on our people. The King sent me to find the dragon and kill it if possible."

"Well, you're still alive, that says something. Let's find something to drink."

Bahbaz led them to a small group of stone benches. He poured small mugs of a frothy drink and then gave one each to Brianna and Zollin. He took a long draught of his own mug and then belched loudly.

"Ah, that's refreshing," Bahbaz said proudly. "Well, go ahead, drink up."

Zollin and Brianna looked at each other as they sampled the drink. Zollin found the drink slightly bitter, but cool on his tongue.

It warmed his body in that familiar way that wine and ale did. It was thicker than most drinks and tasted creamy.

"That's an Oliad clan drink. It's made from root liquor, ewe's milk, and spring water with herbs. We age it in brass vats. As you may have noticed, vegetation is scarce here in the northern highlands, but we take our drink very seriously. It's called arkhi."

"It's very nice," said Brianna.

"Yes, I like it," Zollin agreed. "It's better than ale."

"Of course it is, it's dwarfish made," Bahbaz said happily. "Now, how can I help you, wizard?"

"Please, call me Zollin. We don't really need anything, although we are grateful for your hospitality. We're pursuing the dragon and we shouldn't stay long. We need to get ahead of the beast."

"You want to keep it from attacking the southlands, eh?"

"No, I mean, yes, of course we do. But we're hoping to ambush the dragon. If we can catch it in a canyon or gorge, we have a plan to kill it that just might work."

"What's to keep it from flying away?" Bahbaz asked. "They're wily beasts, after all."

"It's wounded," Brianna said. "I shot it with my bow."

"You would need dwarfish steel to penetrate dragon hide."

"We have dwarfish steel," Zollin said. "I traded for it with Jute of the Yel Clan."

"The Yel Clan is in the southern mountains. Not the wiliest traders. What did you give him?"

"He wanted ale. I brought him over a dozen casks."

"Ale? I knew it. The southern clans are not brewers, and they're always looking for something to supplement their vapid drinks. They want arkhi, but we don't trade it cheap. We have been in negotiations with the southern clans for two decades now, but they're stubborn. The southern mountains have more minerals, but they are loath to trade them to us, because they know we're better brewers and better smithies too."

"You don't have iron here?" Brianna asked.

"Yes, of course we have iron. It's the other minerals that are scarce. Quartz, for example, is very rare, as is wolframite and scheelite. They have the precious gems you southlanders crave, too, but we have little use for them. In the old days we were at a distinct disadvantage to the southern clans. We have the greater skills, see, never doubt that fact, but the southern clans had access to people. You southlanders don't travel into the northern range very often."

"No, I suppose not," Zollin said.

"Well, that's enough history for today. I want to show you something, wizard. Something very special."

"All right," Zollin said.

He knew he needed to continue his journey, but he was fascinated with dwarves. Their tight-knit clans, pride in workmanship, and friendly nature drew him to them. He looked at Brianna and she nodded encouragement.

"It may be that we can help each other," Bahbaz said.

He led them down a long, narrow corridor that sloped down. The air grew warmer and the light faded. There were carvings on the wall that depicted battles and fantastic beasts, dwarf kings and entire dwarf clans. Zollin wanted to stop and inspect the carvings, but Bahbaz hurried past them. Soon the roof of the corridor began to slope down, and Zollin was forced to stoop. Brianna wasn't as tall as Zollin, but she was soon walking bent over as well. They walked with their hands on the walls as the light faded, and soon they were moving in almost total darkness. The only sounds were their boots scraping along the floor of rock.

"There are many ways through the mountains," Bahbaz said. "You southlanders go over or around the mountains, while we go under. But it's been a long time since the Stepping Stones were used by dwarves or men."

"What are the Stepping Stones?" Zollin said.

"You'll see soon enough. Patience, my tall friend. Patience."

"If this roof gets any lower we'll be crawling," Brianna said.

"I'm getting a little claustrophobic," Zollin said. "How much further?"

"Not far, not far," Bahbaz said in a merry voice.

The temperature had grown steadily warmer. Zollin and Brianna in their thick, winter clothes were sweating and panting from the exertion of walking bent over. Just when Brianna thought she couldn't take anymore, the tunnel began to brighten. It took several more minutes, but finally they came out into an immense cavern. The heat took their breath away. It felt like they were standing in an oven. The floor of the cavern sloped down to a vast pool of glowing molten rock that illuminated the giant cave. The ceiling was covered with huge stalactites that glittered brightly and reflected the orange light in all directions.

"Wow," Zollin said.

"It's a rare sight," Bahbaz said. "Very few people not of our race have seen this place. It's the heart of the mountain. The magma is impossible to approach, even for dwarves. There was once a bridge that spanned the pool and allowed us to travel through the mountains and to the south, but occasionally the magma rises. We can never predict how high it will rise or when or even how long it will stay that way. The Stepping Stones are what we call these caverns. They can allow us to move quickly through the mountain range, but with the bridge out we can't risk it. If we get caught trying to circle the pool of magma, we could be trapped if the pool rises. It's just too dangerous."

"What happened to the bridge?" Zollin asked.

"It grew weak from the heat and eventually collapsed. Sometimes the magma rises slowly, and other times it erupts like a pot boiling over. When that happens the molten rock gets thrown up as air in the magma from far below bubbles out. The bridges get damaged and eventually destroyed. In the past, great numbers of dwarves would come together to rebuild the bridges, but it's been harder and harder to get our people motivated. We've grown complacent, and many tribes are isolated."

"That's fascinating, but why show me this?" Zollin asked.

"Well, you're a wizard," Bahbaz said in surprise. "If you will rebuild the bridge, I'll lead you south. You'll be well ahead of your dragon when we're though, provided you don't take too long with the bridge."

Zollin was at a loss for words. He knew that he could build the bridge, he just wasn't sure how to build it or with what. Brianna was watching him, as was Bahbaz.

"You can do it, can't you? I'm mean, a wizard who hunts dragons must have great power," Bahbaz said.

"I guess so," Zollin said. Then he turned to Brianna, "What do you think?"

"If it gets us ahead of the dragon it would be worth it. And we wouldn't have to waste time hunting or making camp. We wouldn't even have to worry about keeping watch."

"Or getting cold," he added.

"So you'll do it?" Bahbaz asked.

"You'll lead us south?" Zollin said. "You'll provide food and drink? How long will it take to get to the Great Valley?"

"Yes, of course, that can all be arranged. If the bridges were all intact we could easily make the journey in a few days," Bahbaz said.

"All right, we'll do it," Zollin said.

Then he scratched his head and wondered just what he'd gotten himself into.

Chapter 9

Kelvich could barely contain himself. The scholars had finally found a section of scrolls that were the work of ancient wizards. Everyone was now busy translating the scrolls. Kelvich had been hoping for documents exactly like this when he found the hidden library at the Ruins of Ornak. The ruins had been the site to which Zollin and the soldiers from Felson had lured the dragon in hopes of killing the beast. As they fortified the site, refashioning a working city from ruins, they uncovered a hidden library with hundreds of clay pots that were sealed with wax to preserve the scrolls inside.

Kelvich had moved as many as he could and, with the help of Jax, a young orphan from Felson, they had transported the scrolls to Ebbson Keep. Kelvich had convinced the scholars who worked in the large library at the Keep to help him translate and preserve the scrolls. The scholars had readily agreed and had begun cataloging the many scrolls. Others had been sent back to Ornak to transport the rest of the scrolls. Kelvich had worked tirelessly to keep the scholars focused on the goal of finding something that would help Zollin battle the dragon. Weeks had passed with no luck. Many of the ancient manuscripts were histories, philosophical treatises, or books dealing with common themes.

When the scholars returned with the second load of scrolls, Kelvich had once again been hopeful of finding something that would aid Zollin in his quest. Unfortunately, most of the scrolls in the second lot dealt with the disciples of the religious community that first formed the city at Ornak. It was fascinating material, and in most circumstances Kelvich would have lost himself in the ancient scrolls. He had spent the better part of three lifetimes learning all he could about the magical and natural world. Before Zollin and his friends had arrived in Brighton's Gate, Kelvich was content to live out his days in quiet solitude. But being a sorcerer, he had felt Zollin approach. He had been drawn to the young wizard and had taken Zollin under his wing, teaching him as much as he could about magic and the Torr.

When the third wagon arrived at Ebbson Keep, Kelvich was worried that his work had been in vain. The third wagon carried all that was left of the scrolls from the hidden library, but it was far less material than the first two wagons contained. Still, the scholars had continued their work with Kelvich, poring over them until finally they discovered several manuscripts that were written by sorcerers and wizards. The finds had been almost simultaneous, and Kelvich now waited impatiently for the translators to finish their tedious work. Kelvich was unfamiliar with languages and couldn't help. The scholars were fastidious, examining every tiny mark on the ancient scrolls and often consulting one another. Kelvich tried to stay busy, but the only distraction that could hold his attention was Jax.

The young orphan had adapted to his new surroundings so quickly that Kelvich thought of him as a local. Jax knew everyone. While Kelvich struggled to keep up with the scholars, Jax knew everyone in the Keep, from his classmates in the essentials school to the servants in the kitchens and even the soldiers who stood guard throughout the large castle. He not only knew names, but he remembered details about their families and interests that people would share with him. Taking a walk though the castle with Jax was almost amusing. Everyone liked the young boy, calling out to him and stopping to talk. He would ask questions and bring up small points of concern with everyone, including the Duke himself.

Kelvich had asked his young ward how he kept up with so much information, but it all came naturally to Jax. His memory was as sharp as a knight's sword. He treated everyone equally, and he had a knack for helping people get what they wanted or needed, even if they hadn't told him they needed it. He suggested that the children run messages through the Keep, which was a large, complex structure. The children were finally able to run through the long castle corridors, which helped burn off some of the restless energy that made sitting and studying so difficult. It also helped the Keep run more efficiently.

Kelvich was pacing outside the translation rooms when Jax came hurrying up to him.

"The Duke wants to see you," Jax said in an excited voice.

"Why?" Kelvich asked. "Is something wrong?"

"I don't know. Come on," he urged.

Kelvich didn't like leaving the translation team. He was anxious to read what they had translated, but of course the scholars rarely came out of the rooms once they started on a project. They stopped only to eat and sleep, often taking their meals in their work rooms and sometimes sleeping in there, too. The scrolls were long manuscripts, and they had been working hard for over a week. Although Kelvich had nothing to do but pace and worry, he still didn't like leaving his post.

Jax led them through the long, stone corridors. Many places in the Keep had high windows that allowed fresh air and light into the rooms and hallways. There were ladders built into the walls that allowed defenders to shoot arrows out of the windows in case of an attack. There were multiple levels to the

Keep, but the staircases only rose one floor. They were spread around in the Keep almost randomly, but the method to the madness forced attackers to fight their way to the top, floor by floor. A traditional stairwell would simply give an invading force access to every floor all at once.

Ebbson Keep had become an important city for scholarly research and cultural advancement, but it was essentially a fort on the border with Baskla. In days gone by, the Keep had played the important role of securing the border. Invaders could bypass the fortress, but in doing so they left their lines of supply vulnerable to the garrison, who could sally forth and harass the supply trains or flank the invaders.

Almost directly across the border was Fort Jellar, a sprawling complex of smaller fortresses that had become a center for trade. Goods moved north up the Great Sea and then took the Weaver's Road, which ran west from Black Bay to Fort Jellar. Merchants who traveled up the western coast of the Five Kingdoms had many options for trade, but goods that were moved north by way of the Great Sea had only two. Fort Jellar had become the biggest city in Western Baskla by virtue of its important location. Ebbson Keep did not prosper as much as Fort Jellar had, largely because the Duke whose job was to maintain the Keep was military-minded and forced all commerce to take place outside of his complex of thick, stone walls.

Kelvich was almost out of breath by the time he reached the Duke's quarters, which were located in one of three massive towers that served as lookout posts allowing soldiers to see for miles across the border in every direction. Kelvich waited in a small vestibule outside the Duke's reception room. There was, of course, a feasting on the lower level, but the Duke did all his business in a large room just below his family's personal quarters. The reception room had large windows with panoramic views. Jax left Kelvich and hurried in to let the Duke know that Kelvich was waiting. Although there were usually no fewer than half a dozen people in the room at any one time, the old sorcerer noticed that the room looked especially frantic today. There were easily two dozen people in the reception room, most gathered around the large conference table or standing near the east-facing windows.

"He'll see you now," said Jax.

"Do you know what's going on?" Kelvich asked.

"No idea, but everyone is very busy," he said cheerfully.

Kelvich followed Jax into the room and found the Duke standing at the conference table. On it was a large map of the Five Kingdoms, held down by heavy brass candle holders.

"Ah, yes, Master Kelvich," the Duke said. "I've been expecting you. How does the translation work go?"

"It's fine, my lord. Slow, but steady," Kelvich said.

"Yes, it's sometimes hard to wait on scholarly men. They seldom understand the need for haste don't they? Well, I've more pressing concerns at the moment. We've had no word from the west, apart from what you can tell me of your travels there. Have you heard word of problems? Political upheaval? Anything of that sort?"

"No, not specifically," Kelvich said. "I know that King Felix is well, or was well. I know that he sent men to escort Prince Wilam home from Osla."

"Do you know why?" asked the Duke.

He was a big man, with round shoulders and a barrel chest. His stomach was large, too, but it seemed to fit his body rather than hinder it. He had a thick beard that he kept trimmed, and his shaggy hair was held in place by a leather strap.

"I was not in Orrock," Kelvich tried to explain.

"But your friend the wizard was, I believe. What did he tell you?"

"Not much really, we were focusing on finding a dragon."

"Please, Kelvich. We seem to be blind here. Troops are gathering at Fort Jellar. They don't seem to be in a hurry and they aren't doing much once they arrive, but it's the first time I've seen troops mobilizing across the border. Any small bit of information would help. Now, why would the King send for Prince Wilam?"

"Well, according to Zollin, Prince Simmeron was poisoning the King. When Zollin healed King Felix, they learned that Prince Simmeron had sent assassins to kill Wilam."

"I see," said the Duke. "That is foul news to be sure. I suppose you've heard that a Council of Kings was called?"

"Yes," Kelvich said.

"It appears that something is afoot in the Five Kingdoms. We've had no word that anything dire has happened to the Prince, but it might be possible that an assassin could have missed his target and harmed someone else. Especially with all Five Kings gathered together. And it does not bode well that King Felix sent for his son when a Council of Kings has been called," the Duke was speaking as much to himself as anyone in the room. "We must be prepared. If the King has withdrawn his support of the Confederacy, we could be vulnerable to attack."

He turned to one of the soldiers standing nearby.

"I want battle stations manned at all times," he said. Then he turned to another man in gleaming armor. "I want the watch doubled, and let's make sure that there are working spyglasses on every watchtower. Gentlemen," he said in a loud voice addressing the entire room. "Be sure your men have their gear ready. As of this moment we are on call. I want everyone to refresh his knowledge of the signal flags. I want all the livestock moved into the Keep, along with as much food, wine, and medical supplies as possible. All leave is canceled. I want everyone on high alert. We may not be at war, men, but we must be ready for it."

There was a chorus of "Yes sir's" and "Aye, my lord's," then most of the men shuffled out of the room.

"Kelvich, stay with me a moment," the Duke said.

He moved over to a large chair and filled a mug with water before sitting down. He rubbed his eyes and then waved to an empty chair.

"Please, sit down. I've forgotten my manners. Would you care for a drink?"

"No, thank you," Kelvich said as he took a seat in one of the many chairs around the Duke's large desk.

"We haven't had much time to get to know one another. I'm very excited about the collection of manuscripts you found. And to be honest, I'm honored that you brought them here."

Kelvich wasn't sure what to say. He wished that he had asked for a drink so that he could use it to stall for time while he thought of the right thing to say. Kelvich didn't feel comfortable around powerful people. He had seen power abused, had even done things he was ashamed of with his own power. As a sorcerer, Kelvich could control and use the power of other magic users. He had little real power himself, but in the presence of a wizard or warlock, he could essentially steal their self control and make them do whatever he pleased. In the past he had used the powers of others for his own ends, but in time he had come to believe that usurping someone's will was wrong, and he had vowed never to do it again.

"I've had two passions all my life," the Duke continued. "I'm a military man, there's no denying that. I love this castle. I love that my family has held the Keep for over five hundred years. But I also love academia. Not that I'm a learned man. I've never had the time to devote myself to one of the scholarly disciplines, but I love books. I used to sit in this room and watch my father read. We would drill with swords all day, then spend our evenings reading. I got those two passions from my father, and I suppose he inherited those same passions from his father. I don't care for court or politics. My place is here, defending the eastern border, even if there hasn't been a threat here for over three hundred years."

He smiled at Kelvich, who nodded encouragingly.

"Young Jax is quite a lad," the Duke continued. "I'd say he's smarter than half the people in this castle combined."

"Yes, he's very bright."

"He's the type of person who combines practical knowledge with genuine concern. His idea of having the children run messages was a stroke of genius. My tutor tells me the classes in the essentials school are more productive than ever. And that's with a portion of the children out of the classroom everyday. I should have thought of that years ago. I know it would have made my life during essentials school much more enjoyable."

"I suppose so," Kelvich said.

"I want Jax to stay here," the Duke said. "As my ward, of course. I think he could be an invaluable asset to the Keep."

Kelvich was surprised and not quite sure what to say.

"Well," he said, struggling to find the right words. "He's an orphan, so I suppose that would be up to him."

"Good," said the Duke. "I was hoping you'd agree. I'll talk to him soon and see how he feels. I've sent messengers to Orrock, letting the King know what we're seeing here. My question for you is, when might we receive your friend, the wizard?"

"I'm not sure," Kelvich said. "I'm supposed to return to the Ruins of Ornak once I learn all I can from the scrolls. He'll only come here if he returns from the highlands and I'm not there."

"I don't suppose I could talk you into staying here then, could I?"

"What do you mean?"

"Well, if war is coming, it wouldn't hurt to have a wizard on our side."

"I really can't believe that war is brewing. We haven't been at war for over three centuries. Isn't it more likely that the troops you're seeing are just replacing the troops normally stationed at Fort Jellar?"

"That's a good point, but the there are no troops leaving the area. More and more come in every day, but none leave."

"Perhaps it's just ordinary maneuvers," Kelvich said.

"I've been the Duke here for over twenty years. I've never seen anything like this."

He stood up and walked over to the large window that faced east.

"Look at this. Tell me what you think it might be."

Kelvich waked over to the window and what he saw surprised him. Fort Jellar was easily over a mile away. There were several tall, stone structures and a long timber wall that surrounded the sprawling compound. Beyond that were rows and rows of small, white tents. Kelvich recognized the tents because they looked exactly like the tents used by the King's legion, which had marched up the Great Valley with the wizards of the Torr in search of Zollin.

"There are so many," Kelvich said quietly.

"More than I've ever seen before," the Duke said. "Now do you understand my concern?"

"I'm beginning to."

"And your friend?"

"Zollin," Kelvich said. He realized that the Duke was hoping that Zollin would come and fight. It made him nervous. He didn't want Zollin to join the Torr, but the Torr had risen to power in the Five Kingdoms by consolidating magical power so that no single kingdom had a military advantage over another by using wizards when they waged war. There hadn't been a wizard aligned with a specific kingdom in centuries. In fact, Kelvich suspected that Zollin's presence was the cause for the Council of Kings. And if he was right and Prince Wilam had withdrawn, that meant that there was no one speaking for Yelsia at the Council. Perhaps it all made sense. Perhaps, Kelvich thought to himself, the King wants war.

"I can't make any promises," Kelvich said. "Zollin could be in the mountains for months. There's really no telling when or even if he'll ever come back. But I see your point."

"I'm not afraid to fight," the Duke said. "I'm not interested in the whys or what happens afterward. My whole life I've trained my body and my mind to hold this Keep against whatever forces come against us. But if I'm right and the other kingdoms join forces against us, we could be overrun. If that happens, we lose the library. All the scrolls could be destroyed. Once the scholars are finished translating the manuscripts you need, I'd like you to leave the Keep and send your wizard to help defend us."

"I'll do all I can," Kelvich said. He was suddenly upset with himself for not insisting that Jax come with him when he left.

"That's all I can ask," said the Duke.

Chapter 10

Zollin considered all the possibilities. He needed materials to make the bridge. There was plenty of stone—he was under the mountain after all—but it would take a lot of time and strength to remove the stone from the cavern walls. Plus he didn't want to have to worry about the structural integrity of the cavern. The molten rock was his best option. It was already heated to a liquid state, so it would be easy to separate and then transmute. The only question was, could he manipulate the molten rock without hurting himself? He had moved incredibly heavy objects before, but he had never worked with anything that was too hot to touch.

"What's your plan?" Brianna asked.

They had asked Bahbaz to bring their packs and gather the supplies they would need for the journey. Zollin was hopeful that by passing under the mountains they could make better time than the dragon, although it was possible that at any moment the beast could take flight and their best efforts would all be for naught.

"I'm wondering about using the molten rock to build the bridge."

"I don't know," Brianna said. "It's already so hot in here I can hardly stand it."

"I don't really have much choice. We need to get this done as quickly as possible. The molten rock is my best option."

"But it could take a really long time to cool enough that we could pass over it."

"No, I'll have to cool it down to a reasonable temperature."

"You can do that?"

"Sure, I think so."

"Can you cool me down?" she asked playfully, waving her hand to fan her face.

Her skin glistened with sweat in the orange light of the cavern, and Zollin thought she looked more beautiful than ever.

"I don't know," he said. "I always get hot when I'm around you."

"Oh, Zollin," she said. "You need to stick to magic. I don't think wooing women is your strong suit."

"I thought it was pretty smooth."

Brianna just laughed, and Zollin turned back to his task. He let his magic flow out and approach the molten rock. He could feel the heat. It wasn't the same as physically being near the heat. It was more like noticing something: the heat registered in his mind but didn't hurt him. He could sense that the surface, although blisteringly hot, was much cooler than the molten rock underneath. He probed the magma and found that the molten rock was thick like molasses on the surface. As the rock grew hotter, it became less viscous until it was almost like water.

He could also perceive the tiny particles that made up the magma. They were the same as the rock all around him, only these particles were spinning and shaking at an incredible rate. Further under the surface of the molten rock the particles crashed into each other, causing even more friction and heat. Zollin realized that all he needed to do was slow down the racing particles and the magma would revert to solid stone.

It took a great amount of concentration to form the shape of the bridge. It had to be arched, both for strength and to allow humans or dwarves to cross over the giant well of molten rock without the heat becoming unbearable.

Brianna watched in awe as the column of magma, at first merely glowing orange and then so bright white it was difficult to look at, rose up from the pool of molten rock. The magma dimmed and took shape as it rose. Zollin first simply made an arch of stone and cooled the rock. Then he levitated more of the molten rock and formed a flat walkway with railings on the side, fusing it to the arch he had already made. The entire process took nearly an hour.

Bahbaz returned halfway through the process and watched in awe as Zollin lifted the molten rock and made a bridge over the pool of super heated stone. When Zollin finished he leaned against the rock wall, tired and hot. His hair was wet with sweat and there were drops of sweat running down his face. He used his shirt to mop up the perspiration.

"That's a fine bridge, wizard," Bahbaz said. "You may have dwarfish blood. How long until we can cross?"

"Whenever you're ready, although I could use a drink," Zollin said.

"How's your containment working?" Brianna said, referring to the barrier Zollin had built around his magic to keep it from sapping his physical strength so much.

"It's fine, I'm just really hot."

"It's warm under the mountain, southlander," Bahbaz boasted. "Spend the day pounding iron near a dwarf's forge and you'll know true heat."

"I'll pass," Zollin said.

Bahbaz handed Zollin a metal canteen that was covered in a thin layer of tanned animal hide. There were four other dwarves with Bahbaz, each carrying a ruck sack, and among them they carried Zollin and Brianna's packs. Brianna hefted hers over her shoulders and offered to carry Zollin's.

"No, I've got it. Let's get moving," Zollin said.

The surface of the bridge was rough under their feet. Zollin had left it that way to give better traction to those crossing the steep inclines. The heat in the large cavern increased as they neared the apex of the bridge. Zollin had to dodge a few of the lowest-hanging stalactites, and soon they were on their way down the far side of the bridge. Beyond that was another tunnel.

The dwarves produced lanterns to light their path. The little lamps were great at illuminating the path, but not so effective at giving light to the ceiling of the tunnel. Zollin hit his head on the uneven stone several times. Brianna put on the helmet Zollin had made for her and the dwarves all marveled at it.

"That's dwarfish steel if ever I've seen it," Bahbaz said. "But who forged it for you? Dwarves don't make human armor."

"Zollin made it for me," she said.

"You're a smith?" asked one of the other dwarfs. He had a gruff voice that was so low-pitched it was almost hard to understand.

"No, I forged it using magic. Just like the bridge."

This seemed to pacify the dwarves. They didn't seem to care that their steel was forged into armor or weapons, but they wanted to ensure it was well made.

They walked for a long time. At certain points the tunnels opened up into larger caverns. At other times, Zollin and Brianna were forced to walk stooped over. Finally they came to another of the large caverns with a pool of molten rock at the center. This one still had remnants of the ancient bridge that once spanned the gap. It was narrower than the one Zollin had built. The pool of magma had built up, too, so that it looked like a tiny volcano in the center of the cavern floor.

"We'll stop here and let the wizard work," Bahbaz said to the other dwarves.

They sat on the stone and began eating. Zollin shrugged off his pack and took a long drink from the canteen. The water wasn't cold, but it was still refreshing. The heat in the cavern was much greater than in the tunnels. He decided to repair the old bridge rather than build one from scratch. He pushed his magic into the molten rock and pulled it up. This magma was heavier, and Zollin could feel that the stone had a high mineral content. As his magic probed the bridge he was surprised to find the ends of the ruined stone walkway seemed almost splintered. Zollin had thought that the molten rock spewing up might have caused the bridge to melt away, but perhaps it just grew weak and collapsed, he thought.

He worked on the bridge for half an hour, then slumped down beside the others.

"Finished already?" Bahbaz said.

"Yes," Zollin said. "I just rebuilt the fallen portion of the old bridge and made a heat shield underneath."

Bahbaz and the other dwarves went to inspect Zollin's work. Brianna brought over a small loaf of bread that was round and flat. She handed it to him and smiled.

"There's also some crumbly cheese they make out of goat's milk, and some meat. How does that sound?" she asked.

"Great, I'm starving."

He ate quickly. The dwarves returned and were ready to push on. Zollin couldn't tell what time it was or whether it was day or night. His body was tired and his feet ached. He sipped arkhi from a canteen that Bahbaz had given him, and they continued their journey. The tunnels they followed rose and fell, sometimes curving and even switching back to head in the opposite direction. There were forks in the tunnels and sometimes the tunnels crossed other tunnels, usually in the larger caverns. Zollin knew he was totally dependent on the dwarves to lead him and Brianna out of the maze of caves.

Finally, they decided they had gone far enough for the day and stopped when their tunnel opened up to a cavern that was so immense that the ceiling and far wall were swallowed in an inky darkness that seemed thick and alive. Zollin felt a strange sensation, as if the darkness were pulling him. It reminded him of being near a sharp drop and the way in which looking down made him feel as if the empty space were pulling him down. They came to a small pool of water, and the dwarves lay down on the hard, stone floor.

"Is there any need to keep watch?" Zollin asked.

A strange look crossed Bahbaz's face, and then he shook his head.

Zollin felt relaxed from the arkhi. He gave the canteen to Brianna and unfolded a blanket from his pack which he spread out on the floor. The dwarves watched them curiously. Zollin spread another blanket for Brianna. They nibbled a bit of dried meat as they lay down, but soon they were too tired to talk or eat or even think. Zollin slept soundly until Bahbaz woke him.

"Time to get moving," said the dwarf.

Zollin had no idea how the dwarves kept track of time, but he stretched and got to his feet. He shook Brianna awake and then folded the blankets. They refilled their canteens with water from the pool. Then they set out again, circling the pool to continue on their journey. As they came to the pool's farthest point from the wall they had been following, they discovered that the water was running out of the pool and falling off a ledge. Zollin saw the gaping abyss and wished more than ever that they were back by the wall.

"What is this?" Brianna asked, peering over the ledge.

"Just a hole," Bahbaz said.

"What's down there?"

"Nothing good."

They waded across the edge of the pool and then circled the far side back to the wall. The rest of the morning they spent traversing the huge, underground cavern. The blackness felt heavy, and Zollin thought it was hard to breathe, as though the weight of the mountains were bearing down on them. He was ready to be back out in the open, to see the sky and feel the sun on his skin.

When they left the big cavern Zollin and Brianna both welcomed the close confines of the tunnel. It took another hour to reach the next Stepping Stone, as Bahbaz called them. This cavern was smaller, and the floor was littered with small rocks. There was no sign of a bridge, so Zollin started from scratch. Once again the dwarves, who were stoic little people, sat and ate while Zollin worked.

He had the arch built when he noticed a change in the magma. It was beginning to churn and Zollin hesitated, watching the molten rock.

"Something's happening," he said.

The dwarves moved quickly past Zollin.

"What is it?" Brianna asked.

"I'm not sure."

"Is it going to erupt?"

Zollin let his magic probe into the magma and felt something strange. The molten rock was still churning, but he could feel something in the pool. It was large, even though it seemed to blend perfectly into the magma.

"There's something in it," Zollin said, noticing the dwarves give each other nervous glances.

"What do you mean?" Brianna asked.

"I can't tell what it is, but there is something moving in the magma."

"Something like . . . ?"

"Like a creature."

"You're saying there's something alive down there? In the lava?"

"Yes," Zollin said.

"It's a luggart," Bahbaz said. "A rock monster."

"You know what it is?" Brianna asked. She was stunned by the idea that anything could be alive in molten rock.

"Aye, lass, we know," said one of the other dwarves.

"And we know how to fight it," Bahbaz said.

"Do we have to fight it?" Zollin asked.

"We can run, but we'll just have to go back the way we came," Bahbaz explained. "You agreed to rebuild the bridges. We can deal with this luggart."

Zollin didn't know what to think. He felt fear digging a sharp talon into his guts. He wanted to move away from the monster instinctively. He felt trapped by the cave. There was no place to hide. He didn't want to be in the tunnel. He had made that mistake with the dragon and it had almost crushed him.

"Come on," he told Brianna. "I don't want to be in the tunnel."

They moved out into the cavern, edging slowly away from the tunnel.

"Don't go too far, I won't be able to protect you if you don't stay close," Bahbaz said.

They watched as the molten rock seemed to bubble and even leap up in bright yellow arcs. The heat in the cavern rose, and Zollin had to wipe the sweat out of his eyes. Then the luggart appeared. It looked like a huge, glowing worm. It flopped up and then fell on the cave floor, sending drops of molten rock flying around the cavern. The dwarves all had short-handled hammers that were shaped like mallets. They brandished the hammers like weapons, each of them swaying on their short legs like runners at the start of a race.

The luggart opened a gapping maw, revealing a wicked-looking eye that focused on the dwarves and several tongue-like appendages. The luggart gave a loud, cough-like roar and then one of the tongues whipped out. It reminded Zollin of a frog's tongue that could shoot out and capture flying bugs that came too close. The tongue hit Bahbaz, knocking the dwarf off his feet. The tongue stuck to him and began pulling him toward the creature's open mouth, but the dwarf next to Bahbaz slammed his hammer down on the tentacle-like tongue. The blow made a sickening, wet thud, and Bahbaz was thrown back as if a blast of air had blown him backwards.

Another tongue shot out and the process repeated. It went on and on, the dwarves hammering the luggart's tongues until finally the giant, worm-like creature retreated back into the molten pool.

"That was the strangest thing I've ever seen," Brianna said.

"It isn't over," Bahbaz said, panting. "It's waiting for us to come closer. Then it'll attack again."

"What can we do?" Zollin asked.

"Just wait it out," said one of the other dwarfs. "Eventually it will give up."

"Or," Zollin said, "we could take the fight to the worm."

Everyone looked at Zollin with surprise, and he smiled.

"I've got an idea," he said.

Chapter 11

"How many creatures are there like this?" Zollin asked.

"Not many," Bahbaz said. "Why?"

"Is it intelligent?"

"I've no idea. I didn't think to ask it any questions."

"I was just wondering what would be the the most effective thing we could do. I got the distinct impression that this fire-worm was trying to protect something. So I'm wondering if we would be better off to kill it, or to teach it to fear coming out of the pools."

"They're killers," said one of the dwarves. "You never know when they're going to come out and strike."

"We've learned how to fend them off as long as there are at least four of us," said Bahbaz.

"Okay, so let's lure it out again. Give me a chance to see what I can learn about it."

"I think we know all we need," grumbled one of the dwarves. "You'd be better off killing it."

"Perhaps, but if the creature is intelligent, we might be able to form a truce that would allow you to travel without fear."

"I'm not afraid, southlander," said the dwarf fiercely.

"I meant no offense," Zollin said, trying to pacify the angry dwarf. "I don't mind fighting or killing when necessary, but it's been my experience that many magical creatures are misunderstood. If I can't reason with the beast, I'll kill it. Or at least hurt it badly enough to make it think twice before bothering anyone again."

The dwarves didn't seem convinced, but they were persuaded to move back into the tunnel and watch. Brianna waited in the cavern. She had her bow in hand with an arrow nocked on the string just in case Zollin needed help.

He walked slowly forward, letting his magic flow out in front of him. He could sense the creature waiting just below the surface of the molten rock. He began to send friendly thoughts toward the creature. He had been able to calm frightened horses and even influence wild mountain lions with this same technique. It worked best on other people, but Zollin hoped he might be able to deal with the luggart peacefully. He wasn't sure what spell to use on this giant worm-creature that was obviously impervious to heat and fire.

When the luggart moved it wasn't slow or peaceful. It lunged out of the molten rock like a fish, sending burning globs of magma everywhere. Zollin raised his shields to protect himself and Brianna, while quickly back-peddling. He tripped over the rough surface of the cavern floor and fell on his back. The luggart's maw opened and Brianna shot her arrow. The wood burst into flame just before reaching the creature and, while it still struck the beast, the arrow shattered into ash upon impact, having virtually no effect.

Zollin was scrambling away from the creature but its tongues were too fast. They whipped out to grab him, but Zollin shoved them away with his magical power. He got back on his feet just as the tongues tried again. This time he used his magic to grab the tongues, holding them fast. The luggart bellowed in fury, but Zollin wasn't through. He levitated the creature, which wiggled and squirmed in the air. It reminded Zollin of his earliest experiments with his magic. He would spend hours trying to isolate and levitate fish from a stream. They, too, had wiggled and fought his power, but he had mastered the technique of holding them in place. The luggart was extremely heavy and incredibly strong, but Zollin held the beast fast, lifting it higher and higher. He could feel his magic roaring inside him, but his magical containment held fast and seemed to channel his power so that it was stronger than ever before. He felt the exertion taking a toll on him physically, but whereas previously attempting such a powerful spell would have left him exhausted after only a few minutes, he could tell that would be able to keep up his strength for a prolonged period of time now.

As the creature rose higher in the air, fear began to break down its will. Zollin hadn't hurt the beast, but he could tell all it wanted was to get as far away from the cavern as possible. Zollin let the creature's head dangle toward the pool of molten rock. Then he let go. The luggart fell into the pool and disappeared, but the splash was massive. Molten rock flew in all directions. Once again Zollin threw up a shield to protect himself and Brianna. The temperature in the cavern rose dramatically. Brianna grabbed his arm and pulled him back toward the tunnel.

"That was impressive, wizard," said Bahbaz.

"That will teach the wormy beast," said another dwarf.

"It's gone now," Zollin said. He reached out and accepted the canteen of arkhi that Bahbaz offered him. "I can't say it won't be back, but I doubt it will come back anytime soon."

"Why didn't you kill it?" asked the dwarf who had challenged him earlier.

"Well, I didn't see any reason to kill it. And to be honest, I'm not sure how I could have. I did try to calm it down, but it was a wasted effort. It's either a very simple-minded creature with no concept of emotion, or a very angry beast."

"Well the good news is that you can now begin to build the bridge," Bahbaz said.

"He needs to rest," Brianna said protectively.

"No, it's okay," Zollin assured her. "The containment is working. I'm not nearly as exhausted as I would have expected."

"Are you sure?"

"Absolutely. We just need to let the cavern cool down before we all go back through, but I think I can get the bridge built from here."

An hour later they crossed the bridge that Zollin had created. It was much like the first bridge, but this time Zollin added a wide barrier between the bridge and the pool. There was no way to keep the cavern from being extremely hot, but the barrier kept the travelers from being exposed to the direct heat from the pool of molten rock.

They traveled on until they came to another dwarven village. This clan lived far underground with no easy access to the surface. Their forges were smaller and the dwarves less hospitable to Zollin and Brianna. Bahbaz explained that Zollin was a wizard and was rebuilding the Stepping Stones, but still the dwarves kept their distance. The travelers ate a warm meal of potato hash with bits of fish and more of the round loaves of bread that the dwarves had brought as rations. The food was warm and flavorful. Zollin was tired and fell asleep right after eating his supper.

Brianna stayed awake longer. They had been given a room in the village that was used as a storeroom, with wooden boxes and barrels scattered around, but it was large enough that they could both stretch out to sleep. Brianna wondered where the wood came from. The dwarves were able to cultivate some root vegetables and tubers, but mostly they subsisted on the strange round bread and animals such as goats. They made almost everything from carved stone or forged metals. Brass, copper, tin, and iron were abundant, but where did the wood come from? she wondered.

The next morning they were given bread toasted over open flames and smoked fish. The fish came from a nearby stream that flowed under the mountain, Bahbaz told them. Then they set off again. They journeyed in this fashion for over a week. Every day, they came to caverns with molten pools, but they encountered no more luggarts or any other monsters. One day, Zollin was called on to repair a bridge that crossed a deep chasm. It was in one of the larger caverns, devoid of any light except for the small lanterns the dwarves carried, and here Zollin felt the greatest fear. He was tired of being constantly in the dark. He was tired of the hot, oppressive air and longed to be back in the mountains. There was a wild freedom in the mountains he had felt no where else. But in these large, dark caverns, the absence of light threatened to destroy him. He had the overwhelming desire to curl up into a ball and cry. Once he completed the bridge, he held onto a bit of hemp and, when they were halfway across the dark expanse, he set it ablaze.

"What are you doing?" Brianna asked.

"I just wanted to check something," he said.

Then he tossed the burning hemp over the rail of the bridge. Zollin and Brianna watched as it tumbled down into the darkness, flickering as it went. The light faded until it was a pin prick, smaller than a star in the night sky. And then, it disappeared.

"Did it burn out?" Brianna asked.

"No," Zollin said. "I don't think so."

"What happened to it?"

"It's still falling," said the gruff voiced dwarf behind them. "It's just too far for you to see."

"Have you ever gone down there?" Zollin asked.

"No. We dwarves are mountain folk. We live in the roots of the mountains. Foul things dwell below, in the deep places of the earth."

They continued their journey in silence after that. Both Zollin and Brianna wrestled with ideas of what could be down deep in the bowels of the earth. The luggart had been horrific, but could there really be worse things? They didn't understand how the dwarves could live exposed to such terrifying creatures, but they kept these thoughts to themselves.

The next day they came to another dwarf village. It was located next to a Stepping Stone cavern that still had an intact but ancient bridge. It was a crumbling structure; the rails were broken down and the edges of the path over the center of the bridge had fallen off, leaving jagged edges that encroached on the path, making it narrow and dangerous to cross. It also left the traveler exposed to the heat from the molten pool below.

"What brings the Oliad clan here without arkhi to trade?" asked a fat dwarf with a dirty beard.

"We are traveling the Stepping Stones," said Bahbaz.

"The Jaq clan has one of the only usable caverns left," said the fat dwarf. "But you can't cross for free. And I don't see anything you brought to trade, Bahbaz."

The fat dwarf said the Oliad clan leader's name with scorn. The other dwarves bristled with injured pride, but Bahbaz just laughed.

"We don't come empty-handed," he said. "The Oliad clan never comes with nothing to trade. We've brought a wizard."

"Bah, there are no more wizards," said the fat dwarf.

"Hammert, your skull is as thick as your belly. Here stands a wizard, and a powerful one at that. He defeated the luggart." Bahbaz pointed to Zollin as he spoke.

"Bah! The only thing the Oliad clan brings is lies. Where did you find the tall folk? Lost wandering in the mountains I expect. We've no use for southlanders."

"Your bridge is crumbling," Bahbaz said. "As is the reputation of your tribe. I'll trade my wizard's work on your bridge for . . ." He let the thought trail off as he pondered what the village had to offer.

"Nothing," cried Hammert. "I wouldn't trade with grifters like you. We've more sense than that."

"No, you don't," said Bahbaz. "In fact you're already proven how very little sense you have. Why don't you welcome us into your village? Are you so poverty-stricken that you can't offer basic hospitality?"

"Bahbaz, you old fool. If you insult us again I'll cave in your skull with my hammer."

"You'll try, but I'm warning you not to threaten me again," Bahbaz said menacingly. "We've repaired the Stepping Stones between here and the Oliad village. Do you really want people to have to try and cross that ruinous relic you call a bridge? Most traders will bypass your village rather than risk it, and your pride will be the reason that your clan suffers."

"What do you know of suffering? The Jaq clan has fought the luggart for decades. We've held the only Stepping Stone bridge in the North. While you Oliads brew your drink and live in safety, we've sacrificed to make sure that trade has prospered in the dark days."

"What's he mean by dark days?" Zollin asked.

"He's referring to the loss of magic in the land and the decay of our way of life. There are fewer dwarves now. Some of the clans have been lost in the darkness. But that's changing now," Bahbaz said this last part loudly, as much to Hammert as to Zollin. "You're the proof of that. The magic is awakening and prosperous times are ahead for the dwarves. Here is a friendly wizard. One who would fix your bridge and share your bread, if you'll but offer it to him."

"He's not welcome," said Hammert. "No one is."

"You refuse us?" Bahbaz said angrily. "What kind of dwarf are you?"

"I'm the kind that knows what it takes to protect my clan," he said. "Move on, I've no more time for your idle talk."

"Hammert!" Bahbaz shouted. "What is wrong with you? Are you so old and bitter that you've lost your senses?"

"You don't know what you're talking about," Hammert screamed back.

"What's wrong?" Zollin said.

"Keep your pet human on his leash," Hammert said.

The group of dwarves traveling with Zollin were angry now. They were prideful people, and while hearing the Jaq headman insult their leader could be excused as poor trading, they would not let Hammert slander Zollin.

"I'll have your head for that," shouted Bahbaz.

"Come and get me," Hammert taunted.

He was standing on what amounted to a balcony that overlooked the tunnel as it opened into a larger cavern. There was an arch of stone with heavy metal doors that blocked their way forward. Bahbaz and his kinsmen were about to charge forward with their war hammers, but Zollin spoke again.

"What is it? Sickness? Plague?" the wizard said loudly.

This made Bahbaz hesitate. Hammert looked crestfallen. His pride was gone, and so was his defiance. He hung his head and leaned heavily on the balcony rail.

"I can help," said Zollin. "Please let me try."

"You can't," said Hammert. "Our best healers have all failed. If you carry this sickness to the other clans, we could all be wiped out."

"What is it?" Bahbaz called.

"It's a wasting disease. Fever burns and food can't be kept down, not even water. We're dying here, Bahbaz. Go and leave us to die in peace."

"Perhaps he's right," Bahbaz said.

"No, I can help them," Zollin said.

"He can," Brianna added. "He can heal people using magic. I've seen it."

"They may not allow us and even if they did, Hammert's right," Bahbaz said. "We could get sick and spread the disease."

"Just let me go in alone," Zollin said. "If I can't heal them, you can leave me here."

"No!" Brianna said loudly. "We're not leaving you."

"You'd never find your way out of the mountains," Bahbaz said sadly. "Even if you weren't killed by the disease. And you might spread it to the other clans. We can't take that risk."

"Then I won't leave. I'll stay here if I can't heal them."

"Think about what you're saying, Zollin."

"I am," he said. "I can't just leave these people to die."

"Dwarves to die," corrected the gruff-voiced dwarf.

"I'm not leaving you," she said firmly.

"You don't have to. Make camp here," Zollin said. "I'll go in and see if I can help them. Then we'll decide what to do."

"I'd rather take you around the village," Bahbaz said. "Then we can repair the rest of the Stepping Stones."

"I can't," Zollin said. "Besides, how long would it take us to go around?"

"Only a few more days."

"We can't risk that," Zollin said. "The dragon would be too far ahead of us."

"Forget the dragon," Brianna said. "I'm not sure you should take the chance. You don't know if you can heal dwarves."

"I don't know I can't," Zollin said.

"But you don't know for sure," she argued.

"It's a risk I'll just have to take," Zollin said sadly.

Chapter 12

The giant metal doors swung open silently on well-oiled hinges. Like all other examples of dwarfish workmanship, the metal doors were well made. Hammert met Zollin at the gate. He had a look of skepticism on his face, but also grave concern. Zollin assumed they had tried everything else to no avail and Hammert was desperate.

"We've tried to quarantine the sick," said the fat dwarf. "This way."

He led Zollin to a large chamber that was used for feasting. The long tables had been pushed against the walls and pallets had been set up for the ill. The room smelled of sweat and vomit, but Zollin had been prepared for that. He didn't waste any time and went to the nearest dwarf and knelt down beside her. It was a young, female dwarf, the size of a newborn human baby. Her face was covered in sweat and her skin looked ashen. Zollin let his magic probe slowly into the dwarf. Their anatomy was completely different from humans'. They had similar organs, but they were in different places, and many functioned differently. Zollin didn't try to understand the anatomy; he was simply looking for something that was causing the illness. It took a long time. There were many hormones and antibodies that were completely foreign to Zollin, but at last he noticed a virus. At first, the virus seemed like a natural part of the dwarfish physiology, but as he spent time watching it, learning its function, he saw it attack and devour a simple protein in her bloodstream and secrete what looked to be a waste product.

Zollin then followed the waste, which found its way to the dwarf's very large liver, but the organ was flooded with the same antigen. It caused the liver to overproduce bile, which accounted for the vomiting and high body temperatures. Zollin continued to search but found no antibodies for the virus; instead the dwarf's body was reacting to the problems in her liver. Zollin stood up and stretched.

"Can you take me to someone who has been sick longer?" he asked Hammert.

"Yes, did you discover anything?" the fat dwarf asked.

"There's a virus and I need to confirm what is happening."

"What's a virus?" Hammert asked.

"It's sort of like a parasite," Zollin said. "Only it mimics a natural part of your body and multiplies by invading and taking over your natural cytokines."

"What's a cytokine?" Hammert seemed suspicious.

"Look, our bodies are all made up of various parts that work together. Dwarves, like humans, produce cytokines, which are various types of proteins that help the different parts work together. They're pumped into your blood by the various lymph nodes and organs. Right now, the virus is attacking the cytokines, feeding on your body's natural protein and producing a waste product that is overloading your liver, causing it to produce more bile. The fever and vomiting are a natural result of the stress on your liver, and my guess is, after a dwarf has been sick long enough, and not eating anymore, the virus is attacking the dwarf's body to get more protein."

Hammert looked at Zollin through narrowed eyelids. It was obvious that he was trying to decide if he believed Zollin or not.

"Just take me to someone who's been sick the longest," Zollin pleaded.

Hammert led the way. He knelt beside a very sick-looking dwarf. After only a few moments he realized that his prognosis was correct. The virus was eating the dwarf alive. Zollin then turned his magic on Hammert. The fat dwarf had no idea that Zollin was probing him to see if the virus had infected him, but it took only a few moments to confirm that it had. The buildup of virus waste just hadn't overwhelmed his liver yet.

"Okay," Zollin said. "Here's what I need. Do you have arkhi, or ale of some sort?"

"We brew potato beer," Hammert said.

"Fine, that'll do. I'll need some of it and food, too. And the patients will need food. Something high in protein, but not too spicy or flavorful."

"I can do that," Hammert said. "But how will we know that you're actually helping anyone?"

"Watch and see," Zollin said.

He let his magic dive back into the sick dwarf. He started with the liver and removed as much of the virus waste as possible. The easiest way was to move the waste into the dwarf's stomach with the excess bile and then cause the dwarf to vomit. Once that was done, Zollin began attacking the virus itself. He needed to slow the progression of the disease so that the dwarf's body could make antibodies to fight the virus. It took over an hour, but when Zollin was finished the dwarf's fever was going down.

"He's still sick," said Hammert when Zollin stood up.

"Yes, he is. But hopefully, his body will have the time to fight the disease naturally now."

"I thought you said you could heal them."

"I am healing them. Look, the virus is basically eating them alive. Your body will naturally fight and kill the virus. It creates antibodies which basically hunt down and kill the virus. Once those antibodies have been developed by your body, the virus can't hurt you anymore. The problem is that the virus has found a way to mask what it's doing so that your body focuses on the waste problem with your liver and all the while the virus is eating you alive. I healed the liver, so now the body will turn its attention on what else is making it sick. Give him a little time and he'll be okay."

"How can I be sure you're not just blowing smoke?" Hammert asked. "We're just supposed to take your word?"

"Hungry," said a very weak-sounding voice.

Both Zollin and Hammert turned to the sick dwarf. His eyes were open and he was licking his dry, chapped lips.

"What was that, Warik?" Hammert said as he bent close.

"I'm hungry," said the sick dwarf.

"I told you," Zollin said. "Feed him something rich in protein."

Hammert hurried out of the makeshift sickroom, and Zollin went back to work healing the dwarves. He spent several hours working with the sick dwarves, using his system for healing their livers and getting the excess bile out of their stomachs. By the time he finished he felt so tired he thought he might just fall over and pass out himself. It wasn't the exertion of magic but the intense mental concentration that taxed his system so much. He ate some of the mash that had been made for the sick, a stew made of goat meat and potatoes. It was bland, but it was warm and filling.

Zollin wanted to lie down and sleep but he knew that Brianna would be worrying about him, and he needed the other dwarves to find a few things for him. He staggered up the short steps that led to the balcony over the gate. He found three of the four dwarves asleep but Bahbaz had stayed awake, keeping Brianna company as they waited for word from Zollin.

"Hey," he said in a tired voice.

Brianna and Bahbaz scrambled to their feet.

"I think I've fixed the problem," he continued.

"Are you okay? You look really tired," Brianna said.

"I am, but it's nothing a little rest won't cure. I'm getting ready to get some sleep. I need something from you," Zollin said to Bahbaz.

"How can we help, southlander?" the stout little dwarf asked.

"The people here are suffering from a virus. It is very contagious, but your body can fight it off if we can boost your liver function. Is there something that dwarves do naturally to help their livers? Any kind of medicine or herb that might be used?"

"Most dwarves have hearty livers," Bahbaz said. "Although I know that sometimes dried cave lichen is used for dwarves who've had a long turn at the barrel."

"I need some," Zollin said. "Can you get it for me?"

"I think so," Bahbaz said. "How quickly do you need it?"

"Rest now and see about it in the morning. I think everyone in this village is going to be sick. If we don't find a way to help the people who aren't showing symptoms yet, it could spread to the other clans."

"We'll find it for you, wizard. Rest assured of that."

"Thanks," Zollin said. Then he addressed Brianna. "You okay?"

"Fine, just anxious for you."

"Things will be fine here," Zollin said. "It's just going to take a little time."

They said their good nights, and Zollin found a warm place to rest and fell promptly asleep. The next thing he knew he woke up feeling nauseous. His stomach was cramping and his mouth was flooding with silva. There was a bucket nearby and Zollin crawled to it, then threw up violently. His body was shaking and he felt hot. He knew the virus had infected him, and apparently his liver was no match for a dwarf's. In the brief respite he had after throwing up, he probed his body. The virus was there and growing, masking its presence with the same waste product that it had used in the dwarves. Zollin worked feverishly to help his liver, which meant another bout of vomiting. Then he fell asleep again. He awoke a few hours later, sick again. Unlike the dwarves', his liver was quickly overwhelmed.

He repeated the remedy and searched his body for the antibodies that it should be producing to fight the virus. There weren't any. He realized he would have to stay awake and keep magically healing his liver to give himself time for his body to recognize the real threat. He sat propped against a stone wall, his body burning with fever and his magic churning inside him. He wanted the potato beer or some arkhi, but he knew the alcohol would only make his liver worse. His stomach cramped and burned as his natural stomach acid scoured the empty organ.

When the village finally started stirring he searched his body again for antibodies and this time found a few. He would need several more hours of work to ensure that his body had what it needed to fight off the disease, but he would live.

Hammert found him an hour later. He looked concerned.

"What's ailing you, wizard?" he said.

"I caught the virus," Zollin said weakly.

"That's unfortunate," said Hammert. "Can't you heal yourself?"

"I'm working on it, but my liver is no match for yours."

"I could have told you that," Hammert said boastfully. "We dwarves have strong constitutions. Humans have us on size, but I suspect we're the hardier race."

"I agree," Zollin said.

"I checked on our sick. They all seem better."

"Good. Once I'm well enough I'll check them again. You're all going to get this virus," he warned Hammert. "You already have it. I suspect most everyone in your village does. Some people will be able to overcome the disease on their own, it all depends on how well their livers function. I suggest you take some dried cave lichen to boost your liver function."

"You know about cave lichen?" Hammert asked in surprise.

"Bahbaz told me about it. He'll find some for your village."

"Good, at least he can do something useful."

"You'll also need to spread the word," Zollin said. "This virus could spread to all the clans. They need the cave lichen and knowledge of how to fight the virus. It would be best if you send dwarves from your village to the other clans; it will expose them to the virus and allow their bodies to create the necessary antibodies to fight it."

"And when should we do that?" Hammert said. "We're short-handed as it is."

"You should wait until the sickness has run its course. Anyone who isn't sick needs to stay here in case they get sick. Let the people who get well spread the word."

"All right," Hammert said. "Can I do anything for you?"

"I need water," Zollin said.

"I'll send someone."

The hours crawled by. Zollin sipped water and was forced to vomit several more times before he felt like his body had enough antibodies to fight the disease. He fell asleep around noon, but was shaken awake by Hammert a few hours later. He hurt all over and his body screamed for more rest, but the look on Hammert's face kept him awake.

"What is it?" he asked.

"Your woman; she's sick."

Zollin stood up and gritted his teeth as a wave of nausea swept over him.

"Where is she?"

Hammert led him to the gate. Bahbaz and the other dwarves from the Oliad clan were gathered around her.

"What happened?" Zollin said.

"She got sick," Bahbaz said in a worried tone. "It hit her hard and fast. She's been vomiting almost non-stop."

Zollin put his hand on Brianna's forehead. It was sweaty and hot. He could feel the magic inside him whipped into a fury by his worry and anxiety. It raged deep in his chest and he fed the powerful magic into Brianna, coaxing her liver back to health. Her eyes fluttered open and she recognized him. Then she was retching, her thin body spasming as every muscle locked hard and her stomach emptied. When the nausea passed, she smiled briefly at Zollin, then fell asleep.

"Will she be okay?" Bahbaz asked.

"Our livers can't handle the virus the way yours can. I'll have to stay with her. Did you find cave lichen?"

"We did, but it will take a while to dry it," Bahbaz said.

"Bring it here," Zollin ordered, then he too vomited.

It took him a moment to regain his composure.

"You're both sick?" Bahbaz said in surprise.

"I'm on the mend," Zollin said in a grim attempt at humor. "The virus is very contagious.   That's obvious since Brianna is sick."

One of the dwarves opened a bag that was full of the lichen. He could feel the power in the small plant, only a whisper but it was there. He let his magic mingle with that of the lichen, and he could feel the life-giving power. It reminded him of the willow tree he had found back in Tranaugh Shire.   It too had magical power, and he had made himself a belt of woven willow boughs to enhance his magical ability. That tree had been strong with the same life-giving magic, a different magic than that in his staff, which was formed from lightning and full of danger.   He smiled as he looked down at the lichen, pale green and thin. Zollin let his magic pour into the bag. In only a minute he had extracted all the moisture from the plant.

"Now it's dry. How do you take it?"

"Powdered, and mixed with drink," Bahbaz explained.

"Bring something to drink," Zollin ordered.

Hammett hurried away and Zollin looked at Bahbaz.   The dwarf looked genuinely concerned for him.

"I'm fine," Zollin said.   "Tired but on the mend.   You should be more concerned with yourselves. I don't know if this remedy will help."

"We are a hardy folk," Bahbaz said. "We shall be fine."

"All right, make sure you all drink some of the mixture and avoid fermented drink for a while. Give yourself time to fight this virus."

Zollin levitated Brianna and moved her to a place out of the way of the busy dwarves. The village was hard at work. There were dwarves seeing to everyday chores and others taking care of the sick. Of course the constant rhythm of hammers on steel and chisels on stone could be heard all over the village. Zollin arranged a pallet for himself and Brianna, with buckets handy for the vomiting that was sure to come. Zollin's body was screaming for sleep, so he positioned himself as comfortably as possible and held Brianna. He knew that she would wake up soon and need to vomit again, but he dozed while she slept.

It took several hours for Zollin to help Brianna past the worst of the virus. Her little stomach seemed to fill with bile so fast that she could last only about half an hour before needing to vomit. Sometime late in the afternoon they both were able to sleep. When they woke up the next day they were weak and famished. Zollin found bread and water beside them and gave some to Brianna, who was sore from the constant retching the day before. They both ate with trepidation, afraid that the food would trigger the nausea again, but it didn't. Zollin probed both of their bodies with his magic and found that antibodies were busy fighting the virus.

"I guess we should find our friends," Brianna said.

"Yeah, I need to see how the dwarves are faring."

They stood up and stretched. They had slept well, but their bodies were busy fighting the virus and they were both still very tired. They walked slowly toward the long room the dwarves had converted to a hospital. There were still dwarves inside, but far fewer than the day before. Zollin checked on everyone and found that their bodies were fighting the illness. Hammert found them there.

"You're up? Good," said Hammert. "It seems that you've been as good as your word. Everyone is improving and we've had no one else fall ill since we drank the cave lichen potion you made."

"That's great," said Zollin. "Do you mind if I check to see how you are doing?"

"By all means, southlander," said Hammert, who was obviously in a much better mood.

Zollin let his magic flow into the fat dwarf. He could feel the liver, working hard to clear the virus waste, but it didn't seem distressed. And there were antibodies already fighting the virus.

"It's working," said Zollin, feeling relieved.

He was tired and ready to lie back down, now that he knew everyone would be okay. He felt a huge sense of relief, like a heavy weight had been lifted from his shoulders. He took a deep breath and let it out, feeling his body sag but also feeling a great sense of accomplishment. This village would have been nearly wiped out by the virus if he hadn't helped. Of all the miraculous things he had done since discovering his powers, this was by far the most satisfying.

"Where are Bahbaz and the others?" Zollin asked.

"They are out gathering more cave lichen," Hammert explained. "There is a cavern not far from the village that is full of it. They plan to take it with them, I believe."

"Good," said Zollin. "I think I'm going to get some rest."

"Is there anything you need?"

"We could use some more water," Brianna said.

"I'll see to it."

Hammert hurried away, his body swaying on his short legs.

"Is there anything else we need to do?" Brianna asked.

"No, we just need to rest and get our strength back."

"Okay," she said, smiling sweetly. "You saved my life you know," she added playfully as they walked back to where they had their supplies and the small pallet they had slept on.

"If you hadn't left Tranaugh Shire you'd have never been in danger."

"And miss all of this?" she said, waving her hand at the dwarf village. "Can you imagine missing this, Zollin? Maybe that never occurred to you, but I think about it all the time. I made my choice. I want to be with you, to experience all these incredible moments. Is it dangerous? Yes, sometimes it is, but it's also worth it. I wouldn't trade this for anything."

"Me neither," Zollin said. "I feel like I'm in a story. As if some greater power that I can't see or touch is somehow guiding me through these adventures."

"God?" Brianna asked.

"Maybe, I don't know what else it could be."

"Well, if it is, you'll know when you need to know. You're a very capable man."

Zollin laughed a hard laugh that made his stomach muscles, which were sore from retching, ache. He bent over laughing, and Brianna couldn't help but laugh too, although she didn't know what was funny.

"What? What's so funny?" she asked.

"You," he said. "I can't believe you just said I'm capable. If only you'd known me better growing up. I was anything but capable. Quinn could do anything, but I was hopeless. I couldn't drive a nail straight. I didn't have the strength to carry the timber. I didn't understand wood grain, or how to use leverage to saw a piece of wood. There were so many things that I was terrible at that I thought I was worthless. Never in all my life did I think that someone would call me capable."

"Well, you are," she said, smiling, her eyes shining as she looked at him. "I love you, Zollin Quinnson."

"I love you, too," he said.

Chapter 13

Mansel was glad to be off the ship. The weather had not been bad, but the wind had made it necessary for the ship to sail in a zig-zagging pattern. The sailors had been busy, but Mansel had languished with nothing to do and no way to help. The idleness had almost driven him mad. His mind was feverish with the desire to get Zollin back to Gwendolyn. The witch was always on his mind. When he closed his eyes he could see her, not her face—which he couldn't picture no matter how hard he tried—but her seductive body and the way she made him feel. He could hear her voice, calling out to him, urging all haste. He had felt a small sense of guilt when he had tossed Quinn overboard, but that had quickly fallen away in his eagerness to complete his task.

At night he dreamed of a lonely cottage. He couldn't remember where the home was. Sometimes he could see the silhouette of a woman, her features pinched as if by grief, and he knew that she was important, but he quickly pushed all thoughts of everyone but Gwendolyn out of his mind. He couldn't think of Prince Wilam without growing furiously angry. Jealous rage fueled him and he wanted to get back to the Castle on the Sea to keep the spoiled Prince from worming his way into Gwendolyn's good graces.

The city at Black Bay was large. It was a major point of trade, with river traffic bringing goods from the Great Valley in the Northern Highlands, and the Sea of Kings bringing goods from the south. The Weaver's Road ran straight to Fort Jellar and Ebbson Keep. Mansel was tempted to spend the night in one of the many inns in Black Bay, where he could get a decent meal and plenty of ale. But they had arrived in the harbor at mid-morning, and Mansel was anxious to get moving.

"Wait for me here," Mansel told the captain of the ship. "I shouldn't be too long."

"I will need to get back to the Castle," the captain said. "Her Highness might need me."

"She won't be pleased if you shirk your task. I'll get the wizard, you wait here."

Mansel's manner was threatening. He had never before used his size and strength to bully people into doing what he wanted. Growing up, Mansel saw his older brothers do their share of bullying, and it had left a bad taste in his mouth. But now he no longer cared what people thought of him. He cared only about pleasing the witch, and she had given him a task. He wasn't about to let the rat-faced sailor keep him from it.

His first priority had been to find a horse. He wanted an animal big enough to carry his weight without growing tired, but fast enough that he could make up for the time he had lost on the ship. He wasn't sure where Zollin was, but he was confident he could find out by staying on the Weaver's Road.

He bought a horse with the coin he had found in Quinn's belongings and set out right away. He still had the sword Zollin had forged for him from the links of chain the army had bound them with in the Great Valley, and he wore it over his shoulder while he rode so that the blade wouldn't constantly slap against his thigh or bother the horse. He had purchased some simple rations: a canteen of water, dried meat, and fresh bread. He was tempted to buy wine or ale, but he didn't want to add extra weight to his horse. The animal was young and spirited, anxious for adventure, and Mansel rode hard.

When night finally forced him to stop, the horse's head was drooping. He hobbled the beast and rolled himself in his cloak to sleep. The next morning he set out at dawn. He passed merchants, most often traveling in caravans that forced him to leave the road so that he could circle around them. There were guards, mercenaries mostly, all with heavy weapons like broadswords and maces. They eyed him suspiciously as he passed. He was tempted to challenge them: it would have felt good to use his sword to wipe the smug looks off their faces, but he didn't want anything to slow him down. He also passed groups of traveling soldiers, usually led by one or two noblemen on horseback with well-made armor. They were the war bands from the Baskla fiefdoms, all traveling west. Their presence seemed odd, but Mansel didn't waste much thought on them. He was focused on his task, which was all that he cared about.

It was difficult to avoid the inns along the road. There were many, each catering to the traveling merchants and their entourages. It seemed as if the aroma of roasting meat emanated from them all. There were buxom maids in the doorways of many, each tempting Mansel to forget his task and give himself to them. He rode stoically past, forcing himself not to look or respond to their pleas for his attention. On the second night he stopped at an inn to eat his supper. He washed the hot food down with cups of ale, and the more he drank the more he wanted. His usual jovial attitude was nowhere to be found. The more he drank the angrier he became.

Most of the wenches in the inn were wise enough to give him a wide berth. They knew a surly drunk when they saw one. But one young girl was not as experienced. She wasn't particularly attractive either, which meant she had to work harder to gain the favor of the inn's patrons and she wasn't put off easily. She brought Mansel more ale and tried to rub his shoulders. He brushed her off but she came back to refill his tankard, leaning her body against him as she poured. Then she stroked his arm, commenting on the large muscles there. Mansel tried to ignore her, but the ale was kindling a fury that he could barely contain. Everywhere he looked people seemed to be mocking him. The wenches, flaunting and flirting, made him think of Prince Wilam, alone with Gwendolyn, trying to steal her virtue. When the mousy wench ran her cold hand inside the open collar of his shirt, he snapped.

"Leave me the hell alone!" he thundered, shoving the young girl, who was thin and clumsy, across the room.

She fell onto the rough planks of the inn floor. A brutish-looking man helped her up and then turned to Mansel with a vicious look on his face.

"Watch your manners, traveler, or I'll beat some sense into you."

Mansel didn't realize it, but he had been waiting for just such a confrontation. His blood began pulsing through his veins and he could hear the roar of it in his ears.

"Shut up and mind your own business," he said gruffly.

"Boy, one more word from you and I'll break that pretty face of yours."

Mansel stood up. He was tall, his waist narrow, but the muscles of his thighs, chest, shoulders, and arms were large. He still had the sword buckled onto his back. He undid the buckle and looked at the other man, who was even bigger than Mansel.

"Swords or fists?" Mansel asked.

For the first time the man seemed hesitant. The aggressive look on his face was replaced with doubt. He wasn't armed so Mansel laid his sword across the table.

"Any man who touches my weapon will die by it," he said in a loud voice.

Then, he lunged forward. It was not the type of finesse that Quinn had taught him. It had none of the careful, patient deliberateness that made his mentor so dangerous. Instead it was an explosion of brute force. His shoulder slammed into the man and sent him sprawling. Mansel roared like a wild animal and jumped forward. Most of the other patrons were now scrambling to get out of the way. The wenches were quick to flee back into the kitchen with the innkeeper.

The shock of Mansel's attack quickly wore off the big man and he scrambled to get to his feet, but Mansel was too quick. He brought up a hard knee into the man's face and sent the local sprawling again. A smaller man joined the fray, leaping nimbly onto Mansel's back and wrapping one arm around his neck and the other behind his head. Mansel felt the muscles tighten and his air was cut off. He reached up and fumbled to find the man's hands, and when he finally did he wrenched hard. Bones popped, and the man on his back dropped to the floor with a howl. Mansel took a big breath and watched his opponent rise in front of him. The big local's face was covered in bright, red blood.

"I'm going to kill you," the man said.

"Do it," Mansel taunted.

The man rushed forward, but this time Mansel pivoted sideways and waited. The big man threw a vicious haymaker punch that would have knocked an ox senseless, but Mansel swayed to the side and then used the man's forward momentum to flip him over. It was a technique that Quinn had taught Mansel, twisting his body and flinging his opponent over his hip. The big man crashed to the floor, but Mansel still had the man's arm by the wrist. He twisted the arm, then brought his booted foot high and slammed it down on the man's elbow. There was a sickening crunch as bones snapped, ligaments and tendons tore, and cartilage popped.

The man passed out from the pain, and no one else moved. Mansel roared again and kicked over a nearby table. Then he stalked out of the inn, grabbing his sword as he went past it. Outside the air was cooler. Fall was approaching, and he was far enough north that nightfall brought cooler temperatures. The cool air felt good on his skin but did nothing to clear his foggy head. He didn't even remember what had started the fight, but he felt like moving on was the best thing he could do. He didn't want to have to deal with locals trying to avenge their friend's defeat or gain compensation for the injuries he had inflicted.

He led his horse until he was too tired to walk anymore. The fight had winded him more than he expected and the ale made him even more tired. He found a small stream that ran near the road and made camp next to it. He hobbled his horse and then fell asleep on the ground. He woke up a few hours later with a boot in his ribs.

"This him?" said the man standing over him.

The man was holding a torch that made it difficult for Mansel to see. All around him the night seemed pitch black and he could just make out the group of horses nearby.

"Yes, that's him. He broke Ennus's arm and crippled Ryker. He'll never swing a hammer again," said one of the men on horseback, just paces away from Mansel.

"Get up, stranger," said the man standing over Mansel.

"Who are you?" Mansel asked.

"My name's Torrence; I'm the town constable."

"What do you want with me?" Mansel asked.

"You assaulted some men earlier tonight," said Torrence. "I intend to bring you back to town. You'll need to make reparations to the men you injured."

"It was a fair fight," Mansel said as he stood up. He was trying to buy some time so he kept talking. "All I wanted was a warm meal."

He was dizzy, and the alcohol in his stomach was only moments from coming up. He recognized the feeling all too well. His head was pounding and his mouth felt incredibly dry and foul. Still, he knew he needed to somehow get away from the men who had come to hold him to account for injuring the men in the inn. He tried to focus his eyes on the group of horses. Were there more men, or just the one who had identified him, he wondered. He wasn't sure and it was too dark to tell.

"You'll have to come with us," Torrence said, in a tone that showed he expected no argument.

"Sure," Mansel said, feigning friendliness. "I don't want any more trouble. I'll just gather my things."

"You can leave all that, my men will see to it," Torrence said.

"I can't leave my belongings," Mansel said. "Someone might steal them."

"Mister, you're coming with me, and I don't care if you come peacefully, or knocked senseless and thrown across the back of a horse. Am I making myself clear?"

"Perfectly," Mansel said.

And then he struck. It was a straight jab right at the man's face, but the constable had been expecting it. He leaned back to avoid the blow, which is what Mansel had anticipated. He moved quickly, grabbing the grip of the short sword that hung in a scabbard from the constable's belt. Torrence moved back quickly, not realizing what Mansel was doing, and the sword pulled free of the belt.

Torrence swung the torch at Mansel, but it was a clumsy effort, and Mansel was already spinning away from him. He knew he couldn't leave his back turned to the other man on horseback. Mansel slashed his sword through the man's reins, startling the horse so that it reared. The man toppled back, still holding the reins that he expected would save him from falling. There was a third man in the group, but he was on the far side of the rearing horse.

Mansel turned his attention back to Torrence, who was ready for Mansel now. The man had a hard look in his eyes, but his only weapon appeared to be the torch, which was really just a tree branch with one end wrapped in rags that had been soaked in oil. The flame fluttered as Torrence swung the torch. The light made things difficult to see, but Mansel acted mostly on instinct. He brought the short sword up to parry the torch, but the branch shattered, and the flaming end flew toward the horses, which reared and nervously danced away from the fight. The man who had identified Mansel was just trying to get up when he was trampled by the skittish horses. The third man was kept busy trying to regain control of his mount.

Torrence was undeterred by the loss of his weapon. He moved forward, obviously intending to fight Mansel with his hands. But the big warrior swung the sword sideways, turning the blade so that the flat side connected with the constable's temple. Torrence dropped to the ground, knocked senseless by the heavy blade.

Mansel finally turned and faced the third man, but it was obvious, even in the dim light, that the man was terrified. Mansel assumed the man had just been conscripted to ride with the two town officials.

"I didn't kill them," Mansel said. "Make sure you remember that when you explain what happened."

He threw the sword into the ground, where it stuck fast, the hilt quivering in the air. Then he walked over to his horse and promptly threw up. The sour smell of alcohol enveloped him and made his stomach cramp again. He retched a few more times, but there wasn't anything left in his stomach. He spit, wiped his mouth with his sleeve, and then untied his horse. His sword was still in its scabbard that was hung on the saddle horn. He had been so tired he hadn't taken the time to unsaddle the horse. He climbed up in the saddle and rode away.

He didn't take the Weaver's Road, but instead rode off into the countryside so that the man who had been too scared to fight him would report that he rode that way. Once he felt he was far enough from the scene of the fight, he turned and rode back toward the Weaver's Road. He came to it over a mile away from where he had made camp. He crossed the road and made his way to a small grove of trees that he hoped would shield him from the sight of anyone traveling down the Weaver's Road. Then he unsaddled the horse and tied it to a tree. He laid out a blanket on the ground and promptly fell asleep again.

Chapter 14

The next day Zollin and Brianna both felt much better, and most of the dwarves were back on their feet as well. They were treated like visiting royalty. Many of the dwarves begged them to take small trinkets to show their gratitude. Zollin repaired the bridge in the cavern that was next to the Jaq clan village, and after getting some rest, Zollin and Brianna were ready to set out later that afternoon.

"You will always have a place here among the Jaq clan," said Hammert.

"He's already an honorary member of the Oliad clan," said Bahbaz gruffly.

"I'm honored," Zollin said, trying to keep the peace.

Bahbaz and the other dwarves with him had worked tirelessly to help the Jaq clan, but now that they were leaving, their old bravado was back in force.

"We have a gift for you," said Hammert.

"You don't have to do that," Zollin said. "Really, we were glad to help."

"It isn't for you," said Hammert.

He held up an intricately woven gold chain. The metal was bright and had a fluid quality as it moved. Hanging from the chain was a brilliant ruby that flashed as if a fire burned inside. Zollin noticed that the stone had magical power, but he was unable to identify it.

"Precious stones are rare," Hammert said. "And we don't normally forge gold, but occasionally we dally with the soft metals. It's my way of saying thank you."

"It's stunning," Brianna said as she took the necklace.

"May it be a lucky charm," Hammert said. "Not many southlanders can lay claim to a dwarfish bauble like that."

"You are too generous," Zollin said.

"Hush, Zollin, you might offend him," Brianna teased, holding the necklace close to her chest protectively. "Here, put it on me," she told him.

He held out his hand and she gave him the necklace. As soon as the ruby touched his hand he felt the power kindled there.

"Wow!" Zollin said instinctively.

"What? Is something wrong?" Brianna asked, concerned.

"This is a firestone," Zollin said.

The dwarves all crowded in for a closer look.

"What's a firestone?" asked Bahbaz.

"I'm not completely sure what it is or how it's made, but it's magical. Here, Brianna, put it on."

"If it has magic power maybe you should use it," she said.

"No, it was given to you. A magical gift often enables the recipient to harness the power. Did you ever notice anything strange about the ruby?" Zollin asked Hammert.

"No, not really. I found it and polished it, but I've done nothing with it since then."

Brianna had turned her back to Zollin and lifted her long, black hair up so he could fasten the clasp at the nape of her neck. When the stone touched her chest she felt a tiny thrill, almost like a shiver of excitement, but she didn't know if what she felt was from the stone or her own imagination.

"What's it do, Zollin?" she asked.

"I'm not exactly sure," he said. "Kelvich told me that many wizards seek out magical objects because they can tap into the object's power and manipulate it. That may be all it is, just a reservoir of magic, but I think it may be more. Try holding your hands together and imagining a fire between them."

Brianna held her hands up and closed her eyes. Her forehead wrinkled as she concentrated. The dwarves gasped when her hands burst into flames, but Brianna didn't notice. The fire was on her skin, but it didn't burn her. She didn't even feel it.

"Wow," Zollin said.

"Is it working?" she asked, her eyes still closed.

"Look and see," he told her.

Brianna screamed when she saw the flames, which promptly vanished. They were attracting a crowd now, other dwarves crowding closer to see what was happening. Zollin took Brianna's hands, but they weren't harmed. In fact, they weren't even warm.

"She's a Fire Spirit," a dwarf said.

"How did she do that?" another asked.

"Are you okay?" Zollin asked her.

"Yeah, I just wasn't expecting that. I thought you said the fire would be between my hands."

"It was just a guess," Zollin said. "I don't even know how I knew what it was."

"Fire spirits can hold and manipulate the flames," said Bahbaz in voice that was clearly in awe of what Brianna had done. "They can touch fire, put their hands right into a forge, and mold the metal in the flames. We've all heard stories of them. Legend has it that Fire Spirits taught the dwarves how to forge steel. I just never thought they were real."

"I'm not a Fire Spirit," said Brianna. "It's the ruby. Anyone can do it. Here," she said, reaching up to take the necklace off, "I'll show you."

"No," the dwarves replied almost in unison. Their collective response froze Brianna before she could unfasten the clasp.

"You've a special gift," Bahbaz said.

"Only you can wield the fire," said Hammert.

"No, I've seen Zollin control fire," Brianna said.

"I can create it and even control it, but I can't touch it," Zollin said.

"But the magic is in the ruby. I can't accept such a valuable gift."

"The stone is yours," Hammert said. "It has chosen you."

"We believe that some objects have a will, a mind of their own, so to speak," Bahbaz said. "You call it magic, but in our experience it is more like a kinship. The stone would not surrender its power to us. Only you can coax the power out of it and wield it."

"But why me? Wouldn't Zollin be a better choice? He's a wizard and I'm just a girl."

"You're so much more than that," Zollin said.

"You're a fire spirt," said Hammert.

"I'm a girl," she said, half-heartedly. "Just a girl."

They said their goodbyes and resumed their journey. Zollin could tell that Brianna wasn't comfortable with her new celebrity status in the Jaq clan. The dwarves who had traveled with them from the Oliad clan had great affection for Brianna and Zollin, but this new revelation didn't seem to surprise them. They treated her the same as always, and Zollin gave her time to think about what had happened. He instinctively knew that she was struggling to accept the power the ruby gave her. He also knew that she wasn't wearing the white alzerstone ring. He had tucked it safely away in his pack so that he wouldn't lose it. At some point Zollin had been planning on giving it back to her, but he wasn't sure if that was a good idea anymore. He didn't know a lot about magical objects, but it seemed unlikely that she would be able to wield fire with the ring on. He wanted her to at least get used to the idea and perhaps even experiment a little to see what she could do, before taking up the ring again.

They made camp in a small cavern, and Brianna sat a little apart from the others. She practiced making fire and controlling the flames. She liked what she was able to do, but she felt like a little girl playing dress-up. She could make fire appear from nowhere, and the flames could lick across her skin while she hardly felt anything. There was no damage to her hands, but even so her power was nothing compared to what Zollin could do. She didn't know if the flames were a weapon or just a tool. She could start a campfire, she was certain of that, but she didn't know if she could do anything else. She needed time to think and explore her gift, but time was the one thing they didn't have. They had not planned to stay with the Jaq clan, but the virus had held them up two whole days.

Brianna slept fitfully. Her body was still sore from being so violently sick to her stomach, and she had trouble getting comfortable on the stone floor of the cavern. The next day they came to the last Stepping Stone. Zollin rebuilt the bridge rather quickly, his skill at levitating and transmuting the molten rock having grown. When he was finished, Brianna went into the cavern. Like the others it had a pool of molten rock at the center, casting an orange glow around the stone walls. This particular cavern had a domed ceiling with no stalactites hanging down. She walked down the sloping floor of the cavern toward the pool of magma. Normally the heat would have seemed unbearable. She remembered how she felt in the first Stepping Stone cavern. It had been so hot she could hardly breathe, the hot air seeming to cook her lungs. But this time things were different. She didn't just tolerate the heat, she soaked it up like a sponge. It seemed invigorating to her, and she wanted to get closer and closer to the source of it.

"Brianna, what are you doing?" Zollin called. "You're getting too close."

"No, I'm not," she said.

She was mesmerized by the heat. It was calling to her and washing through her body in a way that made her feel strong and confident.

"Brianna!" Zollin shouted.

She heard him, but she ignored his shouting. She knew what she was doing. She knew that the heat should be overwhelming, but it wasn't. It felt like getting into a hot bath, when the water feels so good you just want to submerge as much of your body in it as possible and never come out. And there was a change happening inside her, as if some hidden side of her nature was waking up for the first time. She was curious and happy. The long days and nights in the tunnels and caverns had bothered her, making her feel suffocated and claustrophobic. She had fought that feeling for days and longed for wide open spaces. But now, in the intense heat of the Stepping Stone cavern, she felt free. She breathed in the searing heat and then blew it out in a long, scorching blast.

"Brianna!" Zollin screamed. "Your clothes are smoking!"

He ran forward but even with his magical shield raised he simply couldn't get close enough to her. Then he realized that she wasn't wearing the white alzerstone ring. He could levitate her back from the molten pool. But he remembered that he had promised never to use his magic on her against her will. He had manipulated her emotions once, in an effort to help her train with her bow, but she had resented and feared him for it. Would stopping her now do the same thing, he wondered?

In that moment of hesitation everything changed. To Zollin's horror Brianna burst into flames. It wasn't just her clothes, her entire body was engulfed.

"Brianna!" he screamed.

"What's happening?" Bahbaz cried.

The other dwarves were gathered around Zollin, who was now sobbing uncontrollably. He knew in that moment it had been a mistake not to give her back the white alzerstone ring. He knew the magic of the ruby firestone was powerful, but now he was afraid it had lured her to her doom. He had seen the fire on her hands and how it didn't hurt her, but that was fire she had conjured. He didn't know if she was burning alive or not. The heat from the molten rock was overwhelming, and she wasn't responding to him.

Brianna felt light as a feather. Her body, although strong, seemed somehow lighter and more maneuverable. She jumped up into the air and flipped several times before coming back down to land on her feet. Her clothes had completely burned away, but the flames covered her now, wrapping around her body like a living second skin. She took a deep breath and blew hard. Flames billowed from her mouth just like the dragon.

"Oh my God," Zollin said.

"She's truly a Fire Spirit now," Bahbaz said.

"What does that mean?" Zollin asked.

"I don't know," Bahbaz replied. "I've never seen or heard of anything like this."

"I have," said the gruff-voiced dwarf. "I heard that the Fire Spirits of old birthed dragons from the molten rock of the mountains."

"That's just a myth," Bahbaz said angrily. "And I don't recall anything about seeing a woman burst into flames or fly around."

"She's coming back," Zollin said.

He picked up a blanket from his pack and held it out to her, closing his eyes so that he didn't see her naked. The flames still covered her body, but her face, arms, and legs were bare. Her skin, which had always been pale, was now a golden tan. Her raven black hair was now streaked with deep auburn. And her eyes seemed to shine brighter than ever.

"Did you see it, Zollin?" she asked with wonder. "Did you see me?"

"Yes," Zollin said. He had his face turned away from her, and his eyes were squeezed so tight they were nothing but wrinkles of skin.

She took the blanket and wrapped it around her body.

"Thanks," she said.

"What was that?" Zollin asked, looking at her for the first time since she had come walking out of the flames.

"I don't know," she said honestly. "It felt so good to be in the heat and then suddenly, everything changed."

"What do you mean?"

"I mean I'm different," she said, laughing. "Didn't you see me? I must be part dragon or something. I breathed fire."

"Do you think that's normal?" Zollin asked.

166

"No," she said firmly, "of course it isn't. I've never heard of anything like it."

"I mean do you think you're okay?"

"I'm better than I've ever been in my life," she said confidently. "Except I lost my clothes. Excuse me."

She picked up her pack and went back into the cavern. Zollin and the dwarves, all speechless for once in their lives, stood in the tunnel not knowing what to say. When Brianna came back they continued their journey. Zollin decided not to press Brianna for answers. She seemed happy and, for now, that was all that mattered.

Chapter 15

Pain. It was all the dragon could think about. The wounds were festering. It had been driven out of its lair, its gold lost, and now its wounds would not heal. The beast's feet were raw from scrabbling over the rocky mountainous terrain. His mind was feverish, clouded by pain and totally consumed by the voice. It was always there, always calling for him. He no longer tried to fight the desire. All he wanted was to go to the voice, which on top of everything else now promised to heal him.

Every lurching step ached. The wound in its leg was so intense that the dragon could barely lift it to move forward, nor could it support the beast's massive weight. The wound just below its wing was even worse. The muscle that worked the wing was dying. After centuries of near invincibility, the dragon was now reduced to an oversized lizard. Enslavement would be better, the dragon freely admitted it now. The humans had somehow found a way to pierce the black scales that covered the beast's thick hide, and now it was helpless. Of course that wasn't exactly true. The dragon was still incredibly strong, its tail could strike and kill the largest animals in the mountains. Two mountain lions with their huge fangs had tried to ambush the dragon, but its tail had shattered the big cats' backs. It could also still breathe fire, so no foe could come close enough to harm the dragon, but soon it wouldn't be able to move at all. It had been lucky with the lions; together they had made considerable sustenance, but the beast had eaten nothing since. Soon it would grow too weak from hunger to keep moving, and it was too large and slow on the ground to get near any game large enough to support the dragon's massive appetite.

It was the wizard's fault, the dragon thought bitterly. It had been tricked into leaving the cave and lured onto the ledge where it could be wounded. If the wounds had only healed properly none of this would be an issue. It could take to the sky and have its choice of food. The beast's mouth salivated at the thought of finding a mountain ram and devouring the animal whole. It dreamed of succulent fare—elk, or even cows or sheep that the humans domesticated—as it dragged its weary body through the mountains and vowed to have its revenge.

* * *

Zollin pondered how he might bring up the subject of the white alzerstone ring with Brianna. She seemed so happy, and the dwarves who had been kind and protective of her before,treated her with awe now. She had changed, not in a bad way, but she was not the same girl as before. Zollin had known her as the spoiled, self-centered young girl who had treated him as if he didn't exist in Tranaugh Shire. He had fallen in love with her when she had been the girl with an iron will, refusing to be left behind or helpless in battle. Now, she seemed more content than he had ever known her to be. She was happy, laughing and almost prancing as they made their way through the dark tunnels under the mountains. She often let tongues of fire dance on her palms or on her shoulders to illuminate the caverns high above their heads.

That night when they made camp she started their fire. It wasn't a difficult spell; Zollin had been making fire with his magic since the day he discovered his gifts, but with Brianna it was different. She could not only produce the flames, she could touch them without being burned and control them like they were a living part of her.

She didn't flaunt her new power, nor did she use it needlessly. Still, Zollin could tell that it made her happy, and he recognized the feeling. For years growing up in the village as his father's apprentice he had struggled to find his place in the world. He never felt like he fit in, not at home where he never measured up to his father's expectations, not in the essentials school where he chafed under the school master's rigid discipline, not even in their village where he was known only as the carpenter's son. When he had discovered his magical abilities he had found his purpose in life. Brianna now had that same expression, more confident, more comfortable in her own skin.

Of course, the power, which was as evident to Zollin as the sweet scent of a woman's perfume would have been to her suitors, only made Brianna more attractive to the young wizard. Her eyes flashed in the light of her fire and he felt a kindred soul looking back at him. The auburn highlights in her hair and the golden tan color of her skin seemed to fit her perfectly. Zollin was forced to use all of his self-control not to touch her when her shirt rose up and revealed a bit of skin above her hip as she pointed up at some geological formation. Luckily they had been on the move the rest of the day, so he had no opportunity to give in to the desire that Brianna conjured in him. Zollin hadn't felt like he could broach the subject of the white alzerstone with her.

The truth was, he didn't know why he wanted Brianna to wear the ring. He had given it to her on a whim while they still lived in Tranaugh Shire. He called it a wedding gift, but the truth was greater than that, it was an expression of his love for her, even though he barely knew Brianna when he had given it to her and she had been engaged to marry his best friend. He had acted impulsively, but the impulse had been driven by something deep inside him, more elemental than his magic and connected to the core of his being. But if she put the white alzerstone ring on now, would it rob her of her own power? How could he ask her to give up what she obviously felt was her true self?

They made camp at last, and Bahbaz informed them that they would reach their destination on the next day. The dwarves prepared a lavish meal, having been generously resupplied by the Jaq clan. Zollin, always hungry, ate his food without tasting it. Brianna was laughing and joking with the dwarves, but Zollin sat in silence, mesmerized by the girl who was now a Fire Spirit.

Finally they bedded down, but Zollin couldn't sleep. He lay staring up into the black recesses of the cavern they were in. The fire had burned low, and the embers cast only the faintest light. He was lying next to Brianna, but they hadn't really talked about things yet. Zollin was afraid that Brianna wouldn't understand why he wanted her to put the ring back on and he couldn't explain it himself. He just knew he wanted her to try.

"Are you awake?" he whispered.

"Yes, I can't sleep," she admitted. "Was I keeping you up with my tossing and turning?"

"No, I couldn't sleep either. I've been wanting to talk to you, but we haven't had much privacy."

"I know, and even though coming down here has been wonderful, I miss being with you. I don't miss the cold wind, but I miss being miles away from anyone else in the mountains."

Zollin smiled. He hadn't thought about it when they were hunting down the dragon; there were too many other things on his mind, like finding food and staying warm. But he missed the isolation, too. He didn't want to be alone in the mountains with Brianna forever, but there was so much less pressure in the wilderness. He didn't feel like he needed to watch his back for assassins or have whole villages depending on him for safety.

"It was nice. Do you think things will ever be that simple again?" he asked.

"I don't know, maybe."

Zollin wasn't sure what he was going to say, but he felt like he had to say something about the ring. He decided his best option was to just dive right in.

"I've got your ring in my pack."

"The white alzerstone ring?" she asked.

"Yes, you can have it back whenever you want it."

"Wouldn't it disrupt my powers?"

"I don't know," Zollin said truthfully. He waited while Brianna thought about things. He didn't want to seem too pushy on the subject.

"I guess I could give it a try," she said.

"Okay."

Zollin sat up and began rummaging in his pack. He found the ring easily enough. It was a simple bit of jewelry, just a plain band and a small, round stone that was completely white. He could feel that it contained magical power, but even after all of his lessons with Kelvich he still couldn't tell exactly what the white alzerstone was or why it blocked magic.

"Do you think I'll lose my powers if I put it on?" Brianna asked.

"You mean lose them forever?" Zollin said. "No, I can't see that happening. It doesn't take away magical ability, it just blocks it."

"I'm not sure I even need it anymore," she said nervously.

"Maybe, I don't know. I just feel better when you wear it."

172

She looked at him and he saw compassion there. He had to admit in that moment he was afraid she was outgrowing him. When he had come into his magical power, it made sense that she would be attracted to him. Now that she had power of her own, he wondered if she might not feel the same way about him. She might not feel like she needed him. Even worse, she might not want him. He wasn't sure he could live with that. He loved her, but since she had walked into that final Stepping Stone cavern and displayed powers that he had never imagined, he had been afraid.

She slipped the ring on her finger and immediately some vital part of who she was seemed to disappear. She was the same Brianna; nothing about her appearance changed, but it was as if her vitality slipped away, and she seemed to sag. She was still beautiful, but it was like looking at a beautiful painting or a grand sculpture instead of the living model; the essence of who she was had disappeared.

"I can't do anything," she said, holding up her hand.

"Take it off," Zollin said sadly.

She took off the ring and laid it on the floor between them. Then she held out her hand and two small flames appeared on her palm, dancing together. Zollin smiled, but it was bittersweet. He had no reason to believe that Brianna's rejection of the white alzerstone meant anything, but he couldn't help but feel that it did. After a moment their eyes met, and once again Zollin felt a rift opening up between them.

"You seem different," she said.

"You're the one who's different."

"No, I'm not," she said smiling. "I'm still Brianna from Tranaugh Shire. I'm still just a girl. I'm still in love with you."

"But you're not still just a girl, you're a Fire Spirit."

Brianna laughed quietly. Zollin thought she sounded like a fountain.

"No, I'm not," she said. "I just have some powers because of this," she held out the firestone that Hammert had given her.

"Take that off, too," Zollin said.

He had a suspicion that taking off the beautiful ruby on its intricate gold chain would do nothing to dampen Brianna's powers. The stone had awoken what was already inside her, but she didn't need it to retain her powers.

"Okay," she said, almost as if he were daring her to do it. "Why do I get the feeling you don't approve of me having magical abilities?"

"I don't disapprove of anything," Zollin said. "I'm just anxious to learn all I can about who you've become."

"Don't worry, I'm not more powerful than you are, Zollin," she said, and there was a note of resentment in her voice.

"Brianna, please don't say that. I'm not jealous of you. I'm not even worried about you. I'm worried about us."

"Why? Because you don't think two magical people can be together?"

"No, of course not," he said, but there was no conviction in his voice.

In fact, that was exactly what he was afraid of; he just hadn't realized it. Brianna took off the necklace and laid it beside the ring. Zollin could tell immediately that nothing had changed. The necklace was just decoration now.

"There, are you happy?" she said.

"Try your powers," he replied.

"I can't. I took the necklace off."

"I don't think you need it anymore," he said.

She couldn't hide her excitement or the hope in her eyes that what he said might be true. He realized then that her powers, new and wonderful to her, were already every bit as important to her as his were to him. When he had been injured in the snow, his back broken and unable to tap into his reservoir of magic, he had wanted to die. He had felt like losing his powers was a fate worse than death. Of course, he knew logically that wasn't true, but it also gave him a frame of reference for understanding Brianna's hopes.

She held up her hand again, and once more twin flames danced across her hands.

"Oh, Zollin, what does this mean?"

"It means you're a Fire Spirit," he said in an even tone.

"But what is a Fire Spirit? I'm still human. I'm still flesh and blood. Here," she said as she grabbed his arm and lifted his hand toward her face.

The moment his fingers touched her cheek they both felt the shock. Zollin's magic surged out of him, mingling with the fiery might that had erupted from Brianna. They were locked together, neither able or even wanting to move. Zollin felt as if his soul were naked and laid bare before Brianna, but she didn't reject him. Her own soul, just as vulnerable, seemed to entwine with his.

After a few intense moments their powers settled and they pulled back. They were both out of breath, and neither spoke for a time.

"See," she told him, breaking the silence at last. "I'm still me."

"You're more of yourself than you've ever been," he said.

"What do you mean?"

"You know what I'm saying. You didn't just become a fire spirt, you always were. Now, whatever was keeping you from being who you were meant to be is gone."

"You make it sound so dramatic."

"I'm not trying to," he said.

They sat holding hands for a while, both looking down at the white alzerstone ring and the golden necklace with the bright, red ruby that lay on the ground between them. Finally, Brianna broke the silence.

"What does this mean, Zollin?"

"I don't know," he admitted.

"But you've been around other magic users before," she said. "Is this normal?"

She didn't really believe that it was, but she had to ask.

"No, it isn't. With Kelvich and the wizards from the Torr, I could feel them. It was like walking past a fire. I could detect their presence, and the closer they got the more intense the feeling, but nothing like this. When I met Miriam there was a connection, but it was more one-sided, as if my magic were stirring up her own magical abilities. I've never felt anything like what just happened."

They continued talking for a while, but soon both lay back down. Zollin still felt an odd sense of foreboding, but he did his best to ignore it. He was sure that Brianna wouldn't cast him aside, and that was really all he could hope for. He couldn't foretell the future, and so he would take each day as it came.

They slept for a few hours until the dwarves woke them up to continue the journey. A few hours later they noticed that the tunnels were sloping upward and the temperature was dropping.

At midday, they stopped in a small cavern to eat, and Bahbaz announced that he and his clansmen were turning back.

"All you need to do is follow the tunnel. You'll be out on the mountains before you know it," Bahbaz explained. "The Great Valley isn't far."

"Thank you," Zollin told him. "You've been a big help."

"And a good friend," Brianna added.

"You've done us a great service, wizard. Those Stepping Stones will make travel and trade much easier now. Perhaps one day you can come back and finish the job."

"I will, I promise," Zollin said.

"And you," Bahbaz said as he turned to Brianna. "You are always welcome among the dwarves of the Highland Mountains."

"Thank you," Brianna said.

"No, it is you whom we owe thanks to. A living, breathing Fire Spirit! Who would have dreamed we would be so fortunate as to see you in the flesh?"

"I never dreamed I would have the great honor of meeting such noble dwarves."

"We are ever at your service," Bahbaz said.

The dwarves weren't much for sentiment, and soon they were gone, trundling away back down the tunnels. Zollin and Brianna spent the next half hour squeezing through a very narrow tunnel. The floor rose steeply and the ceiling got lower and lower until they were finally forced to crawl the last five hundred feet. The cave entrance was hidden by a large boulder that didn't quite cover the cave, but was close to the mountain and forced them to squeeze between the large rock and the mountain. The sky was overcast and gray, but it was dazzling to Zollin and Brianna just the same. And while the air was far from freezing, they both quickly pulled on the extra clothes they had in their packs.

"We made it," Brianna said. She was glad to be out of the caves but shivering with cold. She wanted to let fire dance across her body and warm herself, but she had to be careful. She was immune to the fire, but her clothes weren't. If she let the fire get too close her clothes would be singed or worse, burst into flames. Then she would have nothing to keep her warm.

"Now we just have to discover where we are."

"Well, what are you waiting for? Work us some magic," Brianna teased.

Chapter 16

The dragon felt the wave of magic as it washed over him. He recognized it, like the roar of some dreaded beast echoing off of the mountains. The beast hadn't moved in over two days. It lay stretched across the rocky ground, pain and the constant call of the voice in its head driving the beast toward madness. But the magic wave meant that the wizard was coming, and the dragon had no delusions about what the wizard wanted.

It rose slowly, first rolling to one side so that it could move its large foot into position on its left side. Then it rolled the other way and moved the other leg. The beast's powerful legs could stretch out behind it, which they did when the dragon was flying or lying down. Now the legs were centered just under its powerful loins and, by raising its head and tail, the beast could stand up. The strain on the dragon's wounded leg was excruciating, but the magic the beast felt was feeding the fear that numbed the pain and motivated the dragon to move.

The dragon stretched its wings. At first the wound under its wing caused by the arrow was simply painful, but the pain soon turned debilitating. After the first week, just holding its wing out was agonizing, and now the muscles in the beast's chest seemed to have atrophied. The wing trembled and then drooped. It was all the dragon could do just to pull the wing back to its body.

It started walking, its head moving from side to side, looking for any sign of danger. The wicked-looking, forked tongue licked the air, but down in the valley the air was tainted with mold and dust, rotting vegetation, and the excrement of scurrying animals. The dragon wasn't sure, but the magic seemed to be coming from the south. How the wizard could have circled around the beast without it knowing was a mystery, but the dragon continued forward. There would be no running away. The beast was too weak to attempt to flee. Its mind too bombarded by the voice that called to it to come south. It knew that if it turned back the wizard would just hunt it down. No, the dragon thought, better to face the threat head on. If the wizard killed the beast, then the suffering would end. And, wizard or no, the dragon could not let anything stop it from going south now, from seeking out the voice in its head that was speaking so powerfully now.

If the dragon's mind hadn't been clouded by pain and hunger, it might have recognized that the mental commands had increased in power. Something was boosting the suggestive force of the voice, but the beast cared only about surviving now. The time when it might have flown to challenge the speaker was past; now it could only obey. It had to move south, to find the voice, to submit.

* * *

"It's that way," Zollin said, pointing northwest. "And pretty close, too. Bahbaz was as good as his word. I can't believe we're still ahead of it."

Brianna merely frowned. She knew that hunting the dragon was their task and that nothing would turn Zollin from his sense of duty, but she was afraid. They had a plan and she thought it was a good one—it had been her idea after all—but still she felt a sense of trepidation. What if the dragon somehow hurt Zollin again? She had seen him battle wizards in terrible displays of magical power, and he'd always come through victorious. With the dragon, he had managed to drive it away twice, but always he had been just a hair's breadth from death. She wished they could turn south and leave the beast in the mountains, but she knew it wouldn't stay there. It had ravaged the northern villages before, and there was no reason she could think of why it wouldn't do so again.

"Let's find a place to fight from," she said, trying to sound braver than she felt.

They walked through the winding valley they were in, and Zollin levitated himself onto a high ridge to look for a place where they could lay their trap for the dragon.

Soon Zollin floated back down beside her, smiling. The use of his magic until recently would have drained all his strength, but since the accident that had almost killed him, he'd been invigorated by the use of his power. He seemed to be full of life and excitement.

"I found a place that will work," he said happily. "And I also found a small stream not far away. There's even some grass growing, and a friend of yours is there waiting for you."

"A friend of mine?" Brianna asked.

"Yes, and she seems none the worse for her vacation in the mountains."

"Who are you talking about?" Brianna asked.

"Lilly, of course," Zollin said, referring to the horse that he had won in a wager with a traveling illusionist after discovering his power in Tranaugh Shire.

Lilly was an older mare, but the horse had carried Brianna to safety when they fled the small village as the Torr pursued Zollin. She and the horse had formed a bond, and Zollin had led the horse from Brighton's Gate all the way to Orrock when Brianna had been captured by Branock. Brianna had ridden Lilly from Orrock all the way into the Northern Mountains, but the terrain had become too steep, and they had been forced to turn the horse loose.

"What about your horse?" Brianna asked.

"He wasn't there. Only Lilly, but one horse is better than none. Come on, we can catch up to her soon."

They moved quickly through the rocky canyons. They grew chilled, but the physical exercise warmed them up. Zollin lifted them up steep inclines and down sheer cliff faces with his magic. When they came to the valley where the stream ran, Brianna was surprised at how emotional seeing her old horse made her. They were afraid that Lilly might shy away after almost a month alone in the mountains, but the horse raised her head and whinnied as they approached, then trotted to meet them. They tied their packs together and laid them across Lilly's willing withers. They had no tack, not even a rope to lead Lilly with, but she didn't need it. It was as if she had been waiting for them, and she followed them eagerly.

It took another hour and a half before they came to a wide valley that ran straight and long before them. The valley narrowed on its southern end. Several other canyons fed into the valley and two massive mountains stood like silent sentinels to the east and west. The mountains had steep cliffs with small terraces that rose like a stair case up the mountainsides.

"This is it," Zollin said. "I'm almost certain the dragon will come this way. We can take a position on one of the ledges up there," he said pointing up at the mountain to his right.

"It looks perfect, but what about Lilly?"

"We'll need to lead her out of the valley. There should be a good place to corral her somewhere."

"How long until the dragon is here, do you think?"

"A few hours," he said. "Hopefully before sunset."

"Okay, I'll take Lilly. You find a good place for the ambush."

Zollin retrieved his canteen and some food. They had refilled their canteens in the stream, so the the water was fresh and cold. Their only rations were some dried goat's meat the dwarves had given them, along with onions and potatoes.

"I'll be back soon," Brianna said.

"Be careful," Zollin said, but there was an element of excitement in his voice.

The truth was, he felt like they could actually finish their task soon. He knew that returning to Yelsia with his task unfinished would be difficult, and after the virus had set them back almost two whole days in the Jaq clan village, he had lost hope of getting in front of the dragon. Now their plan was coming to fruition, and he couldn't help but be excited. He had sensed the wounds on the dragon. Its pain was palpable, and he was sure the beast couldn't fly. There was really no reason why they couldn't defeat it. He rose joyfully into the air, excited to find the perfect vantage point.

Brianna led Lilly through the valley. The horse was the picture of contentment, her horse shoes clipping and clopping on the rocky valley floor. Unlike the Great Valley, which was green and full of life, this valley was filled with loose stone and low, anemic-looking shrubs that managed to take root in the few spots where soil covered the stone floor. The cloud cover overhead was starting to break apart, and a few shafts of sunlight shined through the thick clouds.

Brianna knew she should be positive and hopeful like Zollin. Once they had dealt with the dragon they could return to Yelsia and to their friends. They could be married, and that thought was a happy one, but still she felt a sense of trepidation. She couldn't put her finger on the problem. In her mind she knew that killing the dragon was the right thing to do. The beast had slain countless people and laid waste to entire villages. Still, in her heart there was a spark of hesitation. Somehow she had developed a sense of empathy for the beast. She didn't want to feel sorry for it but she did, and no matter how hard she tried she couldn't shake the feeling.

It took half and hour to walk Lilly through the valley, which eventually curved around one of the mountains and ended in a small, sheltered area that was the perfect place to leave her horse and set up camp. She gathered some dry brush that could be used for a fire later that night and took the packs off Lilly. Then she spent some time talking quietly to the horse and rubbing its soft nose. Then she left Lilly, telling her to stay, which the horse willingly did.

The walk back was more difficult. She knew that she needed to tell Zollin about her misgivings, but she didn't really know what to say. They had a job to do, a duty to their kingdom, but she wasn't sure if she could go through with it.

Zollin had already found what he thought was the best place to wait on the dragon. There were scattered boulders they could hide behind if they ended up needing to do that. They had a perfect view of the valley. When Zollin saw Brianna returning, he used his magic to lift her up the mountainside.

"What do you think?" he asked. "It's perfect, isn't it?"

"Yes, it's just what I had in mind," she replied.

"You don't sound very convinced."

"I've just got a lot on my mind."

"Well, we're going to be just sitting here, waiting for the dragon to come by. You might as well tell me what's bothering you."

"How do you know the dragon will come this way?" she asked, hoping he wouldn't notice that she was changing the subject.

"It's a big valley—several of the other valleys feed into it," he said, his forehead wrinkling with thought. "I guess we'd be better off having something to lure the dragon this way."

He stood up and let his magic flow out. He could sense the dragon nearby, but it was moving slowly and he wasn't sure that it would come into the valley. He began looking for other animals. He needed something big, something large enough that it would be a tempting meal for the dragon. There was a goat on the mountain opposite them, but it was small and scrawny, making Zollin doubt that it would attract the dragon's attention. Then he found an elk. It was a cow, all alone, which Zollin found odd. Still, he concentrated hard and lifted the animal into the air. She kicked and thrashed in terror, but Zollin didn't lift her high. He pushed feelings of peace and safety into the terrified animal and was pleased to feel that she immediately calmed down.

"Is that an elk or a deer?" Brianna asked.

"A cow elk," Zollin said. "I think I can calm her down and keep her in the valley. We can make a few small cuts to get her bleeding. Hopefully that will be enough to attract the dragon."

"It's a bit inhumane isn't it? I mean, the elk will be in pain."

"Not if I do it right. I should be able to keep the pain blocked and after she's bled a little I can heal the wounds."

"Okay," Brianna said.

She wasn't wholly convinced, but she had a bigger issue on her mind. The dragon was coming closer. She could feel the large beast now, through some sort of magical connection, although she didn't understand it. It was like a woman who is close to labor, but hasn't started contracting yet. Brianna knew the dragon was coming, and her sense of empathy was growing with every minute that passed. She could sense the dragon's pain, its raw feet, the festering wounds, its overwhelming hunger. She knew instinctively that it would now come through the valley. It would smell the elk, even if Zollin didn't bleed it. It would come to feed and it would be walking right into their trap.

Zollin had just finished healing the elk and putting it into a deep sleep in the middle of the valley when the dragon appeared. It was hobbling along, obviously in pain. They could hear the scraping of its rough scales as it dragged its body along the ground.

"There it is," Zollin said.

"I see it," Brianna whispered.

"Get your bow."

"I will, it's too far away to shoot at yet."

"You shot game that far away," Zollin said, with a note of suspicion in his voice.

"Think about it, Zollin. Even if I hit it, one arrow won't kill it. And it can easily just run away. We need to let it get closer so that we have time to make sure it doesn't escape."

"All right," he said. "So are you going to tell me what's bothering you?"

"It's nothing," she lied.

"Since when do we keep secrets from each other?"

"We don't keep secrets," she said.

"Well, whatever is on your mind is more than nothing, so why don't you tell me?"

She sighed, an obvious sign of exasperation that Zollin recognized.

"Okay, you don't have to tell me," he said, throwing up his hands.

"It's not that I don't want to tell you," she replied. "It's just that I don't really know what's bothering me. It's just a feeling."

"What kind of feeling?"

"I don't know. Why is it so important?"

"I'm sorry, I can just tell that you're not okay. I want to help."

"Well, you can't fix it. Thanks for caring, but I'll be fine. Let's get on with it."

They watched the dragon for several more moments. The beast was hurrying toward the elk, oblivious to any danger. Zollin couldn't tell if it was so used to being at the top of the food chain that it had no fear, or if it was being reckless.

"What do think?" Zollin asked.

"If we wait much longer it will kill the elk," she said, her voice sounding hollow.

"Okay, do your thing. I'll make sure there's a magical shield up around us, just in case."

She raised the bow and nocked an arrow. There was something reassuring in the familiar routine. Having the bow in her hand again made her feel strong. She pushed down her foreboding and drew the bow, bringing her thumb to her check just below her eye. Her vision narrowed and zoomed down onto the dragon. The beast looked weary. She could see the wounds her arrows had caused at the dragon's lair. The tissue around the wounds was swollen, and there was some type of dirty-looking mucus seeping from the wounds. She focused on the beast's head. It had a row of thick, scaly lumps or ridges running from its snout up across its skull. There were small horns on the dragon's head, and its eyes were cloudy.

"What are we waiting for?" Zollin whispered.

Brianna knew she needed to fire her weapon. She knew instinctively that they could slay the beast now and be done with their task, but she couldn't do it. She not only felt sorry for the creature, she wanted to help it.

"I can't," she said.

"What are you talking about? Shoot it!"

"I can't, Zollin. I have to try and help it."

"Are you insane?"

"No, I'm not crazy. I know it sounds crazy, but it's in pain, can't you see that?"

"I'm glad. I hope it suffers and dies a slow death. It's a dragon, Brianna. You've seen it kill indiscriminately. Don't you remember that it almost killed us both, more than once?"

"Yes, of course I remember that, but I think I can help it."

"Why?"

"I don't know," she said as she laid down her bow. "But I have to try."

"What does that mean?"

"It means I'm going down there."

"No, that is absolutely not going to happen."

They heard bones popping and looked down. The dragon had reached the elk. It had been killed instantly when the dragon bit the animal's neck, breaking bones, before wrenching the head off.

"See that?" Zollin said. "That's what it does. It kills things. If you go down there, even if it doesn't incinerate you with its breath, it will still eat you."

"I don't think it will."

"And how do you know?"

"I don't know, exactly. I just know I have to try."

Zollin was getting angry. He couldn't understand what Brianna was going on about, but he knew her well enough to know that she wouldn't give up. She was determined to go down and face the dragon, and there was nothing he could do to stop her.

"At least let me go down first and be ready to help."

"Okay," she agreed. "But don't do anything stupid. I really think I can help the dragon."

Zollin nodded, biting back all his objections. Every sense of self-preservation he had for himself, and all his protective instincts to keep Brianna safe, were screaming danger. He knew they should just stick to the plan, but he also knew this was important to Brianna. She was still discovering her power, and the dwarves had talked about the legends of Fire Spirits and their connection with dragons. It wasn't hard evidence, but those stories combined with Brianna's obvious empathy for the beast was enough for Zollin to want to find out more. Of course, he knew if something happened to her he would never forgive himself.

He floated slowly down the mountain. The sun was setting and already low behind the mountains. He stayed in the shadows as much as possible, his fears for Brianna churning his magic into a furnace inside him. He could feel the magic testing the barriers he had put in place. If they crumbled, the magic would burst forth and drain his physical strength. He knew he couldn't let that happen. The dragon was dangerous, and any unexpected weakness could mean the difference between life and death.

Brianna didn't wait for Zollin. She jumped off the mountain ledge. It was an impulsive thing to do, but even as her stomach seemed to leap into her throat she she knew she wasn't in danger. It was like swimming. She gracefully aimed her body, twisting and turning through the air, slowing her descent. She could feel the fire inside her, eager to be set free. She had a moment of giddy euphoria and then she landed on her feet, as light as a dancer.

* * *

The dragon recognized the trap the moment it smelled blood. It had no doubt that the wizard was laying a trap, but it was anxious to have the battle over, to kill its tormentor or be killed. Either way, it would soon have peace. The smell of the elk blood was intoxicating. It hurried forward, no longer caring that its tail dragged along the ground like a serpent. Its tongue was hanging from its mouth, and no thought registered in the beast's mind other than feeding.

The first bite was glorious and reminded the dragon of its power. It felt the thick bones in the elk's neck snap between its powerful jaws. It sucked the hot blood into its mouth and swallowed a glorious mouthful before ripping the elk's head off with a powerful wrench. The head had no antlers to deal with, so the dragon crushed the animal's skull in its mouth and swallowed the head in one greedy gulp. Then it moved on, ripping hunks of meat and hide off the carcass and gobbling them down.

It was almost through with the elk when the human girl dropped to the ground not far away. She seemed fearless, standing still and watching the dragon eat. It took a deep breath and spewed flame toward her. There was a shout from nearby, but there was no hope for the girl. She would be burned beyond recognition, or so the dragon thought. The girl's clothes caught flame and burned around her, but she was unscathed by the blast. Her head was thrown back as if she were relishing the blast. The dragon roared in fury, shifting its body and spitting fire again. This time the girl moved into the blast. She jumped into the fire and swam in it, twirling and spinning like fish in a fast moving stream.

The dragon moved back instinctively.

"Don't," the girl said. "I'm not going to hurt you."

The dragon swung its tail, but the girl jumped into the air, flipping over the tail in a graceful somersault and landing on her feet.

"I want to help you," she said.

The dragon was confused. Never before had any human been so bold. Even the wizards of old had shown caution when controlling the beast. It shook its head angrily and roared. Still the girl came forward. Her clothes were blackened rags with gaping holes, but the skin underneath was smooth and unblemished. She reached out her hands, and the dragon saw flames erupt from her palms to flash and wave across her skin. Then the fire moved toward the dragon. It wasn't a blast of flaming power but a slow wave. The fire rolled over the dragon's scaly hide and with it came a feeling of supernatural warmth. It reminded the dragon of the way it felt to lie on the gold in its lair. It felt the pain in its breast and hip begin to ease. The beast's feet, which were raw and bleeding, began to grow stronger.

The dragon lowered its head and stared into the girl's eyes.

"You don't need to be afraid," she said. "I'm a friend."

The dragon made a noise, not a roar but more of a purr. Its tongue flashed out and tasted the air, which was hot and delicious. The elk carcass, what had been left of it, was now burning fiercely. The fat was crackling and the aroma was intoxicating. The girl drew close to the beast's head and then laid a fiery hand on its jaw. It was the first touch the beast had felt in centuries. It was bittersweet, but there was also a jolt as skin touched scaly flesh. The dragon felt strength welling up inside it. It swung its tail back around, but this time, instead of swatting the girl away, it coiled around her and drew her close.

Just then the wizard came charging forth.

"No!" Zollin screamed. "Let her go!"

Sizzling blue energy shot out of the wizard's hands and the dragon leapt backwards instinctively, its wings flapping. The wizard struggled to stand against the downdraft of air that lashed around him. Dust, dirt, and stones were hurled into the air and the wizard closed his eyes against the stinging debris.

Then the dragon realized it could fly again. The wounds were gone, healed by the girl's touch. The beast rose higher and higher into the air. Then it dove, but the wizard was sending white-hot bolts of lightning flashing toward the beast, and it veered away, flying higher and higher, holding the precious girl close to its body.

* * *

Zollin screamed again as lightning shot from his body and filled the air with the stench of ozone. The bright, popping energy lit up the valley, which was falling quickly into the gloom of night, but it served only to allow Zollin to see the dragon flying away. He jumped into the air, levitating himself after the beast, but the dragon was flying too fast and Zollin's energy was quickly draining.   His emotional outburst must have consumed his strength, and he was forced to float back down to the ground where he lay sobbing in the dirt.

He couldn't believe what had happened. He had watched as Brianna approached the dragon, saw the beast breathe fire that should have consumed her, but she was untouched. It had taken all of Zollin's force of will not to shield her from the flames. Even though he knew she was somehow immune to fire, it was difficult to watch the flames envelop her. When she hadn't been harmed by the dragon's fiery breath, he had let down his guard. The dragon didn't seem to want her near him, and Zollin assumed she would pull back. Instead, she had healed the beast. Hers were different from Zollin's own abilities. His power allowed him to do almost anything he could imagine, such as knitting broken bones or reconnecting severed tissue, but Brianna's power was composed of fire. She couldn't heal a person, or even most magical creatures, but a creature whose very nature was fire, such as a dragon, she could heal. Their magic was foreign to Zollin and totally unlike his own, but he could sense that Brianna's magic and that of the dragon were the same. He could only hope that the beast wouldn't kill her. Either way, nothing would stop him from finding the dragon now.

He stood up and brushed the dirt off his clothes. Then he wiped away the dusty tears from his face. He needed their supplies and he could ride Lilly, which would make his journey much faster, but he had flown out of the valley he had been in. His inner defenses felt weak, and the center of his magical power was so hot that he was sweating. He scrambled through the darkness, over the rocky terrain, as fast as he could. It took an hour of climbing for him to reach Lilly. The horse neighed when she heard him approaching.

"It's just me, girl," he said softly. "Brianna's gone, but we're going to find her."

He rubbed the horse's forehead, and the mare nuzzled his shoulder. Then he grabbed their packs and laid them across the horse's withers. He rummaged through one and found something to eat. Then he drained Brianna's canteen of water. The cool liquid tasted sweet and, even though he was tired, it gave him the energy he needed to press on.

He levitated himself onto Lilly's back and set out on the dark, winding path that he hoped would lead him to the Great Valley.

Chapter 17

"Sir, there are simply no ships to be found," said the steward.

King Oveer of Ortis cursed. He was not used to problems. He preferred to stay in his castle where servants and sycophants saw to his every need. His kingdom was run by a small council of nobles, which he oversaw, although he rarely attended that council. He let the tax collectors fill his treasury while he focused on what he found to be most important, making himself happy. And what made Oveer happy was an abundance of nice things. He loved fine clothes, brightly polished armor, and weapons. He also enjoyed fine wine, the best food, and of course, beautiful women. He had a wife, but the Queen's role was to produce heirs. Unfortunately, she had not succeeded in that one responsibility, and Oveer had long ago lost interest in her. She was sickly, and he was waiting for her to die so that he could marry a new, young queen who would give him children.

The only other thing that really interested Oveer was conquest. He had kept up a constant battle with the Norsikans and was constantly on guard against Shuklan raiders who pillaged along the coast. Of course, the King didn't actually do any fighting, but he spent a considerable amount of his fortune building his armed forces. When King Belphan of Osla had shared with him the plan to break the peace and invade Yelsia, Oveer had immediately sent word to his commanders to ready the invasion force. Oveer would not fight, of course; that would involve too much risk. But he would lead the army. Few things entertained King Oveer as much as seeing men fight in pitched battle. He sponsored many tournaments, but the controlled chaos of the melee wasn't nearly as exciting as watching an army at war.

The invasion plan had been simple: the armies of Osla and Falxis would sail up the coast and land on Yelsia's west coast. King Oveer's army would sail north from Blue Harbor, across the Sea of Kings, and rendezvous with Baskla's army to invade Yelsia from the east. Oveer didn't believe that Yelsia could withstand an invasion, much less fight a war on two fronts, but he had to admit the plan was sound. His job was not just leading the invasion on the eastern front, but also keeping an eye on King Ricard of Baskla. The two northern kingdoms had always been close allies. King Ricard could not deny the rumors of a dragon in Yelsia, which was the pretense of the Council of Kings, nor could he deny the charges of espionage and treason at that council. Still, the Baskla army needed to be held in check with a strong leader, and that was Oveer's job.

Unfortunately, the plan had not included instructions on what to do if there were no ships to conscript into his service. Ortis had a small navy, but it was located on the eastern coast, too far away to be of any use. The Great Sea of Kings was a massive, freshwater lake surrounded by three of the five kingdoms. Merchant and fishing vessels were the only ships on the Great Sea, but for some reason, there were none in port. Blue Harbor was an important city and one of the major trade ports on the Great Sea, but the local residents said that no ships had been seen in weeks. There were rumors that all the ships, other than small fishing vessels, were at anchor near Lodenhime. It was all very frustrating to Oveer. He was ready, with over half of his army, to sail north and begin the invasion. It was hot in the late summer sun, and he had been looking forward to enjoying the voyage north, where the cool sea breeze would be a nice change from the weeks he spent traveling south to Osla and back for the Council of Kings.

"So what do you suggest?" Oveer demanded. "I need ships, not excuses."

"Sire, we could send a legion to Lodenhime. I would lead them myself," said one of Oveer's generals. His name was Burgon and he was an older man, very practical and efficient in his duties with the army, but completely boring at court.

"Fine, but you do not need a legion. It would take twice as long for that many men to march around to Lodenhime. I want this seen to quickly."

"I could take a century of heavy horse," said Burgon. "We could be ready to ride in an hour."

"Sire, would a hundred men be enough to commandeer the ships we need?" said another of the commanders.

"It should be plenty," said Oveer.

"But there are rumors of a foul nature," said the commander. He was short and fat, obviously appointed to his position because of family connections at court. His name was Avery, and the King despised him.

"Don't trouble us with your craven nature, Avery," the King said. "Rumors don't trouble us."

"But Your Highness, doesn't the fact that are no ships at Blue Harbor indicate that perhaps the rumors are true?" said Avery.

"Witches, an army of besotted farmers, and what else? Do you think a century of heavy horse could not decimate an army of farmers and merchants? Why do you trouble me with your constant worry, Avery? Go and see to the supplies. Make sure we are ready to board the ships as soon as they arrive in port."

"Yes, my lord," said the fat commander, bowing and hurrying from the tent.

"Take your century and ride," King Oveer commanded. "I will see you back here with enough ships to move the army north in three days. Don't delay, commander."

"Yes, sire," said Burgon. He saluted and then left the tent.

"What of my entertainment?" the King asked.

The steward clapped his hands and a trio of musicians entered the tent, followed by a troupe of dancers, most dressed in silks so sheer that they did little to cover the dancers' lithe bodies. The King and the remaining army commanders settled in as the entertainment began. There was wine and food served, with servants hurrying to meet the smallest need or want. As the King and his commanders filled the rest of the day with debauchery, Burgon rode south along the coastal road that curved toward Falxis and the sea port at Lodenhime.

* * *

"My lord," cried a portly man who was attempting to run across the courtyard. "Her Highness's rider is returning! He is riding fast. Shall I go to the Lady Gwendolyn to give her the news?"

Prince Wilam looked at the man with unveiled contempt. He knew the pudgy merchant was looking for any excuse to get close to the Queen of the Sea. He also knew Gwendolyn hated to wait for anything, and taking her news that she would only have to wait on would put her in a bad mood. He would wait for the rider; after all, sending out scouts had been his idea. Why should someone else get the credit for his work? Of course, it didn't occur to him that he would be taking credit for the work the scout had done.

"Don't be a fool," he said contemptuously. "Get back to your post!"

"Yes, my lord," the man said.

He hurried back to his station on the watchtower while Prince Wilam paced impatiently. He had given the scouts instructions to send men back to bolster their numbers at the Castle but to return themselves only if they discovered signs of danger. Being in Gwendolyn's presence made him forget many things, such as his loyalty to Yelsia. The past no longer mattered to Prince Wilam; he only cared about pleasing Gwendolyn. There were times when she seemed so close to giving in to his advances. He was a crown prince after all. If she married him, all of Yelsia would be hers, but she had so far resisted his charms. He hoped that the scout was bringing good news: victory in a small battle might distinguish Wilam in the witch's eyes, and it was only a matter of time before King Zorlan sent troops from Luxing City to confront Her Highness.

He watched as the gate was opened. The fortifications around the Castle on the Sea had been his idea and had kept him busy for weeks, as had training the merchants, laborers, and farmers who made up Gwendolyn's army. They were as ready as they could possibly be for combat. Defending the fortified Castle gave them a strategic advantage that might level the odds if they had to face regular soldiers, as long as they weren't terribly outnumbered.

The rider came galloping in. He was covered with sweat and dirt and his horse was foaming at the mouth from exertion. The scout swung down off the horse, whose head was now hanging down, almost in the dirt.

"I hope your news is worth the life of that horse," Wilam said. "You've ruined it, you careless oaf."

"I thought the Lady Gwendolyn should know the news as quickly as possible," the rider said.

"What news?" Prince Wilam demanded.

The rider's hopeful look was dashed. He realized then that his hopes of being able to report to Gwendolyn were gone. He raised his eyes to Wilam's with a look of defiance, but saw immediately that he was hopelessly outmatched. The Prince wore a cool look of confidence that was unmistakable, and the rider realized that Wilam was ready to kill anyone who disobeyed him.

"Soldiers are coming. An entire century of heavy horse," the rider said.

"From Luxing City? I'm surprised it took them this long."

"No, sir," the rider said. "Along the coastal rode from Ortis."

"Ortis?"

"That's right, sir. They're flying their colors plain as day."

"How far away are they?"

"A few hours, at most. They're riding fast."

"A hundred of them, you say?"

"That's right. They're riding in formation and I could count them."

"Are there foot soldiers behind them?"

"No sir, not that I could see."

"Did you look?" Wilam demanded.

"I was watching the coastal road. I counted the riders and then came back here as fast as I could."

"Get yourself another horse and go back. I have to know what we're facing. Look for soldiers on foot and for supply trains."

"Can you please let the lady know I brought the news—"

"Yes, yes," Wilam said angrily, interrupting the scout with a wave of his hand. "I'll make sure the Queen knows you were doing your job. I'll also let her know you didn't do it well."

"I'm sorry," the man said, obviously crushed both by the realization that he had not done his duty as well as he had thought and because he had to ride back out again.

"This time, take better care of your horse, or I'll have you beaten and thrown into the sea."

"Yes, sir," the man said.

Prince Wilam didn't wait to see that the man did as he was ordered. He hurried into the Castle to give Gwendolyn the news. He was halfway through the feasting hall when the Queen appeared. Her cheeks were flushed with excitement and she hurried to Wilam.

"There are soldiers approaching?" she asked.

Anger blossomed in Wilam so violently that his vision turned red for a moment. He looked over Gwendolyn's shoulder and saw the gloating look of Keevy, the Castle steward. Obviously the sneaking little bastard had eavesdropped on the scout's report and then hurried to be the first to bring the Queen news, even if it was only a portion of that news. He vowed then to kill the steward.

"Prince Wilam!" Gwendolyn said loudly.

"I'm sorry, my Queen."

"Don't make me wait on news of this magnitude."

"Yes, my lady. A century of cavalry troops are riding this way. Ortis troops traveling along the coastal road."

"Excellent. When will they arrive?"

"They aren't coming to parlay," Wilam said.

"Don't you dare try to tell me my business," Gwendolyn said angrily, her voice rising in volume so much that it seemed supernatural. "I am Queen here, never forget that!"

Wilam was a proud man, a trained warrior, and the firstborn son of King Felix of Yelsia. Still, he cowered under the wrath of Gwendolyn. He was both frightened and worried at having displeased her. She had taken Prince Wilam into her confidence when he had come to the Castle with Quinn and Mansel. She had sent them on an errand but she had kept Wilam close, and he had naturally hoped that she would favor him as her lover. But Gwendolyn showed no interest in romance. A sorceress, Gwendolyn fed off the magical power of her twin sister, who was a warlock, unable to control her own magical power. Gwendolyn used that power to bewitch the men around her, all smitten and helpless in her presence, so that they did whatever she asked. The end result was usually bloodshed. Men could not stand to see those around them favored, and their jealously would eventually erupt in some form of physical violence, but Gwendolyn was determined to hold them in check, at least for now.

"They will arrive in a few hours, if the scout was correct, my lady," Wilam said, bowing in submission.

"Good, we have plenty of time to prepare. Make sure that all the sailors are in the compound. I don't want any of them in the town. I shall confront the soldiers myself. Keep your men in check, Wilam. I don't want to lose any of the soldiers."

"You mean to fold them into your service?" Wilam asked, shocked at the thought. His years of military training in Yelsia had emphasized loyalty, and while he had discarded his own loyalty, the thought of other soldiers joining their number was repugnant to him.

"That's right, my good Prince. They will join us; they will join your army. We must have a large army to fulfill my plans."

"But I could defeat them," Wilam said, trying not to sound like a little boy wanting to impress his mother. "I know that I could beat them in battle. Besides, what good will cavalry do us here? We are in a perfect defensive position. We don't need to sally forth. These walls are our greatest asset."

"No, I am our greatest asset," Gwendolyn said angrily. "Do not question my plans, or I will have you removed from my presence, is that understood?"

She was bluffing. She needed Wilam, but she didn't want him to know that. His desire for her would bring him back in line. He would do anything to ensure that he stayed close to her.

"Yes, of course, my Queen. Forgive my impudence."

"It is forgiven. Now do as I command."

He bowed, then hurried out of the Castle. He dispatched men to ensure that everyone who was loafing in town was summoned immediately back to the Castle. Lodenhime was a busy city in normal times, but Gwendolyn's presence had drawn all of its men to her service so that none of the usual activities were being done. Merchants let their wares rot in warehouses or abandoned shops. Laborers used their skills only as the witch needed them to. The women of the city were terrified but carried on as best they could while their husbands and sons wasted their days plotting ways to win Gwendolyn's attention.

Once Wilam had everyone in the Castle, his conscripted soldiers took every precaution to ensure that the Castle was secure. He gave very specific orders that no one was to fight. Gwendolyn intended to confront the soldiers, and that meant that his men had to stand at their posts and do nothing more than watch.

The courtyard was full of people. The news of the soldiers' approach had everyone on edge. The sailors had not been conscripted and were unruly. They despised Wilam, but they did not challenge him. His royal bearing and the broadsword he wore at all times (except on evenings when he was allowed to spend time with Gwendolyn and Andomina in their private quarters), let the others know he was no one to trifle with.

The scout returned after two hours. He was just as filthy as before, but this time his horse was in better condition. He was admitted into the Castle courtyard and rode up to the Castle steps. Gwendolyn and her sister were sitting on a padded bench at the top of the stairs that led into the large, stone fortress. An awning had been constructed to keep the sun off their flawless skin. The scout dismounted and knelt before the steps until Prince Wilam waved. He was led up toward the Queen to give his report.

"There are no other soldiers," the scout said, having trouble forming his words under Gwendolyn's intense gaze.

"Are you certain this time?" Wilam demanded.

"Yes sir, I watched the riders pass, then rode on. There's no one else on the coastal road."

"How close are they?" Wilam asked.

"They'll be in the city any time now. I wouldn't expect it to take them more than half and hour to find us here."

"Good," Gwendolyn said. "We have time for a drink."

Keevy hurried out of the Castle with a large pitcher of wine. He poured the wine into a crystal decanter filled with fresh fruit, then swirled the concoction around before serving drinks to Gwendolyn and her sister.

"When the soldiers are in sight of our walls, I want to know it," Gwendolyn told Wilam.

"Yes, my lady."

"I shall address them from above the gatehouse."

"What if they attack?" he asked her.

"They won't."

"But if they do, you'll be exposed."

"I'll have you with me," she said flirtatiously. "You wouldn't let them hurt me, would you?"

"Of course not, Your Highness."

"Good, then there's nothing to worry about."

Gwendolyn finished her drink and was deep into her second when word came that the soldiers were approaching. Gwendolyn stood, and most of the men in the compound moved forward anxiously. They wanted to be close to her, but Wilam pushed them out of the way. He had a large shield on which someone had painted two beautiful sirens that looked strikingly like Gwendolyn and Andomina.

The witch was confident and smiling as she walked across the courtyard. She kept her head high and met no one's gaze, as if to say that she was above them all. They were like worker bees in a hive, swarming around their Queen. Andomina followed her sister. She was lovely in her own way, but she had none of the confidence or royal bearing that her sister possessed. She looked only at the ground and never spoke. She followed her sister wherever she went and seemed more like a shadow than an actual person.

Wilam led them up the narrow staircase that led to the top of the guardhouse. Wilam had ensured that the buildings around the Castle's walls had been destroyed and the debris removed. It had created a large open area where attackers would find no shelter from the arrows, rocks, and spears that could be rained down upon them. Wilam called the area a killing field. The century of heavy horse cavalry were in a long line on the far side of the killing field when Gwendolyn reached the top of the gatehouse and could see them.

"Come to me," she said, her voice once again unnaturally loud.

The soldiers didn't move at first.

"I would know you all," Gwendolyn said, her voice as sweet as honey.

Wilam felt his own jealous fears of being replaced loom up in his mind, but he fought them down and looked at the men standing watch on the walls. They seemed steady enough, but one wrong move and they might very well attack. Hearing Gwendolyn seem to be giving favor to anyone aroused the fury of the men already in her service.

"Come to me, please," she said, her voice coaxing and tempting them to move forward.

For another long moment no one moved. Then finally, one lone soldier spurred his horse forward. Wilam braced himself for an attack, but almost immediately the first soldier was joined by others. At first they seemed to come, one by one, but it was only a minute before the entire century of soldiers was hurrying forward.

"Join me," Gwendolyn was saying. "You have a place here, with me and mine."

The cavalry soldiers all wore heavy armor, including helmets with face guards. They were raising their visors and throwing down their lances as they approached, each one trying to speak directly to Gwendolyn. The result was a cacophony of noise as each man pledged his love and his sword to Gwendolyn's service. She smiled down at the men, who were obviously smitten with her, then she turned to Wilam with a gloating look in her eye.

"See, my Prince, there was never anything to fear. Now you have a cavalry to play with. Be a good Prince and take care of them."

Wilam was speechless. He stood, staring as Gwendolyn descended from the gatehouse with Andomina in tow. The crowd below separated, creating a walkway from the gatehouse to the Castle, all while the men below cried out to Gwendolyn, pledging their lives for just one glance from the witch.

Chapter 18

The storm had blown Quinn and Olton so far out to sea that it took them two days to sail back. They finally made shore near a small village north of the Walheta Mountains, which separated Falxis from Yelsia and Baskla. Olton generously shared some of the money he made from the fish they caught while sailing back to land. It wasn't much, but it was enough to get Quinn started. He knew that Mansel had a big head start on him; his only real hope was to head north and hope that he could intercept Zollin as he traveled with Mansel back to the Castle on the Sea.

He couldn't afford a horse or weapons. Instead, he bought as much food as he could and wished Olton a safe journey home. Then he headed north on foot. He followed the coastal road, skirting the Rejee Desert and hoping that he would not be bothered. It was dangerous to travel alone, and even if he didn't have anything of value, he would still be an easy target for outlaws looking for a quick score. The coastal road was a haven for brigands who could hide out in the desert canyons with little risk of being found. The establishments along the coastal road catered to outlaws and sailors, but Quinn didn't have the coins to spend in inns or taverns. He kept to himself and stayed on the move. At night he looked for places where he could sleep concealed from view. He didn't light a fire or try to warm his rations, which were mostly hard bread and a little smoked fish.

He had traveled for six straight days, his feet blistered and sore, his skin burned and peeling from the sun, before he ran into trouble. Two men on horseback met him on the road and refused to let him pass.

"Spare a coin?" asked one of the men.

"You wouldn't begrudge us a few coppers," said the other, a grim-looking man with long, greasy hair and a lurid scar across one cheek. "We'd like to take a rest and perhaps have a drink at a nice inn, but unfortunately we haven't fared well lately. I'm sure you'd like to help."

"I haven't any coin," Quinn said, in honesty.

He tried to keep walking past the men, but they guided their horses to block his path.

"Hey, that's no way to treat your neighbors," said the first man again. He had a long, curved knife stuck through his belt without a sheath. The blade was rusty and nicked.

"I don't want trouble," Quinn said. "I've got some hard bread rations and water, and I'd be happy to share with you."

"Oh, come now," said the greasy man. "Travelers here on the coastal road always have more than some moldy bread. I tell you what. We'll split what you have three ways, if you give it up without a fight."

"It told you, I don't have any coin."

"I don't believe him, do you Wol?" said the greasy man.

"No, I don't," Wol said, drawing his rusty knife.

"Last chance," said the greasy man. "Split your money or we'll split your skull."

Quinn just smiled a cold, deadly grin.

"Give it your best shot," he said.

The two outlaws hesitated for moment. They hadn't expected Quinn to seem happy about a fight. Wol was the first to strike. He spurred his horse forward and slashed at Quinn with his knife. The blade almost caught Quinn's shoulder but he dropped to his knees just in time to avoid the attack. Then, as the first outlaw passed Quinn launched himself at the other man. Quinn was sure the greasy outlaw had a weapon, but he had not drawn it yet. He jumped up and grabbed the man, who tried in vain not to fall off his horse. The horse reared up on its hind legs and both men fell. Quinn managed to land on top of the outlaw, with all of his weight driving the wind from the greasy man's lungs. Then Quinn spotted the small knife in the outlaw's belt. It was little more than a utility knife and probably used for everything, from cleaning his horse's hooves to cutting his own meat for supper.

Quinn snatched up the knife. The blade was no longer than his hand. He turned and saw Wol riding quickly toward him again. He drew back his arm and threw the knife. It was a poorly made weapon, certainly not well balanced for throwing, and Quinn knew he had only a slim chance that the knife would do any real damage. The knife hit the outlaw in the breastbone handle-first, but it was thrown hard. The outlaw dropped his own weapon and fell back, one hand clutching his chest, the other grasping desperately for the saddle horn.

Quinn hurried over and retrieved the rusty, curve-bladed knife from the ground and felt a little better now that he had something to defend himself with. The greasy outlaw was struggling to stand up, while Wol, now weaponless, rode further and further away.

"Get on your knees," Quinn said. "And put your hands on your head."

The outlaw complied without comment, which only made Quinn more wary. He approached the man slowly, from behind. He turned the curved blade around so that it arched back over his forearm in a defensive position. He was just about to search the man for hidden weapons when the outlaw spun around, falling on his back and kicking up at Quinn with a hook motion. There was a blade protruding from the outlaw's boot. Quinn knew it before it struck, but he had no way to stop the blow. The boot tip, with its small, pointed blade, hit Quinn in the thigh. The kick alone was hard enough to cramp the muscle, but the blade gashed into the flesh, causing Quinn to cry out and stagger backward.

His left hand dropped to the wound instinctively, and he felt warm blood welling up between his fingers. The pain was bad, but his adrenaline was pumping, fueled by anger at the outlaw. He lurched forward as quickly as he could, swinging the rusty knife in a wide swipe that caught the outlaw across his back. The man,staggered forward, his back arched in agony, his hands reaching for his back in an effort to stop the pain. Quinn lurched forward again, and this time he slammed the knife down into the base of the outlaw's neck. The greasy man stiffened and then fell dead on the dusty road.

Quinn looked up to find Wol, but the other outlaw had not stopped riding. As he stood, panting from exertion and pain, he knew he needed to do something about his leg. The outlaw's horse was not far away, but it seemed nervous, probably because it could smell the blood. Quinn limped toward the animal slowly, trying his best to ignore the pain in his leg. He held out his hand and made no sudden movements to set the horse at ease. A few minutes later he was leading the horse back to the greasy outlaw's body. Quinn patted the man down and searched his pockets. He found only a few copper coins, but it was more than Quinn had had. He pulled the curved knife out of the outlaw's neck and wiped the blade on the man's clothes. Then he cut the sleeve off his own shirt. It wasn't as clean as he would have liked, but it was certainly cleaner than the greasy outlaw's. He could feel the blood running down his leg and into his boot. The wound was painful, but he doubted that it was serious, as the blade wasn't long enough to have reached the bone. It was painful to walk on, but he now had a horse to ride, so he could rest the leg and perhaps make even better time than walking.

He tied the cloth around his leg, knotting it tightly, and then climbed up into the saddle. The saddle wasn't much more than a leather strap with a saddle horn and stirrups. There were no saddle bags, and the saddle blanket was thin and worn through in more than one place. Quinn pulled his small satchel and canteen over his head and hung them from the saddle horn. He took a long drink of the lukewarm water and then nudged the horse's flank with his boot. The animal set off, walking at a slow pace. Quinn urged it into a trot, but the heavy-footed animal's gait was so jarring that soon he slowed the horse back down.

It took three hours to reach the next village, and the sun was beginning to set when he arrived. He asked a man carrying buckets of water from a well if there was a healer in the town. The man pointed at a small cottage and Quinn thanked him. He rode to the small building and climbed slowly off the horse. His leg was throbbing with pain and was too sore to hold any weight. Quinn tied the horse's reins and hopped to the wooden door. He knocked and waited a few moments before the door opened.

"Eh, can I help you?" the man asked.

"I've got a wound here that could use some tending to," Quinn said, pointing at his leg. "I've got four coppers."

"Well, that's enough for me to stitch you up. Come inside."

The cottage was plain, just a single room with a small bed in one corner, a fireplace in the other, and a sturdy-looking table in the center of the room.

"You can pull your pants off, or I can cut them off for you," the healer said. "One way's less painful, but if you don't have spare clothes I suggest you pull them off. Of course, you might start a new fashion style, one sleeve, one pants leg," he joked.

Quinn nodded and started with his boots. It was difficult but he managed it. Then he untied the makeshift bandage, which increased the pain. His leg had swollen and the wound was still seeping blood. He had no belt, and the pants came off without too much trouble. He nodded at the healer when he was finished.

"That's fine, just hop up on the table there," he instructed.

Quinn did as he was told, and the healer stretched the injured leg out so he could inspect it. He lit a lamp and held it close to the wound. He pressed around the inflamed flesh and smelled the wound. Then he stood up.

"It's dirty," he said. "You get cut with a dirty blade?"

"A knife in the toe of an outlaw's boot," Quinn said.

"Yes, I suspect that's about as dirty as they come. I hope you repaid the bastard."

"In spades," Quinn admitted.

"Can't fault you for that," the man said. "My name's Orval, but most everyone calls me Red. I used to have red hair, back before it all fell out."

"I'm Quinn."

The healer washed the wound first with water, then he poured strong alcohol over the wound. The burning was intense.

"That's strong stuff," Quinn said.

"It's only for medicinal purposes. Pure grain alcohol. I don't flavor it or age it. It cleans wounds and helps keep the flesh from rotting."

Next he mixed a poultice using oats and some other herbs to make a thick paste. Once he had it mixed, he used a curved needle to stitch the wound. Then he plastered it with the poultice and wrapped the leg with a long white bandage.

"That should fix it up. I'd like to take another look at in the morning though, just to make sure there's nothing more serious happening."

"That's fine," Quinn said, as he pulled his pants back on.

He fished out the coins from his small purse and handed them to the healer.

"Ah, well that's kind of you," he said. "Why don't we take two of these to Ned over at the Seaview Inn? It'll be enough for some supper and ale, if that suits you. You can bunk here tonight if you don't mind sleeping on the floor."

"That's very kind," Quinn said.

"It's no trouble," the healer added. "I'll be glad for the company and to not have to eat my own cooking for a change."

Quinn leaned on the older man's shoulder as they walked to the inn. The small village was built along the coastal road. There was a small quay with several fishing boats moored to the ancient-looking pilings. The Seaview Inn was almost exactly like every other inn Quinn had seen as he traveled up the coastal road. It was a rectangular building with a lean-to stable. There was a second story with rooms for guests. The larger first floor consisted of a large common room, kitchen, and store rooms, as well as the innkeeper's quarters.

"Red, you've got a patient," said the innkeeper happily when they entered.

"One who paid in coin," the healer said happily. "We'll have supper and ale, if you don't mind."

214

The innkeeper held out his hand, and Red dropped in two coppers. The man hurried away as Red helped Quinn onto a bench. The healer sat opposite from Quinn and chatted amiably while Quinn took in the room. There was no fire in the hearth, but the room was lit by candles in two large chandeliers that hung from the room's high ceiling. There were several long tables with benches on either side. There were several guests in the room, mostly older fishermen from the looks of them. Across the room, slumped against the wall, was a familiar face. Wol was glaring at Quinn.

"Do you know that man?" Quinn asked.

Red had to turn around in his seat to see who Quinn was pointing at.

"No, can't say that I do, why?"

"He's one of the outlaws who tried to rob me."

"Oh," Red said, dropping his gaze.

"Do you have a constable in this village?" Quinn asked. "Any kind of law?"

"Not here. The coastal road villages pretty much look after themselves."

"I'll be right back," Quinn said.

"Wait, where are you going?" Red asked in alarm.

"I've got unfinished business with that man," Quinn said, getting up from the table.

"But you'll bust your stitches, and get that wound bleeding again."

"I doubt it," Quinn said, as he hobbled away.

The room grew quiet as Quinn approached the man. He was still leaning against the wall, and he didn't move when Quinn drew close.

"Looks like you found Dalson's boot knife," the outlaw said quietly.

"Yes," Quinn admitted, "and he found that curved knife of yours. I think you should leave."

"No, I'm staying," said the outlaw.

"Get out, now," Quinn said. "Don't look back, just keep riding. If I find you waiting on me I'll kill you."

"I said I'm not leaving, and you can't do anything about it. I haven't done anything to you, and there are witnesses here who will back that up."

"I doubt it," Quinn said coldly. "Now, get up."

"No," the man said, sounding like a petulant child.

Quinn struck so fast the outlaw didn't even have a chance to move. Quinn hit the outlaw square in the chest. It wasn't a powerful blow, but the outlaw screamed in pain, doubling over and cradling his chest, struggling to breathe. Quinn put his hands on the table he was standing next to and kicked Wol in the side of the head with his good leg. The outlaw was knocked senseless, and Quinn searched him for weapons. He found a small utility knife and a dagger tucked into the top of his boot. There was also a small money pouch with half a dozen copper coins. Quinn took the knives and coins, then turned to the innkeeper, who had watched the confrontation from the door of his kitchens.

"Has he paid you?" Quinn asked.

"No," the innkeeper said.

"Did he bring in any belongings?"

"Just the clothes on his back."

"What about his horse?"

"It's in the stable."

"Any saddle bags?" Quinn asked.

"No, just a saddle and blanket. My boy took care of the horse and gave it good rubdown and some oats."

"Three coppers be enough to cover that?"

"Sure," the innkeeper said.

"Good, I'll take the horse," Quinn said. "Throw some water on him and send him out."

"What if he tries to fight me?"

"He won't," Quinn said. "His breastbone is broken, or at least bruised. It'll hurt him to breathe for a while I suspect, but that's what happens when you assault innocent travelers."

"Hear, hear," said a few of the men in the room.

"Good riddance, then," said the innkeeper.

Quinn noticed the other men in the room raising their mugs of ale or nodding respectfully to him as he hobbled back to his table. The innkeeper had fresh bread, a crock of butter, and mugs of frothy ale waiting for him.

"Well, now, you're not a man to trifle with," said Red. "I don't think I've ever seen a man felled with one punch. It didn't even look like you hit him very hard."

"I didn't. When they attacked me today I threw a knife at him while he charged me on his horse. The knife butt hit him in the chest and nearly knocked him out of the saddle. He abandoned his partner after that."

"He's lucky to still be alive," Red said. "That knife could have killed him."

"That was the intention," Quinn said. Then he waved for the innkeeper's son to come over as Red took a bite of bread he had just smeared with a thick layer of butter.

"Can you go to Red's cottage and fetch back my horse? Give it a good rubdown and some oats. I'll be riding out in the morning," he said, flipping the boy a coin. If you can have them saddled and ready for me, with their hooves picked and clean, I'll give you another."

"Yes, sir!" said the boy, before hurrying out of the inn.

They spent the rest of the evening talking. Several of the local villagers joined their table, including the innkeeper, after having the outlaw dragged out of the inn. Quinn learned that the coastal villages were not doing well, since most of the shipping vessels had not been seen for weeks. He told them about the witch in Lodenhime and his journey to stop his son from being lured back there with Mansel.

They enjoyed a meal of fish stew. There was more bread and much more ale. On the walk back to Red's cottage the two men leaned on each other. The next morning Red unwrapped Quinn's leg and washed off the poultice. Then he sniffed the wound again.

"No sign of putrefaction," he announced happily.

Then he applied another poultice and rewrapped the wound.

"I'm sure it's painful, but there's no danger of infection, I wouldn't think," Red explained. "Leave the bandage on for five or six more days and don't get it wet. Then wash off the remains of the poultice and have someone remove the stitches. If you don't have any foot races, you should be fine."

"Thank you Red, I greatly appreciate your help," Quinn told him.

"It was my pleasure," said the healer.

They went back to the inn, where the innkeeper insisted they have some breakfast. After they ate Quinn found both horses saddled and waiting. He gave the innkeeper's son another coin and bade the others good-bye. Then he climbed into the saddle, tied the reins of the other horse to the saddle horn, and set off.

The days went by swiftly, and soon Quinn had to make a decision to either continue north on the coastal road to Black Bay, or turn east and ride for Ebbson Keep. He had no idea where Zollin was, and while he knew he needed to get on Mansel's trail as quickly as possible, he also knew the young warrior would be far ahead of him. If he turned east, he could miss Zollin and Mansel entirely. It was a difficult choice, but he felt that he couldn't take any chances. He stayed on the coastal road and traveled north as swiftly as he could.

Chapter 19

The Weaver's Road led Mansel to Fort Jellar. He saw the smoke from the fires long before he was in sight of the city itself. He wasn't sure what was happening but decided to proceed with caution. He didn't want to be held up by city officials who may have heard about his previous run-in with the village constable.

His main concern was getting across the border quickly. He left the road and circled the army encampment. The Weaver's Road ran straight across the border, and Mansel angled back toward it. He recognized Ebbson Keep from the descriptions he'd heard as a child: the towering stone structure was one of the oldest in the Kingdom of Yelsia, and traveling singers would often describe the great battles that had taken place there. Mansel decided to see if he could learn anything about Zollin at the Keep.

There was a long line of scouts spread out along the border, and Mansel decided his best bet for crossing would be to wait for nightfall. It was late in the day at any rate, and so he took the opportunity to rest. When night fell, he resumed his journey, leading his horse as silently as possible, when a cloud passed in front of the moon. He couldn't see the scouts, but there were lights burning at Ebbson Keep, so even in the dark it was easy to keep his bearings, and once he felt he had safely reached Yelsian soil, he remounted and rode to the Keep.

There were guards stationed at the main gate who told him that no one was allowed in the fortress until morning. He saw to his horse and made camp for the night with a few other travelers who had arrived too late to be allowed into the Keep. The next morning, Mansel was questioned thoroughly before being admitted into the fortress. He explained that he was looking for Zollin, the wizard, at which point he was escorted into the Keep's main building and told to wait. He was just beginning to grow restless when a guard led Kelvich into the room.

"Mansel!" Kelvich said in surprise. "This is completely unexpected. How are you? Where is Quinn?"

"One question at a time," Mansel said in a testy voice. "I need to find Zollin. Do you know where he is?"

"No, but you got here just in time. I was getting ready to go in search of him myself."

"Did he slay the dragon?"

"There's been no word from Zollin," Kelvich explained. "We set an ambush for the dragon in the ruins at Ornak. I was sent here with a treasure trove of ancient scrolls that we discovered in the ruins. We did hear that Zollin and the soldiers drove the dragon off and that Zollin and Brianna went in pursuit of the beast on their own. They were headed into the Northern Highlands. The dragon hasn't been seen since, but neither has Zollin or Brianna."

"Then that's where I will go," Mansel said.

"We can ride together," Kelvich said in a merry tone. "This is fortunate indeed."

"Are you ready? I don't want to waste my time here."

"Oh, I'll only be a short while. Tell me, where is Quinn? Did you succeed in escorting Prince Wilam back to Orrock?"

"We'll have time to talk about that later," Mansel said.

He was trying to keep his frustration from showing, but his self control was waning. He felt guilty at having thrown Quinn overboard. He knew that if he revealed that Quinn was dead, Zollin would insist on knowing what happened. He needed a credible story, both about Quinn and Prince Wilam. Simply revealing that the Prince had stayed with Gwendolyn at the Castle on the Sea would surely make his task even more difficult. And just thinking of the Prince being near Gwendolyn made Mansel angry. His only happiness was daydreaming about how his Queen would reward him when he returned with Zollin. But when he tried to picture Gwendolyn his mind grew conflicted and confused. Whenever he tried to think of what Gwendolyn looked like, he saw a lonely-looking woman and smelled the briny scent of the sea. He had to forcefully push all those thoughts away, and each time he did, he felt his rage increasing.

"Oh," Kelvich said. "All right, I'll gather my things and we'll be off."

"Make haste," Mansel said. "I'll see that we have plenty of supplies."

Mansel turned on his heel and walked briskly toward the door where a guard stood sentry. Kelvich nodded to the guard, who opened the door for Mansel. Then the sorcerer hurried up to his quarters. The Duke had been impatient for Kelvich to leave, but Kelvich had wanted to bring the translations the scholars had been working on. If for some reason the dragon did still live, there might be information in those texts that would help them defeat the beast.

He had packed his belongings so that he would be ready to go. He just needed to stop at the scriptorium and get what he could from the scholars working there. He found Jax just outside the scriptorium.

"There you are," Jax said in an excited voice. "The Duke wishes to see you. Come on."

He grabbed the elderly sorcerer's hand and began leading him away.

"Wait, wait, Jax. I need to speak to the scholars first."

"But it's the Duke!" Jax said in surprise.

"This will only take a moment."

Kelvich hurried into the room and told the scholars that he needed to take the translations they were working on. The scholars argued that they weren't finished, but Kelvich insisted, telling them he would return shortly to collect whatever they had ready. Then he let Jax lead him back up to the Duke's audience room. As always, there were several people in the room, some talking to the Duke, others talking quietly to one another.

The Duke looked up as they came in.

"Thank you, Jax, you can wait outside," the Duke said.

Kelvich noticed the crestfallen look that crossed Jax's face, but to the boy's credit he didn't argue. He went quickly from the room, and the Duke waved Kelvich over.

"I assume you know the man who came looking for Zollin?"

"Yes," Kelvich said. "His name is Mansel. He was sent south with Zollin's father Quinn to escort Prince Wilam to Orrock."

"Did he succeed?"

"No, I don't think so. He's alone and he's in a hurry to continue his search for Zollin. I can only assume that he failed and that something happened to Quinn."

"You think the wizard's father is dead?"

"Most likely," Kelvich said sadly.

"Are you leaving to begin your search?"

"Yes."

"Good," the Duke said. "Please convey my sympathies but also share the urgency of our situation. If the army at Fort Jellar attacks, I'm not sure how long we can hold them back."

"I understand," Kelvich said. "I'll do my best."

"Jax is staying with us," the Duke said.

"You've spoken with him about it then," Kelvich said in surprise.

"No, and neither shall you. You know how I feel about the boy. I think it is better for us all if he stays."

"That should be his decision."

"In more idyllic times I would agree. But it appears that we are on the brink of war, and I need every able-bodied man I can get."

"Or perhaps you are using him to lure Zollin here," Kelvich said, and the room fell silent. The other men in the room were all military officers, and none of them had ever heard anyone confront the Duke before.

"Don't be absurd," the Duke said. "I've come to love the boy as if he were my own. I wish him here, where I can keep him safe."

"You just said if the army at Fort Jellar attacks you could be overrun. Wouldn't Jax be safer leaving the fort with me?"

"Somehow I doubt that," the Duke said in a cynical voice.

Kelvich held his temper in check. He respected the Duke and appreciated all that had been done for him, but he despised the fact that he was seen as nothing more than an old man. He had powers that would shock the Duke and, under the right circumstances, destroy his precious Keep without lifting a finger, but he knew his anger wouldn't serve him well now. He needed to get his things and catch up with Mansel.

"Very well," Kelvich said. "I'll leave Jax with you. Is there anything else you need?"

"I don't suppose your friend has any useful intelligence about what is going on?"

"I doubt it," Kelvich said. "My guess is Quinn was killed and Mansel is returning to give his friend the news."

"Fine, go quickly. If you need anything tell my steward," the Duke said, waving his hand in a dismissive gesture.

Kelvich hurried out of the room and found Jax standing not far away.

"I have to leave the Keep for a while," Kelvich told the boy.

"You do? Where are we going?" Jax asked.

"We aren't going," Kelvich said. "That is what the Duke wanted to talk to me about. He said he needs you. I'm just a bothersome old man, but the Duke has come to depend on you and wants you to stay."

"He said that?" Jax said proudly. "He said he needs me?"

"Yes, now I want you to listen to me. Do everything you can to help him. He's a good man, but he's under a lot of pressure. Listen to him, keep your ears open, and pay attention to what is going on. Do you understand what I'm telling you?"

"Yes," said Jax seriously.

"You're a good boy and you have a bright future, but don't try to be a hero. I want you to start looking for a way out of the Keep in case there is fighting. Always have a plan for an emergency."

"Yes, Master Kelvich," he said.

"I will come back for you," Kelvich said. "I'll bring Zollin back here and we'll make things safe again. Until then, you do all you can to help, but stay safe."

"I will. You can count on me."

"I know I can," Kelvich said. He hugged Jax and then looked him in the eye. "I'm very proud of you."

Jax seemed to light up from the inside at hearing those words. Then he was off, hurrying back into the Duke's audience chamber, and Kelvich's eyes blurred with tears. He hadn't realized how fond he'd become of the young orphan.

After gathering his belongings and the copies of the translations the scholars had finished, which had been collected into a stiff, leather portfolio, Kelvich went quickly to the stables. He found the stable master waiting with a fine-looking horse already saddled.

"She's a reliable mount," the man told him. "Her shoes are in good condition, and I've seen to everything."

"Thank you," Kelvich said.

"Take care of her," the man said.

"I will."

Kelvich stuffed his belongings into the empty saddle bags and climbed up onto the horse. He hoped that Mansel had been sincere when he offered to get their supplies, otherwise Kelvich would have to stop and buy them for himself before leaving the Keep. He didn't even have a canteen or water skin.

He rode through the crowded courtyard and found Mansel waiting for him just outside the gate.

"It's about time," Mansel said. "I have the supplies. Let's get moving."

"You have enough for both of us?" Kelvich asked. "I don't have food or water."

"Yes, I have enough. Let's go."

They rode through the day, Kelvich trying to keep up with Mansel, who was in no mood to talk and who pushed his mount as hard as he could. They stopped just before dark and made camp. It was quiet, and the stars were bright and the moon was almost full. Kelvich was sore from riding hard all day. Once he had seen to his horse, giving her a good rubdown and making sure she was hobbled where there was plenty of grass for her to eat, he unrolled his blanket and lay down.

"Should I start a fire?" he asked.

"No," Mansel said. "We don't need one."

He handed Kelvich a few strips of dried meat. Kelvich looked at the rations, his stomach growling with hunger, and sighed.

"I miss the meals at Ebbson Keep already," Kelvich said.

"Sorry this isn't some fancy dinner, but it's enough to keep you going."

"Do you want to tell me what happened now?" Kelvich said.

"What do you mean?"

"I mean, what happened to Quinn?"

"He was captured."

"What happened?" Kelvich asked sadly.

"He was captured," Mansel repeated.

"By whom? The Mezzlyn? I didn't think the assassins took hostages. Where is he?"

Kelvich waited, but Mansel didn't volunteer any other information.

"Is that all you're going to say?"

"It's all that's important."

"Are you mad? Quinn was my friend. I have a right to know what happened."

"No, you don't," said Mansel. "You have a right to be quiet and keep up, or you'll get left behind. I don't answer to you or anyone else. You can help me find Zollin or do whatever you want to do, but don't bother me with questions."

Mansel walked away, into the darkness. He was so angry he knew that if the old man pushed him he would snap, just like he had done in the village and with the constable. He didn't want to hurt people, but he couldn't stand being questioned all the time. He just wanted to find Zollin and get back to Gwendolyn.

Kelvich sat in the darkness, stunned by what he'd just heard. Mansel not only seemed evasive, but dangerous. The elder sorcerer knew better than to push his luck with the young warrior. Mansel reminded Kelvich of a bear that had been cornered by hunters. With nowhere else to turn, the beast was twice as dangerous. Making up his mind to hold his tongue until they found Zollin, he rolled himself up in his cloak and went to sleep.

* * *

For two weeks the armada of ships from Osla and Falxis beat their way up the coast. Offendorl was impatient, and although he had hoped to land at Tragoon Bay and sail up the Tillamook River rather than marching with the armies, he had finally relented and made landfall just up the coast from Winsome on the southwestern edge of Yelsia near Angel's Shelter. The soldiers were rowed to shore and almost immediately met by scouts from the Yelsian army, who watched their every move but did not engage.

Offendorl wasted little time once the soldiers had landed. He met with King Belphan of Osla and King Zorlan of Falxis to plan their attack. They had four legions of foot soldiers and half a legion of cavalry. King Zorlan was a quiet man, content to stay out of the planning. The truth was, he was only participating to save face with the other kings, and he was afraid of Offendorl. Belphan postured and acted the part of the royal commander, but as always he deferred to the Master of the Torr. They sent scouts ahead and began slowly making their way north. Skirmishes between the scouts of both armies were common, but no major action had taken place. They were just south of Valeron when a small company of knights flying a white flag from their lances approached the army.

"Go and see what they wish to do," Offendorl told Belphan. "Go with him, Zorlan, and each of you take one knight with you as an escort. Return to me with their demands and I shall instruct you on how to proceed."

Both kings did as they were told. Offendorl was traveling in a very large wagon with a padded bed and his most valuable books. When the army camped, his mute eunuchs erected a tent next to the wagon and set up camp chairs with thick cushions for the ancient wizard. There was also a trap door in the ceiling of the wagon so Offendorl could sit on top of the large vehicle and have an unobstructed view of the army encampment and beyond. He used a small awning to keep the sun off his almost transparent skin, but that wasn't necessary on this day, as clouds rolled in like a thick blanket being pulled over a bed.

Offendorl climbed into his wagon slowly, then opened the trap door and levitated himself up to the roof. He then used his magic to levitate a small canvas camp chair and a goblet of wine so that he could sit comfortably and wait. He watched as the riders met with the kings from Osla and Falxis. He was glad he didn't have to listen to their pronouncements and over-long introductions. He could guess what was being discussed. King Felix of Yelsia had sent men to find out what this army's intention was, as if that weren't obvious. They would then insist that the army was trespassing on sovereign soil, and so on and so forth, all in a vain effort to scare the kings into retreating.

It was tiresome, but it was necessary. It would allow Offendorl to make his demand of King Felix. He wanted Zollin. Not even the entire Yelsian army could hide the boy. Offendorl would destroy them all if that is what it took to bring Zollin under his control. Then he would let Belphan and Zorlan do what they wanted with Yelsia; it made no difference to Offendorl. Soon the army from the east would force Felix to capitulate, and he would have the insolent young wizard under his control. That was all that mattered.

He watched as the kings and their retinue returned to the camp. The knights with their white flags still flying in the quickening breeze remained on the field. Offendorl waited until the kings were close to his tent before coming back down. He sensed rain coming: he could feel the humidity rising and smell the rain in the distance. Rain would delay their attack. The armies could not march far through wet, muddy fields. Offendorl would stay dry in his wagon, but the others would not be so fortunate. He levitated back down and went into the tent to see what the kings had to report.

"Arrogant bastard," Belphan said loudly. "They threatened us!"

"Tell me," Offendorl said, waving to a servant to bring the kings goblets of wine.

"They said we should turn back and leave Yelsia or they would attack us. They await our response."

"Let them wait," said Offendorl. "Tell your men to make their camp ready for rain. It will be on us soon. Send no word back to Felix. If his messengers are man enough to wait in the rain, I'll send them on their way myself when we are ready to march again."

The kings skulked away like scolded dogs. Offendorl ordered men to march into the surrounding countryside to get food. Soon the rain began, first in fat drops that fell and splashed on the dusty ground, and then in unrelenting sheets. The ground around the camp was quickly transformed into a muddy bog. The army was allowed to rest, with only the scouts and cooks being kept busy in the rain.

Offendorl watched the knights. They stayed in the field, their banners soaked and drooping, their horses pawing at the muddy ground while the knights shivered in their heavy armor. He smiled. Things were progressing nicely, he thought to himself. Then he took a long drink of wine and stretched out on his thickly padded bed.

Chapter 20

Zollin rode through the mountains and finally came to the river in the Great Valley. Unlike the southern range, the northern mountains came down close to the river. He was well south of Brighton's Gate and had to make a decision about which way to go. He could find a vessel to take him west on the river where he could sail south. The only problem with that plan of action was that it did not allow him to track the movement of the dragon. Zollin knew it was moving south, although it had flown out the range of his magic, so he couldn't be sure where the beast was. He had to force himself not to think about what it might have done to Brianna. Fire couldn't hurt her anymore, and while she couldn't fly, falling from a great hight didn't seem to be a major threat either. Still, that didn't mean the dragon couldn't eat her whole. He could still remember the beast's hot breath when it had snatched him up in its jaws from the roof of the temple in the Ruins of Ornak. He could see the teeth with their serrated edges that would have cut him to ribbons had it not been for the magical shield he had thrown up around himself. It took all his strength not to give in to the despair that was eroding his heart.

He levitated himself over the river and then brought Lilly across the same way. It took several minutes after that to calm the horse down, but Zollin managed it. Then he remounted the aging mare, turned her west and rode for Brighton's Gate.

It was late at night when he came to the city that had sheltered him through the winter. It had been almost a month since he had seen it last, and the villagers had accomplished much. Zollin was surprised that the soldiers who had been guarding the Great Valley were gone, but there was no one awake to give him any news. He was tired, and although he would have preferred to push on through the night, he needed to find out what the villagers knew about the dragon. He found a lean-to shed with fresh hay and saw that Lilly was unsaddled and rubbed down before he wrapped his cloak around him and made a bed for himself in the hay.

He woke up the next morning at dawn, his whole body hurting and wanting nothing as much as more sleep, but he forced himself to rise. He saddled Lilly and led her through the main street. There were people living once more in the homes that had been destroyed by the dragon's attack in the spring. Most of the buildings had been rebuilt, and to his surprise Zollin discovered that work was now being done to rebuild the Valley Inn. The Gateway's owner must have given up and moved on, since most what was left of that establishment was now being scavenged to help rebuild the other town structures.

"Well, well," came a familiar voice. "Look what the cat's dragged in."

It was Buck, the innkeeper of the Valley Inn. He had come from behind the inn carrying a bucket of fresh milk. He smiled and waved to Zollin.

"Come inside and have some breakfast," said the rotund innkeeper. "Where's your lady friend? You're both welcome in the Valley Inn. Although we may not be up to your standards quite yet."

"You're too generous," Zollin said. "But I really can't stay. I just need some information."

"Well, an inn's the best place in town to find out what there is to know. If it won't hurt, you can take a load off and enjoy a bite while you learn what you need to know. The army left us a few animals. We've got fresh milk and Ollie's making a nice porridge. You look like you could use something warm in that stomach of yours."

Zollin had to admit he was hungry. He still had a meager supply of goat's meat, but it felt like chewing leather and tasted even worse. He tied Lilly's reins to a post outside the inn and followed Buck inside.

"Heavens!" said Ollie when she saw Zollin. "You're even thinner than the last time I saw you. Where's Brianna? I suspect she could use a bath and bite to eat, too."

"She's not here," Zollin said.

"Oh, no," Ollie said. "She didn't get hurt in the mountains did she?"

"No, not exactly. It's a long story, really, but the gist of it is that the dragon has her now."

"The dragon has her?" Buck said in surprise, as he set a glass of fresh milk down in front of Zollin.

He took a drink and nodded.

"Have you heard or seen the dragon?"

"No, we haven't seen it, thank heaven," said Ollie.

"But we did hear that some others did," Buck added, "further down the valley. They say it just few over, headed south.

"That's what I thought. I'm going after it; that's why I'm in a hurry. Thank you both for your kindness," he said, standing up.

"No," Ollie said. "You'll sit down and eat. It won't take but just a few minutes, and it'll do you a world of good. It's ready, just hang on there."

"You heard her," Buck said. "No use arguing. I've learned that one thing at least in the last twenty years. What can I do to help you?"

"I could use some supplies, food mainly. And I need a better saddle for Lilly."

"We haven't got much, but I can get you some fresh bread, if that'll help."

"That would be great," Zollin said.

Ollie quickly brought him a bowl of porridge, with a few bits of meat stirred into it, along with a hunk of warm bread.

"I'm sorry, I'm low on butter at the moment," Ollie said.

"This is more than fine," Zollin said, his mouth full of food. "It's delicious, thank you."

"You're welcome. Things took a turn for the better after you healed folks last time you were here. People began believing that some good was coming their way again. The army pulled out a week or so ago and we've been able to trade for the supplies we needed. There's men driving up some sheep and pigs that will get us through the winter. We'll be okay as long as the Skellmarians don't come back."

"I doubt they will," Zollin said. "We ran into them on our way north. It turned out for the best. I think we convinced them not to raid anymore, at least for a while."

"I don't see how anyone can reason with those savages, but if you're right we owe you another debt of gratitude."

"You don't owe me anything," Zollin said.

"Well, that may be so," Buck said, coming back in from outside as Zollin finished the last of his breakfast, "but I tied a small keg of ale to your horse anyway. Now, before you thank me, just keep in mind it's the first batch I've brewed since we started rebuilding. It might be a bit sharp, but there's no time to age it, and it'll be better than water."

"Thank you," Zollin said as he stood up.

"You go find that girl of yours," Ollie said.

"And tell your father to come see us, when you see him, that is," Buck added.

"I will. Thank you both."

Zollin hurried outside and found that Buck had saddled Lilly and tied a small keg of ale behind the saddle and a bag of small loaves of bread to the saddle horn. He swung up onto Lilly's back and set off through the village.

People were peeking out at him from behind closed shutters, but none tried to stop him. Zollin was flooded with memories as he rode out of the village. It seemed like ages ago when he and Brianna had taken this same path, only then it had been through the snow. They had fought that day and Zollin regretted it. That had been before he had been willing to admit how Brianna made him feel, before they had fallen in love. He wished he had followed his heart sooner so that they could have had more time together, but he couldn't change the past.

He saw that there were still some tents around Kelvich's old cottage. Many of the trees that had once surrounded the small home had been cut down and milled using the big saw that Quinn had set up behind the cottage. Zollin had learned to control his magic in that cottage, and he felt his heart swell as he thought of Kelvich. He missed his old mentor and wished the old sorcerer was there to tell him everything was going to be okay. This was really the first time Zollin had been on his own in his whole life, and while he knew he could manage, he discovered that he didn't care for solitude. He missed Brianna most of all, but also Kelvich and Quinn, even Mansel. He wondered how Quinn and Mansel were doing returning Prince Wilam to Yelsia. He wished for a minute that he had gone with them. He would like to see the southern kingdoms, but that would have to wait. Summer was almost over and soon it would be too cold to travel.

As he rode into the mountains on Telford Pass the sky was covered with clouds. He knew it would rain before too long, not by any supernatural sense, but because that was the way his luck had been running lately. He repacked his extra clothes so that they wouldn't get wet and then kept riding.

It was late evening when the rain started. The rain was cold, and even though Zollin was exhausted, he knew he wouldn't be able to sleep. He dismounted and led Lilly through the pass in almost total darkness. The rain fell hard and soaked his clothes in a matter of minutes. Zollin shivered as he walked, occasionally kindling a flame with his magic. The fire would sputter and hiss in the rain, and then Zollin would let it go out. His body ached with cold and fatigue. Lilly walked with her nose almost touching the ground. The sun was just beginning to rise when the rain stopped falling, but it still ran down the sides of the mountain and turned sections of the trail into streams of water. They continued walking, hoping that the sun would appear to dry them and give a little warmth to their frigid bodies, but the sky was full of clouds that threatened to dump even more rain on them. By noon, Zollin couldn't go any further. He ate a little bread, but it, too, was wet and tasted gummy in his mouth. He tapped the small keg that Buck had given him and sampled the ale. It was a little sour, but it warmed him up a bit, and soon he was asleep on the wet ground.

Lilly's frantic neighing woke Zollin up. There wasn't much light left, but he could see the big mountain lion that was slinking toward them. Zollin had tied Lilly's reins to his own ankle so that she wouldn't wander off while he slept. If she had, the lion might have killed and eaten Zollin before he woke up and realized the danger.

He got to his feet quickly and let his magic flow out. He could sense the mountain lion he had seen in the twilight gloom, but that beast was only a distraction from the real danger: there was another cat much closer, its body tense as it prepared to leap down on them from a short cliff. Zollin brought up his defenses just as the lion jumped. The weight of the lion was tremendous, but Zollin's magic was churned into a frenzy by his fear. He flung the lion away as the other cat sprang toward them.

"Blast!" Zollin shouted, sending a wave of crackling, blue energy directly toward the lion. It hit the cat in the face and the animal's body locked up, its muscles spasming from the shock. Then it collapsed dead on the trail.

Zollin turned his attention back to the other lion that was now charging back toward him. He sent out another wave of energy, but directed this one into the ground just in front of the lion, and it spun around and bounded away in fear. Then Zollin sagged against Lilly. The horse was still frightened, her large eyes looking around so wildly that the whites showed.

"There, there, girl. It's okay," he told her. "We're all right. Those lions won't bother us anymore."

Zollin walked over to the dead mountain lion and looked at it. There were dark burns across its face, the huge fangs blackened and sooty. He pulled out his dagger and cut a large hunk out of the lion's thick haunch.

"I wonder what roasted lion tastes like," Zollin said to Lilly.

He led the skittish horse a couple miles down the trail and then stripped off his wet clothes. He laid them on the rocks and pulled on his dry clothes. They felt good on his cold, clammy skin. Then he picked up the raw lion meat and sent his magic into it, cooking the meat from the inside out. It took only moments, and then he was able to eat the lion meat. It was stringy and tough, a little like the elk meat he and Brianna had eaten in the northern range of mountains, only gamier. Still, it was hot and filling. Zollin felt bad because he had nothing to feed Lilly. There was almost no vegetation in the mountains, and the villagers at Brighton's Gate couldn't spare any oats for Lilly. He drank some more ale and dried a spot on the ground, then went back to sleep, keeping Lilly tied to his boot.

He woke up just before dawn and continued his journey. It took them two more days of hard travel to get through Telford Pass. Zollin was temped to stop and see Jute and the other dwarves of the Yel clan, but he had no reason to. He needed to find out where the dragon had gone after leaving the southern range of mountains. They stayed on the road that led them through Peddingar Forrest. Once again, Zollin saw lights and strange noises as night fell, but then the rain started again, and it was all Zollin could do to keep putting one foot in front of the other. Around midnight he crawled under the thick limbs of a massive fir tree. It wasn't completely dry under the tree, but it wasn't soaking wet either. And the soft fir needles were a nice change from the rocky ground in Telford Pass.

Once again Zollin woke up shortly after sunrise. He was nearly out of rations. He finished the keg of ale and left the small barrel behind as he set out for the day. He was almost out of the forest when he saw a familiar sight. He almost didn't believe his eyes. He had been alone for several days now, and he thought at first he was just seeing what he wanted to see, but soon he heard a voice hailing him and arms waving for him. Lilly seemed excited, too, and she sped her trot into a fast canter.

"I don't believe it," Zollin said, as tears stung his eyes.

"We found you!" Kelvich said.

"It's good to see you," Zollin replied.

"Where's Brianna?" Mansel asked.

"That's a long story," Zollin answered. "Where's my dad?"

Kelvich looked down, waiting for an answer of some type, but nothing came.

"I'll tell you about it on the way. We need to go to Lodenhime," Mansel said.

"I can't, at least not yet. The dragon has Brianna."

Kelvich's mouth fell open, but Mansel didn't seem to hear.

"Well see about that when we get back. I really need you to come with me. Your dad's in trouble."

"What?" Kelvich and Zollin said at the same time.

"He's a prisoner in Lodenhime. You've got to come and see if the lady of the Castle on the Sea will release him to you."

Zollin looked at Kelvich.

"Did you know about this?" he asked his old mentor.

"No, he wouldn't tell me anything."

"You have to come," Mansel said. "We need to get going. I've been gone too long as it is."

"I can't," Zollin said. "I have to track down the dragon."

The three men sat on their horses staring at each other, no one speaking. Finally, Zollin broke the silence.

"I love my father," he said. "But I love Brianna, too. I've asked her to marry me. I have to find her first."

Mansel looked frustrated, but Kelvich kept silent.

"I could use your help," Zollin said to both men.

"After you find Brianna, will you come south with me?" Mansel asked.

"Of course," Zollin said.

"All right, let's get going."

They turned their horses and set off, heading south. Kelvich was full of questions, but he kept silent. There was something wrong with Mansel, but he wasn't sure what it was. The young warrior had been short with him on the trip to find Zollin, but Kelvich had chalked it up to remorse over what must have happened to Quinn. Now, finding out that Zollin's father was being held in Lodenhime, by someone Mansel called the lady of the Castle on the Sea, he felt that there was more to the story than Mansel was telling them. But Kelvich also remembered the way Mansel had reacted when the sorcerer had pushed him for more information. He knew that Mansel was dangerous—not just a skilled warrior, but a dangerous man for reasons he couldn't quiet explain yet. He decided to wait and speak to Zollin when he could tell the young wizard how he really felt.

Chapter 21

Mansel knew that he was taking a risk, but it was a calculated risk. There was virtually no way for Zollin to discover what Mansel had done to Quinn before reaching the Castle on the Sea. Once there, Gwendolyn would have her prize, and nothing else mattered. The only thing Mansel had to worry about was the ship captain. If the ship captain spoke up too soon, everything would be ruined. He would have to ensure that the roguish sailor couldn't spoil his plans.

"Tell me what happened to Quinn," Zollin said as they rode along.

They were nearly out of the forest and could cut cross-country in hopes of finding a village or homestead that was still occupied. He needed to discover where the dragon had gone and find Brianna. It was hard not to feel as if he were being drawn and quartered. Brianna's need took precedence, but he could not deny that he was worried about his father as well.

"We went south and got the Prince," Mansel said, deciding to leave out his problems with Quinn and how he'd been left behind at Cape Sumbar. "But we were warned about trying to sneak him out of the country by sea, so we traveled overland into Felxis and made for the nearest harbor, but there were soldiers there as well."

"Wait," Kelvich said. "Why did you need to be concerned about soldiers? I thought you were sent to save him from the Mezzlyn assassins."

"We were, but apparently the Council of Kings sent troops to stop him from returning to Yelsia."

"Why would they do that?" Kelvich asked.

"How the hell do I know?" Mansel said angrily. "I'm not privy to the whims of kings."

"Calm down," Zollin said. "We're all a bit frazzled. There's a lot going on, and biting each other's heads off won't help."

"I only ask because there are troops massing at Fort Jellar," Kelvich said. "The Duke there is worried about war. He sent me to find you in hopes that you would come and bolster his position."

"War? Why would there be war?" Zollin asked.

But even as he asked the question he remembered what King Felix had said to him before Zollin had left on his quest. Felix had hinted that a time might come when Zollin's help would be needed against the other kingdoms. At the time, the King's hints had made Zollin nervous, but now he could see that he had some major decisions to make.

"It's against the treaty for wizards to side with one kingdom over another," Zollin said.

"That's true," Kelvich agreed, "but it seems as if perhaps the treaty has already been cast aside. What use would the Council of Kings have had for detaining a crown prince serving as an ambassador? And if troops were mobilized to stop Mansel and your father from bringing Prince Wilam home, it seems probable that plans for war were already under way."

"So what do you think it all means?" Zollin said.

"It means that the world is changing," Kelvich said. "But we knew that already, didn't we? You said yourself that you've seen things you would never have believed were real."

"Like those creatures in the forest," Mansel said nervously, looking around to see if they were being followed.

"Forest dryads," Kelvich said. "Nasty creatures, but they are the guardians of the forests. They wouldn't have bothered you alone, Mansel."

"They tried to kill us," he insisted.

"They wanted Zollin," Kelvich said. "In times gone by, some wizards devoted their entire lives to the study of forest lore. They made their homes with dryads, even fought wars with them. But that was long, long ago, in wilder times."

"Is that where we are headed?" Zollin asked his mentor. "I mean, I keep running into creatures, some of which are absolutely deadly. It's as if they're attracted to me."

"Not to you, but to your magic," Kelvich said. "For hundreds of years the Torr have controlled all magic in the Five Kingdoms. And they have consolidated their power and knowledge in the tower of the Torr. I'm sure you saw the tower in the Grand City of Osla," Kelvich said to Mansel.

For a moment the warrior felt a wave of panic. If Kelvich questioned him about the Grand City he would not be able to answer the sorcerer's questions. He realized he should have dealt with the nosy old man before finding Zollin.

"Yes," Mansel said.

"It's quite a sight, isn't it?"

"The tower or the Grand City?" Mansel asked.

"Both," Kelvich said merrily, but his eyes were studying Mansel intently.

"Yes, they are."

"The tower is a marvel, especially the three-pronged, upper tier. It looks like a giant trident, as if some ancient sea god were thrusting his weapon up toward the sky. Tell us what you thought of it, Mansel."

Zollin recognized the question in Kelvich's voice. The old man had used the same sort of technique as they had worked on recognizing various plants with magical qualities. He wondered what his old mentor was up to.

"We have things to do," Mansel said. "We should ride more and talk less."

He spurred his horse forward. Zollin looked over at Kelvich, who was watching Mansel with a critical eye.

"We need to talk," Zollin said.

"Yes, but not now," Kelvich said.

He gave Zollin a reassuring smile and they both nudged their horses to catch up with Mansel. It took a few more hours to finally exit the forest. Zollin immediately turned his horse west.

"What is your plan?" Kelvich asked him.

"I need to find out where the dragon was last seen," he explained. "It was headed south; surely someone must have seen it."

"But the farms and villages have all been abandoned this far north," Kelvich reasoned. "We should ride to the Ruins of Ornak. The soldiers there will know as much as anyone. I'm sure Commander Hausey has scouts out, combing the countryside for even the slightest rumor of the dragon."

"All right, but we'll need to ride hard," Zollin said. "Are you up for the challenge?"

"I think I'll be okay," Kelvich said, a little hurt that Zollin would think he might be a liability.

"I'm not worried about your heart," Zollin said. "I know you would never give up. I just have to ride as hard as possible. I don't want to force you to do something you don't want to do."

"Just try and stop me," Kelvich said.

They ate in the saddle and walked their horses once night fell. They slept without a fire. The weather outside of the mountains was warmer than Zollin had been used to, but as summer waned the nights turned cooler. They hobbled their horses and slept a few hours, resuming their journey with the dawn. Zollin wanted to find out why Kelvich seemed so suspicious of Mansel, but there was never a good time to talk. Mansel did seem irritable. He was even less talkative than usual, but Zollin thought he was probably worried about Quinn. On the second day he asked the young warrior to finish telling them what happened.

"So, there were soldiers in Felxis, too," Zollin prompted. "I suppose my father suggested you head north."

"Yes, we rode for Lodenhime," Mansel said gruffly. "We ran into a pair of assassins along the way, and if not for the Prince's mercy, we'd have dealt with them."

"What do you mean?" Kelvich asked.

"They came at us as a pair. We killed one, but the idiot Prince released the second assassin. I told him the Mezzlyn don't accept failure. The one we caught had a poison tooth, just like the one in Brighton's Gate. But still, the Prince insisted and Quinn wouldn't countermand him. So we let the devil go, and, sure enough, when we reached Lodenhime, the assassin tried to kill the Prince again. Your father saved his life and received a nasty scratch from the killer's knife to boot. If it had been poisoned like those darts in Brighton's Gate, he'd have been killed."

"So how was he captured in Lodenhime? Was it the Mezzlyn?"

"No, there is a woman in the Castle on the Sea."

"The what?" Zollin asked.

"It's a fortress. Not really a castle, but it was built like a castle, and it sits on a small peninsula that juts out into the Great Sea of Kings. The people in Lodenhime call it the Castle on the Sea. She's building an army. I left your father and Prince Wilam while we were still in the city. After killing the second Mezzlyn assassin we assumed we were safe. I was sent for supplies while Quinn and the Prince saw about booking us passage on a ship heading north," Mansel lied.

The truth was fuzzy, he thought. He had left Quinn and Prince Wilam in Lodenhime, he remembered that, but he couldn't remember why.

"They went to the Castle but never came back. I went to find them but realized I couldn't rescue them by myself, so I came to find you," Mansel explained.

It seemed reasonable enough to Zollin, but he was completely absorbed in his grief over losing Brianna to the dragon and wasn't thinking critically. He still had hopes that Brianna was alive, and nothing seemed as important as finding her and rescuing her from the dragon.

They rode on in silence after that, each man occupied with his own thoughts. They passed several abandoned villages, but saw no people. It took them three days of hard riding to reach the Ruins at Ornak. They could see from a distance that the soldiers had rebuilt the ruins once again. There was an air of mystery to the ancient settlement, made even more haunting by the fact that it was, once again, entirely abandoned.

"Where is everyone?" Zollin asked out loud.

"I don't know," Kelvich said. "I can't believe Commander Hausey would have abandoned this post with leaving at least a small contingent of men."

Zollin rode into the village and saw the statue of gold he had built. It stood forlorn in the middle of the ancient ruins, the gold glinting in the late afternoon sunshine.

"The relic hasn't been touched. There haven't even been looters here stealing the gold," Zollin said.

"It's as if we're the only people left in Yelsia," Mansel said.

"That's ridiculous," Kelvich said.

"Well, we won't find any answers by wasting time here," Zollin said, spurring his horse forward.

"Where are we going?" Kelvich cried out as his horse jumped forward with the others, reluctant to get left behind.

"We'll ride to nearest village," Zollin called back over his shoulder. "Surely someone will know what happened."

They rode late into the night. The next day they were met shortly after dawn by a group of riders. Commander Hausey was with them. He called out when they were close enough to identify one another.

"Hello there!" he shouted. "Zollin! Kelvich!"

"Commander Hausey," Zollin said, reining in his horse as the two groups approached each other.

"I have orders from the King," Hausey said. "He requests that you join him in Orrock."

"Why?" Kelvich said, not waiting for Zollin to reply. "What made you withdraw your troops from the Ruins at Ornak?"

"We have been invaded," said Hausey. "Ships landed near Winsome, and soldiers are marching north. The King has recalled the army from Felson and the legion he sent to the Great Valley. Men have been sent to strengthen the forts at Ebbson Keep and Mountain Wind, but every able-bodied man is needed in Orrock."

"I'm searching for the dragon," Zollin said. "Has there been news of it coming back out of the mountains?"

"That task must wait," Hausey said.

"It can't!" Zollin said angrily. "The beast has Brianna. I must find it."

Kelvich put his hand on Zollin's arm.

"The King insists that you come," Hausey said. "I regret the news about Brianna. She was a special girl."

"She isn't dead," Zollin said.

"Why does the King want Zollin?" Kelvich said.

Hausey looked at Kelvich for a long moment before answering. They both knew that enlisting a wizard to fight with a kingdom's army broke the treaty signed by all five kingdoms over three centuries ago. They also knew the tactical advantage of having a wizard during battle. One wizard could lay waste entire legions under the right circumstances.

"We must push back this invasion," Hausey said to Zollin. "Surely you understand that."

"But is it wise to break the treaty?" Kelvich asked.

"I leave those kinds of decisions to my King," the Commander answered. "We have been sent to find you and bring you to Orrock."

"But surely the King's Army is capable of withstanding an invasion. We can take defensive positions and fend them off. There's no need for Zollin to get involved and break the treaty."

Zollin noticed the disdain in the eyes of the knights who were with Commander Hausey. They didn't like that Kelvich was questioning their orders or the King's plan, but Zollin understood. If he chose to get involved, he ran the risk of destroying a peace that had lasted over three hundred years. It also gave King Felix precedent for commanding Zollin. The young wizard had no desire to disobey his King, but neither did he relish the idea of becoming someone's puppet. He had to make a decision soon, he knew that. And if he refused the soldiers, he might have to fight them, which he did not want to do. If there really were soldiers from the south invading, he didn't want to make matters worse by injuring or slaying five of the King's knights.

"You are correct," Hausey said. "We do have the strength to withstand this invasion. We have equal numbers, and the defenses at Orrock would make a siege difficult, but not impossible for us to weather. We could easily hold out through the winter, if worse came to worst, and then drive them back in the spring after they have been weakened by the cold and lack of resources. But that does not take into account the people living near Orrock. Their homes would be pillaged and burned, their crops and livestock stolen. And if a force were to invade from the east, we would be helpless. They could ravage their way to Orrock and reinforce the siege, which would put us at a distinct disadvantage. All might be lost. We need Zollin."

"We'll ride with you," Zollin said, and the words felt like gravel being ground into the wound of his grief. "If we hear news of the dragon, though, I must turn aside, at least temporarily."

"You would disobey your King?" said one of the knights in a haughty tone.

"Do not question his loyalty or courage," said Hausey angrily. "If finding his beloved is what it takes to get him to Orrock, that is what we will do. We will support you, Zollin."

"That is all I ask," he said.

Mansel felt his rage burning more fiercely than ever. He had understood that Zollin needed closure, perhaps even revenge against the creature that had stolen Brianna away from him. But now he would have to persuade Zollin to leave his King and country in order to go south to Lodenhime. The muscle in his jaw flexed so hard it felt as if his teeth would break under the pressure.

They turned and rode hard through the day. They passed a few villages where people still made their homes, although there were many empty homes and farms even in the occupied villages. No one had heard any news of the dragon in weeks. It was a discouraging sign for Zollin. The beast may have taken refuge in another mountain lair, or it may have doubled back to its original cave far to the north. Either way, Zollin knew he would not be able to rest until he had tracked the dragon down and discovered what had become of Brianna.

Chapter 22

"You want war?" Prince Wilam said angrily. "You want to take the riffraff forces we have here and march against King Ortis's entire army?"

"Yes," said Gwendolyn. She was pouting at Wilam, using all her charms to break down his resistance to her plan.

In most other cases, she would have merely replaced a man who showed any doubts about her plans, but she knew she couldn't lose the Crown Prince of Yelsia. He was important and so she coddled him.

"We have their cavalry," she said.

"We have a portion of their cavalry," Wilam corrected her.

"You have to remember that I don't want to kill them," she said. "I want them to join us. I want to build a grand army and march south."

"But why? Is what we've given you here not enough?"

"Of course it isn't," she giggled. "Don't be silly. I'm a woman, I can never have enough. Besides, this will be your chance to show me what you've been able to do with my army. I'm anxious to see the fruits of your hard labor and reward you."

Wilam knew that Gwendolyn had great power over men, even if he couldn't recognize that he himself was bewitched by that power. He had been in awe when the cavalry force surrendered to her and pledged their swords to her service. It had been an incredible feat, and although he was jealous of the men and the way Gwendolyn fussed over them, he was glad to have a stronger fighting force. He doubted that an entire army could be won over so easily, but he couldn't resist the temptation to show off the army he had built for Gwendolyn. The scouts had returned with more men, and with the contingent of cavalry from Ortis, they were five hundred strong now. Each man knew his duty and each was eager to fight for Gwendolyn. Wilam was not eager to fight, but he was desperate for the reward, which he assumed would be a place in the witch's bed.

"I shall not disappoint you. We will be ready to leave at dawn."

"Not dawn, no, that won't do," said Gwendolyn. "Have your men ready, but make it midday. That sounds much more pleasant."

Wilam was at a loss for words. He bowed and hurried from the room. He was walking across the long feasting hall on the way to inform his troops to gear up and prepare to escort their Queen to Blue Harbor when he was met by Keevy, the Castle steward.

"I shall be leaving with you tomorrow," he said, doing his best to sound confident.

"Oh, no," Wilam corrected him. "This is a military matter. Your place is here," he said in mock sympathy.

"I serve Her Majesty," Keevy said angrily. "I'll not leave her alone with you."

"You'll do as you're told, or we'll find a new steward while your head decorates the Castle gates."

"No!" he shouted, his pudgy face red with indignation. "You've been trying to get rid of me since you arrived. I won't let you. I won't let you worm your way into Her Majesty's good graces."

"Do not forget who you are talking to," Wilam said in a low voice that was brimming with anger. "I have not forgotten how you went behind my back and told the Queen about the force from Ortis. You are a snake in the grass, and I'll have your head if you cross me again."

"You can't kill me. The lady Gwendolyn needs me," he said haughtily.

"Don't test me."

"I'll do more than that, I'll slice your throat while you sleep. I don't fear you. You've had everything handed to you your whole life. You're nothing but a bag of hot air."

In most circumstances the entire exchange would have been laughable. Prince Wilam was not the kind of man who bandied words with anyone, and no one who knew him would ever accuse him of being lazy or spoiled. If anything, the Crown Prince was too dedicated and suffered from an inflated sense of responsibility to his people. But the steward's constant scheming chafed Wilam, as did the steward's access to Gwendolyn. His fist shot out so fast that Keevy never saw it, just felt his head snap backwards from the blow.

The Castle steward staggered back and fell over the long feasting table. Even though he was much older than Wilam and had no experience fighting, he bellowed in rage and launched himself at the Prince. The fight didn't last long. Wilam used the steward's own momentum to flip him over, and Keevy landed on the stone floor with a bone-jarring crash. In any other circumstances the fight would have ended there, but Keevy was insane with jealous rage. He picked himself up off the floor, his face twisted in anger and pain. Wilam didn't wait for the steward to launch another attack, instead he kicked Keevy hard between the legs. The older man folded over in pain and fell back onto the floor.

The fight should have ended then, but Wilam was caught up in battle lust. He grabbed the steward's head and slammed it into the flagstone floor of the feasting hall. The skin on Keevy's forehead split, sending blood streaming from the wound. The man was unconscious as Wilam slammed his head into the floor over and over again, shattering Keevy's skull and pounding his brains to jelly. When Wilam stood up, he was covered with blood and bits of gore. Several other servants had come running to see what had happened. They had heard Keevy's bellow of rage and seen Prince Wilam beat him to death.

Wilam was still angry and would have gladly continued fighting but Gwendolyn had come down when she heard the steward screaming in rage. As soon as Wilam saw her, his blood lust evaporated and he stood still.

"Clean up the mess," Gwendolyn said icily.

Then she spun on her heel and marched back up to her rooms, her gown billowing out behind her and Andomina following silently behind. Wilam was unsure what to do. He turned and left the hall, stopping at a barrel of fresh water to wash himself. Then he sent word for his officers to join him.

The next day their small army assembled in the courtyard. The cavalry from Ortis would lead the army, followed by Gwendolyn and Andomina in their carriage and then by the foot soldiers and supply wagons. Wilam had not returned to the Castle that night. He normally slept in a small anteroom outside of Gwendolyn's quarters, in case she needed him in the night. But after killing Keevy, who had served as Gwendolyn's steward since she arrived at the Castle on the Sea, he was ashamed. Even though he would gladly have killed any number of men just to get close to Gwendolyn, his sense of honor was shaken that he had given into his rage and killed a civilian as helpless as Keevy. He didn't miss the steward—they had been enemies since their first encounter—but he had never lost control like that before and he didn't like the result.

He organized the army and then waited with his troops until Gwendolyn was ready to leave. When Gwendolyn and her sister finally came out of the Castle, they went directly into their large, wooden wagon, outfitted with thick drapes and padded benches. Gwendolyn didn't speak to anyone, so Prince Wilam ordered the army to set out.

They marched without stopping until sunset. It was a hot and dusty day, but they were traveling on the coastal road, and the wind off the Great Sea of Kings was cool. At dusk they made camp, pitching tents and starting fires. Food was taken to Gwendolyn's carriage, but neither she nor her sister Andomina were seen.

They broke camp shortly after dawn and continued their trek. It took three days to reach Blue Harbor, where the army of Ortis, a little over two full legions, was camped around the city. Wilam rode at the head of the cavalry, and ordered the column to stop when he could see the sprawling army from Ortis. He rode back to the carriage and gave Gwendolyn the news.

"I need my horse," she said from inside her wagon. "And have my tent set up where I can meet with the King and his generals."

"Yes, my lady," said Wilam, trying to sound more confident than he felt.

Prince Wilam was so afraid that even putting one foot in front of the other was difficult. Questions were swarming around his brain like a hive of angry bees. Would Gwendolyn reject him in favor of King Oveer? What about the generals, would she give them leadership of the army? And what if King Oveer or his troops weren't convinced to join them? Their small army could be massacred, and Wilam might not be able to protect his Queen.

Still, his sense of duty propelled him forward. He had Gwendolyn's tent set up and made sure that a squad of his most capable men were set to guard it. Then he retrieved the horse that they had brought along specifically for Gwendolyn to ride. The horse was white all over. The skilled saddle makers in Lodenhime had crafted a fine leather saddle that was pale ivory. When Prince Wilam had saddled the horse and ensured that everything was just the way Gwendolyn wanted it, he led the horse to Gwendolyn's carriage.

"Your Highness," he called. "Your horse awaits you."

Gwendolyn opened the door of her carriage and stepped out. She was wearing an ivory gown that showed off her figure. She moved her feet lightly from the carriage step into the stirrup and sat down gracefully on the saddle.

"Let's go meet the King," she said playfully.

Wilam rode beside Gwendolyn, and the Ortis cavalry soldiers fell in behind them, their armor, polished especially for this meeting, glinting in the afternoon sunlight. They rode along the path toward the army encampment and were met by a small group of knights who had been riding out to find out who they were.

"We wish to see King Oveer," Wilam told the knights.

"Who wishes to see the King?" the lead knight said.

"Queen Gwendolyn of Lodenhime," Wilam said, "and Prince Wilam Felixson, of Yelsia."

The knight nodded and turned his horse. Then he led Wilam and Gwendolyn to the large tent where King Oveer had been lounging for the past week. They waited patiently as the group of soldiers around Gwendolyn grew and grew. She did not even speak, but the men jostled to get near her.

"What is this?" came a frustrated voice from inside the tent.

King Oveer was a short man with long brown hair and a full beard. His crown was propped back on his head when he emerged from the tent, and his clothes were wrinkled. He wore a sword, but it was buckled too high on his hip to be useful, and the hilt was encrusted with precious gems.

"Prince Wilam is wanted for treason," King Oveer said loudly, as he looked up at Wilam.

Oveer and Wilam had met in the Grand City, but the King couldn't say for sure that this Wilam was in fact the Prince of Yelsia who had gone missing before the Council of Kings. Oveer rarely paid much attention to anyone but other kings.

"Arrest him and send for the executioner," he added, trying to sound more royal than he did.

"No," said Gwendolyn, "that won't be necessary."

None of the men around her moved. Normally the order of a king, even one as pompous and unpopular as Oveer, would have sent men scrambling to obey, but Gwendolyn held them all in her spell.

"And who exactly are you?" Oveer thundered, furious for having been countermanded. "There is no queen in Lodenhime, unless you're Zorlan's latest excuse for a wife."

The men around Oveer started to grumble, taking offense at their King's insult, but Gwendolyn didn't seem to mind. She slid off her horse and stepped in front of King Oveer, whose eyes narrowed angrily at first and then slowly relaxed.

"I require your assistance," Gwendolyn said. "I need an army and capable commanders. I was hoping you might be persuaded to join me."

"My lady," Oveer stammered, suddenly at a loss for words. "I am sorry, please forgive me. I don't know what got into me. An army, you say?"

"That's right, King Oveer. I want your army," she said in a pouting voice. "Will you give it to me? I'd be ever so grateful."

"Of course," Oveer said. "Anything you want, anything at all."

"That is so generous of you," she said raising one hand and allowing King Oveer to bow forward and kiss it.

The gesture made Wilam's blood boil. As far as he knew, he was the only person to have touched Gwendolyn's fair skin. She occasionally allowed him to rub her shoulders or her feet. The small gestures made him feel as if she cared for Wilam more than anyone else, and now she was giving her hand to the fumbling King of Ortis.

"Gather your generals," Gwendolyn told Oveer, "and meet me at my tent in one hour. Can you do that?"

"Of course, my lady," Oveer promised.

"Good, then perhaps we can finalize our plans. I would like to move as soon as possible. Your camp smells dreadful."

"It's the heat," Oveer said in a lame attempt to excuse the stench of the army's camp. "And Blue Harbor is full of raw fish. We shall ensure that not a breath of wind carries to your tent, my love."

Gwendolyn's eyes flashed angrily in response to the King's last endearment, but then she brought herself swiftly under control, although her voice carried an icy tone that was hard to mistake.

"Good, that would be a welcome change," she said. "Do not keep me waiting, King Oveer. I am not a patient person."

"We shall make haste," the King said.

Gwendolyn reached up, and Wilam extended his hand to help her back onto her horse. She climbed into the saddle lightly and then turned her horse. The men who had crowded close to see her now parted so that she could ride back toward the carriage and her tent. They cheered for her and called out for her attention as she rode. Their unbridled fervor to be near the witch made Wilam uncomfortable. He rode with one hand on the pommel of his sword just in case he needed it.

When they arrived back at the carriage, Gwendolyn called to her sister, who came meekly from the wagon and walked behind her sister's horse. They rode to the tent, which had been lavishly furnished during their absence from the camp. Food was being roasted nearby and the aroma was delicious.

"I want you to join us just before the King arrives," Gwendolyn said to Wilam. "We shall be making our plans, and I want you to lead the army. I trust that is a task you can manage, or do I need to find someone else who can fulfill my needs?"

"No, I shall not disappoint you, my Queen," Prince Wilam said.

"Good. Make sure you are not late."

Then she slid off her horse and walked briskly into the tent, followed by her sister. Wilam spun his horse and set about ensuring that their camp was efficiently managed. He made sure that the men camped downwind of Gwendolyn and warned the men not to do anything to embarrass the Queen. He washed the grime of the road off his face and hands and made sure his clothes were neat and his weapons accessible before returning to Gwendolyn's tent. She told him to wait on the party from the Ortis army, and, when they arrived, he escorted King Oveer and five of his generals into Gwendolyn's tent. She had wine and cheese waiting for the men. Once everyone had a goblet, Gwendolyn sat down on a throne-like chair and waited while the men found places on benches around her.

"Now," she said. "I want a large army. How many soldiers do you have, King Oveer?"

"More than two full legions here at Blue Harbor," the King said. His lust was so profound he was almost drooling. He sat leaning toward Gwendolyn, and it took all of Wilam's self control not to draw his weapon and attack the arrogant ruler.

"Two legions?" Gwendolyn said, frowning. "That isn't enough. Can't you get more? Surely you have more troops than that."

"I'll send riders north to rally our reserves guarding the border and the Wilderlands. It will take a few weeks, but we can gather another three legions."

Wilam saw the nervous looks the generals gave each other as they listened to their king. He was obviously overestimating his forces. Wilam didn't mind; in fact, he saw the King's exaggeration as a point in his favor. If Oveer couldn't keep his word, then Gwendolyn would find out how untrustworthy he really was. In contrast, Wilam would seem all the more honorable, and, he hoped, attractive.

"Good, but that still isn't enough," Gwendolyn said. "I want you to send your troops to Luxing City. We shall meet there after gathering troops from Falxis, and then march south to the Torr."

"That is fine, my lady, but I'm afraid you won't find many troops in Falxis. King Belphan and King Zorlan are sailing to invade Yelsia as we speak. I doubt there are many troops left in reserve."

Prince Wilam's chest tightened at hearing this news. His devotion was to Gwendolyn alone, but he couldn't help but feel worried about hearing of an invasion in Yelsia, even if he couldn't say exactly why it had him worried.

"Why are they invading Yelsia?" Gwendolyn asked.

"The wizard Offendorl insists that it must be done. He fashioned his plans with King Belphan to invade Yelsia. He thinks there is a wizard there, being harbored by King Felix. He sailed north with the armies to make sure he gains control of the wizard."

"The master is not in the Torr?" Gwendolyn said to herself. Her face had gone pale and Wilam waved for her servant to refill her wine goblet.

Gwendolyn took a long drink and then stood up.

"Did you hear that, Mina?" she said to her sister, turning her back on the men in the tent.

Andomina was sitting in a camp chair, twirling the ends of her hair around and around. She made no sign that she heard her sister at all.

"The master has left the Torr at last," Gwendolyn said. "This is better than we had hoped."

She spun around and looked at Wilam.

"We ride immediately," she told him. Leave a few people here to gather what we can't move immediately." Then she turned to King Oveer. "I want all your troops, every last one, to march south to the Grand City. We shall take the tower and gather all our forces there. When the master returns, he will find that his house is no longer his own."

Chapter 23

"These guerrilla tactics pose no serious threat to our efforts," Offendorl said.

"I did not say they were a serious threat," King Belphan said defensively. "I said they were worrisome. We still have heard no news of the attack from the eastern front. I did not come to this backwards kingdom to fight an all-out war. You said we would overwhelm them."

"And we shall," said Offendorl. "I admit that you are right, we should have heard of our forces invading from the east. Perhaps we underestimated King Ricard's ties to Yelsia. But our plans have not changed. We shall lay siege to Orrock."

"What about the dragon?" said Zorlan.

"I'll worry about the dragon," Offendorl said in a snarl. "You are both beginning to sound like nagging old women. Act like men. We are here, and in any battle there will be things that do not go as planned. We must see things through. You act as if you want to run back to your kingdoms. What message would that send to Yelsia? They have broken three centuries of peace by harboring a wizard. What will they do next, I wonder, when they see you running home with your tail between your legs like a whipped dog?"

"Do not dare to speak to us so, wizard!" said Belphan angrily. "We are kings, not your vile, tongueless servants."

"And I am Master of the Torr," Offendorl said in a low but deadly voice. "Do not fool yourselves. I can kill you with a thought. I can usurp your throne and make your kingdoms worship me if I so choose. Neither of you has seen war; you do not know its horrors or hardships. I have seen battles between beasts and men and wizards. I have lived in these Five Kingdoms for over three hundred years. Do not dare to question my authority on this venture, or you will find yourselves in the same position as King Felix."

It was not the first time King Belphan and King Zorlan had complained. Offendorl had sailed to Yelsia on a separate ship from the kings so he didn't have to listen to their constant complaints as they traveled. When they first landed in Yelsia, the excitement of war made them tolerable companions. But it hadn't taken long for them to begin complaining. The food was not to their standards. They weren't used to long journeys or living in tents. They were spoiled tyrants whose every whims were fulfilled in their kingdoms, but not on this campaign. So they whined like children and Offendorl grew weary of it.

"We are less than two days from Orrock," he told them. "We shall surround the city and pillage the countryside. Your troops will have gold, women, and ale. You can spend your days drunk in your bed if you so desire, and when we are through you shall divide Yelsia's spoils. Until then, stop complaining and find your courage."

Offendorl stalked out of the tent. They were camped on a wide plain, south of the Tillamook River. The army had made good time moving north, despite the fact that King Felix had sent skirmishers to harass them. The small bands of soldiers were well mounted, and, because they knew the land, they could strike an ambush and then flee before a proper counterattack was mounted. The main body of their army had been harried with volleys of arrows. If a unit or group strayed far from the larger group, it was attacked by men on heavy horse. The casualties weren't significant enough to deter them, but their inability to strike a blow wore on their morale. It became apparent very quickly that this was a deadly business, and while the soldiers endured, their kings howled about every minor assault.

Offendorl had a tent that was every bit as lavish as that of Belphan and Zorlan, but he preferred to meet with the kings away from his personal space. Spending time with the kings and their generals each day was wearying, and he made sure that he could escape to his own quarters after he'd made his daily rounds.

Once he was ensconced in his wagon, he lit two lamps to give his ancient eyes enough light to read by. He was propped on cushions and sipping a goblet of wine while he read the book he had brought with him. It was so old the paper had to be handled with the utmost care to keep it from crumbing to pieces. In some places the writing had faded and was difficult to make out, but that didn't deter Offendorl. He was determined to learn all he could about controlling the dragon. He continued to call to the beast day and night, and he sensed that it was moving closer.

The entire first half of the book was a history of the dragon species. Very little was known about where dragons came from or why they seemed to spring up in groups throughout history. The translation of the text was tedious, but Offendorl had grown patient in his long life. A younger man might have been tempted to skip ahead, past the history and care of dragons, but Offendorl was nothing if not thorough. Reading and learning where the only things he still cared about other than power. He read to learn to increase his magical abilities, but he still found pleasure in a quiet, comfortable place with a thick tome or ancient scroll before him. He was awake late into the night reading, and at last he had discovered exactly what he needed to bring the dragon under his control.

He was fascinated to learn that crowns worn by kings had their origins in dragon lore. There was no explanation for why dragons were drawn so strongly to gold, although the precious metal not only worked to heal the beasts, it could also be used to control them. Offendorl sat studying a picture of a wizard with a long beard and helmet made of pure gold. The helmet had a name inscribed on it, and, according to the book, if Offendorl could learn the dragon's name, he could have total control of the beast. It was exactly the kind information he had been hoping for, that elusive last piece to the puzzle he needed.

He slept for only a few hours before his servants woke him. He rose early each morning and met with the commanders of both armies. He had to make sure their invasion moved forward smoothly. In fact, it had been his idea to send the knight who had approached them under the banner of truth back to their king empty-handed. After the group had sat through the long, rainy night, Offendorl had sent them away without a reply while King Belphan and King Zorlan slept. This morning he needed riders to go in search of anyone with information about the dragon. They had passed by and plundered many villages on their way north, and already they had heard reports of people claiming to have seen the beast, or to have fled from their homes to escape the dragon. Offendorl knew the dragon was communicating, and what he needed was someone with knowledge of the beast's name.

By midmorning, once the kings had slept off their excess from the night before, the army began its daily march. It was late afternoon when they spotted the Yelsian army spread out before them. Offendorl was surprised by King Felix's daring. Unlike Belphan and Zorlan, Felix was not content to sit in the castle. He brought his army into the field, and now they would fight. At least,

Offendorl thought, there would not be any more skirmishing. A full-on attack would mean that thousands would die, on both sides, but Offendorl put little value on the lives of mortal men. The army halted, and they made camp less than a mile from their enemy.

"In the morning, we shall attack them," Offendorl told King Belphan and King Zorlan, as they met for their nightly report.

"I thought you said Felix would hide in his castle," Belphan said.

"I did, but in this instance I was wrong," Offendorl admitted.

"He's making a bold move," said one of the generals. "I can't imagine what would make him fight us in the open field."

"Perhaps he has an advantage that we know nothing of," said Zorlan.

"It's possible," said Offendorl, "but if the wizard Zollin is with them, they would still be better off fighting from behind the high walls of their city."

"So, why would he do it?" Belphan asked.

"There could be any number of reasons," Offendorl said angrily, he did not like being questioned. "The most likely being there is something between us and Orrock that he cannot move and does not wish us to find. It forces him to fight us here, and we shall use that to our advantage. He will find that we shall not be beaten back so easily."

"What do you have planned for them?" Belphan asked again.

"Nothing," Offendorl said, "we cannot break the treaty."

"You will not fight for us?" Belphan's face was turning red. "This invasion is entirely your idea, and now you will leave us defenseless?"

Offendorl looked at King Belphan. His generals were all staring at the ground, their faces red with shame.

"You have an army, my King. You are not defenseless. You want the spoils of war without doing the work. Do not fear, you shall be safe. We will keep you and King Zorlan far from the fighting."

Just then a tremendous crash shook the ground. The camp erupted with shouting and screaming.

"What have you done?" King Belphan shouted.

Offendorl didn't bother to answer. Instead he hurried out of the tent with the generals of the armies. The camp was in chaos, and another crash shook the ground. Someone shouted for them to take cover, and fires were flaring up in the darkness all around the camp. Offendorl let his magic flow out so that he could discover what was happening. He felt the next boulder hurtling through the air and the truth dawned on him.

"Trebuchets," he told the generals. "Pull your men back. Do it quietly. No torches; they will only give the Yelsians something to aim at."

The soldiers moved quickly away, while King Belphan and King Zorlan crowded closer to the master wizard.

"They have trebuchets?" Belphan said. "It is dishonorable to fight at night."

"I don't think they are concerned with honor," Offendorl said. "Get your servants moving. We need to pull back out of their range."

The next hour was frantic. Offendorl stayed with the kings, even raising a defensive shield around them when one boulder came crashing down not far from their position and sending shattered bits of rock flying toward them. The officers of the army shouted themselves hoarse trying to get their men organized in the dark chaos, but eventually the army had fallen back and reformed beyond the range of the trebuchets. The camp burned, including many of the soldiers' tents, and much of the plunder they had taken on their march north was lost. Both of the kings' tents were burned, but Offendorl's servants feared their master more than death. They worked tirelessly to ensure that the ancient wizard's possessions were moved out of harm's way.

When dawn finally arrived, the invaders' camp was in total ruins. There were smoldering piles of ash where tents or wagons had burned. Shattered stone was everywhere, and the earth was torn into muddy gashes. Nothing that had been left behind was intact. Offendorl could still see the Yelsian army in the distance, but the trebuchets were not visible.

"The ground must slope downward on the far side of their forces," said one of the generals who was standing nearby waiting for orders.

"Yes," Offendorl said. "I imagine the Tillamook river is nearby, and they are using the river to ferry in stone for their artillery."

"What do we do now?" King Belphan asked.

"We wait," said Offendorl.

"But sir," said one general in surprise, "we have more than enough men to take their position." The soldier turned to King Zorlan. "Send us forward, sire, and we shall destroy them."

"Don't be a fool," said Offendorl. "After marching for nearly a mile across open ground while they drop stones on your forces, you'll be in no shape to fight anyone."

"We can see their boulders now," the general argued angrily. "We won't be such an easy target as that."

"They won't use boulders now, you imbecile. They'll use rocks about the size of your fist, hundreds of them. You won't be able to dodge them. Your shields will be smashed to pieces. Even the knights in full armor will be killed. This invasion would be over before the day is out."

"I disagree," the general began to argue, but those were his last words.

Without warning, the soldier, dressed in chain mail and a thick jerkin with a wide leather belt, burst into flames. He shrieked, but the fire consumed him so quickly that no one could help him.

"We do not need senseless bravado," Offendorl said as the men around him stared at the burning corpse. "I have other plans, but until they come to fruition or until our forces from Baskla arrive, we stay here."

"Begging your pardon, my lord," said one of the other generals. "You don't want to flank them. We could divide our forces and march around their position."

"No, they will have thought of that, and I don't want to play into their hands," Offendorl replied. "Set up a defensive perimeter and send scouts to ensure they don't move those trebuchets any closer."

The generals all hurried away. Offendorl knew they were glad to have an excuse to get as far away from him as possible. The smell of the burned man was horrible, and he left the kings gawking at the corpse. He returned to his wagon; he was exhausted and needed to rest. He had a lot of work to do, work that would tax his ancient body. Transmutation was not something he did on a regular basis, and while he had the skill and more than enough power, he would need all of his strength.

He called for one of the servants while he lounged in his wagon.

"See that my tent is set up for King Belphan and King Zorlan, but not next to the wagon. I want some space from those sniveling potentates. And begin gathering lead. I need as much heavy metal as you can find. Bring it to me here and see that I am not disturbed."

The servant bowed low and left the wagon. Offendorl leaned back and closed his eyes. He had instructed another servant to prepare him food and wine, but it would be a while before the meat was cooked. He would nap for a while, then eat, before working on the golden crown he was making to control the dragon.

Chapter 24

Brianna paced back and forth in the small confines of the cave. It wasn't a true dragon lair; the beast had spotted it from the air as they flew over the southern range of mountains. But it was deep enough that the cold winds were held back. The dragon had carried Brianna carefully, letting its flaming breath roll back over her to keep her warm. For her part, Brianna held tightly to the beast. She wasn't sure what their connection was, but she felt as though they were the same. She knew she wasn't a dragon, but she also knew she was more than just a girl.

For days they had sheltered together in the cave. The dragon was wary, but open in its way. Brianna found that the dragon could talk, although its voice was sometimes difficult to understand. It was just as curious about what Brianna had become as she was. She had hoped at first that the dragon might be able to explain what she was becoming, but it had no knowledge of Fire Spirits. For her part, Brianna understood the dragon's desire to be free. She could feel the beast's uncertainty and its nagging desire to fly south to find the owner of the voice that was continually calling for it. Brianna had been able to calm the beast and allow it to rest. For days the nagging pain of its wounds had tormented the dragon. It had been able to sleep only in troubled fits. It had been in constant fear, which seemed odd to Brianna for such a large, powerful creature. It had no natural enemies, and yet Zollin's constant pursuit and the wounds she herself had inflicted on the creature had created a sense of constant paranoia. Only now that she was with the dragon did it feel safe enough to rest.

They spent hours debating what the dragon should do. She knew that it had been moments from death when she went to it.

Even if Zollin hadn't been there to fight the dragon, it would have starved or succumbed to the infections from its wounds. She had healed the dragon's body in the valley far to the north, but it took many days to heal its mind. Brianna wanted the dragon to stay in the mountains, but the nagging voice in the beast's mind was slowly driving it mad.

It was gone at the moment. The dragon went out hunting at least once a day. It often brought back small portions of meat, which Brianna cooked simply by holding the raw meat in her hands. She was growing extremely tired of eating nothing but meat and longed for vegetables and fruit, but there was no way to get what she wanted without leaving the dragon.

She experimented every day with her power. At first she could conjure fire as if it were part of her body. The fire came out of her skin and didn't burn, even though she could feel the heat. She wasn't cold, even though they were high in the mountains where the temperature never got far above freezing. The heat from her fire, or from the dragon, felt luxurious to her, and since she had no clothes she often let the flames dance across her skin and cover her nakedness.

After a few days, she began to be able to control the fire, not just conjure it. She could move it just by thinking, intensify the heat until it was so hot it began to melt stone. And as her powers grew, so did a strange desire for offspring. She had heard women in Tranaugh Shire talk as they grew older about their intense desire for children and Brianna had always looked forward to being a mother, but this desire was different. She knew she wanted to have offspring, she just no longer thought of them as children. She didn't know what it meant, but in her dreams she saw eggs formed from the most intense heat. There was no mating involved, no birth process in the traditional sense. Brianna imagined it more like forging offspring, of coaxing hatchlings from the heat. It was a mystery, but the desire grew day by day.

She was still pacing when she heard the telltale whoosh of the dragon's wings. She felt a little better now that it had come back. She was afraid that it would abandon her, simply fly out for food and never return. Not that she couldn't get down the mountain on her own: she couldn't fly like the dragon, but the uncanny sense of lightness had grown stronger as her power did, and she now felt so light that it would take only a little effort to soar up into the sky and sail about on the wind.

The dragon landed gracefully at the mouth of the cave and folded its wings back flat against its body. It had a young goat in one talon. The animal was still alive, but clearly so frightened that it was in shock.

"You were gone a long time," she said to the dragon. "I was afraid you weren't coming back."

The dragon eyed her balefully, but Brianna had come to recognize the look not as one of hate or distrust, but simply the dragon's natural mannerism. She wondered if their ferocious appearance was what caused men to fear them, when it was possible to live in harmony together.

"I am leaving," the beast hissed, its forked tongue whipping out of its mouth as it spoke.

"Why?" Brianna said. "You don't have to go."

"I must," it said. "The voice is growing stronger."

"I can keep you safe," she said, still not sure why she said it.

"Then come with me," it pleaded.

"No, you said yourself that wizards enslave dragons. I know that isn't always true—Zollin would never do that—but whatever is calling you south can't be good for you. Stay here. Fight it. I know you can."

"No, I must go. It is no longer in my control."

Brianna put her hands out and the dragon, hesitating for only a moment, thrust its head forward so that she could stroke its cheeks.

"You are good, I know that," she told the dragon. "You don't have to give in to hate. You don't have to let evil men use your great power."

"I cannot change," the beast said. "I will fly you down to the lowlands."

"No," Brianna said. "I can't leave yet. I have something to do here. I can't say what it is, but I have to stay."

"And I have to leave."

"Be careful," she told the beast.

It nuzzled her shoulder then moved swiftly past her. She followed it to the mouth of the cave, the cold air whipping her hair around her face. Then the dragon jumped high into the air, its wings flapping, and it soared away. Brianna felt a twinge of regret. She had a strong sense that she would never see the dragon again. It was an odd feeling, she thought. It wasn't like the dragon was a pet or even a friend. It was an incredibly powerful creature that somehow she had connected with.

She walked back into the darkness of the cave. The goat was bleating, and she realized that it was afraid. She didn't like the thought of killing the animal. Death had become part of her life, and she had never even questioned it. She was tired of death, and the more she thought about it, the stronger her desire to create life became. She missed Zollin, but she knew she still had things to learn and things to do. They were things he could not help her with. In time, she would return to Zollin, she was sure of it. But for now, she had to discover what it meant to give life.

* * *

Quinn was more tired than he could ever remember being. He had ridden north to Black Bay, then turned east and taken the Weaver's Road toward Ebbson Keep. He rode day and night, alternating mounts, eating in the saddle, stopping only to catch a few hours' sleep in the late watches of the night. At first he had stopped to ask if anyone remembered Mansel, since the boy was hard to miss. He was larger than most men, both in height and build. But the people who remembered seeing Mansel only remembered seeing him pass by, so Quinn pushed on.

At Fort Jellar, he skirted the army encampment. Although it was tempting to check on Mansel at Ebbson Keep, Quinn decided to keep moving. He wasn't sure if it was a desire to find Mansel, or if he just really wanted to see Miriam again. His desire to see the healer in Felson had been growing in him since Mansel had thrown him overboard and the shock of the cold water broke the spell Gwendolyn had cast over him. He decided to push on for Felson and kept a wide berth around Ebbson Keep. He had little difficulty easing through the line of scouts in the dead of night. Once back on the Weaver's Road, he resumed his demanding pace.

The weeks went by in a blur of constant movement. His body ached from riding so long, and his mind wandered for long periods. He was a day's ride from Felson when the cough began. At first it was merely a tickle deep in his chest. But the tickle nagged at him, and his discomfort grew stronger. Soon, he was coughing so hard that his sides ached, and he had even caused himself to vomit at one point. When he approached the city, late that night, he smelled the stench of too many people trying to live in a small area. He rode through a shanty town, where people were camped on either side of the road, some under makeshift shelters and others exposed to the elements. He could smell the trash and the unmistakable odor of the latrines that had been hastily dug as refugees from the north flooded into the city.

He was leaning heavily on the neck of his horse as he entered the city proper. There were still a few people roaming the streets at that late hour, but none of them looked to be up to anything good. After a while, Quinn was finally met by a small squad of soldiers.

"It's past curfew," said the ranking soldier.

"I just got to the city," Quinn said. "I'm looking for Miriam, the animal healer. Can you direct me to her home?"

He coughed so hard after speaking that he had to bend over double, his breath coming in wheezing gasps.

"Sounds more like you need a physician than an animal healer," said the soldier.

"She's a friend," Quinn managed to say.

"Well, I'm sure she wouldn't appreciate being roused out of bed by a sick man."

"Please," Quinn said. "I don't have much time."

"All right," said the soldier. "I'll take you to her home, but don't try any funny business. We're not in the mood."

Quinn nodded, thankful that the soldiers were going to help. He felt guilty that he had shirked his duty to Prince Wilam. When he'd finally come to his senses after being rescued at sea, he'd immediately thought to travel north to save Zollin. He should have gone south to rescue the Prince from Gwendolyn, he supposed, but no matter how strong his duty to King and country, his family would always come first.

They arrived at Miriam's home after only a few minutes of travel through the city. Even in the dark Quinn could tell that Miriam's home was filled with refugees. There were tents around the small corral, and pushcarts lined the front of the house. Quinn climbed out of the saddle, being careful not to fall. His arms and legs felt so heavy he had trouble moving them, but he managed to shuffle toward the house.

The soldier stood back as they approached and watched Quinn with an experienced eye. He had one hand on his sword while the other held a torch high, letting the light spill onto the small porch. Quinn knocked on the door with slow, heavy thuds. There were sounds of movement in the house, then a light came shining weakly through the front window.

"Who is it?" came Miriam's voice. It was cautious, but clear and exactly as Quinn remembered it.

"It's Quinn."

There was the sound of a heavy bolt being lifted, and the door opened just a crack. Light from a candle shone through.

"Oh, Quinn," she said, throwing the door open wide. "Come in, please. Are you okay?"

Before he could answer the soldier spoke up.

"You know this man, lady Miriam?"

"Yes, he's a friend."

"Fine, we'll be moving on then," said the soldier.

Quinn turned to say thank you, but he was racked with a fit of coughing. Miriam helped him inside and into a chair.

"You're sick," she said.

"No," he managed to respond. "Just tired. I've had a long journey."

"Well, you're here now and you're safe," she said. I've got one bed left, and you're going right into it."

"No," he said again. "I'm filthy. I'll sleep on the floor."

"Don't be ridiculous," she said. "This is my house, and I don't let people sleep on the floor. Now come with me."

"I'm sorry," he croaked, "to intrude like this."

"I'm glad you're here," she said. "I haven't heard from Zollin or Kelvich in weeks. I did hear that they were headed to Orrock recently. Some of the soldiers were talking about it when I was at the fort."

"Orrock?" Quinn asked. "How recent?"

"I heard it a few days ago. There's rumors of war, but we haven't heard anything for certain. The legion, what was left of them, were called to Orrock. Things have been tense here for the last few weeks. A small contingent of soldiers have been working hard to curb the crime, but it's getting worse despite their efforts. We can talk about all that tomorrow, though. You need to rest."

"I have to catch up with Zollin," he said.

"You said that the last time we met," she said, smiling.

"You've been on my mind ever since," he admitted.

She smiled and helped him into a bed. He noticed the covers were rumpled and thrown back hastily. There was no candle by the bed.

"This is where you were sleeping," Quinn said.

"And now it's where you are going to sleep."

He wanted to protest but he was too tired. He sat heavily on the bed and before he could stop her she pulled his boots off. Then she pushed him back onto the soft mattress and he felt himself swooning. As his head hit the pillow, he could smell the fragrance of Miriam's hair. It was intoxicating and he couldn't help but smile as he fell asleep.

Miriam watched Quinn for several long minutes. His face was gaunt, his beard overgrown and patchy. It was obvious that he hadn't been eating well. His clothes were dirty, stained with sweat and blood, not to mention ragged, with several holes and rips in the fabric.

She was tired and wanted to settle into the chair she kept by her bed, but she remembered the horses she had seen outside. There had been two, both saddled and looking almost as tired as Quinn. She knew that not only would it be bad for the horses to stay saddled overnight, but there was also a strong possibility that they would be stolen if she didn't move them into the barn.

She hurried outside after lighting a lantern. The horses were waiting out front. Although neither was tied up, they seemed content to stand and wait on Quinn. She took their reins and led them into her barn, which was filled with animals and people. She had one stall left, and luckily it was big enough for both horses. She removed their tack and brushed them both down before giving them a bag of oats and leading them into the stall. When she got back inside her house she collapsed into her chair and fell asleep.

It seemed like only a moment later that the sun was peeking through her window. She yawned and stretched. Sleeping in a chair, no matter how comfortable, was hard on her. When she moved her neck a sharp pain ran down her arm. She tried to stretch the soreness out but it wasn't very effective. Still, she knew she had things to do, so she forced herself to get moving.

Miriam started her days by feeding and watering the animals she had in her charge. She went out to the barn, enjoying the crisp, cool, early-morning air. The nights had finally started getting cool again, after weeks of very hot weather. In the barn, only a few of her guests were stirring. They were all temporary residents. She made sure that they knew she didn't want long-term guests living in her barn. Most were refugees, and she refused to take what little payment they offered.

There were sick animals, but none seemed critical. Since that first meeting with Zollin months ago, she hadn't faced a problem she couldn't solve when it came to sick animals. She had always considered herself to be a talented animal healer, but now things seemed to come to her more easily. After she checked on the sick animals, she looked in on her own. She had three horses, several chickens, and a milk cow. The goats stayed outside in a small corral.

She milked the cow, spraying the warm, frothy milk into a wooden bucket. Most of the milk would be given to children of the families she allowed to stay in her barn, but she planned to save a little for Quinn. Once she had seen to her animals, she returned to the house and went into the kitchen, where she brewed coffee and toasted a little bread for her breakfast. She had two permanent house guests who traded room and board for work. Both were young and happy to have a place to call home. When they rose and found Miriam in the kitchen, she sent them both on morning errands. The girl was sent to get the eggs her hens laid overnight. The boy was sent to fetch the doctor. Miriam could hear Quinn coughing in his sleep. His breathing was labored, and she was beginning to worry about him.

When the young girl returned with the eggs, Miriam set about making breakfast for her two boarders. They ate eggs and toasted bread before hurrying off to start their chores. The healer from the fort arrived while they were eating, and Miriam showed him where Quinn was still asleep. The healer listened to Quinn's breathing with a funnel-shaped instrument and then he gently woke Quinn.

After an brief fit of coughing, Quinn was able to answer the healer's questions.

"I've been traveling pretty hard," Quinn admitted. "I had a wound on my leg, but it was treated and seems to be mending just fine. It's this cough I can't get rid of."

"You've got fluid in your lungs, and it could get worse. I've got some herbs that will help, but you really need to stay off your feet for several days," the physician said.

"That's the one thing I can't do," Quinn admitted. "I've got to find Zollin and Mansel."

"They're headed to Orrock," the healer said. "Commander Hausey was sent for Zollin, and scouts reported that there was a group traveling together. Zollin, Kelvich, and a big lad."

"That would be Mansel," Quinn said bitterly. "I have to go."

"You'd do better to wait at least a few days and give your body time to heal."

"Yes, you should stay, Quinn," Miriam said, almost pleading. "You're in no shape to go after Zollin."

"It can't wait. He's in danger."

"I'll go for you," Miriam suggested.

"No, Mansel's my problem. I don't know if I can stop him or not, but I have to try."

He related how they had been bewitched in Lodenhime and how Mansel was operating under the witch's influence. Quinn coughed again, and the healer went to the kitchen to brew a drink with the herbs he had with him.

"This is lunacy," Miriam said. "You're in no shape to travel. Your horses aren't either. You've run them into the ground."

"I have to try," Quinn said. "He's my only son."

"I understand that, but you aren't going alone."

"What?"

"I'm going with you."

"No, you can't. You have people here who need you."

"I have people here who can look after things while I'm gone," she insisted. "I'm going to get things ready and then we'll leave. Until then, you stay in this bed."

Quinn wanted to argue, but he knew it was futile. He had no reason for not wanting Miriam to go with him. She wouldn't slow him down, not in the state he was in. Their chances of catching up to Zollin and Mansel were slim, but they had to try. And the truth of the matter was, he wanted Miriam with him. Now that he had seen her again, he knew without a doubt that he wanted to be with her, not just right now, but always. He had to save Zollin—that was his first priority—but after that, he would stay with Miriam for as long as she would have him.

Miriam called her young helpers into the house, just as the physician was taking Quinn the hot drink he had brewed. The boy was fourteen and Miriam's unofficial apprentice. He knew enough to take care of the animals in the barn. Miriam put him in charge of her small practice and to see to any repairs around the house that needed to be made. The girl, a bright, young orphan who thought she was eleven, although she couldn't be sure, had lost both parents when the dragon attacked her village. She was found by a band of refugees and brought to Felson. Miriam had no children of her own. Jax had filled that role to some degree, but with his absence Miriam was only too happy to bring the girl into her home. She put the girl in charge of the house, including fixing meals and helping with the refugee children.

Then Miriam went to the barn and saddled three horses. She left the two Quinn had brought in, and they looked relieved when she left them in the stall. It took nearly an hour to make sure she had enough food and medical supplies. Once she had everything packed neatly on two horses, she went to get Quinn.

"Miriam," the young girl called. "The healer told me to pour this up for Quinn. Is that the man sleeping in your bed?"

"Yes, child," Miriam said, blushing a little at the implication. "He's very sick."

"This is his medicine," she said holding up the canteen. "And here are the herbs. The healer said to boil them in water to make more medicine."

"Thank you," Miriam said smiling at the girl's enthusiasm. "I'm very proud of you. We shouldn't be gone too long, a few weeks at the most."

"I'll make sure everything is okay here," the girl said.

"I'm sure you will."

Miriam went to get Quinn and found him sleeping. She wanted to wait, to let him rest and recover, but she had promised they would leave as soon as she was ready. She moved to his bedside and shook him gently.

"Quinn," she said in a soft voice. "Can you wake up?"

His eyes fluttered open and they took a moment to focus on her.

"Is it time?" he asked.

"Yes, if you're ready."

"I just need a little time to get up here," he said struggling out from under the covers. "I'm afraid I've soiled your bed with my filthy clothes."

"It's okay," Miriam said. "We can wash them later. Just take your time," she added as she took hold of his arm.

Another coughing fit shook him, but it seemed less severe than the ones before. Then he was out of the bed and stretching.

"That brew your healer gave me was one of the worst things I've ever tasted," he said. "And the taste it leaves in your mouth afterward is even worse."

"Well, the good news is that it should help you feel better," Miriam said.

"I feel like you're leaving something out," he said, smiling.

"Of course the bad news is," she continued, "the healer left a whole canteen for you to drink today."

"Oh no."

"And the worse news is I've been instructed to brew more when that's gone."

Chapter 25

Zollin was tired. Emotionally he was a total wreck, but he hid the damage as best he could. Riding with Commander Hausey had one positive benefit: it allowed Zollin the freedom not to worry about pushing the pace or finding his way. Mansel was brooding and quiet, preferring not to speak unless he was asked a direct question. Zollin was too caught up in his grief over Brianna to take much notice, but Kelvich was worried.

Not only did the big warrior seem different somehow, he refused to drink. They passed several inns, but Mansel didn't recommend they stop. When ale or wine was offered by villagers, he declined. It was the last straw in Kelvich's case against Mansel, and once he was sure that something was wrong, he began looking for an opportunity to talk to Zollin about it.

That night they made camp a few hours after dark. Commander Hausey had pushed the pace, but he knew his men needed sleep. They all took turns standing watch, and Kelvich made sure he knew when Zollin would be awake in the night. They ate a dinner of beans and bread, with stream water to wash it down. Then, during the last watch of the night, several hours before dawn, Kelvich roused himself.

"What are you doing?" Zollin said without turning around. "You aren't on watch tonight."

He had been up for over an hour and he sat as still as possible, letting his magic flow out around him. He trusted his magic much more than his eyes and ears, especially in the dark.

"I couldn't sleep," Kelvich said. "Old men don't need much anyway."

"Well, if you're staying up I don't mind getting a little more rest," Zollin said.

"I was hoping we could talk," Kelvich said.

"Hausey wouldn't approve. He doesn't think we take watch seriously enough as it is."

"Let me worry about Commander Hausey," Kelvich added in a whisper. "I'm more concerned about Mansel."

"What's wrong with Mansel?" Zollin asked.

The truth was Zollin was having trouble caring about anyone but Brianna. Commander Hausey was intent on doing his duty and getting Zollin back to Orrock, but all Zollin could think about was Brianna. They hadn't found anyone who had seen the beast, and Zollin was beginning to lose hope. It felt like part of him was dying. He knew Kelvich had been wanting to talk with him for days, but he just didn't want to talk. He was grateful that Mansel seemed more quiet than normal, because at least Zollin didn't have to pretend he was okay around the big warrior.

"Don't you think he's acting strange?"

"He's just worried about Quinn. He probably feels guilty."

"He doesn't act like someone who feels guilty."

"What do you mean?" Zollin asked.

"It's as if he's angry."

"Of course he's angry," Zollin said, exasperated by the conversation already. "Quinn was his mentor. We've been like a family to him."

"But that's just it, he doesn't seem angry at what happened. It's as if he's angry at us for keeping him from returning."

"That makes sense," Zollin said, thinking that he felt the same way about having to break off his search for Brianna.

"No, it doesn't. He doesn't act like he's anxious to save Quinn. He just wants to get back to Lodenhime."

"That doesn't mean anything is wrong with him."

"He stopped drinking; have you noticed that?" Kelvich said.

"No, I guess I haven't, but I wouldn't say that's a bad thing. Perhaps he finally just realized that drinking isn't a good idea for him."

"I wish I could believe that," Kelvich said. "Look, he's very evasive about the details of what happened. I don't think he ever set foot in the Grand City. When I asked him about the trident at the top of the Torr, he blew me off. There is no trident on top of the tower, I just said that to see if he was telling the truth. I think there's more to his story than he's telling us."

"So ask him, if you're concerned about it."

"He won't talk to me," Kelvich said. "I was hoping you might try."

"That's probably not a good idea," Zollin replied. "I'm not really in the right frame of mind to be questioning anyone."

"So you're not worried about this?"

"No, I'm not. I have enough to worry about. I'm leaving everything else up to you and Hausey."

They sat in silence after that. Kelvich felt sorry for Zollin. He knew his world had been turned upside down when Brianna was taken. He was fascinated by the story of Brianna's transformation and wanted more than ever to see the young girl again, but just like Zollin he was starting to lose hope. He had read the partial translations of the scrolls from the Ruins of Ornak, but unfortunately, he had learned nothing useful from them. The scrolls talked of dragons, but there was very little known about where they came from or where they went for long periods of time when no one saw them.

And Kelvich had to admit he was jealous of Zollin's experience with dwarves. He had never met the people under the mountains, although he had read about them in the past. Dwarves were known in other places around the world, where Kelvich had traveled in his efforts to escape the Torr. Still, he had never met a dwarf and badly wanted to see their underground caverns.

When the sun came up they continued their journey. The days were cooler and more comfortable for everyone. Under other circumstances they might have greatly enjoyed being out on the open road together. They had only recently returned to the Weaver's Road, which ran through the heart of Yelsia. They had ridden north of Felson and were now only a few days' hard ride from Orrock. Commander Hausey grew more grim by the day, convinced he would return too late and find the city overrun.

Mansel, as usual, brooded quietly, keeping his own company and riding several paces behind everyone else. It made Kelvich nervous to have Mansel behind him. He felt a rising sense of dread over the last several days. He didn't know if the feeling had something to do with Mansel or if it was because they were riding to war. He knew at some point he would need to stay behind, as he would be no use to anyone in battle. But he hated the thought of leaving the others without first discovering the truth about Mansel.

They stopped at midday to rest the horses near a small farmstead. Mansel went to relieve himself behind the stable, and Kelvich took the opportunity to speak with Zollin.

"This would be a good time to talk to Mansel," Kelvich whispered.

"Oh, please don't bother me with your constant worrying," Zollin said, his aggravation obvious. "If you want to talk to him, go do it yourself."

"Fine, I will," Kelvich said. He was angry, but he quickly got control of his emotions. He understood Zollin's pain and why he had been so short with everyone of late.

Kelvich found Mansel just behind the stable.

"Ah, Mansel, may I have a word?" the sorcerer asked.

"What?" Mansel said gruffly.

"Well, it's just that I had a few questions," Kelvich said. "It just seems a bit odd that you left Quinn in Lodenhime."

"He was captured," Mansel said without a trace of emotion.

"Yes, I understand that, but why didn't you try to rescue him?"

"What are you trying to say?"

"I'm just wondering what's really going on. You don't seem like yourself."

"Keep your nose out of my business or I'll bloody it for you," Mansel warned.

"Mansel, I'm your friend. I only want to help."

"You can't help, you're just an old man who doesn't know when to butt out."

"Why aren't you drinking?" Kelvich said, pressing Mansel for answers. "Why didn't you tell us from the outset that Quinn had been captured? I doubt he would have left you behind."

"I'm warning you . . ."

"To what, stop digging for the truth? Look, I'm on your side, but you've got to level with us."

"I don't have to do anything."

"I think you're lying," Kelvich said. "I think something happened in Lodenhime that you aren't telling us. Is Quinn dead? Why are you so anxious to—"

Kelvich never saw the knife that Mansel had slowly drawn. The thrust was quick, and it seemed to suck all the strength out of Kelvich. At first there was no pain, just surprise. Mansel stared deeply into Kelvich's eyes with a look of deadly intent. He was just about to rip the knife upward when someone shouted.

"There! Look there!"

Mansel looked up, thinking he had been discovered. He let Kelvich fall, the small knife handle protruding from his stomach. He ducked around the stable and saw Zollin and the soldiers looking up into the sky. Mansel glanced up and saw the dragon flying overhead. It was high in the sky and moving at speed, but even from a distance it was obvious that it was the dragon.

Zollin ran and jumped onto his horse. Before anyone could stop him he was galloping away. Mansel ran to meet the soldiers, who were hurrying to catch up. They rode away from the small farm without a word about Kelvich. In the excitement he seemed to have been forgotten.

The elderly sorcerer lay in the grass, his stomach on fire with a searing pain that made it difficult to breathe. It took two hours for the farmer to stumble upon him.

"What happened?" the farmer asked, but Kelvich couldn't answer.

The farmer removed the knife from the sorcerer's stomach. The blade was short, only slightly longer than the farmer's middle finger, but it had done the job. He carried Kelvich inside the farmhouse and tried to make him comfortable. The farmer's wife fussed over him, but there was nothing to be done. Kelvich was slowly bleeding to death.

"Parchment," he told the farmer's wife.

Writing-quality parchment was rare on a rural farm, but after a frantic search she found some. She brought it back and waited.

"Can you write?" Kelvich whispered.

"A little," she said.

"Write this down," he said, panting for breath.

His body cavity was filling with blood, which pressed against his lungs and made it hard to breathe. His mind was growing foggy from lack of blood. He knew his time was short, and his only regret was that Zollin was exposed. He didn't know what Mansel had done, but Kelvich was certain the young warrior had killed Zollin's father. Kelvich had lived a long life, easily three times as long as most men, still time seemed short.

"To Zollin," he began. "Mansel killed me. Don't trust him. I'm proud of you. Don't let death," he was having trouble speaking, and it was taking the farmer's wife a long time to write the words down, "make you bitter. You will wake up the magical world. That is your destiny."

"Give it here," he said weakly.

The farmer took the paper from his wife and held it up. It took Kelvich a full minute to read the words. They were poorly written and his eyes kept losing focus. He was dying and he knew it. He was ready for it. Ready for the pain to end. The pain, growing worse every minute, was threatening to rob him of the capacity to finish his task, but the old sorcerer was determined. The farmer's wife dipped the quill in their small supply of ink and handed it to him. His hand shook as he signed the paper.

"You have to take it to Zollin," he said. "He's a wizard. Take it to Zollin."

"We will, you have my word on it," said the farmer.

Kelvich lay back then. He had done all he could hope to do. The world grew dim, and he could see the farmer and his wife fussing over him, but he no longer cared. There was a light shining on him from somewhere that he couldn't see. His body had grown cold, but the light was warm and inviting. He wanted to go to the light, to let it shine on him, to feel its warmth always. Nothing else mattered. He let the world grow dark around him.

He died peacefully despite the pain. His eyes were open and his body composed, but he was clearly dead. His features that had always been so animated, were now waxy. His eyes lost all their vibrancy and grew dull.

"What shall we do with him?" the farmer's wife asked.

"We'll bury him," the farmer replied.

"And the note?"

"We'll send it west with the next traveler that passes by."

"But you promised him you'd deliver the message," she insisted.

"And I'll send it along, but I can't leave the farm. There's work to be done."

They folded the note and sealed it with candle wax. The farmer's wife wrote Zollin's name on the paper and set it on the windowsill by the door. The farmer dug a grave and then returned to his fields. The farmer's wife fixed supper and shortly before they ate, together they laid Kelvich in the ground and buried him.

Chapter 26

Zollin slapped his horse with the reins to coax as much speed as he could out of her. It was dangerous, he knew, but in that moment all he was thinking about was Brianna. He strained to see the dragon but there was no sign of Brianna.

"Wait!" he screamed, but the dragon was too high to hear his voice.

Then his horse stumbled and Zollin was thrown though the air. He reacted magically on instinct, sending up a shield to protect his body and levitating himself higher into the air. The fall only lasted one terrifying moment. He came floating down on his feet and turned to see Lilly, Brianna's beloved horse. She was lying on the ground, neighing in agony. The horse's right foreleg was broken and lay at an odd angle. Zollin felt a sense of hopelessness. The poor beast was dying because Zollin had rushed after the dragon and wasn't paying attention to where they were going. He'd ridden far from the Weaver's Road, and neither it nor the farm they'd just recently stopped at were in sight.

Zollin knew that a horse with a broken leg would never be able to hold a rider again. It would be unable to pull a wagon or a plow. It would spend weeks in pain and then become a cripple. The humane thing would be to put the horse down, but Zollin refused to even think of that. He had won Lilly from a traveling illusionist, and the aging mare had carried Brianna when they fled Tranaugh Shire. In his mind, as long as he had Lilly, there was still hope that he might find Brianna. He knelt by the horse's head.

"It's going to be okay," he said in a soothing voice.

He immediately pushed feelings of peace and rest toward the horse with his mind. At the same time he let his magic flow into the animal's leg. He felt the bone, broken and splintered. It was beyond hope of being set by traditional methods, but in moments Zollin was hard at work repairing the damage. There was muscle damage and torn tendons and ligaments, which all took time to heal. He was almost finished when he heard the other horses cantering toward him. He finished his work without looking up, his magic churning inside him. He felt a deep sense of hopelessness and white-hot anger that was boiling just beneath the surface. His magic felt like a caged beast just waiting to be released. It took all of his control and concentration to hold himself together.

"If your horse's leg is broken," said one of the knights who had come with Commander Hausey, "you should put it out of its misery."

"Zollin, are you okay?" Hausey asked.

"I'm fine," he said, standing up.

He had finished healing the animal and she, too, scrambled to her feet. Zollin rubbed Lilly's nose and looked up at the knight on his horse.

"The horse is fine, too, thanks," he said in an icy tone.

"It seems the dragon is headed in the same direction we are," said Hausey. "That is good news, at least."

"Good news?" Zollin said. "Did you see Brianna with the dragon?"

"No, but that doesn't mean she wasn't. The beast was so high in the air, it was hard to make out much detail," Hausey said.

Zollin knew the hardened soldier was trying to be positive for his sake, but the effort fell short.

"No, she isn't with the dragon, which probably means she's dead," said Zollin, his eyes stinging with tears. "My only course of action left is to avenge her death."

"Well, let's push on," said Hausey. "The dragon might be headed for Orrock."

Zollin doubted it, but he kept his thoughts to himself. The last thing he wanted was to go to the King and be pressured into fighting a battle he had no desire to be involved with. But he was determined to follow the dragon: it was the only link he had left to Brianna.

"Is your horse suitable to ride?" asked one of the other knights.

"Yes," Zollin said, as he swung up into the saddle. The trauma Lilly had suffered with her leg had left her skittish, but the leg was completely healed. She circled nervously as Zollin settled into the saddle, and he took control of the horse's reins.

"Right then, I guess we're ready," Hausey said.

Zollin should have noticed that neither Mansel or Kelvich was with the soldiers, but his fear for Brianna blinded him. He rode along behind the soldiers and was reminded of leaving Tranaugh Shire. That had been a cold day, and he'd just watched his best friend die. The pain of that memory loomed up again, and he couldn't stop the tears that streaked silently down his cheeks. Now Brianna was gone, and he knew he had to face that fact. There was nothing else he could do. He would probably never know what happened to her, but he would spend the rest of his life finding out.

Mansel joined the group silently, riding up behind Zollin and falling in without a word. He'd expected Zollin to ask about Kelvich, and he had a lie ready, but Zollin didn't even look up.

They rode late into the night, and Mansel was given first watch. Zollin didn't speak or eat; he just saw to his horse and then rolled himself in a blanket. The other knights were busy fixing something to eat when Hausey approached Mansel.

"Have you seen Kelvich?" the commander asked him. "We rode away from the farm so quickly, I'm afraid he got separated from us."

"No, he stayed behind," Mansel said. "That's why I was late catching up. I tried to change his mind but he said he never had plans to go to Orrock with us. He's not a warrior."

"No, I suppose not," Hausey said, "although his healing skills would surely have been an asset."

"Zollin can heal anyone," Mansel said. "I wouldn't worry about the old man. He'll be fine."

Hausey didn't question Mansel further. The night passed without incident, and Zollin was the first one ready to ride at dawn the next day. The others were tired from their hard journey, but Zollin felt as hollow as a reed. His body ached from lack of rest and sleeping on the ground night after night. Exhaustion had become a familiar state, but he was also crushed emotionally. He didn't speak and rarely made eye contact; he just rode along with the others, occasionally nibbling some stale bread or sipping water from his canteen.

Mansel stayed beside him, as quiet as a shadow. The big warrior was frustrated by the delay; all he could think about was getting Zollin back to Lodenhime. He hoped that this sad turn of events would make his task easier. Once they dealt with this invasion, he would take Zollin south, and Gwendolyn would give him his reward. The thought of being with the witch made his skin tingle and his head light. It was a pleasant fantasy, and even though he had no proof that Gwendolyn would reward him by becoming his lover, in his foggy mind that was the only way he imagined she could respond.

Zollin was the most powerful person Mansel had ever seen, and he could not imagine a greater gift being given to his Queen. He felt sorry that he had thrown Quinn overboard to drown in the Great Sea. He felt guilty for having stabbed Kelvich, too, but he considered both these to be necessary steps to get what he wanted. It was more than just base desire: Mansel felt he deserved Gwendolyn, and the more he thought about her, the more he felt like she was his destiny. He still saw the lonely woman by the sea when he tried to imagine what Gwendolyn looked like. His heart ached when he saw the woman even though he could not remember who she was or why he couldn't get her out of his mind.

They rode hard all day, not even stopping to rest the horses, and it was almost midnight when they finally saw Orrock in the distance. There was very little to be seen; the city seemed like a dark shadow.

"Where is the invading army?" Zollin asked. It was the first time he had spoken since healing his horse.

"I don't know," Hausey said. "King Felix must have found a way to delay it."

They were pushing their horses along the Weaver's Road when a savage cry rang out, and four men rushed forward. They had pikes with hooks that they used to pull the knights from their horses. Zollin sat on his horse, watching Hausey and his knights struggling. He heard the crunch of metal and bone as the knights fell off their horses. Mansel drew his sword beside Zollin, but neither attacked. They sat watching, and then the arrows came. Two thick bolts, racing toward them, one aimed at Zollin, the other at Mansel. Zollin raised his hand and both projectiles bounced back after hitting his invisible shield.

"Crossbows," Mansel said calmly.

"That means we have a minute or so before they can reload."

"More than enough time," Mansel said, smiling wickedly.

Zollin sent a ball of fire shooting into the air, which lit the entire area in bright light. There were half a dozen horses, all tied to single tree. The ambushers had made a cold camp, and two men were busy trying to reload their crossbows. They were bent over, with one foot in the stirrup of their weapon as they pulled the thick cord up toward the nut. They had stopped and looked around when Zollin's fireball lit up the sky, but quickly they realized that they needed to reload their weapons quickly, before the men they were ambushing turned on them.

Mansel didn't hesitate. He kicked his horse into action and charged at the two crossbowmen. One dropped his bow and ran for his own horse. The other got his weapon loaded and raised just in the nick of time, but his nerves got the best of him, and his shot went wide. The bolt flew harmlessly past Mansel, who brought his sword down on the crossbowman's shoulder as he galloped past the man. The blade cut deep and sent blood arcing up into the air. As Mansel turned his horse, Zollin looked back at the knights who had been pulled off their horses. They were well armored, which protected them from the weapons of their attackers, but it also made it difficult for them to get back onto their feet. The assailants had closed in and were hacking at the knights with their pikes. Zollin levitated the ambushers into the air. The men were totally surprised and dropped their weapons as they shouted in fear.

Zollin tossed them away from the knights the way a bored child might toss dolls.

"Get up, Hausey!" Zollin shouted. "Let's see how they like a fair fight. Mansel, let them be."

Mansel was anxious to renew his attack, but he angled away from the ambushers. He wanted to see how the knights would fight, and although he hated to move away from the action, he knew better than to cross Zollin. He reined in his horse and sat watching.

Hausey was the first on his feet. He moved stiffly, drawing his broadsword and taking a defensive stance while his comrades struggled to get up. The ambushers were terrified. It was obvious that they were Oslian soldiers and should have been familiar with displays of magic, but they had not anticipated Zollin's attack. Being lifted into the air had terrified them and they weren't anxious to rejoin the fight. Two of the men broke and ran.

"Mansel!" Zollin said, which was all it took to get the big warrior moving.

He was like an attack dog let off his chain, kicking his horse into action and screaming a battle cry as he rode forward. His bloody sword was held high in the air as he raced toward the first deserter. He leaned forward and swung his menacing weapon in a level slash that chopped cleanly through the man's neck. The head flew away from the body, which ran on for several more steps before crashing to the earth. The other man had angled away from his fleeing companion and when Mansel's horse veered in his direction the man dropped to the ground. Mansel rose straight for him, trampling the man under his horse's hooves so that blood splashed up on the animal's belly.

One of the knights was injured in the fall and couldn't get to his feet. The other two were helping him when the last of the four assailants rushed toward Hausey. They had short swords and daggers, but the commander was a veteran fighter. He moved quickly to the right and thrust his broadsword at the nearest attacker. The man lurched back, and Hausey quickly spun around and slammed his sword into the other attacker's shoulder. The blade stuck fast in bone, and when the man scrambled backward Hausey lost his grip on the sword. The first attacker moved forward again, bringing his sword around in a vicious slash that would have gutted Hausey, but the blade couldn't penetrate the commander's mail coat. Hausey punched the attacker with a straight, right-handed blow to the nose that crushed cartilage and bone. Blood poured from the man's nostrils, and he dropped his sword as he staggered back, holding his face. Hausey drew his own dagger and swung it at the man's face. The attacker raised his hand in a defensive reflex that cost him three fingers. The attacker fell to the ground in shock, and Hausey dropped to one knee as he slammed his dagger into the man's heart.

The other attacker was screaming in pain as he writhed on the ground, desperate to get the sword out of his shoulder. He had dropped both of his weapons, and Hausey put his booted foot on the man's head before wrenching his broadsword free. The man passed out from the pain, and Hausey sliced open his throat in one efficient move with his dagger.

"Neatly done," Zollin said.

"Thanks for the assistance," the commander replied.

Mansel came riding up, wiping a cloth across his blade. It was the same sword Zollin had crafted using the steel links of chain the soldiers in the Great Valley had used to detain them. It was the one possession Mansel treasured. Everything else could be replaced, but not the sword. He made sure that it was well maintained and razor sharp.

Zollin helped the injured knight onto his horse. The knight refused Zollin's offer to heal him, insisting that his leg was sore but not broken. Zollin levitated the knight into the saddle, and everyone else got ready to finish their journey.

"Is there any need to search them?" one of the knights asked Hausey.

"No, they're obviously a scouting unit. Let's get moving. Our orders were clear: we need to get Zollin to King Felix."

They rode for another hour before finally reaching the main gate. It was closed, of course, and the soldiers guarding it were wary, but one recognized Commander Hausey and they were allowed inside.

"Where is King Felix?" Hausey asked one of the guards.

"He's in the field," the man explained. "He took the whole army and marched south."

"We need fresh mounts, then, and supplies," he ordered. "We'll ride to join him at dawn."

* * *

For three days there was a stalemate. Offendorl held his forces in check, and King Felix was content to hold his position. Then one of the many scouts sent out to find people who had seen the dragon returned with an old man.

"You've seen the dragon?" Offendorl asked him.

"No, but I've seen the Priestess," said the man.

"Who is the Priestess?"

"She's the one who warned our village that the dragon was coming. Most folks didn't believe her, but I did. She had wild hair and her clothes were all singed. She weren't acting, that I could see right away. Most folks in my village thought the rumors weren't true, but the Priestess made a believer out of me. I left Tucker Hill that same day and from what I heard the dragon burned it to the ground that very night."

"What did the Priestess tell you?" Offendorl asked.

"She said that the dragon, Bartoom she called it, wanted our gold and that if we would leave all our gold it would spare our village. I didn't have any gold so I just left. Better safe than sorry I always say."

"Bartoom," Offendorl said, trying out the sound of the word. "Bartoom? Are you sure that's what she called it?"

"Of course I'm sure," the old man said. "I've lost a lot of things but my memory is just fine. To be honest, she gave me a fright with her spooky-looking eyes. She had no emotion, just dreadful words, and she spoke in a strange voice. I'll remember it to my dying day."

"Get him food, drink, whatever he wants," Offendorl told the soldiers who had found the man.

He had hurried back to his wagon after that. The golden helmet was almost complete. He drank more wine and felt the warmth of the wine spread through his body and give him strength. Then he focused on the lead that his servants had brought to him. He could move his mind quickly down into the metal and feel the spinning essence of it. Soon the lead seemed to blur, then melt, and finally it transformed. The dark, dull lead was now bright, gleaming gold.

Once Offendorl had transmuted the lead into gold, he had to stop and rest. He wasn't as strong as he once had been. His knowledge was greater than ever before, and that is what always separated him from the other wizards of the Torr. In small bursts he could summon great power that no one could fathom, but his physical body simply couldn't hold up to the stress of wielding such power for long. But he'd learned to deal with his limitations and how to position himself so that only his strength was visible.

He drank more wine and ate again. He was in no hurry; the Yelsian army posed no threat at the moment. The reports of casualties from the bombardment were grievous but not alarming. They had lost over two hundred men, although many of those were reported as missing, and Offendorl guessed they were deserters. Once he felt strong again, he used his magic to fashion the gold he had transmuted into a crown-like helmet. It was large enough to cover only his skull, but it was still very heavy, and he knew he would be able to wear the helmet for only short periods of time. It only took moments to inscribe the dragon's name into the gold. Then, even though he was tired and hungry, he put on a leather coif to give his head some protection from the heavy gold helmet. He had to boost his strength with magic, levitating the hemet rather than just lifting it up. When the helmet came down on Offendorl's head, he felt a jolt as his magic rose up and joined the golden crown. Offendorl had collected many magical objects, but he'd never discovered how to create one. Now he could feel his magic join with the helmet crown, and his mind seemed sharper somehow.

Offendorl sent out his summons to the dragon. He had felt it approaching for days, but it had not come within sight. It moved mainly at night now, hunting and flying high overhead where Offendorl guessed it could see the army camp. Now he called the beast by name, pushing out the mental commands with his magic to give them power.

He felt the dragon moving, it was flying now, hungry and angry, but submitting to Offendorl's will just the same. It would be here soon, he thought. It was close, and now he could understand the dragon's thoughts. They were like mental images, streaming from the helmet into his brain. He saw the countryside passing beneath him, felt the ecstasy of flight and the anguish of the beast's loss of will.

Offendorl tried to stand up, but the weight of the crown was just too much. The muscles in the ancient wizard's neck stood out like taunt ropes under the weight of the helmet. He wanted to take it off, but he didn't want to lose his connection with the dragon. He called to his servants, who hurried into the wagon wordlessly.

"Send for the generals," Offendorl said through gritted teeth. "Tell them to prepare their troops."

How the mute servants would communicate that message was not Offendorl's concern. He was sending the dragon along the Tillamook River to spy on the enemy encampment. Things were finally turning in his favor, he thought. Then he sent the mental command to the dragon to attack the Yelsian army.

Chapter 27

The dragon had been cautiously moving closer to the source of the voice in his head. Since leaving the mountains and the girl who was more than just a girl—the dragon thought of her as dragonkind—he had flown south. He could feel the wizard who called to him; he was different from the one who had hunted him far into the northern highlands. This wizard spoke with authority, and there was a sense of arrogance that reminded the dragon of its masters from ancient times.

When the beast guessed it was near enough to the wizard, it landed, waiting for nightfall and hiding during the day. The wizard was with a large army that, fortunately enough for the dragon, had scared the local inhabitants away. When night fell, the dragon flew over the army's camp, searching for the wizard whose voice the beast couldn't get out of its head. The dragon was torn between two intense desires: on one hand the dragon wanted to destroy the wizard and return to freedom. Not that freedom had been all that great—it had been hounded and almost killed—but it hated the wizard who wanted to control it just as much it hated as the wizard who was trying to kill it. But the dragon also wanted to give in; the voice was so alluring and it never seemed to stop. The idea of giving up the fight and giving in to the voice was intoxicating.

For two days the beast had swung back and forth like a pendulum between the desire to kill and the desire to give in. Then, something changed. The voice, which had always been enticing, suddenly became undeniable. The dragon knew immediately that the wizard had discovered its name. He could no longer help but obey the voice of the wizard. It had been preparing to fly over the army camp again, but now the voice was ordering it to turn toward the river. There was another army ensconced there, and the voice compelled the dragon to approach it. The sky was bright with stars but the beast couldn't change that. It circled the second army's camp, which was divided into three parts. Nearest the river were large wooden devices with mounds of stone beside them. Up a slight hill were the tents and cooking fires of the army, and then further out from this was a line of soldiers standing stiffly, facing into the darkness.

The dragon was angry, but the voice in its mind now had total control. The beast dove toward the river. Once it was close enough, it breathed fire onto the wooden structures. It was easy work: the wood was like kindling and caught fire immediately. There were five of the structures and in moments they were all ablaze, casting a dancing, yellow light out over the river and toward the camp. Soldiers were rushing toward the fires, but they had no way to get water up to the top of the structures. Then the dragon revealed himself fully. He dove toward the army and carved a blazing trail of death through the men crowded below. It took only one pass to scatter the army. Humans fear what they cannot see, and Bartoom the dragon was hiding in the thick, black smoke from the burning trebuchets. Like a viper the dragon would strike, diving down and snatching up a soldier in each talon and one in its gaping mouth. Then it would climb back up into the sky and drop the soldiers like bombs onto any massed group of soldiers.

The delicious thrill of battle was hampered by the voice in the dragon's head. It was constantly directing the beast, which had no choice but to obey. The army below was scattering, and the beast was called south to the wizard's army, but as it flew it saw that the wizard's soldiers were hurrying from their camp to attack the other army.

The voice told the dragon to land, and it set down lightly near a large wagon. The door of the wagon opened and the wizard appeared. He was old, his skin wrinkled and his head bowed by the weight of the golden crown that it was using to control the dragon. The wizard made his way slowly down the steps before looking up at the beast. The dragon wanted to destroy the wizard. Its fury was so intense its vision was turning red.

"You want to kill me, eh?" the wizard said, his voice echoing in the dragon's mind so loud it was like the tolling of a giant brass bell.

"Well, that won't do, not at all," the wizard said. "I am your master now. We have much work to do, but you will find that I am not a harsh task master. Make your lair here, with me. It is time to restore order to these lands."

The dragon stalked around the wizard and then blew a fiery gout of flame along the ground, burning away the vegetation. It would have to sleep in the dirt like an animal, the dragon thought, shame making the human flesh in its stomach rise up and almost gag the beast.

"Good," said the wizard. "Now rest. Do not move until I summon you."

The dragon curled up on the ground, its black scales gleaming, its golden eyes shining as brightly as the stars overhead. It couldn't move. It would lie there until it died of dehydration unless the wizard with the crown freed it. But it watched the old wizard's every move, waiting, biding its time to break free and escape, perhaps exacting revenge along the way.

* * *

The battle began, not against the enemy or the dragon that was burning his precious trebuchets, but just to control his own men. King Felix had known that war was coming. He had known that his harboring Zollin would incite the Torr to stir up the other kingdoms against him. But the opportunity was just too great; no one had resisted the Torr in centuries. The treaty had been necessary just to keep the Five Kingdoms from tearing each other apart. When the Kingdoms were fighting, raiders pillaged unchecked, and no one prospered; yet consolidating all magical power in the Torr had given the wizards too much control. Felix remembered his father's caution, wrestling over every decision, not to determine what was best for his kingdom, but what would keep him out of the Torr's bad graces.

Now he had a chance to restore the balance of power. King Felix recognized that his son Simmeron had been greedy for the throne, but he couldn't fault the boy for trying to harness Zollin's power. Unfortunately, Simmeron had also been trying to kill Felix, but that had been dealt with. Simmeron was under control and now Zollin, too, was almost completely in Felix's control. No, he thought, control isn't the right word, he didn't want to control Zollin, but he did want the boy on his side. He wanted to get full use of Zollin's ability, to have someone on his side who didn't cower in fear at the sight of the other Torr wizards.

Regardless, all his plans were for nothing if he didn't survive this battle. Felix knew Offendorl was behind the dragon's attacks. In all likelihood, the Master of the Torr had sent the dragon to raze the Yelsian villages in the first place. The summons to the Council of Kings, which Felix had ignored, hinted at the dragon's presence as the cause for the council. It wasn't surprising to see the beast doing Offendorl's dirty work now.

"My lord," said General Yinnis, head of the Boar Legion, which built and maintained the   in the King's Army's engineering projects, such as the trebuchets and temporary bridges used to move troops across the Tillamook River. He came rushing to King Felix to give his report. "It is too late to save the trebuchets."

"What of the bridges?" King Felix asked. "We need to fall back beyond the river."

"The bridges are intact, my lord."

"Good, organize a retreat. We've got to get control of this situation. I'm sure the wizard's army will be marching down on us at any moment. That's the only reason he would have called off his dragon."

"I'll see to it personally, my King," the soldier said, snapping a salute before rushing away.

Felix hurried over to where two servants were holding the King's charger. The beast was a massive shire horse, a breed normally used for pulling rather than riding, but this particular line of horses had been bred specifically for war. It wasn't as fast as most horses used as cavalry mounts, but it had no trouble carrying the King in full battle armor while being covered with heavy metal plating itself. The King normally stayed well back from the fighting to ensure that he was never in danger, but the big shire horses were bred specifically to carry the royal family away from an attack unscathed. The horses were trained for war, so fire and even the presence of a dragon didn't make the horse skittish. The servants had saddled the horse and fitted armor over the horse's head, withers, and rump.

The King had thrown on his chain mail but couldn't wait for his servants to dress him in full armor. He went over to the horse and used a set of three wooden steps to mount.

"Here we go again, Specter," said the King, patting the horse's brawny neck.

"You men, gather what you can and head for the river," he told the servants. "Take what we need, nothing else."

"Yes, sire," they replied.

King Felix rode to the crest of the hill, where the scouts were positioned. The burning trebuchets were lighting up the field behind them and making it even more difficult to see across the dark expanse toward the invading army.

"Any sign of the enemy?" King Felix called.

"No, sire," said one of the scouts.

The King rode his massive horse along the line and ordered his scouts to keep their shields raised. He expected a volley of arrows at any moment and he strained his eyes in search of any sign of movement.

A group of Felix's commanders came galloping up the hill and reined in their horses beside the King.

"You are too close to the front, my lord," said one of the knights, a tall man with thick blond curls hanging from his battle helm. His name was Corlis of Osis City.

They were all noblemen who served the King as generals and commanders. Generals were tacticians, one serving each legion of the King's Army. Commanders usually oversaw smaller groups and actively led their troops in battle. They all wore armor of some type and all carried lances with their legion's identifying emblem.

"Never mind where I am, sir," Felix said. "What is the state of our army?"

"We have all the troops except for the scouts heading across the river," General Sals said. He was the third son of Duke Shupor and commanded the Fox Legion.

"Our bridges are holding, sire," said General Yinnis. "The trebuchets are a total loss but we still have ships that can ferry you back to Orrock."

"I expected to be pushed back at some point," King Felix said. "Offendorl is no fool. At least we held them up these last three days. I want the scouts ready to fall back on my command, and let's get another century ready to cover their retreat. They can then commence a fighting retreat. I also want the bridges ready to burn. I doubt Offendorl would be so foolish as to send his troops onto our bridges, but it's worth a try."

"I volunteer the Heavy Horse to cover the scouts' retreat," Corlis said in a superior tone.

"No, if something happens to our bridges I want the cavalry on our side of the Tillamook," King Felix said. "What legion are these men from?" he said, indicating the scouts.

"They are Eagles," said General Tolis.

"Fine," said King Felix, "get another century of your Eagles up here to cover their withdrawal, Tolis. General Yinnis, see to the bridges. I'll cross over and oversee the retreat back to Orrock myself."

General Yinnis and General Tolis both saluted and then galloped away.

"Sire," said General Sals. "If the dragon attacks again, you'll be exposed. We can't protect you from fire."

"No, you can't, but I'll still cross over and lead our troops back. They need to see this as a strategic maneuver, not a military defeat."

"The Orrock Heavy Horse will protect you, my liege," said Corlis.

Felix bit back the angry retort that almost jumped out of his lips. The last thing he wanted was to take his anger out on a capable commander. They would need everyone at their best if they were going to face the dragon. Felix didn't take it as a good sign that the beast had shown up and attacked his army. He needed Zollin, but what if the boy had been killed by the dragon? They were lost against Offendorl and his army without a wizard of their own. Even so, those fears couldn't play a part in how he made decisions now, or in how he treated his men.

"No, that isn't necessary," Felix said. "The Heavy Horse should pull back to Orrock with the rest of the army. The light cavalry can guard our retreat, and the Royal Guard will accompany me at all times. Gentlemen, make no mistake: we are at war. So far we've done little to check the enemy's progress into our kingdom. But we will stop them at Orrock, one way or another."

Just then a familiar whistling sound was heard, and General Sals screamed to the troops around him.

"Arrows!" he shouted, raising his shield to cover King Felix.

Most of the arrows flew past them, but some found their marks. The scouts had been ready with their shields held above their heads to protect them from the falling projectiles. They dropped to a squatting position so that the shields covered most of their bodies. A few scouts were hit with arrows, but they were mostly superficial wounds in their legs or feet.

Corlis raised his own shield in an effort to protect the King, but his horse was hit with an arrow and it reared suddenly, throwing the young commander from the saddle and charging away, neighing in pain.

King Felix waited for the arrows to fall, which took only a moment. The projectiles sounded like demonic hailstones, but once that volley was over the King and General Sals kicked their horses into action, each riding in a different direction down the line of scouts who were spread out thirty paces apart. Both riders shouted orders for the soldiers to pull back and join their respective leader.

The scouts didn't need to be told twice; they sprinted down the hill in the direction of either the King or General Sals. When the telltale whistle of a second volley was heard, the men dropped to their knees and raised their shields. King Felix raised his own shield, but had to trust the chain mail to protect his thighs and legs. Several arrows hit him, two on his shield and one on his foot, punching through the stirrup and into his boot, gouging through the flesh below his ankle bone. The pain was spectacular, and King Felix cried out, but he managed to keep from falling off his horse.

Despite the danger several of the scouts ran to their king. One was killed when an arrow tore through his neck. Several more arrows hit the King's horse, but the heavy plate armor protected it from harm.

"Are you hurt, sire?" shouted one of the troops.

"Damn arrow got my boot," Felix shouted back. "I'm fine. We have to form a shield wall. We'll move slowly back down the hill, but we have to be able to withstand their initial attack."

As the scouts moved into position in front of King Felix, they began to hear the screams of the invading army. Their commanders had sent them forward, and the men were running flat out, planning to use their momentum to break down the defenders' shield walls. Felix looked over and saw that General Sals had formed a shield wall of his own. They would move down the hill and converge at the bridges that the Boar Legion had constructed.

Fear was rattling its icy breath on the back of King Felix's neck, but he also felt the pride of knowing that the men around him were willing to fight. It made him proud that General Sals had acted in the same manner that the King had done, even without any orders. He knew that his officers were well trained. It was true that some were young and inexperienced, like Corlis, Commander of the Orrock Heavy Horse, but there was something to be said for a hungry fighter looking forward to his first taste of glory.

Many of the leaders of the King's Army were noble born and appointed as much for their family connections as for their ability in the field, but most had fought the Skellmarians who trickled out of the mountains to attack settlements in the Great Valley, or Shirtac raiders who sailed their long ships down from the northern tundra and pillaged along the western coast of Yelsia. Felix hoped that experience would give them an edge in this battle and the ones to come.

The first invaders crested the hill and renewed their battle cry when they saw the Yelsians. King Felix knew that at any time his Royal Guard would arrive to whisk him away, but he needed to stay and support the fifty or so scouts who were slowly retreating down the hill. He drew his sword and shouted to his men.

"Hold that wall! Here they come."

The first few soldiers threw themselves against the shields of the Yelsians. The scouts combined their strength and held the wall firm. The attackers were knocked back and then cut down.

When the invaders rushed down in groups, the defense became more difficult. The scouts did their best to hold their shields together, but the weight and momentum of the invaders running into them at full speed knocked several backwards, and the wall quickly dissolved.

The melee that ensued could have been disastrous, but King Felix charged forward on his giant horse. He struck out with his sword a few times, but the real danger was Specter's thrashing hooves. No one could stand against the mighty horse in his plate armor. Felix directed him in a circle around his small band of scouts. Several of the soldiers had been wounded or killed, but the space created by King Felix's charge gave them time to reassemble. They set up their shield wall again just as Felix circled behind them. There were too many invaders for the ones cresting the hill to charge through. They had to depend on their superior numbers to push down the wall of shields the Yelsians were using to defend themselves, and it took almost three minutes before the sheer number of invaders gave them the strength to push back the shield wall.

King Felix was calling out orders from the back of his massive horse. He was calling the scouts into a steady retreat. They moved slowly down the gently sloping hill. As they withdrew, the light from the burning trebuchets increased. The invaders were just about to flank them when arrows went whistling over King Felix's head and fell among the invaders. The volley, fired by Yelsian archers shooting from the river bank, was just enough to give the invaders pause once again, as the battle lust that had sent them charging down the hill evaporated and the terror of death settled over them.

The Royal Guard charged up the hill and surrounded the King, but he sent them to reinforce the scouts' shield wall. The Royal Guard were elite fighters, both with short swords and throwing knives, but they didn't carry shields. Instead they ranged behind the scouts and used their weapons to cut down the invaders by thrusting their swords over the scouts' shields. It was a grueling effort, and the invaders were slowly overwhelming the scouts even though their attack was unorganized.

King Felix could hear the enemy commanders shouting orders and trying to arrange the invading troops into a shield wall of their own, but then a full century of foot soldiers from the Eagle Legion rushed forward with their spears leveled at the invaders. The long reach of the spears caused the invaders to stop their push onto the shield wall of the scouts.

"My lord," called General Tolis as he rode toward King Felix. "We shall hold them here; please begin your retreat."

The space the Eagle soldiers made was enough to allow the scouts and Royal Guard to retreat back with King Felix. He led them several hundred yards closer to the river until they could feel the heat from the burning trebuchets at their backs, then he ordered them to renew their shield wall. There were fewer than thirty scouts left, but it would be enough to cover the retreat of the Eagles.

"General Tolis!" Felix shouted. "Begin your withdrawal."

The General shouted orders, and his men moved with quick efficiency. The invaders were darting forward now, trying to find a gap in the line of soldiers. Another volley of arrows arced over the line, and once again the invaders were scattered in panic. As the Eagle troops moved back, King Felix looked to the top of the hill. The soldiers there were massing for a concerted push. The King realized he needed to get his men down the hill and across the bridge as quickly as possible.

"Move, General!" he shouted at Tolis.

King Felix looked over to where General Sals had been and saw that the other group of scouts were now surrounded. General Sals was nowhere to be seen, but Corlis had the scouts formed up in a circle that was fighting ferociously. But they weren't moving down the hill, and they had no avenue of escape. Felix turned toward his archers near the wooden bridges.

"Archers!" he shouted. "To me, archers. To your King!"

The archers jogged forward. Their commander, an older man named Verhok, came with them.

"Verhok, can you clear a path for those soldiers to join us?" King Felix asked.

The veteran archer nodded and called for several of his men by name. They lined up and fired their arrows in rapid succession, each one hitting its mark. King Felix made a mental note to reward each of the talented archers when time permitted.

Felix stood in his stirrups and waved his arms as he called to Commander Corlis.

"Lead them this way, Corlis!" he shouted. "We'll cover you."

The young commander met Felix's gaze and then began shouting at the scouts around him. They broke from their position and ran toward the King. The archers picked off several of their attackers and over half of the dwindling group survived the run, including Commander Corlis.

"Where is General Sals?" Felix called to him.

"He was cut down in the initial charge," Corlis shouted back.

319

Felix nodded grimly. There was no reason to continue the fight now. He needed to move his troops back quickly. The archers went first, resuming their position beside the bridge. They were followed by the scouts led by Commander Corlis. Then King Felix's group of scouts and Royal Guard joined with the remaining soldiers from Eagle Legion and moved slowly back toward the bridge. The archers fired volley after volley, but most of the invaders had their shields up now and the rain of arrows had little effect.

Once the soldiers reached the bridge the archers crossed over first. The battle became fierce once the invaders saw their enemy escaping. They pressed in hotly, their timidity cast aside. The Royal Guard surrounded King Felix and General Tolis, who were shouting orders. Then arrows came raining down from the invader's archers, forcing King Felix to retreat back over the bridge. Over half of the troops on the south side of the Tillamook River died in the fighting. The other half sprinted across the bridge then turned to hold the crossing against the enemy fighters who were crowding across the wooden structure. There was a wide drawbridge close to Orrock, but it had been raised and the draw lines severed, so that the bridge couldn't be lowered onto the stone pilings. The bridge the soldiers now defended was a temporary structure, and as soon as his troops were across, King Felix order the bridge to be fired.

Arrows were lit with torches and then shot into the planks of the bridge. The Boar Legion had soaked the bridge in oil as they crossed, so when the flaming arrows hit, the fire spread rapidly. At least fifty enemy soldiers were wounded or killed by the fire, while King Felix completed his retreat.

The army was half a day's ride west of Orrock, but the army would march through the night. It was imperative that they reach the safety of Orrock's walls before the invaders crossed the river and caught up to them.

King Felix had left the Wolf Legion, commanded by General Griggs, to man Orrock's defenses and to see that the city was prepared in case of a siege. He only hoped that General Griggs had everything ready for their return. Griggs was a capable leader, but more suited for administration that military strategy, which was why King Felix had left his legion in reserve.

"What are your orders, my King?" asked General Yinnis.

"See to our retreat back to Orrock," Felix ordered, wiping the sweat from his brow and then taking a long drink from his canteen. We must arrive before dawn. Get these troops moving before Offendorl finds a way across the river and cuts us off.

"But Sire, you are wounded. Surely you need medical care."

"It's nothing that can't wait. Our priority is getting these troops moving. We can rest once we get into the castle. Am I making myself clear?"

"Yes, my lord," said Yinnis.

"And, General, give Commander Corlis temporary command of the Fox Legion."

"Is General Sals dead then, sir?"

"I'm afraid so," said King Felix.

The King saw a wave of emotion pass across Yinnis's face, but the general nodded and rode away to oversee the retreat. Many of the officers in the King's Army were friends. Their bonds stemmed not only from fighting side by side, but also because they were all the youngest children of noble families and understood one another. General Yinnis had obviously been grieved by the news that General Sals had been killed, yet he did his duty. King Felix and his officers knew there would be time for grief once the invasion had been turned back.

Felix took another drink and then turned his horse. He was surrounded by Royal Guardsmen who had found horses somewhere. The King didn't question their methods. The Royal Guard had the right to commandeer whatever they needed to protect the King.

"Gentlemen," King Felix said to his men, "let's ride."

They galloped away, following a path that angled away from the river but toward Orrock. The pain in Felix's foot grew worse as they rode. In the battle, he hadn't had time to think about the wound, but in the tedium of their ride through the night, the pain grew so bad it was all he could think about. His boot was leaking blood, but not as fast as it was filling his boot. The foot was swelling, and every jolt his horse made sent a spasm of pain up his leg. He tried propping his foot across the horse's back but couldn't find a position on the big animal that was comfortable. As the night wore on, hours in the saddle and lack of sleep made his whole body ache. His eyes felt gritty and his stomach soured. He longed for a bottle of wine and a soft bed, but his entire kingdom was at stake, so he forced himself to keep riding. It was the only option he had.

Chapter 28

Quinn didn't complain, even though his body ached so bad he couldn't hold down food while they were riding. Still, he rode as long as there was daylight. Zollin was moving toward Orrock, which meant he wasn't going south with Mansel, so Quinn allowed Miriam to dictate their pace. She nursed him as often as she could. When they made camp she did everything, from rubbing down their horses to starting the fire and cooking their dinner. The first night they had stayed at a small inn, but after getting separate rooms, they both decided that they would prefer to camp so that Miriam could keep a closer eye on Quinn. They also enjoyed the privacy.

The fluid buildup in Quinn's lungs didn't improve quickly. The cough that racked his body from time to time made every muscle in his stomach and back incredibly sore. Just riding a horse became difficult, but Quinn refused to stop. On the third day, Miriam talked Quinn into getting a wagon. He had no coin, but Miriam was able to barter for an old wagon. They didn't have much in the way of supplies, so they folded their blankets across the wagon bench and rode side by side. Miriam tried to get Quinn to lie down in the back but he flatly refused.

"I'm not an invalid," he argued.

"But you might be if you get any worse," she said.

"I'm drinking the gruel that hack of a healer gave you."

"He's not a hack. He said you needed bed rest."

"I can't, not while Zollin's in danger."

"You could lie down in the wagon," she pleaded.

"No, I'm too stubborn to do that. Besides, I prefer sitting close to you," he said, winking at her.

"You are stubborn, like an old mule. I guess it's good that I've spent my whole life working with animals."

They flirted shamelessly, but Quinn's condition didn't allow them to pursue what was obviously a very strong physical attraction. Quinn still felt twinges of guilt over Zollin's mother, even though he knew that feeling guilty was senseless. Still, there were times when his happiness felt wrong. He liked Miriam, she was smart and attractive. Under different circumstances he would have wooed her with gifts and perhaps taken a more conventional approach to courting her, but he didn't have the freedom to do things the way he would have liked. For the last nine months he had lived with the threat of constant danger, to himself and to his son. He longed for a time when he could relax and not worry about Zollin, but he knew that day would never come. Too many powerful people wanted Zollin, and, until that changed, Zollin would never be truly safe. Still, Quinn felt his time was over. His body just couldn't keep up with the constant demands he was making on it.

They rode through the day, often waking before dawn and setting out as soon as it was light enough to see their way. They didn't pass many travelers, and fortunately they weren't accosted by outlaws. It seemed that the closer they got to Orrock, the emptier the land became.

"Do think there is really an invasion?" Miriam asked, trying to keep the worry from her voice.

"It's difficult to say," Quinn answered. "I think it is entirely possible, and the people who live here seem to think it's true. I'm assuming that's why they all left."

They were riding through a small village that was empty of its residents. The inn was locked up, but the windows had been broken, and someone had obviously looted the establishment, most likely looking for ale.

"War seems so improbable," Miriam said. "I mean, there hasn't been a war in over three hundred years."

"There hasn't been a war between the kingdoms," Quinn said. "But, there has always been fighting. We battle the Skellmarians and the Shirtac raiders. Baskla has fought the Shuklan forces trying to cross the North Sea. Ortis has held the Wilderlands against the Norsik. Even Osla has trouble with pirates raiding along the eastern coast at times. There will always be fighting to some degree."

"That's a very cynical point of view," Miriam said.

"Maybe, but I've been there. I served in the King's Army and fought Skellmarians up in the Great Valley."

"You were a soldier?" Miriam asked.

"Yes, for a time, and promoted to the King's Royal Guard. Then I met Zollin's mother and decided to settle down."

"What happened to Zollin's mother?"

"She died giving birth to him. Something tore, and the midwife couldn't stop the bleeding," Quinn said sadly.

"Oh, Quinn, I'm so sorry."

"Me too. It was a tough time. The village had a wet nurse who helped with Zollin, but it took me years to get over the loss. I'm sure I wasn't a very good father."

"Zollin is strong. I think you must have done a very good job raising him."

"The fact that you would describe him as strong makes me incredibly happy. That boy couldn't hammer a straight nail to save his life. He was absolutely miserable as my apprentice, and I was afraid I was going to lose him. I didn't think he would make it in the army, he just seemed too fragile. Then he discovered magic and everything changed. All the things I thought were weaknesses became strengths."

"That's probably not uncommon. I think parents are often too close to see their children for who they really are. Then, when they grow up and begin life on their own, you get to see them the way they are, not just the way you want them to be."

"It sounds like you've had a lot of experience," Quinn said. "Were you married?"

"No, I never married, never had a family," she said wistfully. "My parents both passed away when I was just coming of age. I had apprenticed with my father, unofficially of course, but I was a daddy's girl. I was learning how to care for animals when I was just a toddler. By the time I was finishing up essentials school I could do most of the work my father did. Then, when they passed away, I just kept his practice going. People kept bringing their sick or injured animals, and when they got the results they wanted, they didn't question what I could do."

"But you never fell in love?" Quinn asked. "I find it hard to believe that none of the young men in Felson found you attractive. I think you're beautiful."

Miriam looked down, blushing. She wasn't used to someone treating her like a woman. She had spent most of her life trying to be seen as the equal of any man. She could shoe a horse, set broken bones, and help any number of animals give birth. Romance had always been a distant, impractical dream.

"Most men aren't looking for a wife with a career," Miriam said sadly. "I was too busy to be of much interest to most boys. There were a few that came snooping around, but they were lazy louts that only cared about drinking, and they thought marrying me would mean they could lay around all day doing nothing."

"It seems like that's all you want me to do," Quinn teased, but then burst into a fit of coughing.

"That serves you right," Miriam said in a mocking tone when Quinn had finished coughing.

"That isn't funny," he said, panting and holding his side. "I think I broke a rib that time."

"Nah," Miriam said. "Your ribs are fine. That's just the meanness coming out of you."

"Seriously," Quinn said, looking at her. "I'm interested, and I'm not just looking for a free ride."

"That's hard to believe while I'm driving this wagon."

"Well, believe it. I don't know what you want in life, Miriam, but I know what I want. I want to be where you are. I'll do whatever I have to do to make that happen. I've given Zollin all the help I can give him. Once I make sure that he knows Mansel is leading him into a trap, I'm through."

"What about Prince Wilam?" Miriam asked.

"That's the King's problem."

"And if the King calls on you again?"

"I've served my country. I've taken care of my family. Now it's time for me to get what I want. And what I want is you."

"Don't beat around the bush," she said, blushing. "Tell me how you really feel."

"I feel like the luckiest man in the world when I'm with you."

"Quinn, you hardly know me," she argued.

"And I can't wait to learn everything about you. I haven't been with anyone else since my wife died. I thought that part of my life was over. I just didn't care for anyone else, but all that changed when I met you."

Miriam didn't reply. She was driving the wagon with her head down, letting the horses find their own way. It was getting late and she knew she needed to begin looking for a place to make camp for the night, but it was difficult to think about anything clearly. She had given up hope of ever finding a partner in life. When she had been young she had thrown herself into her craft. Animals were her passion, and without her father to find a suitable match, she had thought that she would always be alone.

"There's a farm up ahead," Quinn said. "Might be a good place to make camp for the night."

Miriam looked up. There was a farmhouse and a small stable. It looked like the perfect place to rest for the evening. And she realized that she needed time to consider her feelings. It had been exciting to see Quinn again. She had felt an instant connection to him when they had met months before, but then Quinn had been sent to Osla, and Miriam had been busy in Felson. She had almost forgotten the way she felt until she saw Quinn at her door. Even though he looked sick, all her feelings had come rushing back to her. His insistence on continuing his quest to find Zollin had propelled her into action. She couldn't let him go alone, and to be honest, she had been excited by the prospect of spending time with him, but now she had to decide what was best for her future. Quinn obviously had strong feelings for her, but it could merely be infatuation. She needed to set the record straight with Quinn. No matter how much fun being with him was, she was too old for romance. She had responsibilities in Felson, and Quinn had responsibilities to the King.

"I'll see if we can make camp here for the night," she told Quinn.

She went to the farmhouse and was greeted warmly by the people inside. The farmer went out to make space for them in the small barn. He had only one milk cow, so there was room for Miriam to bed down their horses for the night. She decided to make camp under a large oak tree, where she spread out their blankets and started a fire. The farmer's wife brought them food, a hearty stew, and some ale. Quinn drank his medicinal brew and soaked his bread in the thick stew.

They had just finished eating when Miriam decided she couldn't wait any longer. She was afraid of her feelings, and going home would be simpler. She could return to life the way it had always been. That was the prudent thing to do, she told herself.

"Quinn," she said softly, just loud enough to be heard over the crackling of their small fire. "I don't think I can go with you to Orrock. I think I need to go home."

"Oh," Quinn said, unsure what Miriam was hinting at.

"I've enjoyed being with you, but you're on the mend now, and I've got responsibilities in Felson."

"Yes, of course you do," he said, suddenly finding it hard to breathe.

"I mean, what are we really doing here? We don't know each other. We have completely different lives."

"What are you trying to say, Miriam?"

"I'm saying, this just isn't going to work."

"What isn't?" he asked.

"Us... you and me, we're from two different worlds. You know the King; I'm an animal healer. You travel all across the Five Kingdoms and this is as far from Felson as I've ever been."

"So? All that matters is how we feel," Quinn said.

He felt as if an emotional knife were being twisted in his stomach. His body ached from his racking cough, but that pain was nothing compared to what he felt as he heard Miriam say she was leaving.

"Quinn, we both know that feelings come and go. We can't base our future on feelings that could change tomorrow."

"My feelings won't change," Quinn said.

"You don't know that."

"I meant what I said. Once I find Zollin I'm going back to Felson. I'm not giving up."

"We'll see," was all she managed to say. "I better go check on the horses."

She hurried to the barn, and Quinn was left alone. He wanted to go after her, but he knew it wouldn't do any good. Miriam had made up her mind, and words wouldn't change it. It was one of the things he admired about her. She put more stock in action than words, just as he did. The only thing he could do was to complete his task and then make good on his promise.

Miriam was gone for over an hour. When she finally came back, Quinn was lying down but not asleep.

"I think I can pull the wagon with just Ajax," she said, referring to one of her horses. "You can take Meela on to Orrock or wherever you need to go."

Quinn didn't respond right away. He was tired and knew he needed at least a little rest, but he had some things to say before he went to sleep.

"Miriam, I'm sorry if I've put you in an awkward position. That was never my intention. I do have strong feelings for you, but I don't want you to feel pressured or uncomfortable. If you want to go back to Felson, I won't stop you. I have to go on and find Zollin, and I know you understand that. But I will come back to Felson, because I want to be near you. I want to get to know you better. I want to show you that I'm sincere in my feelings. Nothing is going to change that."

Miriam didn't answer, and Quinn was worried he'd said too much. He lay on his back and looked up at the stars through the leafy branches of the big oak they were camped under. The fire had died down and the nocturnal insects were singing. It was a peaceful moment, but neither Miriam nor Quinn felt at peace.

"I just think it's for the best," she said at last.

"All right," Quinn said, his heart aching. "Be careful going home. I'll see you as soon as I can."

Quinn had never expected to feel the pain of heartbreak again. It was like a dark cloud had enveloped him, and he felt as if he would never be okay again. He rolled onto his side and tried to sleep.

Miriam was sad too, but she was also afraid. She had been practical all her life. She had learned to be responsible when her parents died, and she had been forced to fend for herself. For years she had been afraid, especially at night. She would bolt the doors and windows, even on the hottest summer nights, and lay quaking in bed. Finally, she had grown used to being alone, and now she was afraid of what a future with Quinn might entail. What if he discovered that she was not the person he wanted to be with? What if there was something about her that was somehow wrong and that he would discover as they got closer? She didn't want to turn her life upside down only to be crushed if Quinn changed his mind. Being practical had seen her through a life of hardship, and she saw no reason to change now, no matter how badly it hurt her.

It was a few hours before dawn when Quinn woke up coughing. The ground seemed to be filled with stones under his blanket, and even though he ached all over, he decided to get up and leave. He checked on Miriam. She was sleeping, or at least pretending to sleep. It was difficult to leave without saying goodbye, but he thought it might actually be easier than seeing her face grow stiff with resolve and bid him farewell in some formal way that would make him feel like a stranger.

He rolled his blanket and gathered his canteen. He stuffed into his belt the packet of herbs the healer had given Miriam to use when making his medicinal drink. There was some salted beef and hard crusted bread, which he carried with him to the barn and put into one of the saddle bags they carried in the wagon. All their tack was neatly arranged behind the seat of the wagon. Quinn hefted his and carried it into the barn. Meela was an older mare, but she was surefooted and happy to see him. She nickered softly as he approached.

"Hi girl, ready for a ride?"

The horse bobbed her head as if to say yes. He arranged a blanket on her back, then set the saddle on top of the blanket and adjusted the straps that wrapped around her stomach. He fit the bridle over her head and put the bit into her mouth, then lead her out into the cool night air. He was chilled, but he knew it wouldn't take long to get warm riding. He stopped one last time and looked back at the campsite. Miriam was still lying down, not moving. It took a great amount of strength to climb onto the horse and leave Miriam behind, but that had been her choice.

He rode out as the stars twinkled in the sky and the moon quietly set. It would be light in a couple of hours, he estimated. He wanted to be as far away as possible when Miriam awoke. He wanted to complete his task and return to her, to prove his feelings were real and that he was someone she could count on.

When dawn came, Miriam rolled over and saw that Quinn was gone. She had expected as much. She knew he was the kind of man who kept his word. She had fully expected him to leave as soon as he could. But she hadn't been prepared for the way his leaving made her feel. She couldn't help but think that she had made a mistake. Perhaps Quinn had been her chance for happiness, and now he was gone. He might never return. She hated the thought of going home and waiting, not knowing if Quinn was hurt, or even dead, but she had made up her mind. Going home had been her choice. She had pushed him back onto his dangerous path alone. She had to live with that decision now.

She got up and began breaking camp. Quinn had taken his own blanket and supplies when he left, so there was very little for Miriam to do. She was hungry, but she decided she would be fine eating their dry rations on the road. She wanted to get home as soon as possible, where perhaps she wouldn't feel so guilty, she hoped.

She was walking around the farmhouse with Ajax, who was pulling the wagon, when the farmer stepped out to greet her.

"I hope you had a good evening," he said.

"Oh, we did, thank you."

"Where's your man?"

"He set out before dawn," she explained. "I'm going back home to Felson."

"Oh, no. I wish I'd known he was leaving so early. I have a message that needs to be delivered to Orrock."

"I'm sorry, he would have been happy to deliver it," she said.

"It isn't my message. Here, read it."

He handed her the small piece of paper. As she read her eyes went wide.

"Is this true?" she asked.

"We buried him ourselves. He was with a group of soldiers, and they rode off when they saw the dragon. We found him a couple hours later, stabbed in the stomach and left for dead. He lived a few more hours. There's not a healer within a day's ride or we'd have sent for help."

"I've got to go," Miriam said, fear straining her voice.

"Oh, okay," the farmer said.

"I'll deliver the message."

"Are you sure?" the farmer asked.

"Yes, I have to do it. Will you keep this wagon until I return?"

"Sure, be glad to do it. Here, let me help you unhitch it."

Moments later she was charging down the road after Quinn.

Chapter 29

Zollin and Mansel were given a tiny room with two narrow beds that was located in the military compound just inside the walls of Orrock City. They immediately went to sleep. They were roused an hour before dawn, and both men washed themselves using small basins that were provided for them. The water was cold, but neither complained. They had traveled hard, and it was the first time either had been able to wash in a long time. When they were dressed they emerged from their room with their gear, preparing to set out at first light, but instead they were met by Commander Hausey.

"The King is back," he said to Zollin. "He's asking for you."

"All right, lead the way."

The city was already crowded. Many of the people from the surrounding villages had now moved their belongings inside the city walls. They slept wherever they could find space. The streets were clogged with people, most still sleeping, wrapped in blankets and huddling along the buildings for what little shelter they provided. The military compound was in a part of the city Zollin had never visited, but the castle was easily the tallest building in Orrock, and he could have found his way to the royal residence without Hausey to guide him.

Mansel followed Zollin, although his presence wasn't requested, and he didn't relish seeing the King. Felix had sent Mansel and Quinn to escort Prince Wilam home from Osla, but they had made it only as far as Lodenhime. The King would want answers, and Mansel didn't want anything to keep him from being able to return with Zollin as soon as possible. Gwendolyn wouldn't be pleased if he arrived leading a legion of troops.

The castle walls were heavily manned, and the gate was shut and barred. Only the narrow, side doorway was open, and every person going in and out was searched. Zollin submitted to the intrusion. He had a dagger in his belt, but no other weapons. Mansel, on the other hand, had his sword and was not happy about giving it up.

"Let him have your sword," Commander Hausey told Mansel. "You'll get it back in due time."

"They didn't take your weapons," Mansel said in a growl.

"I'm a commander in the King's Army."

"I don't let anyone touch my sword," he said defiantly.

"Fine, you don't have to join us," Zollin said. "Why don't you wait in the tavern you stayed in before? I'll come and get you when I'm done."

"All right," Mansel said.

The truth was, he didn't like Zollin being out of his sight, but this way he got to keep his sword and avoid the King. He turned and headed to the nearby establishment while Zollin followed Hausey into the castle.

Servants were hurrying everywhere inside the castle courtyards. There were animals being fed and watered and even more servants cleaning the dung from the courtyard cobblestones. There were men stacking crates of supplies. There were piles of arrows and tables laden with swords, shields, and spears. The castle was heavily guarded as well, but this time Zollin and Hausey were waved through without incident.

They climbed the wide staircase to the third floor. The castle was familiar to Zollin; he had stayed there for nearly a week after healing King Felix from the poison Prince Simmeron and his surgeon had been administering the King. When they reached the large royal chamber, they found the wooden carved doors propped open. The room was full of military staff and servants. On the King's desk food had been laid out: eggs, bacon, fruit, and freshly baked bread were laid out for anyone who wanted them, although Zollin didn't see anyone eating. His own stomach growled at the sight of such rich food just waiting to be eaten. He couldn't help but think that Mansel would have gone straight to the food. The thought made him smile, and it was the first truly happy thought he'd had since losing Brianna to the dragon.

"You're here just in time," the King said from across the crowded room.

The military men parted, and Zollin saw the King propped in a chair, with healers examining his foot.

"What can you do for an arrow wound?" the King asked. "Some fool got a lucky shot that hit me in the only place I didn't have armor. Right in the damn boot."

The foot was elevated, and the boot had been cut away. The arrow had been severed, as that was the only way to get the King's foot free from his stirrup, but the projectile was still in his flesh. It penetrated just below his ankle bone and protruded from the bottom of his foot.

"That looks painful," Zollin said.

"It is," King Felix said. "I damn near passed out when they were cutting my boot off."

"It was necessary, my liege," said one of the healers. "You should have let us give you a sleeping potion."

"No, we haven't got time for that," the King said. "Zollin, can you heal it? If not, I'm going to have the arrow pulled out and the wound tended by my healers."

"Yes, I can help," Zollin said. "Give me a little room, please."

The healers and medical staff stepped back, but they were all watching with fascination. Zollin's first move was to block the pain receptors in King Felix's foot from sending their electrical message of pain up to the King's brain.

"Oh, that's better already," Felix said.

"Pull out the arrow," Zollin told the healers. "Do it very, very slowly."

One man took hold of the King's leg, another held the foot still, and a third man began to pull the arrow using a set of tongs. Zollin let his magic flow into the swollen foot. He passed through blood and antibodies that were causing the swelling, and focused on the damage the arrow had caused. He could sense the wooden shaft of the arrow being pulled slowly down through the bottom of the King's foot. As the end of the arrow disappeared into the King's foot, Zollin began to heal the wound. He mended the skin, causing the crowd in the room to gasp, but then the real healing began. First was the muscle that had to be knit back together. Blood vessels were rejoined to each other, nerves restored. Finally the arrow came free, and Zollin finished his work. The magic inside him was as hot as a fire, but the inner levies he had constructed contained the heat and focused his power.

"That was miraculous, Sire," said one of the healers.

"I didn't do it," Felix said, trying to flex his foot, which was slowly resuming its normal shape and size as Zollin moved the fluids that had built up in the tissue and joints around the many bones.

"I could use some breakfast," Zollin said when he finished healing the King's foot.

The King was standing up, gently testing his weight on the recently healed limb.

"Bring me a fresh pair of boots," the King said loudly.

Servants hurried around the room as Zollin poured himself a mug of fruit juice. He was just taking a long drink of the cool, sweet drink when the King came up to him.

"Thank you, Zollin," he said.

Zollin took a bite of bacon and waved his hand as if to say the act had been nothing special. The King stayed near the table, but he drank wine instead of juice and didn't eat. The other military officers gathered around the table as well.

"You did well, Commander Hausey," the King said.

"We had very little trouble, Your Highness."

"We'll hear all about that another time. Right now we have to focus on the attack that is surely coming soon. As you both probably know we've been in the field. Your old friend Offendorl has led an army to our doorstep in an attempt to force you to join him, Zollin."

"I don't know the man," Zollin said around a mouthful of food.

"I'm guessing you know the dragon well enough. Well, now we do, too. It attacked our trebuchets and cut a swath through the Boar Legion as well. We'll be lucky to have three thousand men to defend our city when the army returns."

"The dragon is with the army?" Zollin asked. "Or did it just attack and leave?"

"I can't say for sure where the beast is. It's too bad you weren't able to conquer it, but it was as I expected, under the control of the Torr."

Zollin's mind was racing. He couldn't believe his ears, and yet it made perfect sense. If the Torr controlled the dragon, Brianna might be under their control as well. The dragon could have delivered her right to them.

"I should go and deal with it," Zollin said firmly.

"No, that's not a good idea," the King said. "I know you have a history with the beast. Hausey gave me a brief report before bringing you here. We need to consolidate our forces. The army will be here soon. They've marched all night. They'll need rest and healers to help the wounded. If you leave the city, you'll be exposed, and we won't be able to help you."

"That's all right," Zollin said. "It's my choice."

"And you won't be able to help us," the King said pointedly. "We've done our best to stop this invasion, to push the enemy back and make their progress too painful to continue, but they outnumber us, and there are reports from Ebbson Keep of military forces building up at Fort Jellar. If Baskla or Ortis marches against us from the east, we'll be hard pressed to survive."

"Without their dragon, they won't have much chance of defeating you inside the city," Zollin said.

"That's true enough, but I doubt defeating us is what they're after. They want you; they want our resources. All they've got to do is lay siege to the city, and wait. In the meantime they can pillage the towns and villages at will, while we slowly starve to death. And if they have reinforcements coming in from Baskla, they could have enough troops to overrun the city."

"If they're after me, why not just send me to them?" Zollin asked.

"We aren't giving up that easily. We can fight. With your help, we can hurt them badly enough to withdraw."

"What about the treaty? I thought that using wizards in the military was banned when the Five Kingdoms formed the confederation."

"It was, but you have to understand we didn't start this fight. The Torr pushed this invasion because we weren't willing to turn you over to Offendorl," the King said.

"You're saying it's my fault they invaded Yelsia?" Zollin asked.

"Not your fault. No, you are just one part of their plan. Offendorl can't let you go free. He's here to take you back to the Torr or see you dead. The other kings want to crush me and divide Yelsia between them. They drew first blood; they invaded our kingdom. That gives us the right to fight back however we choose. They have a wizard, and we have a wizard. There is no unfair advantage to that."

Zollin found a nearby stool and sat down. Once again he felt the desire to just give in. Why shouldn't he join the Torr? Perhaps it was for the best, he thought. If he had, this army wouldn't have invaded Yelsia, and if this Offendorl had Brianna, or at the very least the dragon, he could finally get some answers. On the other hand, if Brianna was still alive somewhere, he could never go to her if he joined the Torr. And neither could he go with Mansel to save his father.

"Gentlemen," the King said, speaking to his generals. "I want weapons and supplies stocked in every part of the city. For now, the Wolf's Legion remains on watch, but I want the Fox,

Boar, and Eagle Legions assigned to various sections of the city. We need clear lines of communication and contingency plans in place to move soldiers across the city if needed."

He continued giving orders, mainly for the rest and nourishment of the troops he was expecting to arrive at the city. Zollin heard little of what was being said, but soon most of the military personnel had left the room, including Commander Hausey. Zollin had finished eating the food he had picked up, but he didn't remember eating it.

"I think you need something a little stronger than fruit juice," King Felix told him. "I know you've got a lot on your mind. I need you here, though. I need you to fight with us," he said as he poured a goblet of wine.

Zollin sipped the drink. It was strong and it burned all the way down to his stomach. The magic inside of him seemed to react to the wine, his power growing with each hot sip.

"I'm certain of two things," King Felix said, sitting on a chair opposite Zollin, with a goblet of wine in his own hand. "First, I'm certain that Offendorl means you harm. He may not kill you if you give yourself up, but he will enslave you. The Torr was meant to be a society of wizards, a place where people like yourself could grow in your skills and benefit the Five Kingdoms. Instead, it has become Offendorl's personal menagerie of magic users, each answering to him and increasing his own personal power. He's old and he's devious. We can't trust him. You should never trust him.

"Secondly, I'm sure he means to give Yelsia to the other kings as payment for their troops. He doesn't have to of course; he has the power to force them to do his bidding, but I'm sure King

Belphan and King Oveer were all too willing to join his little invasion."

"So what do you want from me?" Zollin asked. "I have things to do besides pull Yelsia out of the fire every time I turn around."

King Felix was shocked by Zollin's tone. He wasn't arrogant, but clearly frustrated. It was a tone that the King was not used to hearing from his subordinates. He had to swallow his own frustration and remain calm. Zollin had not been in the field with the army, but he had suffered loss and endured hardship. He had earned the right to question the King, at least this one time.

"I am your King," Felix said. "Even wizards are beholden to their rulers. I don't have your power, and I'm not the type of man who would make you use your magic against your will. But Yelsia needs you, now more than ever."

"I don't know," Zollin said, throwing his hands up into the air. "It seems like I cause more problems than I solve. I don't mean to be rude, Sire, but it's hard for me to wonder what I can do that would actually be of service."

"That's a good question, and to be honest, we won't know until the invaders arrive. But I know one thing for certain. If the dragon returns, we will need your help. You've done nothing wrong. You had every right to refuse the Torr. The treaty said that we, the kings of the Five Kingdoms, would turn over our wizards. In other words, that we would not keep wizards in our armies. But the Torr has changed, and you have never been part of the King's Army, at least until now. We have done nothing wrong, certainly nothing that would warrant sending an army onto our sovereign soil. Had you been here in Orrock when the wizards of the Torr first found you, I would have counseled you to do as you did. It was not their place to take you from your home by force."

"So what do you want from me?" Zollin asked.

"I want you to stay close until we know exactly what we're dealing with. I want you to help, where and when you can. For now, that is all I want. Once we know more, we can make a decision together. And whatever your decision, I'll support you."

Zollin wondered if the King really meant what he was saying, but he had no reason to believe otherwise. Still, he sensed that the King wanted Zollin within his control. That was always behind their seemingly genial conversations, as if Zollin were just a tool to be used by King Felix, instead of a person with hopes and dreams of his own.

Zollin agreed to stay in the city, and the King insisted he have his old quarters in the castle. Zollin went back to the rooms and found them just as he had left them, which was much the way Branock had them when he had been conniving with Prince Simmeron. They had been cleaned, but the furniture was familiar and brought back memories of his time there with Brianna. His heart ached fiercely just thinking of her. He wanted to ride out of the city and find the damn dragon. It felt too much like he was simply writing Brianna off by staying in the city, but he knew better. He didn't expect to get answers from the dragon; it was a wild creature, after all. Instead, he wanted it to suffer, the way he was suffering, although he knew that was impossible as well.

He wandered out of the castle and was thinking of going to find Mansel when a soldier came hurrying up to him.

"Master Zollin," the soldier shouted.

"That's me," Zollin confirmed.

"Commander Hausey sent me to find you," he said, between gasps for breath. "The army has returned and they have wounded. Commander Hausey requests your help."

Zollin sighed deeply. He wanted to be left alone, but he knew that staying busy was a healthier alternative to brooding in the streets. He nodded and followed the soldier, who led Zollin back to the military compound. A makeshift hospital had been set up, and healers were hurrying around. Zollin found Commander Hausey, who looked relieved that he had come.

"Zollin, thank you for coming."

"Of course, Commander," Zollin said. "Take me to the most critical soldiers first."

Hausey showed Zollin into a building that was full of men, most lying covered with blankets, unconscious or in shock. There were several with severe burn wounds. The dragon had made a pass through a large group of soldiers; most of those unfortunate enough to be close to the dragon had been consumed by the fire, but many others were just badly burned. Zollin didn't mind working on burns. The heat affected the tissue beneath the skin, but it was easier to heal than most wounds. He worked as quickly as he could, healing the worst of the wounds and leaving the minor burns for the healers to handle. By midday, most of the critical patients were healed, and Zollin had lost only a few men who had succumbed to their wounds before he could get to them.

Commander Hausey brought Zollin lunch.

"As I recall, you prefer wine," he said with a smile. "The army cooks are roasting sheep. I have mutton, bread, and vegetables. Are you hungry?"

"Famished," Zollin admitted.

They ate outside. The streets were crowded and busy, but in the military compound there was still space on the drilling ground were they could sit and eat undisturbed. Most of the soldiers were sleeping. He assumed they had traveled all night and would be allowed to rest a while. He was tired too, extremely tired. He and the knights had pushed their pace trying to get to Orrock. Zollin had been relentless once he'd seen the dragon. He had slept for a few hours, but as he ate the rich food and sat still, fatigue drifted over him like a dark storm cloud.

"So, the healers say you are working wonders," Hausey said. "Thank you for that. We'll need every man we can get once the fighting starts."

"Has there been word of the enemy army?" Zollin asked.

"Scouts report they are moving this way. They'll most likely lay siege to the city. That's what the King thinks. Duke Ebbson has sent word of troops massing at Fort Jellar, but we've no word that Baskla has invaded. If they do, though, we'll be helpless to stop them."

Ebbson Keep made Zollin think of Kelvich. He missed his old friend and wondered why he hadn't joined them. At the time when Mansel had mentioned it, he didn't think much about it. Kelvich was no fighter. He had left the Ruins at Ornak before the dragon arrived and hadn't come to Orrock with Quinn after they left Brighton's Gate. But Kelvich didn't seem like the type to shy away from a fight. He fought with Zollin against the wizards of the Torr at Brighton's Gate.

"And then there's the dragon," Hausey said. "That's a whole new wrinkle that will be hard to deal with. That bloody beast could burn Orrock to the ground if we aren't careful."

"I'll deal with the dragon," Zollin said. "This time it won't get away."

"What happened in the Northern Highlands?" Hausey asked.

"We tracked it down, far into the northern range of mountains. I went into its den, but the beast caught me in a small passage and almost killed me. It probably would have except that Brianna was able to wound it."

"Brianna wounded it . . . how?"

"We got dwarfish steel and made arrow heads. They penetrated the dragon's hide."

"Dwarfish steel?" Hausey said skeptically.

"Yeah, I had the idea after Ornak. I met a dwarf in Peddingar Forrest, and he traded us ale for steel. It's a long story," Zollin said when he saw the commander's look of disbelief, "but there really are dwarves living under the mountains, just as there are dragons and other magical creatures."

"I don't mean to doubt you, but you have to admit, it sounds more like a bard's tale than actual fact."

"It's true. There are a lot of things I can't explain. We saw a giant after that," Zollin said, skipping the part of the story where he and Brianna fell off the mountain and Zollin broke his back. "Met more dwarves and fought a rock monster. Like I said, it's a long story."

"What happened to Brianna?"

"I honestly don't know," Zollin said. "Have you ever heard of a Fire Spirit?"

"I've heard of sprites. Aren't they elves of some kind?"

"I don't know. The dwarves were convinced that Brianna was a Fire Spirit from their own stories. I can say this, Brianna is more than just a girl. The dwarves gave her a magic ruby, and it woke up some type of latent magical power in her."

"What type of magical power?"

"Dragon magic," Zollin said.

"What is dragon magic?"

"I wish I knew. I can sense magic, Commander. In people and objects. Some plants have magic abilities: they're generally used in medicines. There are people who can manipulate or recognize magic, such as healers or alchemists. And there are magical creatures, like dwarves and giants and dragons. I can sense their magic too, but it's like a foreign language. I know it's magic, I just don't understand it and can't manipulate or control it."

"And Brianna suddenly had dragon magic?" Hausey asked.

"Yes, that's the best way to put it. The ruby had the same type of power, and when she put it on, it either woke up that power that was dormant in Brianna already or transferred its power to her. At first it seemed harmless. She could manipulate fire. That's no big deal; I've been doing it every since I discovered my own powers."

Zollin held up a hand and with a thought conjured a flame, which waved and danced just above his palm.

"The only difference was, Brianna could touch the fire and not get burned. We were crossing through these deep chambers under the mountains where there were these pools of molten rock. You couldn't go near the pools; the heat was just too intense. But Brianna could. She went so close her whole body burst into flames and she could dance around in the fire, jumping like an acrobat—only better. She even breathed fire. It was unbelievable."

"You're making this up," Hausey said.

"No, I'm not. When we caught up with the dragon, she was supposed to kill it. I made a bow for her with my staff and she could shoot incredible distances with it. The dragon was wounded from her other arrows and couldn't even fly, but instead of killing it she wanted to heal it. I don't know why," he said, seeing the question in Hausey's face. "Like I said, she changed. She was still Brianna, but she could relate to the dragon maybe. I don't know. She went to the dragon and somehow healed its wounds. Then it wrapped its tail around her and flew away. I chased it, but I couldn't catch it."

"That's dreadful," Hausey said.

"Yes, it absolutely is. But the dragon won't get away from me this time. I'm going to kill it."

"But how? What's your plan?"

"My plan is to kill it," Zollin said. "I won't stop until I find a way."

"That's no strategy," Hausey said. "You need a plan, some sort of tactics that will allow you to kill it."

"I don't know any dragon tactics," Zollin said. "Do you?"

"No, I don't," Hausey said excitedly. "But Kelvich sent me a scroll. I was supposed to give it to you, but by the time I got it, you had already gone north. Let me get it for you."

The commander hurried off, and Zollin sat dumbfounded. Had Kelvich really found a way to defeat the dragon? If so, why hadn't he told Zollin? And why wouldn't he have come with them to Orrock? Nothing made sense. Zollin needed more answers from Mansel. He would have to go and find the big warrior, but first he wanted to read the scroll that Kelvich had sent to Commander Hausey.

He waited impatiently, eating more food, although he wasn't really hungry for it. The wine was good, but Zollin didn't want to dim his wits so he drank the wine sparingly. Finally, Hausey returned and handed him the scroll.

"Sorry, it was in my luggage and it took a while to find," said the officer.

Zollin took it and unrolled the scroll. It only took him a few minutes to read the story that had been translated by the scholars at Ebbson Keep. He was puzzled when he read it. The story it contained seemed inconsequential. He read it again, then he let Commander Hausey read it.

"It's just a story," Hausey said. "What do you think it means?"

"I don't know," Zollin said. "I sure wish Kelvich had stayed with us."

"Yes, that would have been helpful. Surely it means something, though. Why else would he have sent it?"

"I have no idea. It seems like just an historical record."

Zollin read the scroll again, his mind struggling to understand what it meant. It was the story of a group of dragons who came north into Yelsia from the Walheta Mountains. They pillaged villages in search of gold, just like the dragon from the Northern Highlands. And then a massive storm blew in from the ocean and the dragons left. There was nothing else. No notes from Kelvich, no explanation.

"Are you sure this is all he sent?" Zollin asked.

"Positive," Hausey said. "I remember the messenger saying this might help."

"Might help or would help?" Zollin asked.

"I don't remember for sure," Hausey said.

"So this could be nothing? It could have just been the only reference he found to dragons in that horde of scrolls he carried back to Ebbson Keep."

"I know that the scholars came and carried the rest of the scrolls to the Keep," Hausey said.

"And Kelvich had some translations with him," Zollin said. "He was reading them by the fire, but he said they only talked about the history of dragons and that the scholars hadn't finished translating the text before he left Ebbson Keep."

"So, maybe this scroll doesn't mean anything," Hausey said.

"I don't know," Zollin said, his mind buzzing. "It seems like there is something here, I just can't figure it out."

"Well, I'm not much for puzzles," Hausey said. "I need to see what else I can do to help prepare the city for what lies ahead."

"Thank you for lunch and the scroll," Zollin said.

"Thank you for helping with the wounded."

Zollin nodded and watched the commander go. He reminded Zollin of his father. Hausey was taller, but wiry like Quinn and just as practical. If he were with Zollin now he'd have said much the same thing. Zollin knew he needed a plan to fight the dragon, he just couldn't figure out if the scroll helped at all.

He stood up and gathered the wine bottle and cups that Hausey had left behind. Zollin was sure someone would clean up the mess, but he didn't like leaving work for other people to do. He was just going into the infirmary area to see if there was anything else he could do when an idea struck. He was thinking about his old staff and how it had formed when lightning struck a tree in the forest outside Tranaugh Shire. The storm seemed like it might have been the thing that drove off the dragons in the story

Kelvich had sent him. And when Zollin had fought the dragon in the Ruins of Ornak, he had blasted the beast with electrical energy that seemed to have an effect, if he remembered correctly.

He turned and sprinted back through the city. He had an idea and he need to get to the library in the castle to see if it would work.

Chapter 30

It was twilight, and Quinn was one of the last people admitted into the city. Orrock was closing its gates for good. Scouts had reported that the invading army was close, and after sending out word to the people in and around Orrock, the King's Army was now preparing for a siege.

Quinn made his way through the crowded streets toward the castle. Zollin had been given an apartment in the royal residence once before, and that seemed like as good a place as any to start. There were soldiers everywhere, and for the first time since leaving Miriam at the little farm, two days ago, he was glad that she wasn't with him. He had pushed himself hard the first day, staying on the road until well after dark. His cough was worse now, but he had made it to his destination. He only hoped that Zollin was still here, although he couldn't imagine where else the King would have wanted him.

The idea that King Felix would use Zollin to fight an army made Quinn angry. He couldn't imagine what dangers a wizard might face in a military engagement. He had fought in several skirmishes with the Skellmarians and Shirtac raiders, and it had always seemed like controlled chaos from Quinn's perspective. No matter how disciplined the army was, there were things that couldn't be controlled. A shield wall was only effective if the man beside you held his position. If he was killed, the entire line could dissolve, and then it became every man for himself.

Quinn pushed those thoughts away. He loved carpentry because it was so manageable. Even if something went wrong, he could look at the problem and fix it. War wasn't like that. In war, anything could happen, and the consequences were life and death.

He hated to think of Zollin facing that, and hated to see Zollin's incredible power used for military purposes. If he could just find Zollin, he could at least stay with his son and do everything in his power to protect him.

The castle was surrounded by guards. There were messengers running to and from the huge stone castle, but the residents of Orrock were giving the royal residence a wide berth. Quinn went to the main gate and was stopped by two very serious-looking sentries.

"No one is allowed into the castle except authorized military personnel," the guard said.

"I'm trying to find Zollin the wizard," Quinn wheezed. He had to fight hard not to start coughing again. "I'm his father."

"I'm sorry sir, but I can't allow you in."

"Is he in there? I've been trying to find him for a long time."

"I'm not at liberty to give you that information."

"Look, I'm Quinn, Zollin's father. The King sent me on an urgent task—" he couldn't finish without coughing.

"Sir, the best I can do is to allow you to send a message to him."

"Fine," Quinn said. "I'll get a note written and bring it back. Thank you."

The guard nodded and then resumed his scan of the passing crowds. There was an inn close by, the same establishment Mansel had made his home when they were in Orrock before. Quinn didn't have much money left. Miriam had given him a little, but it might not be enough for a night's stay and a stall for his horse. He would have coin again once he was granted an audience with King Felix, but he didn't relish telling the King that his son, the Crown

Prince of Yelsia was now bewitched by Gwendolyn in Lodenhime. He had no ability to save Wilam by himself, and if Zollin had fallen under her spell, there was no telling what damage the witch might have done. Getting to Zollin had been Quinn's first priority, and he wasn't ashamed of that. As far as Quinn knew, Prince Wilam was safe for the moment, and the King would have to be satisfied with that.

He led his horse to the inn, and tied the reins to a post just outside. The inn wasn't as posh as the one in which he'd met with Prince Wilam's advisor in the Grand City of Osla, but as inns went, it was still an upscale place. He went in through the thick, oak door and found the common room well appointed. There were lanterns along the walls, a fire in the massive hearth, and a large chandelier on the ceiling. The burning beeswax candles gave the inn an inviting smell. There was more wine being consumed than ale, and the wenches who worked the room were beauties.

"Have you got room for one more tonight?" Quinn asked the innkeeper.

"Have you got coin?"

"I have a silver mark," Quinn said. "I can have more tomorrow."

"What's you're business?" the innkeeper asked suspiciously. He obviously didn't want any trouble in his establishment.

"Zollin the wizard is my son," Quinn said. "I'm trying to get word to him that I'm here."

"You know the wizard? Then you should know his companion," the innkeeper was obviously testing Quinn, but he had no idea what effect the question would have on the master carpenter.

"Is Mansel here?" Quinn asked in a low voice.

"He is," the innkeeper said. "I take it you know him."

"I do," Quinn said, feeling his stomach twist into a knot, and he had to hold back a fit of coughing that he could feel trying to claw its way out of his chest.

"He could get a message to the wizard for you," the innkeeper said. "I've got room in the stable, if you don't mind sleeping with a few horses. Space is at a premium with the siege coming, but your silver mark will get you food, wine, and a bed of hay to sleep on."

"That's fine. Have you got room in your stable for my horse as well?" Quinn asked after coughing a little.

"There's plenty of room in the stable at the moment. Most of the horses in the city have been commandeered by the army. I'm sure to have more people bunking in the stable soon, but for now, your horse is welcome there."

"I'll just see that he's taken care of," Quinn said, holding out his last coin to the innkeeper.

"I'll let Mansel know you're here."

Quinn's first instinct was to stop the innkeeper, but then he decided that at this point he had no choice. He would have to face Mansel. He couldn't hide through the night and hope to catch Zollin alone the next day. He wasn't the kind of man who cowered from others, and although he was weak and sick, he owed Mansel a fight. This time he wouldn't be taken off guard.

* * *

The wenches were surprised by Mansel's coldness. They all remembered him from his last visit to the inn, and he had been fun and generous with them. Now he was surly and sat alone in one of the private rooms, drinking and eating. He had coin, they saw that, but he had no interest in them. After being shouted at, the serving girls were all giving the big warrior a wide berth.

When the innkeeper came into his room, Mansel looked up angrily. He hated sitting around in Orrock while Zollin played the hero. If he had to be here, he wanted to be left alone. He wasn't interested in fighting a war, he just want to get Zollin and go south. He was almost ready to knock his friend over the head, throw him across the back of a horse, and take him to Lodenhime by force, but he knew that wasn't a good idea. Even if he could manage to get Zollin out of the city, if the wizard didn't come willingly, Mansel wouldn't be able to force him to go anywhere for long.

"What do you want?" Mansel said. "I've paid you."

"You have a visitor," the innkeeper said, still standing in the doorway. "The wizard's father, Quinn, is here. He needs to get a message to his son."

"Quinn is here?" Mansel asked. "That's impossible."

"Well, there's a man claiming to be the wizard's father. He knew you by name. I told him I would let you know, and I have. I'll leave it to you to work out who he is, but don't do it inside the inn. I'll throw you out," the innkeeper said in an shaky voice, "if you cause trouble."

"Don't worry, I won't," Mansel said. "Where is he?"

"He's in the stable, seeing to his horse."

"Good," Mansel said, standing up.

He started to buckle on his sword belt, and the innkeeper hurried away. Mansel's mind was racing. He couldn't believe that Quinn had survived being thrown overboard in the Great Sea, but it was just like the wily old carpenter to survive and show up here. Mansel was sure Quinn wanted to take Zollin back to Gwendolyn. If his mentor didn't try to kill Mansel outright, he would certainly reveal Mansel's treachery to Gwendolyn. Mansel couldn't let that happen. Whether the person in the stable was actually Quinn or not, he needed to die.

The fury that had been building in Mansel was white-hot now. Normally he would have relished the opportunity to fight, to let his aggression go and vent his frustrations, but it was unnerving to think that Quinn could have survived after being thrown overboard. Mansel remembered seeing Quinn sink under the waves, and there was nothing but water in every direction as far as the eye could see. It was impossible to think that Quinn could have swum to shore, he told himself.

The nervousness only made him more anxious to fight, to exert his strength and let the tension that had been building up go. He stalked through the inn, the guests and staff giving him plenty of room. There was murder in his eyes and everyone saw it. Voices fell silent as he passed. Their fear made Mansel feel invincible as he stepped outside and turned toward the stable.

* * *

Miriam was frantic when she reached Orrock. The city was locked down and no one would allow her in. The invading army was making camp around Orrock, and she was trapped between their forces and the city walls. The guards looked at her with pity, but they couldn't take a chance that she was a spy.

"Please," she begged. "I must get in. There are people in danger."

"Ma'am, we're all in danger," the sentry at the city gate told her. "Your best bet is to get across the river. You might be safe there, if you can get across."

"No, I have to get in. You don't understand."

"I have my orders, I can't break them for you or anyone else."

"Please," Miriam begged. "I have to see Zollin. He's in danger, grave danger."

"I'm sorry," the soldier's face had gone stony, and Miriam knew she had lost him.

"Wait, can you take a message to Zollin?"

"I can pass it along, but I can't make any promises," the soldier said.

"Here," Miriam said, handing up the note that Kelvich had left at the farmhouse for Zollin. "It's very important that he get his note. It's life and death, do you understand?"

"I'll pass it along," he said.

The soldier disappeared for a moment and then he was back.

"I sent it to Zollin the wizard. It's the best I could do," he said.

She thought he sounded sincere, but he had been gone from his post for only a few seconds. For all she knew he might have tossed it in the dung heap and was just telling her what she wanted to hear.

"Thank you," she said.

The soldier nodded, and then Miriam was left with a difficult decision. She could see the invading army, spreading out across the plain that surrounded Orrock. There was no place for her to take shelter, and if she tried to go back toward Felson, she would surely be captured. They might let her go, she was just a woman after all, but armies had a reputation of not being very polite to women. She didn't think she could take that chance.

On the other hand, the Tillamook ran close to the city. If she could get across it she might be able to get home, but she couldn't swim, and the river was wide. The thought of trying to cross a river really frightened her. Ajax was a strong horse, and perhaps he could swim the river with her on his back, but what if she slipped off? She was suddenly terrified, and she realized she was all alone.

* * *

The soldier gave the note to another guard who happened to be passing by. That guard gave the note to man who was officially off duty, but with the army now starting to surround the city, no one was leaving his post without good reason. That soldier passed the note to one of the healers who was on his way back to the military compound.

The healer gave the note to one of the volunteers who was helping in the infirmary. The healers hadn't had much to do, since Zollin had healed the most critically wounded soldiers, but they were busy preparing for what they expected to be a major influx of wounded once the fighting started. The healer gave the volunteer instructions to take the note to Commander Hausey.

It took nearly half an hour of searching before the volunteer found Commander Hausey, who saw that the note was addressed to Zollin and then tucked it into his belt. He would have to go to the castle to give a report soon. He would pass on the note then.

* * *

Quinn was giving his horse a good rub down. He had already taken off the saddle and blanket, and the horse was busy munching on the hay that Quinn had put in the stall. There wasn't much light in the stable, just a single lantern that Quinn was using, but he heard the door open and guessed immediately who had entered.

"Mansel," Quinn said. "I thought you might find me here."

"You're alive," Mansel said. "I should have known you'd find a way to survive."

"You don't need to kill me," Quinn said. "We were under a spell. The woman in Lodenhime is a witch. You don't really love her."

"Stop trying to deceive me, Quinn. I know you want Gwendolyn to yourself. Why do you think I threw you overboard? Not that she would want an old man like you."

Quinn felt a cough coming. He knew that he couldn't avoid it, but he didn't want to appear weak in Mansel's eyes. The big warrior hadn't moved from the doorway of the stable, and Quinn had continued rubbing down his horse. He wished he had a better weapon. He still had the curve-bladed knife he'd taken from the outlaw. He had scoured off the rust and honed the blade so that it was razor sharp, but it was still a poorly made weapon.

"You aren't yourself, old friend," Quinn said. "Let me help you."

"I don't need your help," Mansel said, his voice rising with anger. "That's your problem, Quinn. You never trusted me. I'm not your apprentice anymore. I'm a man. I'm a warrior. I'm going to kill you and take Zollin to Gwendolyn, and there's nothing you can do about it."

"When we were on the road with Prince Wilam, you mentioned a girl," Quinn said. He was searching frantically for anything that might break the witch's spell. He didn't want to fight Mansel. He would probably end up dead, or Mansel would, neither of which was an option he wanted.

"Shut up. I've committed myself to Gwendolyn. Don't try to smear my honor."

"I'm not," Quinn said, then he coughed quietly into his hand.

"I'm sorry it has to be this way," Mansel said.

Quinn heard the quiet hiss of a sword being drawn.

"If you had just gone away," Mansel said, with a note of grief in his voice, "no one would have been the wiser. You could have had a long life, but now you have to die."

"Why?" Quinn asked.

"I can't take the chance that you might warn Zollin not to come back with me."

"He can't go," Quinn said. "I can't let that happen."

"You can't stop it."

"Are you sure about that?"

At that moment a coughing fit racked Quinn. He couldn't stop it, and he had to hold onto the stall wall to keep from falling over.

"You're in no shape to fight Quinn," Mansel said. "Don't make this harder than it has to be."

Anger welled up Quinn. He was tired, his body ached from the constant cough, and he had given up everything to be here. He was so close to reaching Zollin, and he wasn't going to just lie down and give up now.

"If you've got something to do, have at it. Otherwise, get out of my sight."

"If that's the way you want it," Mansel said.

"I would have forgiven you," Quinn told him. "But now I'm going to kill you."

A hard look crossed Mansel's face.

"You're like a rabid dog, and it's time someone put you down. I made you; I guess it's up to me to unmake you."

"You're a foolish, sick, old man. Killing you will be easy," Mansel said.

Quinn stepped out of the horse's stall and closed the door. Then he drew his long knife and bent his knees slightly. For an instant Mansel looked unsure.

"You know I can do it," Mansel said.

Quinn didn't answer, he just looked at the young man he loved like a son. A shadow of grief crossed his face. He knew that Mansel wasn't in his right mind, but he couldn't help but feel as if he had failed Mansel somehow.

Mansel charged forward, and all the pent-up rage and frustration and fear came boiling out in a terrifying battle cry. Quinn didn't move; he just waited for the charge. He knew he had to get inside Mansel's reach to neutralize his sword, but Mansel would be expecting him to do just that.

Mansel feinted to his left and then swung his sword in a tight arc with his right hand. Quinn danced away from the blade and let Mansel charge past him. The young warrior spun around, expecting an attack from behind, but Quinn stood quietly. His chest was burning, his arms felt weak, and his legs were heavy, but he did his best not to let Mansel see that anything was wrong.

"You still fight with your emotions," Quinn said. "That's gonna get you killed."

"Not by you."

He raised his sword and then stepped forward, bringing the blade down in a chopping motion. Quinn ducked, and the end of the sword struck the wood of the stall door behind him, sticking fast. Quinn dove forward, slashing with his curved knife at

Mansel's stomach. The big warrior dodged back, but he wasn't quite fast enough. The blade cut through his thick woolen pants and into the flesh of his hip. Mansel shouted in pain and staggered back.

"You bastard," Mansel shouted. "I'll cut your heart out."

He drew his own daggers, one from his belt and the other from his boot, and moved forward more cautiously. Quinn knew his young enemy had the upper hand now. Quinn couldn't even rely on his speed to give him an advantage. The sickness had sapped him of that. Even now, his eyes watered and his chest erupted in a coughing fit.

Mansel dashed forward, his daggers a blur. Quinn shimmied backward, blocking one blade with his own and ducking under the other. He spun and threw his left elbow into the side of Mansel's head, but it only glanced off the bigger man's skull, causing no damage. Mansel spun and Quinn dropped to the ground, scissoring his legs in an attempt to trip his protégé, but the younger man anticipated the move and dove forward. Quinn felt the steel slam into his left shoulder; the pain was exquisite and caused him to cry out in pain. At almost the same time Mansel hit the floor and rolled over his shoulder, coming up on his feet. He spun around as Quinn struggled to get up. He knew he needed to get the wicked-looking knife away from his mentor, so he kicked out at Quinn's right hand.

His survival instinct gave Quinn the speed he needed to avoid the blow. His arm darted back and then forward again, cutting a nasty gash up Mansel's calf muscle. The top of Mansel's boot folded down across his shin and Quinn saw the muscle, red and fibrous, bulge from the wound. Mansel hopped back, howling in pain, and Quinn staggered to his feet. He knew that now was his only chance. His left arm was worthless, but Mansel was having trouble putting weight on his wounded leg.

Quinn stepped forward and threw a kick at the side of Mansel's good leg. Perhaps Quinn was weakened from the nasty wound to his shoulder, or perhaps he just underestimated Mansel's strength, but the kick landed solidly without doing any damage at all. Quinn thought it was like kicking a tree, and then Mansel's hand lashed out, the blade flashing in the light of the lantern that Quinn had hung over his horse's stall. He dodged backward but wasn't fast enough. Mansel's dagger caught him in the cheek. He felt the blade puncture flesh and rattle off his teeth. Quinn fell back, dropping his blade and clutching at his wounded face. Then he felt Mansel's weight land on him, and the muscles in Quinn's back spasmed so hard they forced the air out of his lungs. He tried to turn as Mansel grabbed his hair and yanked his head up so that his neck was exposed. Quinn knew what was coming and threw his right hand across his throat. He felt the blade sawing through the muscles and tendons of his hand. He screamed again as Mansel released his hair.

"Fine, have it your way," Mansel said.

Then he slammed the dagger into Quinn's back.

Chapter 31

Zollin was in the small library of the castle. He was reading books about weather when the King came in, followed by his entourage. Zollin looked up and took in the grim look on the King's face.

"They've arrived," King Felix said. "We're going up to the watchtower to see what we can see. Come with us."

Zollin stood up. He would have liked to continue his study, but he had enough information for now. He followed the group of soldiers. Most were noblemen, although a life of military service was the best they could hope for. The noble families still oversaw the larger cities in Yelsia, but for the children who did not rule, the military was seen as an honorable place to earn a reputation and bring glory to the family name.

Zollin felt out of place with the men. He followed silently as they made their way up the winding staircase to the tallest tower of the castle. The youngest of the men, a commander not much older than Zollin himself, swung open the trap door that led onto the roof of the tower. The roof had a crenellated railing of stone and was large enough that all the men could stand easily on the tower's surface. There was a cool breeze, almost chilly. They could see the dark shadows of the enemy army spreading around the city. The dark ribbon of the Tillamook ran across the south side of the city, though the city walls didn't reach out that far.

"They'll have us completely cut off by morning," said General Yinnis. He was a large man, with long, dark hair that was turning gray. He still wore a sword, but he carried plans of the city under his other arm. On the front of his tunic was the image of a running boar.

"That's what we expected," said King Felix.

"We've men all along the city walls and more guarding the castle," said General Griggs. "The remainder of the Boar Legion and Fox Legion will bolster that force on the walls. Sir Tolis's Eagle Legion will remain in reserve. The Light Horse Legion from Felson is still under Commander Hausey's direction and is serving in the infirmary."

"And your Wolf Legion?" Felix asked.

"We are divided, half on the city walls, half guarding the castle," General Griggs said.

He was a middle-aged man who looked too small for his brightly-polished armor. He had a pinched face and small eyes that gave him the appearance of a rodent. His breastplate bore the emblem of a growling wolf's head.

"Zollin, tell me what you think," Felix said.

Zollin let his magic flow out. He could feel the people and animals inside the city, sensed their fear and anxiety about what was happening, but he pushed his perception farther. He could sense the men in the field. They were busy, but excited to finally be at their destination. Then he felt something odd. A lone person, edging closer to the river. There were no more Yelsians around the city, they had all either fled or taken refuge inside the city walls. The soldiers were moving in groups, and the woman all alone stood out to Zollin. He concentrated on her and recognized the spark of magic in her. It was familiar to him, an animal healer's power, stronger than when he'd last seen her, but he was sure it was Miriam.

"I don't know," he said to King Felix. "I don't sense anything strange. I can't feel the Master of the Torr or the dragon. The beast isn't close by."

"Odds are good it will attack us by night again," said General Tolis. He was the leader of the Eagle Legion, a short man with heavy features but bright eyes. His hair was cut close to his scalp and his emblem was a spread-winged eagle.

"I'm working on that," Zollin said, looking up at the night sky.

"Well, there's little more we can do here now," said King Felix. "I want men posted here with runners who can inform us of anything they see."

"I will see to it personally," said General Griggs.

They started filing down back down through the trap door, but Zollin focused on the lone woman again. She was terrified, both of being caught in the open and of the water. She was sitting on her horse facing the river and Zollin realized she needed to cross the river but was afraid to. He felt his magic blowing hot through him, like the billows of a blacksmith's forge. He lifted her, the horse and rider both panicking as they left the ground. He levitated them over the river and sat them down safely on the far side, sending them both reassuring waves of peace and safety as he did so.

He saw the horse turn, and the rider was now facing the city from across the river. He couldn't see her in the dark, but he could feel her sense of relief. Then she turned and rode east toward Felson.

"What were you doing?" the young commander asked him.

Zollin realized that they were alone on the tower. The other men had gone on without them, but the young commander had waited.

"I was helping a friend across the river," Zollin said.

"No really, you looked like you were in pain."

"I was helping a friend. She was caught between the city and the river. I levitated her across."

"I've heard of you," the commander said. "I'm Corlis, Commander of the King's Heavy Horse and third son of Duke Shupor."

"Zollin Quinnson," he said, holding out his hand.

The commander took it and smiled.

"Zollin Quinnson, not the *Wizard of Yelsia*?" he said, emphasizing the title.

"No, I'm a wizard from Yelsia, but I don't serve an official position here."

"You're an interesting person, Zollin Quinnson."

"Thank you," Zollin said, not certain if the young commander meant what he said as a compliment or an insult.

"Shall we?" Corlis said.

"Sure," Zollin agreed, walking first through the trap door.

Zollin wasn't sure if the young commander liked him or distrusted him. They descended back into the King's chambers. He was pacing in front of the dark fireplace. The room was warm even without a fire, and lamps had been lit and placed around the room. Commander Hausey was giving the King his report. The healers were ready and well equipped for whatever they might face. His troops stood ready to assist the healers and help move the wounded to the infirmary when they were needed.

Once he finished giving his report, the other generals started talking, and Hausey moved over to where Zollin was standing next to Commander Corlis. Hausey reached into his belt and removed the message.

"This came for you today," he whispered.

Zollin took the note. It wasn't sealed, and there was no name on the outside. He unfolded the paper and took in the contents in just a few seconds. He felt the blood drain from his face and his hands began to shake from fear and rage.

"Are you well?" Corlis asked.

Zollin didn't answer; he just handed the note back to Commander Hausey and ran from the room.

"Where is he going?" King Felix asked.

"I think he may be going to check on his friend," Commander Hausey said, his eyes still on the note.

"Well, go with him, Commanders. See that he gets back here quickly."

"Yes, my King," they said in unison and then Corlis and Hausey ran from the room.

Zollin was already halfway down the stairs. His heart was pounding. He simply couldn't believe what he had read. At first he thought it was a prank: the handwriting wasn't Kelvich's, but the signature at the end certainly was. Mansel had killed Kelvich. Zollin couldn't fathom why, and his mind simply refused to believe it, but he would get answers. Mansel had been evasive and distant. Zollin had chalked it up to shame over not being able to help Quinn. Zollin's father had been like a father to Mansel, too, taking him as an apprentice and then allowing the big warrior to travel with them when they left Tranaugh Shire. Quinn had taught Mansel to use a sword, and it made sense that Mansel would be grieved by Quinn's capture. But Kelvich had seen something else. Zollin had let his own grief blind him, and his need to find Brianna had kept him from listening to his mentor. And if the note was right, Kelvich was dead. Zollin couldn't wrap his mind around the fact.

His magic was churning, and he didn't notice the snapping, blue energy that was running up and down his arms as he ran from the castle.

"Open the gate!" he shouted.

The guards had strict orders, but the sight of Zollin, his power rippling over him, was all the motivation they needed. They lifted the heavy beam from the side door and opened it for him. He rushed out. They were just locking the door again when Commanders Hausey and Corlis came rushing after Zollin and called for them to open the door again.

Zollin crossed the wide street that ran around the castle walls and made his way to the inn where Mansel had said he'd wait. He was almost to the inn's door when the innkeeper stepped out.

"Good God!" the man shouted. "Don't hurt me."

"I'm not going to hurt you," Zollin said, realizing for the first time that his magic was getting away from him. He reined in the snapping energy, clamping down hard on his magic.

"I'm Zollin Quinnson—" he started to say.

"I know who you are. You're the wizard. I guess you got the message," the innkeeper said, thinking that Quinn had managed to get word to his son.

Zollin thought the man was referring to the message about Kelvich's death.

"What do you know of it? Did you send it?" he said angrily.

"No, not me. The man's in the stable."

"What's going on, Zollin?" Hausey said.

"Mansel's in the stable," he answered.

"No," said the innkeeper, "not Mansel. He's in his room. The other man was in the stable."

"What other man?" Zollin asked.

"The one who said he was your father."

Zollin felt the icy tendrils of fear wrap around his heart. He sprinted for the stables.

"What is going on?" Corlis shouted.

Zollin burst into the stable and saw Quinn lying in the hay, Mansel's dagger still protruding from his back.

Chapter 32

The dragon was soaring again. The wizard, now its master, had left it in the dirt all night and day. The humiliation had been crushing, and the beast was full of rage. The wizard had marched away with his army in the night and then traveled on to the big city near the river. The dragon had seen the city when it flew south. It was made of stone and wood, the buildings sprawling all over each other. It was full of men and beasts, and now the master wanted the dragon to fly to the city and burn the walls.

The beast could feel the wizard inside its head. It had forgotten how much it hated that feeling, every thought exposed, and the realization that it was no longer a free creature. The dragon had no idea how the wizard had learned its name. The dragon had been careless. The woman it had used to warn the villages must have spoken the dragon's name. Now it was carved in the wizard's crown and the dragon was a slave again.

When it had awakened from its hibernation, the dragon had thought only of more gold. Now, the dragon thought of the girl, too, but she was more than just a human, she was dragonkind. The dragon didn't know how that was possible, but as the wizard's commands pressed on its will, the beast dreamed of being back in the mountains with the girl. She had been the dragon's only companion, after centuries alone. She was a fiery spark of hope. If the dragon could escape the wizard's bondage, it would return for her.

The summer night was cool, and the feeling of wind in the dragon's wings made it feel powerful. It approached the city from a great height. The walls were easy to see, as were the soldiers on top of the wall. They were the same soldiers it had attacked by the river. Their armor was repulsive, and the dragon would not try to feed on the soldiers: the taste reminded the beast of the wizard who had come into the mountains to kill it. In the dragon's own lair the wizard had sent small shards of razor sharp metal flying into its mouth. The pain had been intense, but the dragonkind girl had healed that, too.

It dove, pulling its wings close to its scaly body. The wind roared against the dragon's eyes, causing the beast to squint, but that only helped it focus on a single target. It flared its wings at the last possible moment. The air caught in the leathery wings and stretched the dragon's breast muscles almost to the ripping point. Two hard flaps and the dragon's fight had stabilized enough for the beast to roar before spewing fire across the southern wall of the city.

* * *

Offendorl watched with glee as the dragon breathed fire and death onto Orrock's city walls. The dragon was massive and at first almost invisible. It was like a shadow above the bright city, but then the dragon's own fiery breath illuminated the scene. Offendorl could see the gleaming scales, the long, curved talons, and even the horned ridges on the beast's head.

"Send the message," Offendorl told the kings.

King Belphan seemed offended, but King Zorlan was now a true believer in the Torr's power. Using the dragon was the perfect loophole, Offendorl thought. He could let the dragon do the carnage and still claim not to have taken part in the battle.

King Belphan disliked that Offendorl used a golden crown to control the dragon. The King's jealousy was perfectly understandable to the wizard. Offendorl hadn't planned things this way, but with the dragon he felt invincible. He would force King

Felix to turn Zollin over to the Torr and then there would be nothing to stop their total domination. King Belphan recognized that the crown represented Offendorl's superiority over even the kings of the Five Kingdoms. His rule would be more direct from this point. The die was cast and there was no stopping it.

"King Felix must concede to our terms," Belphan said. "This has to be about more than the wizard, Offendorl."

"The boy is just the first step, Belphan, how often must I explain this?" Offendorl said cruelly.

"*King* Belphan, if you please, Master Wizard. I am the sovereign ruler of Osla. The problem with your plan is that it does not address our concerns."

"Without Zollin, the Yelsians are doomed. They cannot venture out of their city, and the threat of the dragon will keep them in line with whatever demands you place on them."

"We have your word you will support our demands?" King Belphan said.

"Yes, of course, just send the messenger."

The dragon had made three fiery passes and now Offendorl was calling the beast back. He fully expected King Felix to reject his offer. Perhaps he did not have Zollin after all. Offendorl could no longer feel the young wizard. Somehow the boy had learned to shut himself off from other magic users. But if King Felix didn't have the boy yet, he would move mountains to get him. That was all that mattered.

* * *

Zollin ran to Quinn. His father was still alive, but just barely. The knife had come down just below the heart, but it had punctured Quinn's left lung, and the bleeding was on the verge of causing heart failure.

"He's alive!" Zollin shouted.

Then his mind dove into his father. He rerouted the blood that was filling his father's lungs. Slowly he drew out the knife and began healing as much of the damage as he could.

"The dragon!" came a terrified shout.

Even inside the stable they could hear the beast roaring. It shook the ground like thunder and then followed the screams of panic. The horse reared in the stall, kicking against the wooden door.

"What the devil is it now!" cried Hausey as he and Corlis ran outside.

Zollin stayed focused on his father, but it was only seconds before Hausey was back at his side.

"It's the dragon, Zollin. The beast is here. Come quick!"

"I can't, my father could die."

"It's breathing fire on the walls," Commander Corlis shouted. "Get the men off those walls!"

"This is why the King sent for you, Zollin," Hausey said. "I'll see to your father, but you have to stop the beast."

"I just have to get him stable," said Zollin.

"It's coming round again!" Corlis shouted. "It's hitting the north wall this time."

Zollin was having trouble concentrating. He knew he was doing only a mediocre job on his father, but it would be enough to buy him some time.

"Zollin!" Hausey shouted. "We can't wait any longer."

"Move him into the castle!" Zollin shouted. He had pulled the knife completely out and sealed up the wound, but Quinn's lungs were still in bad shape and he was bleeding from gashes in his hand, face, and shoulder, too.

"He's stable for the moment, but I want someone with him all the time."

"I'll see to it personally," Hausey said. "You have to stop the dragon."

"It's heading for the east wall," shouted Corlis.

"I need someone to stop Mansel. I want him alive."

"I can do that," said Corlis. "What's he look like?"

"He's a big warrior with shaggy hair," Hausey said.

"The innkeeper should be able to point you to him," Zollin said. "But be careful. He's skilled in combat."

"As am I," Corlis said with a smile. "I won't let you down."

Corlis rushed off as Zollin tore down a stall door to use as a stretcher for his father. He levitated his father onto the board and then levitated it up and out of the stable. Hausey had to run to the castle to get men. They came rushing to Zollin and took hold of the corners of the door his father was laying on.

"Get him inside and safe, Hausey."

"You have my word," said the commander.

Zollin rushed back into the castle and levitated himself to the top of the watchtower. The guards there were terrified, but Zollin explained who he was.

"The dragon's veered off," said one of the lookouts.

Zollin let his magic flow out. It was as if he had unlocked a dam. The magic rushed out forcefully, and Zollin could feel the beast circling high over head.

"All right, it's going to take me a while, but tell the King I'm working on the dragon problem."

"Yes, sir," said one of the lookouts, before running down through the trap door with the news.

There were already clouds high in the sky, blocking some of the starlight. There wasn't enough that rain would be an issue, but Zollin didn't care. He didn't need rain, he needed electricity. He sent his magic into the clouds and began to focus on the tiny particles of water in the clouds. He pushed them with his magic and swirled them. It was like waving his hand through smoke, but he knew almost immediately that his plan was working.

The tiny water particles were made up of two different forms of gas that were stuck together to form the water. Each of those gas particles had an electrical charge. It was like rubbing his hair and then touching a metal spoon. As a kid he had loved to build up static electricity and give Todrek a shock by touching him. Now the cloud was charging up, and the amount of movement within the cloud's trillions of particles was creating an electrical power that was stronger than Zollin could produce using magic. He knew that when the dragon came again, he could, if his theory was correct, at least drive the beast away. The dragon may have iron-like scales that most steel could not penetrate, and it might be impervious to fire, but lightning was a different matter.

"What the blazes are you doing?" King Felix said angrily.

"I'm brewing up a storm for the dragon," Zollin said, trying to maintain his concentration.

"Where were you? I knew something like this was going to happen. Do you know how many people were killed because you shirked your duty?"

Zollin spun on the King then and stared at him angrily.

"This is not my fault," he shouted. "Don't blame me. I didn't send the dragon. If you were afraid of this, why did you station men on those walls? I was seeing to my father, who was almost killed. Don't you dare speak to me as if I'm your slave. I am here now. That is all that matters."

"And what will you do if the dragon comes back?"

"I'm going to hit it with lightning," Zollin said. "If you'll leave me in peace long enough to prepare it."

"Sire, there's a messenger coming from the enemy," came a voice from down below. "He's coming to the city gates."

"Are you sure you can deal with the dragon?" King Felix said to Zollin.

"Absolutely," Zollin said, sounding more confident than he felt.

"Generals, with me," King Felix said.

Zollin went back to stirring his storm cloud.

* * *

It took less than half an hour for the messenger to return. Offendorl was on top of his wagon, while King Belphan and King Zorlan waited anxiously below.

"Well?" King Belphan said when the messenger bowed before him.

"King Felix's response to your demand for the boy wizard was, 'Hell no.'"

"Good," Offendorl said. "We can have some more fun."

"Shall we send in troops?" Zorlan asked.

"No need for that," Offendorl replied. "We'll just continue to soften them up. By dawn they'll be begging to surrender."

He levitated the heavy, gold crown onto his head and felt the instant connection with the dragon. The beast was high in the night sky, circling just as Offendorl had instructed him to do. He sent the mental order to strike again, this time directly at the castle. Offendorl wanted King Felix to feel the heat personally.

He watched with the eagerness of a school boy waiting to see a shooting star. His hands were clasped in front of him, and his body was leaning forward. The dragon dropped, diving like a falcon toward its prey. Then suddenly, a bolt of white-hot lightning erupted from the night sky. It was there and gone in an instant, but Offendorl felt the shock of fear from the dragon. Then the thunder boomed. It wasn't a rolling wall of sound, but a sharp crack, followed by a massive slap that shook the ground.

The dragon veered away from the city, but another bolt of lightning surged out toward it. Once again the beast felt fear, but this time the lightning was close enough that it shocked the dragon, burning its tail. Offendorl felt fear, then pain, then panic, as a thunderclap once more shook the ground.

The dragon disappeared into the night, and Offendorl was forced to remove the helmet to break the link he had with the beast's mind, which was so crazed with fear it was scrambling the wizard's own thoughts.

"What is happening?" cried Belphan.

"Zollin," Offendorl said angrily. "The boy knows how to defeat a dragon."

"What do we do now?" Zorlan said.

"Now we do what I should have done all along," Offendorl said. "I'll go after the boy myself."

But not now, he thought, now I need rest. He raised himself from his chair, and for the first time in centuries he felt fear. He shook off the fear, angry with himself. This upstart boy had some skill, but no one could stand before Offendorl. For over two centuries he had been the most powerful wizard in the Five Kingdoms. Tomorrow he would prove that he still was.

"Ready your troops," said Offendorl. "We attack at dawn."

Chapter 33

Mansel was in his room. One of the wenches had been enlisted to tend his wounds. Mansel had removed all his clothes except for his undergarment which he had pulled down on one side. He had a deep cut on his hip, and the gash on his lower leg was even worse. The girl, not quite as old as Mansel himself, washed the hip wound with cool water. Her eyes kept darting up to his wide shoulders and the thick muscles in his chest. Then, she began to stitch the wound with practiced movements.

"You're good at that," he said through clenched teeth.

"My mother taught me to sew," she said in a flirty tone that was completely lost on Mansel. "She took work as a seamstress but made me and my sisters do all the sewing once we learned how."

It took half an hour to stitch up Mansel's hip wound. When the wench turned to the leg, she frowned. The muscle was swelling and bulging out of the gash.

"I can't stitch this one," she said. "You need a healer."

"Just sew it up," Mansel said, taking a long drink of the innkeeper's strongest wine.

"I can't, the muscle is sticking through."

"Daft girl!" Mansel shouted at her.

He raised his leg up, groaning with the pain, and poured wine over the wound. Then he used his fingers to push the swollen muscle back into the skin. Blood poured onto the floor.

"Start stitching," he said, his voice straining from the pain.

The girl looked woozy, as if she might pass out at any moment, but she stitched up the wound as neatly as she could. The wound was bright red and looked hideous as it curved up his calf.

"That's a damn ugly job," he said in a hateful tone. "No wonder your mother sent you off to be a whore."

The girl ran from the room, and Mansel took another long drink of wine. The alcohol didn't numb the pain, but it dulled his senses enough that he didn't notice it as much. He was about to curse that the girl had left the door open when a man stepped in. He was around the same age as Mansel, but not as big. He had long, curly, blonde hair that fell around his shoulders and a boyish-looking face. He had a neat mustache that he obviously trimmed and combed daily. His eyes were bright and he wore a military uniform.

"Are you Mansel?" the man asked.

"Yes, what's it to you?"

"You're wanted at the castle."

"By who?"

"A lot of people, actually. The King's at the top of the list, though."

"As you can see, I'm busy at the moment. I'll swing by in the morning."

"Oh, no," said the stranger. "That won't do. I've been sent to fetch you. I wouldn't want you trying to slip away since you're wanted for murder."

"What the hell are you talking about?" Mansel said.

"I have it on good authority that you killed a man on your way to the city. Almost killed another one in the stable. I'll have to take you in," he said. He was talking so nonchalantly that it was hard to tell if he was serious or joking.

Mansel reached over for his sword.

"Oh, I was hoping you'd do that," the stranger said.

"Who are you?" Mansel asked. "I like to know the names of the people I'm killing."

"I'm Commander Corlis, of the King's Heavy Horse. I come bringing tidings of your friend Zollin and his father."

"Go to hell," Mansel spat, rising to his feet.

"Oh, no, I'm a gentleman. We go to heaven."

Mansel drew his sword from its scabbard in one quick motion and attacked, swinging a vicious cut toward the commander's thigh. Corlis jumped back and drew his own weapon. It was a longsword, well made and light, much like Mansel's.

"It's too bad you're wounded," Corlis said. "I was hoping for a fair fight."

"You'll get more than you can handle," Mansel said.

He lunged forward, thrusting his sword out in front of him. Corlis parried with his own blade and thrust out a light slap of a kick that landed on Mansel's bandaged hip. He cried out in pain and staggering back.

"Ah, just as I suspected," said Corlis. "This is going to be easy."

Mansel's vision went red. All he could hear was a roaring sound in his ears. He grabbed the wooden chair he had been sitting in and threw it at the Commander, who side-stepped out of the way. It was exactly what Mansel expected the soldier to do; in fact, he had thrown the chair wide to the far side so that his opponent would dodge toward Mansel, who flicked his sword forward and up, slicing through Corlis's shoulder. The commander cried out in pain and staggered backward, but Mansel showed the man no quarter. He hammered Corlis with blow after blow from his sword. Corlis blocked the blows but was pushed back into the corner of the room. His shoulder was bleeding, and he was forced to fight using both hands to counter Mansel's power.

After several hammer-like blows, Mansel feinted high then shifted to a low thrust that cut across the Commander's thigh, skidding off the thick femur bone. Corlis cried out, almost dropping his weapon, and Mansel moved forward wearing a wicked grin.

He didn't feel the dagger stab him at first; he just realized that something was wrong because his sword seemed too heavy in his hand. He looked down at his hand, and saw Corlis yank the narrow blade free. Then fire erupted in his gut and Mansel's legs gave out underneath him.

"You stabbed me," he said in surprise.

"You're lucky Zollin wants you alive, you bloody oaf," Corlis said.

Then he spit on Mansel, who wanted to fight back, but his body wasn't obeying his commands. He felt warm liquid running over his thigh, and he realized it was his bladder emptying itself.

"Try not to die, bastard," Corlis said as he hobbled from the room.

Mansel laid his head back on the wooden floor of his room. The ceiling was plaster and a bit dingy from candle smoke. He thought of Nycoll for the first time in months. Nycoll with her little cottage by the sea. He wanted to go there, to be with her, but he was in Orrock. He was dying on the floor of an inn in Orrock and he didn't know why. What had happened, he wondered to himself as the room began to spin around him. His stomach lurched, and he rolled over to vomit, the bile burning his throat and smearing across his cheek when he couldn't hold his head up any longer. The lights were going dim and there was a ringing in his ears. Mansel knew he was dying, and his biggest regret was that Nycoll would not know what happened to him. He had promised her that he would return.

* * *

"You're wounded!" the innkeeper cried when he saw Commander Corlis. "You're bleeding on the floors."

"Not as badly as your patron," Corlis said in vile tone. "He's bleeding all over your precious floor. I think I smelled urine too. That's too bad for you. I'll send some men to collect him soon. Try to see that he lives."

Corlis staggered out of the inn and was met by several soldiers who helped him toward the castle. It took six men to carry Mansel, now unconscious, to the castle. Commander Corlis was helped into a room where Quinn's father was already being examined by healers.

"You've got another patient coming, but it may be too late for him," Corlis said bitterly. "The fool gave me no choice."

A few minutes later Mansel was hauled in and laid on a table.

"He's alive," said one of the healers, "but there's precious little we can do for him, Commander."

"Send for Zollin," Corlis said. "He'll know what to do. And give me something for the pain."

Zollin was on his way to the makeshift infirmary to check on his father when a healer hurried him into the room. Mansel was unconscious, and Zollin looked over at Corlis angrily.

"I told you not to kill him," Zollin said.

"He's still alive," the commander said. "He gave me very little choice."

"Yes, it looks that way. Are you all right?"

"I'll live, although I won't argue if you want to heal me the way you did the King."

"Give him something for the pain," Zollin said to one of the healers. "I'll get to him when I can."

Zollin let his magic pour into Mansel. The wound in his stomach was deep. Blood was flowing into his abdomen, and his small intestines were lacerated in several places. It took nearly half an hour to stop the bleeding. When Zollin was finished knitting together Mansel's abdominal muscles, he was forced to sit down. He was tired and hungry.

"I need wine," Zollin said. "And some food, please."

One of the castle servants ran to get the food as King Felix entered the room.

"Well this is a fine mess," said Felix. "At least your plan with the dragon worked."

"Partially, I meant to kill the beast," Zollin said.

"At least you know how to fend it off," said the King. "I don't suppose either one of these two fools was able to save Wilam."

"I don't know," Zollin said honestly. "I need to work on healing my father. Mansel should come around shortly. You can question him, but I'm not sure you'll get any useful information."

"And why is that?"

"Because he lied to me. He told me that my father and your son had been captured in Lodenhime. Now my father shows up here. I'm just not sure what is going on."

"Well, we can be sure of one thing," the King said. "Those troops will still be outside in the morning. We need a plan to defeat them."

"That's not my highest priority at the moment," Zollin said.

The King's face grew red. His eyes narrowed, and he stepped close to Zollin and spoke in a low voice.

"Well then, you'd better get your priorities straight," he said. "Orrock isn't your personal playground. Either get on board with what we're trying to do, or I'll hand you over to the Torr myself."

Zollin looked at the King in surprise.

"You did a good job with the dragon," the King said loudly, "but this is war, not some demonstration or parade. Those soldiers outside these walls have killed your countrymen. They have burned homes, stolen crops, done unspeakable harm to the innocent. Yet here you sit, like a spoiled child who only cares for himself. Yes, I understand your father is gravely wounded, but people died in this city tonight. Don't you care?"

Zollin stood up. He was so angry the blue, electrical power began snapping up and down his body. When he spoke, his voice was supernaturally low and forceful.

"And what have you done, oh King? You hide here and push others into a fight they had no part in starting. What did you do to your son, Prince Simmeron, after he poisoned you and sent assassins to kill his older brother? After he recruited a wizard from the Torr and kidnapped an innocent girl to force me into his service? Has Simmeron been brought to justice, or does he live in luxury in one of your many palaces? I am not your slave. I am not in your service. Do not speak to me again, King Felix," he said the ruler's name with such disdain that the King cowered back. "Your presence is not required here."

"This is my castle," the King said.

"No, this is the castle of a king, not a sniveling, selfish coward. Don't think I was not aware of your greedy attempts to bring me into your service. You are no different than your son. You wanted to use my power for your own gain. You could have stopped this war, but the truth is you wanted it. You want me to wipe out that army so that you will rise in power among the Five Kingdoms. I am no fool. Stop treating me like one."

"Zollin," came a weak voice from behind him.

The wizard turned quickly and saw his father, looking at him through glazed eyes. The power that had been building in Zollin waned, the energy stopped flowing, and his voice became normal.

"Father," he said, rushing to Quinn's bedside. "How do you feel?"

"Like I should be dead," he said.

"I need to do more work on you," Zollin said.

He started to send his magic into Quinn again but his father stopped him by taking his hand.

"Wait," he said. "You need your rest. Tell me what is happening."

"Brianna is gone," Zollin said. "The dragon took her." There were tears in Zollin's eyes. "Mansel is here, but he killed Kelvich. What has happened to him?"

"There's a witch in Lodenhime," Quinn said. "We were there looking to sail north with Prince Wilam."

"Does my son live?" King Felix asked from over Zollin's shoulder.

"Yes, he lives. But he has been bewitched. We all were. She casts some type of spell over men, and they forget everyone and everything else but her. She sent Mansel and me to bring you to her, Zollin. She wants you. You have to stay away from her."

"I will, I promise," Zollin said.

"We will deal with this witch once we have pushed Offendorl back into the sea," King Felix said. "See to your people, Zollin. I will see to the defense of our kingdom."

The King left the room and Zollin felt a wave of guilt wash over him. He wasn't proud of the way he had acted. It seemed like the world was against him. At one point, not long after he had discovered his powers, when he was still living in Tranaugh Shire, he felt as if the world was his for the taking. He had never heard of anyone who could do the things he was able to do. But now, despite all his powers, he felt helpless. Brianna was gone, his father was still not well, and Mansel had betrayed him. Now, he had been forced to confront his own King and fight a war he did nothing to start.

"Kelvich told me something about you, Zollin," Quinn said. "He told me you would wake up the magical world. Everything is changing and change can be hard, but you aren't alone. You can make the world a better place, but it won't be easy. Making things better takes work, but you've never shirked a task, son. I'm very proud of you."

"Oh, no," Zollin said, as tears came pouring from his eyes. "I've ruined everything," he moaned.

"No, you haven't. Sometimes you have to clear away the rubble before you can rebuild something good. We have to do what we can to make things better Zollin. You and I."

"I can't do it alone," Zollin said.

"You aren't alone. I'm here. I'll always be here for you. I love you."

"I love you, too, dad."

Quinn feel asleep after that and once Zollin had eaten he healed his father, Mansel, and Commander Corlis completely. It was late, well past midnight, when he finished. He was tired but he knew that he couldn't rest until had made one thing perfectly clear.

He climbed slowly up the steps to the King's personal quarters. The big, wooden doors, both elaborately carved with horses, were still open. The King sat with a goblet of wine, staring into a fire that had been kindled in the large stone fireplace.

"May I come in?" Zollin asked.

King Felix looked up and then nodded.

"What do you suspect the army will do?" Zollin asked.

"I don't know," the King said. "Offendorl is a powerful wizard. He may have plans up his sleeve that we can't imagine."

"If I take him out, what will happen?"

"Again, that depends," said King Felix. "If Baskla or Ortis sends troops to reinforce the armies from Osla and Falxis, then we'll be lucky to survive at all."

"How did this happen?" Zollin asked. "Is it really all because of me?"

"You know, I'm not a very wise man, Zollin. I've had the benefit of being King, but I didn't earn this position, I inherited it. My choices, good or bad, have long-lasting consequences that impact thousands of people, most of whom I don't even know. That's just the way life is for me, and for you."

"We have to stop the fighting," Zollin said. "Do you think the army will leave if you turn me over to the Torr?"

"Not without exacting a great number of concessions from Yelsia."

"Still, people might live," Zollin said.

"Surrender would allow people to live, that is true. I thought we could beat that army. I thought you would come in and fight for us, but that was foolish of me. I'm afraid I haven't been very kingly when it comes to you, Zollin. I thought I could use you to elevate Yelsia, but what I really wanted was to elevate myself. To do something my father and his father hadn't been able to do. I wanted to stand up to the Torr and be truly independent once more, like the kingdoms of old. Yet here I sit, defiant and surly, but still just a man. I don't know what I want anymore."

"I know what I want," Zollin said. "I want peace. I want to live my life without being hunted by the Torr. I've wrestled with what to do since Branock led the wizards of the Torr to my village. It seems like death and destruction follow me wherever I go."

"I don't know what is best for you, Zollin," the King said. "But I know this: Offendorl rules the wizards of the Torr like they are his slaves. I don't know much about magic, but I doubt you'll find what you're looking for with him."

"So how do we get out of this mess? I don't want to slay armies. That's a road I'm not willing to walk down. I know that in the past wizards were used to fight battles, but I don't want to kill people. That's not who I am or who I want to be."

King Felix looked at Zollin for a long time without speaking. Then he sighed and nodded his head.

"No, it isn't. I'm sorry I pushed you toward that, Zollin. I let my own ambitions cloud my judgement."

"And I have let my grief cloud mine. I'm sorry too," Zollin said.

"I will send messengers to seek peace in the morning. I would appreciate your help in that matter," the King said, "if you are comfortable serving as a counselor to your King. I promise I won't force you to do anything against your will."

"Well, I'm going to get a little sleep, then," Zollin said. "I'll see you in the morning, Sire."

"Sleep well," King Felix said as Zollin left.

The King waited for an hour before he rang the little bell that summoned his personal servant. The man was still wiping sleep from his eyes when he appeared.

"I want you to find Commander Hausey for me," he said. "I want to see him here, and I don't want anyone else to know about it. Is that clear?"

"Yes, my King," said the servant.

"Good, go quickly. He should be in the military compound."

The servant bowed and hurried from the room. King Felix stood up and drained the last of the wine from his goblet. Then he went to his desk and used one of the many large quills to write a message on thick parchment. He folded the paper and sealed it, pressing his ring into the soft wax to make an impression.

He was just pouring himself another goblet of wine when Commander Hausey came into the room. His face was puffy from sleep, but other than that he looked ready for any task his King might give him.

"I understand that you put Zollin on trial when he was in Felson," the King said.

"Yes, my King. I felt it was necessary because of the crimes my soldiers were accusing him of."

"Oh, I understand completely," the King said to reassure his commander. "I believe you drugged him, is that correct?"

"Yes, my King. It was the only way to keep him under control."

"What drug did you use?"

"It was just lavintha combined with milk thistle. It's what the healers use to dull pain. Enough of it renders a patient unconscious."

"And how did you administer the drug?"

Commander Hausey was torn between his friendship with Zollin and his duty to his King. He knew he had to answer; the only question was, could he live with himself if he answered truthfully?

"We mixed it in some fruit juice, which we gave him the morning of the trial," Hausey said, the words tumbling out of him and causing him to sag.

"Fine. I need you to take this message to the enemy," King Felix said. "Give it only to the wizard Offendorl personally, and wait for his reply. This task is of the utmost importance. Complete it well and you shall be richly rewarded," the King said.

Commander Hausey snapped to attention and saluted his King.

"Go quickly. I must have the answer before sunrise," said King Felix.

He watched as Hausey hurried from the room. Then he sent his servant to prepare a mix of lavintha and milk thistle. He closed his eyes and slept as he waited for the response to his message.

Chapter 34

Offendorl sat brooding in his wagon. Sleep would not come, but he had not expected it to. He was frustrated at the way things had turned out. He had not expected Zollin to know that lightning was the one thing dragons feared, nor how to conjure a storm. Someone must have instructed the young wizard, and Offendorl, like his minions before him, had underestimated Zollin's magical skills. Now he would have to fight the boy, and that was not what he wanted. It was so much easier to usurp power when it was given willingly. Now he would have to take the boy's power, and Zollin would be constantly striving to get it back.

The dragon had fled north again. Offendorl was coming to think of the beast as a skittish creature. It ran to the mountains at every opportunity. The distance was not a concern for Offendorl, as he still had the golden crown that enabled him to call the beast whenever he wanted. He was certain now that the dragon could not resist his commands, and that knowledge was enough for him at the moment.

There was a knock on the wagon's door. Offendorl scowled and stood up, his ancient joints popping as he did so. He opened the door and found one of the many military aides waiting for him.

"Excuse me, Master Offendorl, but there is a messenger from Orrock with a letter for you. He says he can only give it you and has to wait for your answer. It has the royal seal."

"Fine, bring him to me," Offendorl said.

He didn't know what sort of trickery this was, but he was willing to play along for now. Curiosity had always been his weakness. He simply wanted to know everything, and in some ways that passion had aided him. He had grown in power as he increased his knowledge, but there were, of course, times like this when his curiosity seemed like more trouble that it was worth.

Commander Hausey came striding purposefully toward the wizard. He was surrounded by no fewer than eight guards, all with weapons drawn. Hausey handed Offendorl the message. The seal was genuine, and the ancient wizard slid a crooked finger under the wax, popping it free from the paper. He unfolded the message and read it, his eyes narrowing gleefully as he read it.

"My answer is yes," he said. "If your King can deliver the boy as promised, I shall withdraw my forces."

"I shall convey your reply personally," Commander Hausey said. "With your permission," he said as he turned and strode back toward his horse.

Offendorl smiled wickedly. Things were turning out better than he thought. King Felix was obviously frightened, and that was exactly what the wizard needed. The King had just offered to turn Zollin over to Offendorl in exchange for the wizard's withdrawal from Yelsia. Of course, Offendorl had promised that King Belphan and King Zorlan could make their own terms for peace, but without his presence, he doubted the two bumbling rulers would be much of a threat to anyone.

Now, the Master of the Torr had only to wait for dawn. It was still a couple of hours away, but he suddenly felt like he could rest. There were no more worries to keep him awake. He returned to his wagon and lay down, his aging body relived.

* * *

Commander Hausey was troubled. He had come to respect Zollin. The boy had considerable power, but more importantly he was bright and compassionate. Now it seemed that King Felix was simply going to turn Zollin over to the Torr. Hausey knew that the treaty signed by all five kingdoms centuries ago forbade any kingdom from drafting a wizard into its military, but he didn't think that meant that Zollin should be forced to join the Torr.

His conscience fought a brief but desperate war. He knew that if he warned Zollin, he could be tried and executed for treason, but it wasn't just his friendship with Zollin that gave him pause. He had looked into the old wizard's eyes. He prided himself on being a good judge of character and what he'd seen in Offendorl was a man who could not be trusted. From a strategic point of view, handing over Zollin might seem like a good idea, but in reality it only strengthened their enemies and weakened Yelsia. Still, he was just a commander in the King's Army. His duty was to his King, and if Felix felt that this was the best plan of action, who was he to second-guess his sovereign?

He was allowed into the city without fuss, and he made his way to the castle. Once again he was not hindered from entering the royal residence, despite the late hour. The city was quiet and so was the castle. Hausey passed by the sick room where Quinn, Mansel, and Commander Corlis were sleeping. He knew he should have gone straight to the King, but he stopped at the room anyway. He told himself if they were all sleeping he wouldn't wake them, but would go on to deliver his message to the King.

He pushed open the door to the dark room and light from the hallway fell across the three prone figures. He sighed and was about to close the door when a voice spoke.

"Is all well, Commander?" Quinn asked.

"It is, at the moment," said Hausey. "Will you see your son this morning?"

"I imagine. I'm not sure where he is."

"Will you allow me to escort you up to his quarters?"

"Oh, is he staying here again?" Quinn asked. "I can find it on my own. I don't want to trouble you."

"No," Hausey said quickly. "It's no trouble. Come with me."

Quinn hadn't been able to sleep very long. He woke up in the darkness, but he felt so much better that he didn't want to sleep. Not only had Zollin healed his wounds, but he had also cured the cough that had plagued him since before he reached Felson. He wasn't even sore anymore. He felt strong, almost young again, and he had no desire to sleep.

Now that he had seen that Zollin was safe from Mansel, Miriam was constantly on his mind. He wanted nothing more than to set out as soon as possible and return to Felson. He had meant his promise. He was through chasing his son and serving his King. He wanted a quiet life, and he was determined to get it.

"I couldn't sleep," he explained to Commander Hausey.

"I'm Commander Hausey, of the Felson cavalry. Did you know I put your son on trial?" he said as they walked through the castle.

"No, I didn't," Quinn said surprised.

"Yes, I drugged his breakfast so that Zollin couldn't fight me. It was actually very effective. It seems if he can't think, he can't do magic. He becomes as helpless as a baby."

"Why are you telling me this?" Quinn asked.

"No reason," Hausey lied, not trying to hide his deception. "I'm afraid I must leave you here," he said outside Zollin's quarters. "I have a message to deliver to the King."

Quinn looked at Hausey, who stared right back. It was as if the commander was trying to communicate through that look, but

Quinn wasn't getting the message. Then Hausey walked away, and Quinn was left standing in the hallway. He opened the door to Zollin's rooms. They were dark and quiet. He went inside and found Zollin sleeping. His son hadn't bothered getting into the bed, he had just lain down across the covers, fully dressed, and fallen asleep.

"Zollin," Quinn hissed. "Zollin, wake up."

"What?" Zollin said in a groggy voice.

"Wake up, son, we don't have much time."

"Time for what?" he asked.

"Listen to me. Commander Hausey just had a talk with me. I didn't understand it all, but he was obviously sending you a message."

"What?" Zollin said rubbing his eyes.

"I need you wake up, son. This is important."

"Are you feeling okay?"

"I feel fine. Better than I have in weeks actually, thanks to you. Now listen. Commander Hausey was going to see the King, but he stopped by the sick room, and I was awake. He asked if I was going to come and see you. I told him I didn't know where you were and he offered to walk me up, insisted on it really. Then he told me he put you on trial and that he drugged you. Do you remember that?"

"Yes, it was in Felson, when we were going to fight the dragon."

"Good. He told me he put the drugs in your breakfast, and then he said he had to deliver a message to the King."

"So? What are you trying to say?" Zollin asked.

"I don't know," Quinn admitted. "But after the shouting match you had with the King, I think you may be in danger."

"No, I talked to King Felix last night. We both apologized, everything is good between us."

"So why did Commander Hausey feel like he needed to tell me about drugging you?"

"I don't know," Zollin said.

"Well, we'd better figure it out fast. Breakfast won't be long in coming. The kitchen staff were already hard at work when we came up here."

Zollin couldn't imagine why Hausey would tell his father about the trial at Felson. It had been a difficult time for Zollin, but he'd slept through the trial, he remembered that. Kelvich had to use some foul-smelling drug to rouse him. He wondered if it was really possible that someone he trusted, like King Felix, could betray him. Then he thought of Mansel. Whatever his friend's purposes were, he had slain Kelvich and tried to kill Quinn. Zollin wouldn't have thought such betrayal was possible, but obviously it was.

"Okay, well, at the very least I'm not eating breakfast," Zollin said.

"What could happen if you were drugged again?" Quinn asked.

"Kelvich said I was helpless. I suppose they could do anything they wanted with me if I were drugged."

"Yes, but what would they want to do? How would it benefit them?"

"I don't know," Zollin said. "I mean, they could hand me over to Offendorl, but I practically volunteered to do that already, and the King said that it wouldn't really help matters."

"You giving yourself up to the Torr might not, but perhaps if the King hands you over he has a better bargaining position. Or maybe he isn't planning on giving you to the Torr; maybe he wants to throw you in the dungeon or give you to one of the other kings."

"Either way, we can't let that happen," Zollin said. "We could sneak out of the city. I can get us across the river."

"That's only a short-term solution," said Quinn. "We need to think this through."

"We don't have much time. It'll be dawn soon. And the King told me he's planning to start negotiations at dawn."

"But Commander Hausey was returning with a message for the King when he woke me up."

"What are you saying?"

"I think whatever the King is up to, he's already at it. He may have been working on it before you even came to see him."

Zollin was frightened. He didn't like intrigue; it was foreign to him. He had always been an honest person by nature, and dealing with someone who wasn't intimidated him. He realized the only way to discover what the King was doing would be to play along.

"I'll have to fake it," Zollin said. "I'm supposed to join the King at dawn. He asked me to give him counsel in the negotiations. Whatever he's got planned, I'll just have to play along until they unfold."

"But by then it might be too late," Quinn said. "I don't like it."

"We don't have a choice. If things get out of hand, you'll have to help, but don't do anything that could get you hurt. I don't want you taking any more chances on my behalf."

"Zollin, you're my son. I would die if it would save you. That's just the way it is. When you have children someday you'll understand that."

"I doubt that I'll live long enough to have children."

"Don't say that. We're going to get out of this. What if we just confront the King? There's nothing he can do to you."

"No," Zollin said, "but he might do something to you. Besides, we don't know how deep this deception goes. For all we know, he may have surrendered the city. The castle could be surrounded by enemy troops right now."

"So who do we trust?" Quinn said.

"Commander Hausey, maybe. I just don't know."

"What about Mansel?" Quinn said.

"What about him? He tried to kill you, dad. He killed Kelvich. He killed Kelvich and I didn't even know it. I was so busy chasing the damn dragon that I let Kelvich die and I didn't suspect a thing."

"You couldn't have known that Mansel would do something like that. Mansel has been under a terrible curse. When I was under the spell I was planning on handing you over to the witch. I doubt Mansel even knew what he was doing."

"That doesn't make it okay that he murdered Kelvich," Zollin said, his voice rising.

"No, it doesn't," Quinn said in a calming tone. "And I doubt that Mansel will be able to forgive himself once he realizes what he's done."

"Why do you always take his side?" Zollin said. He could feel the old resentments and jealousies that had plagued him in Tranaugh Shire rising to the surface once more. "I'm sorry I'm not like him, but I'm your son. He's just your apprentice."

"Don't misunderstand me," Quinn said patiently. "I'm not excusing Mansel and I'm not taking his side. He threw me overboard in the Great Sea and all I had was a wooden bucket to keep me from drowning. He has a lot to answer for, but when he threw me overboard, the shock somehow broke the witch's spell. Maybe almost dying did the trick for him. If it did, then we may have an ally that no one knows about and that we know we can trust."

"But how can we know that the spell's broken? How can we really trust him?"

"It's easy," Quinn said. "If he can say anything bad about the witch, we'll know her hold on him is broken. When you're under her power, nothing seems important except being with her. If he's still in her power, he won't say anything negative about her, or let us say anything."

"All right, let's go. But we need to be careful. I don't want to lose you, dad. I love you."

"I love you, too, Zollin. I'm incredibly proud of you. We'll figure this out together, okay?"

Zollin nodded and the hurried from the room. The sky was just beginning to lighten, and only the servants seemed to be moving around the castle. They made it back down to the sick room without being questioned. Inside, Zollin lit a lamp so they could see. Commander Corlis and Mansel were still asleep.

"Wake him up," Zollin whispered.

Quinn shook Mansel and said his name in a whisper by the big warrior's ear. Mansel's eyes fluttered open. He looked at Quinn and the shame on his face was plain to see. Tears welled up in the warrior's eyes.

"Are you all right?" Mansel asked.

"Yes, I'm fine, thanks to Zollin," Quinn said.

Mansel looked at Zollin, and the wall that held back his grief broke. He sobbed quietly. Zollin was surprised. He had never expected to see Mansel cry.

"I'm so sorry," he said. "Oh, God, I killed Kelvich. Oh, no."

"Pull yourself together," Zollin whispered. "We've got trouble and we need your help."

"What you did was terrible, but you were under the witch's spell," Quinn said. "She's a vile bitch, that one. She deserves to burn in hell."

Quinn was looking at Zollin when he spoke, and they both looked at Mansel.

"I was a fool," he said. "I would have done anything for her. How is that possible, Quinn?"

"Magic is powerful," Zollin said. "And we need to be sure the spell is broken, Mansel. I need to hear you denounce her."

"Denounce her? I'll kill her if I ever see her again, even if it means my own death. She can't be allowed to go on. There's no telling what she can do, Zollin."

"We'll deal with her when we can, but first we have a situation here."

"What sort of situation?" Mansel said.

"We're in Orrock; did you know that?" Quinn asked him.

"Yes, I remember everything," he said bitterly, as if the words were acid in his mouth.

"Then you know there's an army laying siege to the city," Zollin said.

"And I think there's a plot against Zollin," Quinn said.

"What are we going to do?" Mansel said.

"Play along for now," Zollin said. "But I need you to watch Quinn's back."

"I will. I won't let anyone near him."

"All right, good. Give me a little time. I'm supposed to meet with the King soon. I'll be pretending to be drugged. I want you guys ready to move at a moment's notice. Don't worry about me, just make sure you get out of the city safe, if you have to."

"All right. And Zollin, I'm sorry."

Anger fought with sympathy inside Zollin as he looked at Mansel. He could see the contrition on Mansel's face, but it didn't bring Kelvich back. The old sorcerer had been Zollin's mentor and a good friend. The thought of Kelvich dying with strangers was incredibly painful, but he didn't have time to grieve. He'd made that mistake with Brianna, and it had cost Kelvich his life. He didn't want anyone else to die because of his anger or rage. He put it from his mind and nodded.

"Just stay safe," Zollin said.

* * *

Commander Corlis lay as still as possible. His eyes were closed, but he heard every word that was spoken. He knew that Zollin suspected the King of foul play and that he intended to go along with the King until he knew what was happening. Corlis wasn't sure what he should do. If he went to the King, Zollin would be in danger, and Corlis was fond of Zollin. He had hoped they might become friends, but his first duty was to his King.

He had to figure out a way to get to the King without arousing suspicion that he was privy to Zollin's plans. When Zollin hurried from the room, Corlis had hoped that Mansel and Quinn would follow, but they decided staying put was their best option. Corlis waited, impatiently. He knew he needed to convince Quinn and Mansel that he was just waking up and hadn't heard their plans, but he also knew the longer he waited, the more time he was giving Zollin to betray the King.

Finally, when he couldn't wait any longer, he yawned dramatically.

"Whose idea is it for sick people to have to sleep on a wooden table?" he said in a lazy voice.

"You're awake," Quinn said. "Zollin healed your wounds."

"Yeah, now I just need someone to work the kinks out of my back from sleeping on a wooden table all night."

"You're lucky to be breathing," Mansel said. "If Quinn hadn't wounded me in our fight, I would have chopped you into bits."

"Speaking of which, I think it's time the castle guard put you where you belong," the commander said. "I'm sure a dungeon cell will make this place seem like the King's own chambers in comparison."

"There's no need for that," Quinn said. "He was under a witch's spell when he attacked us. The spell has been broken."

"Oh, okay," Corlis said. "If he was under a spell from an evil witch, then everything's fine. Oh, wait, this isn't a children's story. This is real life, and he attacked an officer. That's a hanging offense, I believe."

"You can't be serious," Quinn said.

"I can," Commander Corlis said in an arrogant tone. "You both stay here."

"Okay," Quinn said.

Then he punched Corlis on the chin with a right hook that snapped the commander's head to the side. His eyes rolled back as he collapsed in a heap on the floor.

"Help me get him up," said Quinn. "We'll put him on the table and lock the door from the outside."

"And where are we going to go?" Mansel asked.

"Somewhere we can be of help if we're needed."

Chapter 35

Zollin hurried up to the King's chambers, where he found the King eating with his generals and Commander Hausey. The King stood up when Zollin entered.

"Ah, Zollin. We're just about to talk strategy," the King said in a warm tone. "Someone get Zollin a plate of food. It's going to be a long day, and we may not get the chance to eat again anytime soon. You need to eat to keep up your strength."

Zollin nodded and took the plate of food he'd been given by a servant. He tried desperately to remember what had happened in Felson when he'd been drugged. He remembered eating and then being woken up hours later by Kelvich. The King was already talking to his generals, discussing plans for King Felix to ride out with Commander Hausey and General Grigg under a flag of truce to sue for peace.

Zollin walked among the men, pushing out thoughts of seeing him eat, but he didn't touch the food. Instead he scraped bits and pieces off his plate, just letting them fall on the floor. He wasn't sure what else to do with them. He hoped his portrayal of a drugged person would be convincing enough to fool the King and his generals.

"I think perhaps Zollin should ride out with us," King Felix said. "It will give us a chance to catch up on what we've been planning."

"Not to mention he might prove useful in dealing with this wizard from the Torr," General Grigg added.

"That's fine with me," Zollin said casually, but he was looking at Commander Hausey when he spoke. The look in the soldier's eye wasn't lost on Zollin. It was obvious the King was planning something.

"Let's go, then," Felix said. "The sooner we break this siege the better."

They walked down the stairs together and Zollin moved slower and slower. Commander Hausey took his arm once they were several paces behind everyone else.

"Why did you eat?" he hissed in Zollin's ear.

Zollin looked at him and winked. Then he leaned on Hausey.

"Master Zollin," Hausey said loudly. "Are you well?"

"Just tired," he said, shaking his head as if to clear the cobwebs.

"The boy needs more sleep," said King Felix in a patronizing tone.

"I'll be fine, Sire," he said.

"Yes, I'm sure you will. Let's get mounted."

"What can I do?" Hausey asked in a hushed tone.

"Just stay close and alert."

Commander Hausey helped Zollin onto the horse that a servant was holding for him. They rode through the city just as the citizens of Orrock were starting their daily chores. Zollin made a show of sagging lower and lower in his saddle. When they arrived at the main gate, General Griggs raised a lance with a white banner. The other generals rode through the gate first, followed by King Felix, then Zollin and Commander Hausey.

"Sire, I believe there is something wrong with the wizard," said General Griggs in a mocking tone.

Zollin was now slumped onto the neck of his horse. He pretended to be completely senseless.

"Sire," Hausey said. "What's happened to him?"

"I took your advice, Commander, a little lavintha and milk thistle."

"But why?"

"We're making a deal," King Felix said, "the one you brokered last night. Don't act so surprised; we all knew this was inevitable. The boy had his uses, but he is a liability. This way, we end the siege in one master stroke."

"Stay with him, Commander," said General Griggs. "Make sure he stays on his horse. We don't want the prize spoiled."

They rode out toward the enemy lines. Zollin tried his best to look senseless while taking in as much of the scene as he could. The sun was just high enough to shed light on the army surrounding the castle. They were already up and in formation, as if at the slightest command they could attack the city.

King Felix stopped less than fifty paces from the opposing army. They had to wait only a few moments before a similar delegation rode out from the enemy lines to meet them. Zollin didn't have a good view, but Commander Hausey held up five fingers beside his leg, and Zollin guessed that meant that five riders were approaching.

"King Felix, thank you for coming," said Offendorl.

"I have the boy," the King said. "He is drugged and will offer no resistance."

"Excellent thinking," Offendorl said. "I will take him with me and leave the negotiations to you kings."

"I thought I made myself clear," said King Felix said. "Once you have the boy, you are to take your army and leave Yelsia."

"Ah, but there is the matter of expense," said King Belphan. "This venture to ensure the peace was costly, I'm afraid. Reparations must be made, both to Osla and Falxis."

"Bring your demands before the council, King Belphan. I will not hear of your squabbling for coin while your army besieges Orrock."

"I find that we are in the best bargaining position now," said Belphan.

"Finish your negotiations without me," Offendorl said. "The sound of your voices wearies me."

"Give him the boy, Hausey."

Commander Hausey hesitated, but Zollin gave a slight nod. Hausey led Zollin's horse to Offendorl. The ancient wizard took the reins of Zollin's mount and turned his own horse as if to lead them away. They had gone only ten paces or so when Zollin saw the old man nod, and a group of fully armed knights came charging forward.

"It's a trap!" Hausey shouted.

King Belphan and King Zorlan turned their horses and raced away, while their knights came charging forward.

"Surround the King," General Tolis shouted.

"We must retreat!" General Griggs shouted.

"There is no time," Hausey cried.

Zollin waved a hand and a wall of invisible power slammed into the charging cavalry. The horses were knocked backwards, and their riders flew forward and crashed into the barrier.

Offendorl turned, throwing up a shield between himself and Zollin, but the young wizard was already attacking.

"Blast!" he screamed, thinking of his first attack on the wizards from the Torr in Tranaugh Shire. His attack then had surprised them, but it had not hurt them. Zollin expected no less from Offendorl, so he purposely let his attack go wide. Two thick beams of crackling energy shot from his hands. They bounced off the elder wizard's defenses and then slammed into Offendorl's wagon. The large wooden vehicle exploded and wooden shards flew into the air. The shockwave from the explosion rocked Offendorl forward as Zollin grabbed as many wooden shards as he could and sent them hurtling toward the master wizard.

Offendorl's shield held the wood back, so that not even a splinter touched him, but his horse was a different matter. Several large slivers of wood sank into the horse's hindquarters, causing the animal to buck and jump. Offendorl was thrown from the animal, and Zollin expected to see him land in a heap of broken bones on the hard ground. Instead, Offendorl rose up in the air and sent balls of fire hurtling toward Zollin.

Zollin kicked his horse and sent the mount charging forward so that the fireballs flew over his head.

"Get back to the castle!" Zollin shouted.

"Ride!" Commander Hausey bellowed, turning his horse and galloping back toward Orrock.

The other generals and King Felix followed, just as Zollin rode directly under Offendorl. He held up a magical shield over his head and pushed it up toward the elder wizard. The fireballs were bouncing off the shield now, each impact like a hammer blow on a knight's shield, but the fire was also getting closer to Offendorl so that he was forced to move away.

At that same moment the army surrounding Orrock took the explosion and fire to be their signal to attack. The troops hurried forward, slapping their swords on their shields and stomping their feet. Clouds of dust rose in the air around them, and horns sounded on every side. Zollin was momentarily distracted and Offendorl's next attack, a stunning whirlwind conjured in midair and sent hurtling toward Zollin, blew him off his horse as the mount reared its hooves, pawed at the air, and then stumbled backward.

Zollin landed on the ground with a massive crash that sent pain shooting through his back, but he didn't have time to stop moving. The ground shook and began to split under him, so he jumped into the air, using his magic to shoot himself like an arrow straight at Offendorl. He didn't know that wizard battles rarely brought the combatants close enough for hand-to-hand fighting. Offendorl was surprised at the move and flung up his magical shield for protection, but Zollin had his own shields raised. The two wizards crashed together, their magics surging.

Zollin felt his own power coursing through the containment field he had constructed. It was blindingly hot, but the containment held and didn't allow the magic to drain his physical strength. Offendorl, on the other hand, was sweating. Zollin could see the strain on his opponent's face and doubled his efforts to get closer to the elder wizard. It was like the intense struggle when two warrior's blades lock together and the battle becomes a test of strength. Zollin could feel the barrier around his magic starting to break apart. He knew that pushing himself this hard was dangerous. If his containment broke down, he could easily be killed by the magnitude of his magical exertion. At the very least he would be knocked unconscious by the strain.

Offendorl felt as he was being pressed down by a giant. He was shocked at Zollin's raw power. He had expected the boy to fight as other wizards fought. Most were loath to do anything physically, so they kept their distance and used their magic to fight.

But Zollin was drawing ever closer and there was a look of murder in his eyes. If Offendorl let the boy get close enough, his young, physical strength would certainly spell doom for the elder wizard. Offendorl tried to pry himself away, but the boy just kept coming. Offendorl felt his own magic tearing away at him on the inside. His body was shaking, and the effort he was exerting with his magic was more than he had used in years. Normally, if he had difficult magic to perform, he could stop, rest, and get refreshment. But now he was trapped with no way to end the onslaught of Zollin's ferocious attack.

Hausey led the retreat. He was an active cavalry soldier and was at home on a horse as much as anywhere. He rode hard, bellowing for the soldiers to open the gate for their King. The gate was rising slowly, and Hausey glanced over his shoulder to see the other generals riding hard to keep up with him. King Felix looked frightened, but he was staying in the saddle. General Griggs, on the other hand, was falling further behind. He was more focused on hanging onto the saddle horn than coaxing more speed from his mount.

At the gate, Hausey spun his horse around. The gate was a huge grid of metal with the lowest parts of the vertical bars ending in sharp points. Behind the actual gate, which was raised straight up, there were two large wooden doors. The doors were hung on massive iron hinges that shrieked as the doors were slowly swung open. King Felix and his generals hurried under the gate and through the huge doors as Hausey looked for Zollin.

The young wizard was reaching for Offendorl with his left hand, straining to reach the elder wizard's throat. Then suddenly he twisted in midair and swung a looping punch with his right hand. The magical barriers slowed the blow, but it hit the older man behind his ear. The blow was hard enough to interrupt Offendorl's concentration, and his magical defenses were knocked away by Zollin's power. The Master of the Torr dropped. They were perhaps twenty feet off the ground, and Offendorl slowed his descent on reflexes alone, but his brittle bones were still rocked by the rough landing. Both ankles rolled and ligaments snapped, causing the wizard to fall to the ground.

Zollin immediately began trying to bury the old man. Dirt and rocks flew from all sides, falling on Offendorl as Zollin slowly descended to the ground several feet away. Then fire erupted from the mound of dirt, like an angry volcano, shooting up toward the sky. Zollin sent a massive, magical shove at the mound, and the dirt flew in all directions while Offendorl rolled along the ground like a tumble weed.

The elder wizard knew that once again he had underestimated the boy. Whether King Felix was in on the deception or not, the Master of the Torr had been duped into thinking the boy was being turned over to him, drugged so that he would not resist. Zollin had taken him by surprise, and now Offendorl was close to defeat. He did the only thing he could think of that might save him. With the last of his considerable strength he reached out to the main gate of the city and ripped it apart.

Zollin heard the rending of stone, iron, and wood as the gate was pulled down. Commander Hausey had just ridden through and the soldiers were trying to close the gate when Offendorl's attack came. Had the gate been closed it would have been more difficult to destroy, but now the city was vulnerable and the invading legions were rushing forward. Zollin threw up a dust cloud to screen him from the elder wizard's sight and sent himself hurtling back toward Orrock.

Hausey was just leading a group of soldiers into the gap in the wall when the enemy army arrived. Hausey was outnumbered, but he had formed his soldiers into a solid shield wall. The invaders crashed into the shield wall but were held in check. Zollin smashed into the invaders with a magical dive that sent the enemy soldiers flying backward. He came to stand on his feet in the midst of the destroyed gate. He looked back toward Offendorl, expecting the Master of the Torr to be in the middle of his own counterattack, but the wizard was nowhere to be seen.

"Get up to the tower!" Hausey shouted at him.

Zollin looked up and realized that from the lookout tower the could see where Felix's army was having difficulty and help turn the tide. He didn't need to be in the midst of the battle physically; he could work his magic from a distance.

"I'll send reinforcements," Zollin shouted as he sprinted through the soldiers who opened the shield wall for him to pass by. As he ran he heard Hausey shouting for his troops to form up and prepare for the next attack.

Zollin jumped up and levitated himself up over the city and came to land once more on the watchtower of the castle. He turned and looked back at the main gate, but Hausey was holding his own against the invaders.

"Send reinforcements to the main gate!" Zollin shouted at the runners who were waiting down the stairs from the tower's trap door. "At least half a legion. We need to hold the gap in the wall."

He turned and surveyed the battle. It was now taking place on all sides of the city. Archers were raining down arrows, and soldiers were using long poles to push off scaling ladders that were being thrown against the walls. He took a deep breath and tried to calm the fire raging inside of him. He knew the siege would last a long time, and he was already at his magical breaking point. The Master of the Torr had been incredibly strong, and Zollin knew that he had gotten lucky in the fight. The next time he would need to be more prepared.

"He's my son, now let me through!" Zollin heard from down below.

Quinn and Mansel came charging up through the trap door, both looking shocked.

"What happened?" Mansel asked.

"The King tried to drug me," Zollin explained, "and turn me over to the Torr, but the old wizard double-crossed him. I saved the King and his generals, but not before the old wizard tore the gates down. We'll be lucky not to be overrun."

"I say let them come," Mansel said.

"You won't see much action up here," Zollin said.

"We're staying with you, son," Quinn said. "Look, they need help there on the south wall already."

Quinn was pointing to an area where enemy soldiers had gained the ramparts in several places using ladders.

"Where are the defenders?" Mansel said.

"Caught off guard, I suppose," Quinn answered.

Zollin was already delving into his magic. It was like walking through an inferno. His containment field was holding, but just barely.

"I need wine and food, Mansel," Zollin said.

"How can you think of eating at a time like this?"

"Just get it. Hurry!" Zollin shouted.

Mansel rushed down the stairs as Zollin sent a shock wave of magical power hurtling toward the invaders who had taken up a position on the southern wall of the city. The power was invisible, but the results were undeniable. The enemy soldiers went flying off the wall, knocking their climbing comrades off the ladders as they fell. Yelsian soldiers came running from both directions to secure the wall.

"We need more men on the south wall," Zollin shouted down the trap door.

"Here comes the King," said Quinn, who was leaning over the wall and looking down into the castle courtyard.

"He won't be happy," Zollin said.

"I should kill him for betraying you," Quinn said.

"No, that isn't our place. We're going to help the city survive and then we'll figure out the next thing to do."

"What if the King turns on you again?"

"We'll deal with that if it happens."

He began using his magical power to push the scaling ladders off the wall wherever he saw them. The ladders weren't heavy, but leaning against the wall, especially when a man was climbing up the ladder, made them especially difficult to cast back down.

King Felix arrived on the tower before Mansel returned with food for Zollin.

"What the devil are you doing?" King Felix said.

"I'm saving your city," Zollin said angrily. He felt his magic on the verge of overcoming his control, and he sagged against the wall, hunger and fatigue finally taking their toll despite the adrenaline pumping through his veins.

"You had no right," said King Felix.

"No right to do what, not eat the food you drugged? Or maybe save your life when the Torr wizard betrayed you? Or maybe you mean I have no right to risk my life for this city. Which is it?"

"How do I know you didn't destroy the gate?" King Felix said. "This could all be part of some elaborate plan."

"Don't be a fool," Zollin said. "I've done nothing but help, but I'll be glad to leave the city and let you fight this battle on your own."

"No, no, no!" King Felix shouted. "Stay, help us. We'll deal with all of this madness later."

"You're right, we will," Zollin said.

The attack began to falter after an hour or so. Mansel finally arrived with a large bottle of wine. He also had bread, cheese, and some roasted chicken.

"Sorry it took me so long, but I couldn't find anyone in the kitchens," Mansel said.

Zollin tore into the food like a starving man. He started with the meat, ripping off huge chunks with his teeth, hardly chewing at all, and then swallowing it down. He gulped the wine and felt his strength returning.

Reports began coming in to the King that the enemy was pulling back. They weren't retreating but rather halting their attack. They began moving toward the main gate, which didn't surprise Zollin.

The King sent a large portion of his soldiers to hold the gate, and Zollin thought it best he go there, too. Mansel was happy to be getting into the action. He wanted to fight, and Zollin knew it was a way for him to deal with the frustration and shame he felt for his actions while under the witch's spell. They hurried down to the main gate, or where the main gate had once stood. It was completely destroyed, but most of the rubble was there.

Commander Hausey was still organizing the defense. He had a dent in his helmet, and blood was trickling down from under it.

"Zollin, it looks like they're going to push hard here," Hausey said.

"I expected as much," Zollin replied. "We need to be ready for them. What can I do?"

"Can you heap this rubble up, so that it makes the entrance narrower?"

"Sort of like a bottle neck?"

"That's right, and if we can station men on top of the rubble, the enemy will try to break through the center and we won't have to fight so many at once."

Zollin was feeling stronger, although his magic was still churning like a forest fire. He let his power flow out and began to levitate the rubble. Quinn helped him figure out how to build up the piles so they were most secure, and, when they were finished, the opening where the gate had been was now wide enough for only five men to pass through walking side by side.

"Do you think they'll attack?" Mansel asked.

"They should," Hausey said. "They won't have a better opportunity. We beat back their attempts to scale the walls. Am I right in assuming you had a hand in that, Zollin?"

"I did what I could."

"It was a big help. If they had gotten inside the city all would have been lost. We simply don't have enough men to cover every part of the wall, not now that most of our reserve troops were called in to help hold the main gate. To answer your question, Mansel, I think they will attack again, but they could revert to a siege. If they do, though, we'll need to find a way to drive them away. A siege would allow us to make this gate stronger, but we can't fully rebuild it."

"And if we give them too much time their wizard will recover and nullify the advantage that Zollin gives us," Quinn said.

"That's absolutely right. We need to end this, as soon as possible."

"Can you tell what the wizard from the Torr is up to?" Quinn asked Zollin.

"No, I can't sense him. He's got defenses as I do," Zollin admitted. "What if we could get our heavy horse cavalry out to attack them? Could we disrupt them enough to drive them back?"

"It's possible, but we would need a way to get the horses out of the city," Hausey said.

"I think I can manage that. And then, I can use magic to mimic the sound of charging cavalry and disrupt them more. At this stage I think illusion is a better weapon than anything else we've got."

Commander Hausey gave the order for the heavy cavalry to form up at the main gate. Half an hour later, Commander Corlis in full armor rode up and raised his visor.

"Tell me what you have in mind, Hausey," he said.

"Zollin is going to create a distraction for you, then do your best to kill as many as you can," Hausey said.

"I'm going to create a massive dust cloud to hide your troops," Zollin told him. "Then I'm going to do my best to scare the hell out of them, but it's up to you to get them scattered and running."

"That should be no problem, if we can get out of the city. From what I've heard you put most of their cavalry out of commission earlier."

"Yes, I hope that was most of them," Zollin said. "Where were you, by the way?"

"Ask your father," Corlis said, turning his horse and riding back to his men.

Zollin looked at Quinn who just shrugged his shoulders.

"What?" Quinn said, trying his best to sound innocent.

"Do I want to know?" Zollin asked.

"Let's just say your old man has a mean right hook," Mansel said.

"Oh, boy. Let's get started."

Chapter 36

Offendorl was moving as quickly as his withered legs could carry him. Healing his sprained ankles had taken what little magical power he had left. He was sure that Zollin had moved back toward the city, but that didn't mean he was out of danger. His chest was heaving, and his center of magic felt as if it were eating him alive. He hadn't been tested in magical battle in decades, and the effort it had taken to withstand Zollin's unrelenting attack had almost broken the ancient Master of the Torr.

He could see the kings and their generals, all still on horseback. None seemed interested in coming to his aid, which only made the elder wizard more angry. He had been caught off guard, and even though he knew it was a simple mistake, he felt embarrassed. In the Torr he maintained total control over himself, his circumstances, and the other wizards. It had been years since he had been forced to work the kind of magic he had used just to survive his duel with Zollin. Now he was exhausted, his mouth parched and his tongue stuck to the roof of his mouth. His legs shook, so that with each step they felt as if they might collapse beneath him. His arms ached, and worst of all, his breathing was becoming difficult. He needed to stop, to rest, to eat and drink, even take the time to heal himself, but he had no time. Nor did he have the magical strength to do any sort of magic at the moment. All he knew was pain and urgency.

When he finally drew close enough to the group of kings and generals they took note of him. King Belphan looked down his nose at the ancient wizard.

"It seems you were wrong again, Offendorl," he said.

"Don't . . ." the wizard said between gasps for breath, "mock . . . me."

"I'm not mocking. I'm simply stating a fact. Every step of this entire invasion has been a disaster. Now it is up to our armies to do what you could not."

"What is happening?" Offendorl said.

He turned back to look at the city for the first time since he had fled the battle with Zollin. He watched as the army marched toward the city. Seeing thousands of troops storming a castle was a spectacle, but the wizard had no interest in the battle.

"I need a horse," Offendorl said.

None of the officers moved.

"What happened to yours?" Belphan said in a mocking tone.

"You know what happened," Offendorl said. "Or were you too busy running away to notice?"

"Do not try me, old man. I've listened to your condescension for the last time."

"And I your impudence."

"General Varlox, bring me the wizard's head!" Belphan shouted.

One of the men next to King Belphan drew his sword and spurred his horse forward. Despite the intense heat and pain it caused, Offendorl reached out with his magic and snapped the general's neck. The soldier toppled backwards off his horse, dead before he even reached the ground. The horse, sensing it no longer had a rider, trotted to a stop next to Offendorl, who took hold of the animal's bridle.

"You are a fool, Belphan," Offendorl said.

Then Belphan, King of Osla, burst spontaneously into flames. He shrieked in agony, and his horse bolted away from the city, its rider roasting to death on its back.

"What the devil are you doing?" King Zorlan cried.

"I am finished dealing with your kind," Offendorl said, but even as he said it he felt something deep inside of him break. It was like a dry twig that snaps under foot. Offendorl doubled over in pain as his magic spread like fire through his gut.

"What does that mean?" Zorlan said. "Are you meaning to kill me, too? I am of royal blood."

There were three generals from Osla and two from Falxis. They looked at one another anxiously, their horses stamping nervously and resisting the riders who tried to calm them down.

"I need food," Offendorl snapped. "Get it," he said through teeth clenched in pain.

He wanted to lie down, but there was no place but the filthy ground. His wagon was gone, and the tent he had given to Belphan and Zorlan was too far away. One of the generals went to bring him something to eat, but Offendorl could tell that he had pushed himself too far. He still had great power, but his physical body could no longer handle the strain.

"Someone help me onto this horse," he groaned.

Another of the generals dismounted and helped Offendorl climb up into the saddle. The wizard's skin was pale.

"I need rest, Zorlan. I trust you can manage this siege with me."

"Yes, of course," King Zorlan said.

"Good, I will be in your tent. If I am needed, come to me there."

Zorlan nodded.

As Offendorl rode slowly away, another rider came galloping up. He threw up a quick salute and then reported on the army's efforts on the far side of the city.

"We have been repelled on all fronts," the soldier said. "Our scaling ladders are pushed off the walls and no one has been successful in breaching the city's defenses."

"Stop the attack," said one of the generals. "Have everyone form up here, on this side of the city. There's no need to waste our strength trying to scale the walls. The main gate's been destroyed for us. We can concentrate our efforts there."

"If we are going to continue the attack," said another general, this one from Osla.

"And why wouldn't we?" Zorlan asked.

"Our King is dead," said the soldier.

"But you heard the wizard. He wants the attack to continue."

"I don't fight for him."

"Well," said King Zorlan, "you can certainly be the one to tell him that. As long as you remain on the field of battle, you will carry out your duties as I command you. Now, I agree with General Wessel. Let's concentrate our attack here, at their ruined gate."

* * *

Offendorl wasn't sure if he could climb down off the horse. His body was shaking and he could barely hold his head up. Then, one of his tongueless servants appeared. There was blood soaking the left side of his head, but he was walking normally and seemed well enough to help.

The servant supported Offendorl as the wizard slid down off the horse and then helped him into the tent. The general who had gone in search of food returned to the tent with wine and bread.

"It's all I could find," the general replied.

"It will do," said Offendorl in a weak voice. "Return to your post."

He sipped wine, but the drink only made his stomach hurt worse. He needed to heal himself, but he didn't have the magical strength to do it. He lay back, fearing the worst.

"Go and get the golden crown," he told his servant. "It was in the wagon. You must find it."

The servant hurried away. Offendorl felt his stomach; it was stiff and painful to touch. Something had split apart in his abdomen, and he was bleeding internally. He needed to get help, but he wasn't sure what to do, or where he could get someone to help him. Perhaps if he gave himself time, he would be able to heal himself, but he didn't know. Never in his life had he been so helpless, and the feeling terrified him.

He forced himself to eat, even though he knew he would only vomit the food back up. Still, eating and drinking had always been the way he restored his magical powers in the past. The wine burned down his throat and set his stomach on fire. He waited as long as he could, but soon he felt himself growing sleepy. He knew if he fell asleep he could die or become too weak to work magic. He had to heal himself now, or he was lost.

He let his mind look into his stomach. The effort was excruciating, but he managed to see the problem. His stomach had torn loose from his small intestines. Blood and food were filling his body cavity. He would have to deal with the blood later. He focused on healing his organs. It took longer than he expected, but he was able to repair the damage. The pain eased considerably, and he passed out.

* * *

Zollin and Quinn had climbed up to the ramparts of the city wall, near the destroyed main gate. They had a clear view of the army that was regrouping along the vast plain that spread out in front of the city. Zollin remembered seeing the city for the first time from the high hills in the distance. There had been a sprawling village of makeshift homes and shops in the plain, but they had been destroyed in anticipation of the siege. Now it was a killing field that the troops would have to cross in order to attack the city.

Zollin looked back, just inside the city gate. Commander Hausey had soldiers lined up, ready to make a human wall across the expanse left vacant by the ruined gate. He also had men stationed on the mounds of rubble that Zollin had built up against the city walls. The King had arrived only moments before with his generals. They were inspecting the lines of defense with approval. Commander Hausey had done his work well.

Zollin turned back to the empty plain and began stirring up an immense cloud of dust. The dirt rose into the air, swirling and churning until it blocked Zollin's view of the opposing army. Then he sent fear and panic through his magic toward the invaders. Soon he could feel their terror as the dust cloud approached.

"Now," he told Quinn.

His father signaled to Commander Corlis, who had been waiting with the entire force of Orrock's Heavy Horse. Whereas the cavalry in Felson were considered light horse, meaning their horses were smaller and built for long-distance riding, the Heavy Horse squad consisted of half a legion of fully armored riders.

427

Their mounts were large warhorses, slower than the light cavalry but bred for war: they would kick and trample anyone who got in their way. The horses' massive weight made them difficult to bring down in a melee, and when they were moving at a full gallop, nothing could stop their charge.

Quinn waved his arms, and Commander Corlis lowered his visor and raised his own arm. The cavalry filed out of the ruined gate and formed a long line between the city and the opposing army. The riders were completely hidden by Zollin's dust cloud. Commander Corlis gave another command, and the horses started at a trot, quickly accelerated to a canter, and then reached a rumbling gallop. They covered the ground between the city wall and the opposing army in less than a minute. Zollin's dust cloud had moved out in front of the cavalry, enveloping the opposing army, and he could sense that the invaders' panic had devolved into chaos. The enemy soldiers were turning on one another.

"Havoc!" cried Commander Corlis to his troops, ordering them to fight as wildly as possible.

The horses smashed into the unprepared soldiers. Their officers had heard the thunder of hooves, but in the cloud of dirt they couldn't control their own troops. The cavalry soldiers used long lances, dealing death en masse to the foot soldiers across the plain.

The thunder of hooves diminished as the horses slowed in the throng of soldiers, to be replaced by the cries of the wounded. Men screaming in agony was a sound that Zollin knew he would never forget. It made the hair on the back of his neck stand up, and his bowels felt watery. He was glad that he was high on the city wall, rather than trapped between the panicking soldiers and the massive horses. Once their lances snapped, the soldiers drew long swords. The heavy blades were finely honed and cut indiscriminately through armor, flesh, and bone.

Five hundred men faced well over four thousand, but the Heavy Horse soldiers were practically unstoppable, and Zollin's dust storm terrified the invaders. More men were killed by their brothers in arms, either due to sheer panic or mistaken identity, than by the Yelsian cavalry.

* * *

"What is that?" King Zorlan asked his generals, who were gathered with him behind the massive army that was forming in ranks ranging along the plain before Orrock's main gate.

The dust cloud was just beginning to form, and a sense of unease was settling over the army. They watched as the cloud thickened and moved toward them. Some men broke and ran, only to be cut down by others. Desertion was not tolerated in any army.

"I do not know, my King," said the Falxis general. "But it is coming this way."

"We need to fall back," said King Zorlan.

"But, Sire, we were told to attack."

"Send the army. Send them all forward. I don't want that cloud to reach me."

"All ranks move forward!" the general shouted, but the order was only half-heartedly repeated down the line. The rows and rows of soldiers didn't move.

"I said, send them forward!" King Zorlan said in a high-pitched, frightened voice.

The general beside him grew angry. He turned and threw a punch at his King, who fell from his horse.

"You send them forward!" the general screamed at him.

Then the gathered generals heard the sounds of the army as it began to panic. The dust cloud had reached them, and the men were breaking and running. Some were using their weapons on their own countrymen. It was a total disaster.

When the cavalry broke through the cloud, the army offered no resistance. Even after the cloud dissipated and Zollin stopped casting his spell of dread and fear, the invaders were terrified. They ran screaming in all directions.

The noise woke Offendorl. His eunuch had just returned with the heavy golden crown. It had been in the wizard's massive wagon that Zollin had destroyed. The soft metal had been dented and bent out of shape on one side by the blast, but it still fit on Offendorl's head.

"What is happening?" the wizard asked.

The eunuch had no way to communicate what was happening, but Offendorl didn't expect a reply. He sat up, and the pain in his stomach made him dizzy. He knew he needed more time to rest and heal himself, but from the sounds of things, he didn't have any time left.

"Put it on my head," he ordered.

The servant raised the helmet and settled it over the wizard's wispy, gray hair. Offendorl felt a shock of power that once again wrenched his physical body, but he held himself together. The dragon was not as far away as Offendorl had feared. Obviously the beast wasn't able to venture far from its master now.

"Come to me," he ordered the beast.

He left the golden helmet on his head only long enough to make sure the dragon was obeying, then he ordered his servant to lift it off him.

"Get my horse ready. We can't stay here," he said.

The servant hurried out of the tent, and Offendorl sagged back onto the bed. Fear was taking root in the old wizard's mind. He was losing this war, he recognized now. He wasn't sure if he would be able to restore enough of his physical strength to match Zollin in direct combat again. He knew he certainly couldn't anytime soon. He needed to get away from the boy. He needed to get back to where he was strong. Somehow he needed to get back to his tower in Osla, before Zollin could find him and kill him. Every second that passed now was agony. He was terrified that he would be discovered at any moment. The fear of death pressed in on his mind, and Offendorl fled.

* * *

Horns sounded, and the invading army began to retreat. Zollin could see the men fleeing in all directions. Just then King Felix came hurrying up beside him and took in the state of the battle in seconds.

"It's working," he said. "I never would have believed it."

"Never underestimate fear in a battle," Quinn said.

"You can dissipate the dust cloud," Felix said. "We need to communicate with our cavalry and tell them to herd the enemy toward the river."

It took less than two hours to push the invaders back to the Tillamook River. Most dropped their weapons and swam to safety on the other side. King Felix sent a delegation to sue for peace. He graciously offered to escort the armies back to Winsome, if they promised to board their ships and sail for home. Over three thousand men had been killed or wounded in the battle.

Zollin was riding out with Quinn and Mansel, looking for a sign on the battlefield of the wizard he'd fought, when the dragon appeared again. It swung low, but far away from the castle.

"There's the dragon!" Mansel shouted.

Zollin was riding one of the large horses from the King's stables. He kicked the horse into a frantic gallop, but he wasn't fast enough. The dragon wrapped its long tail around someone and took to the air. Zollin knew who it was. Offendorl had called the beast. Zollin could only watch in frustration as the beast flew south.

"What was that?" Quinn said.

"I think it was the wizard," Zollin said.

"The dragon got him?"

"No, he's found a way to control the dragon," Zollin said. "He's using it to escape."

They rode on and found the tongueless eunuch who had seen to Offendorl's needs. He was standing alone. The dragon had eaten the wizard's horse and terrified the servant before taking Offendorl to safety. The Master of the Torr had left his faithful servant to die.

"What do we do with him?" Mansel asked.

"Leave him," Quinn said. "He's just a servant."

"No, he might have useful information," Zollin said.

He dismounted and approached the man. Offendorl's servants were broken, pitiful creatures. They served because they feared their master, and now the man was distraught.

"It's okay," Zollin said. "I'm not going to hurt you. In fact, I can help."

The eunuch shook his head vigorously.

"Please," Zollin said soothingly. "Did you serve the Master of the Torr?"

The man looked like a dog who had been repeatedly beaten by a harsh kennel owner. His eyes were large and terrified. He opened his mouth and bellowed a wordless shriek.

"Oh, please, put him out of his misery," Mansel said.

"No! No one is going to hurt him," Zollin said. "Come with me. I'll look after you."

The man looked relieved, but still skeptical. Zollin mounted his horse and pulled the servant up behind him.

"So what now?" Mansel asked.

"Now we go back to the castle to see if King Felix has any useful information. And then we ride south. This won't be over until the Torr either gives up on me or is destroyed."

"We have to try and save Prince Wilam, too," Mansel said.

"Yes, and perhaps we can learn what happened to Brianna."

Back in the city, the people were celebrating. There were huge bonfires where animals were being roasted and barrels of wine, ale, and cider were being tapped. There was music and dancing in the streets. It reminded Zollin of the harvest festival in Tranaugh Shire, only on a much larger scale.

Zollin rode back to the castle with Quinn and Mansel. All were quiet, each lost in his own thoughts. Quinn was thinking of Miriam. Zollin had shared with his father how he had lifted her across the river the night before, but Quinn was worried that she might not have gotten far enough from the city before the fighting started, or that some of the soldiers who fled across the river might find her. Mansel was filled with guilt. He had murdered an innocent man, and although Quinn and Zollin seemed ready to forgive him, he was having trouble forgiving himself. He wanted revenge on the witch in Lodenhime, but he also wanted to return to Nycoll's cottage on the coast of Felxis. He understood now why she stayed in the forlorn home all alone. There was something peaceful about the cottage and the solitude. He longed to lose himself there and perhaps someday come to terms with his guilt. Zollin was eager to travel south. He wanted desperately to catch up with the dragon and perhaps learn the fate of his beloved. Brianna was never far from his thoughts, and sometimes it took all his will power not to give into the crushing grief and fear that he would never see her again.

At the castle, the officers of the King's Army were feasting in the great hall. King Felix was on his throne with a great banquet table spread before him. Zollin was amazed at how quickly the kitchen staff had prepared food. The battle had only been over perhaps two hours, and yet there were cakes, roast fowl, and mountains of vegetables, bread, and cheese. A huge roasted pig sat carved on one end of the banquet table, and two huge venison hams were on the other. Wine and ale flowed from giant barrels that the servants had tapped and were constantly using to refill pitchers for the tables.

Zollin stood for a moment, gazing at the festivities. He noticed that Commander Hausey wasn't present, nor was Commander Corlis. But the King, his generals, and many of the leading families in Orrock were present. Zollin turned and led the way up to his quarters, followed by Mansel, Quinn, and the eunuch. Inside their rooms Zollin poured a goblet of wine for everyone, even the eunuch.

"Well, to victory I suppose?" Zollin said, holding up his cup.

"To peace," said Quinn, and they drank.

The eunuch didn't raise his own cup. He looked frightened and unsure of himself.

434

"Have a drink, friend. You are safe now. The wizards from the Torr cannot hurt you here."

The eunuch still looked unsure, but he sipped a little of the wine.

"I can't believe how fast it ended," said Mansel.

"Once they lost their advantage in numbers, they had no choice but to retreat," Quinn said. "We're fortunate Zollin bested their wizard."

"Fortunate, indeed," Zollin said. "I got lucky."

"Don't sell yourself short," Mansel said.

"I'm not, but you should have felt the power radiating from him. He was old, but he was strong. I don't think things will be that easy a second time."

"So why not leave it be?" asked Quinn. "No one says you have to go after him."

"I can't just pretend he doesn't want me. If I do that, how long will it be until disaster visits the people we care about again? I have to go. I have to end this, one way or the other."

"Well," Quinn said sadly. "I understand. When we left Tranaugh Shire, things were changing so fast I didn't know what to think. But I can see that you're a man now. I couldn't be more proud of you. But I'm though adventuring. I'm going to Felson, to find Miriam and hopefully settle down."

"I think that's great, dad," said Zollin. "You deserve to be happy."

"Well, I won't be truly happy until you are."

Zollin smiled sadly. He couldn't imagine ever being happy again. Then Mansel spoke up.

"I want to go with you, Zollin. I have unfinished business in Lodenhime, and I owe it to you to help," he said sadly. "And then, when all this is over, if I'm still alive, I'm going back to Falxis. I met someone there that I care deeply about. I promised her I would return, and I mean to keep that promise."

"You don't owe us anything. I'm as much to blame for Kelvich's death as you are," Zollin said. "He warned me that something was wrong with you. If I had just listened he might still be alive."

"You are both being too hard on yourselves," Quinn said. "The thing to remember is that Kelvich lived a good life, and we were a part of making it a good life. He was a grown man, who lived longer than most men can dream of, and he was one of the wisest people I've ever met. You don't have to act like his passing isn't a tragedy, but you mustn't take on the blame. Remember him for the man he was, not the unfortunate way he died."

Zollin and Mansel pondered this for a moment. And then Zollin turned to eunuch. The timid servant was sitting in one of the thickly padded chairs and sipping his wine, obviously grateful to be alive.

"And now it's time to finish this," said Zollin to the eunuch. "And you, my friend, are going to help me."

* * *

The next morning, as the four men were preparing to leave, King Felix arrived and asked to see them. He was bleary-eyed, but alert. It was early morning, and most of the city was still sleeping off the excesses of the night before. Their celebrations had lasted long into the night, but Quinn and Mansel had stayed busy preparing their supplies for the journey ahead while Zollin questioned the eunuch. It was difficult to communicate, since the servant had no tongue to speak with and could not read or write. They had to use hand signals, but the eunuch was able to tell Zollin how many servants there were at the Torr and how many other magic users. It wasn't the most valuable intelligence, but it was better than nothing. The man, whom Zollin had named Eustace, was willing to travel with them and help them in their quest to defeat the Master of the Torr.

King Felix found them in the stables. He was hurrying to catch up with them before they left.

"Where are you going?" he asked. "We missed you at the feast last night."

"I'm sure you did," Zollin replied. "But we didn't feel like celebrating. Orrock is safe for the moment, but the Master of Torr escaped. It's only a matter of time before he comes after me again."

"And we shall defeat him again if he does," said King Felix. "There is no need to run and hide."

Zollin spun on his heel, and Mansel drew his sword.

"Boys!" Quinn said loudly. "Don't do anything rash. Mansel, put that sword away."

"We aren't running away," Zollin said. "We're going to finish what we started."

"What do you mean?" King Felix asked.

"I mean we're going to stop the Torr from ever coming after me again."

"What about my son?" the King said. "Where is he?"

"He's alive and well, Sire," Quinn said. "But he's under the spell of a witch in Lodenhime."

"And you three are going to free him?"

"Not me," said Quinn. "I'm retiring."

"We will go to Lodenhime after we deal with the Master of the Torr."

"But what if something happens to Prince Wilam?"

"You have an entire army," Zollin said. "Send someone else to rescue the Prince."

"You are refusing me?" the King said angrily. "After all I've done for you? I gave you rooms in my castle. Everything in this kingdom is yours if you need it."

"I know you think of everything in this kingdom as your own personal possession," Zollin said angrily, "including the people who live here. But we are not your slaves. I have not forgotten the drugs you put in my food or your intentions to hand me over to the Torr."

"You volunteered to go," said King Felix.

"Are you mad? I offered to go and you counseled against it. If you thought I was truly willing to go, why did you drug me?"

"I only did that at the urging of my generals. They thought you might change your mind."

"You are a liar," Zollin spat. "You do not deserve to wear that crown. You are no different than Simmeron."

"You overstep your bounds, wizard!" King Felix said angrily.

"And you yours. We are leaving," Zollin said as he climbed onto his horse. "Step aside."

"If you leave, you shall never be welcome in this city again."

"Goodbye, Your Highness," Zollin said sarcastically.

They rode out of the stable and out of the castle courtyard.

"Well, that was awkward," Mansel said.

"He's a pompous fool," Zollin said.

They rode through the city, and their horses' hooves clipping and clopping on the cobblestones was the only sound. At the city gate, which was now guarded by an entire century of soldiers, they passed out of the city and reined up their horses.

"So what's your plan?" Quinn asked.

"We ride south," Zollin said. "I guess we'll retrace your route to Osla."

"Well, be careful. When this is all over I expect to see you in Felson," Quinn said. "Goodbye, Mansel. I hope you find happiness."

"And you as well, Quinn," Mansel said, his voice thick with emotion. "You've been better than a father to me. I'm sorry again for the pain I've caused you and your family."

"I have no regrets," Quinn said, smiling. "You're a good man. Never forget that."

They embraced, and then Quinn turned to Zollin.

"I love you," he said.

Zollin smiled. "I know, dad, I love you, too."

They shared one last embrace, and then they turned their horses and went their separate ways. Zollin led Lilly, laden with their supplies. Eustace the eunuch and Mansel followed him. Quinn followed the Weaver's Road east, toward Felson.

* * *

Far to the south, Offendorl was being rowed out to a ship. Bartoom the dragon had carried him to the coast and then stayed with him through the night. Offendorl had sent the beast away to wait for him in the Walheta mountains while Offendorl booked passage south on a trade ship. He had been forced to pawn part of his golden crown in order to pay for his passage and buy supplies.

The old wizard was physically spent. His abdomen was swollen from the internal bleeding, which the wizard had healed, but he had not had time to clear all the old blood and bile from his body. He needed time to rest and mend, which Offendorl planned to get during his journey on the ship.

He also needed time to think. Offendorl was angry at himself. Nothing about the invasion had gone the way he expected, and he couldn't help but wonder if he had somehow lost touch with reality. The power Zollin possessed was not as great as his own, but perhaps he had come to rely too much on knowledge. His vast intellect had not helped him in his battle with a younger, faster opponent. Offendorl knew he needed to hone his skills and build his strength if he was to face Zollin again. And that prospect was all he could think of. He was not giving up, now that time and distance had eased the fear that had driven him away from Orrock. He was the Master of the Torr, he thought reassuringly, and he wouldn't stop until all the magical power in the Five Kingdoms was his, including Zollin's. He would bring the boy under his control, or see him dead.

Epilogue

Brianna had been working for days, perhaps weeks; she wasn't sure. She was neither hungry nor tired. She was focused on one thing only, the task at hand. Her fire had burned through the mountain, straight down into the deliciously warm bowels of the earth. And there she had begun to create life. It was not a child, not a human or even a Fire Spirit baby. She was giving life to her own kind, to dragonkind.

She heated the stone until it was more fire than rock. She formed the dragon's shape, from its horned crown to the tip of its tail. She labored over every detail, lovingly working and shaping the molten ore until it glowed with heat, which was life to her kind.

Finally, she had to give the dragon the spark of life. It was not an easy task, and she could not explain how she knew what to do. She breathed fire onto and into her offspring. Over and over again she breathed life into the beast. She felt it coming to life, felt its awareness growing. The beast was almost alive. All that it needed now was gold and a name: then the dragon would live, and they could leave the mountains together. She knew that the time for her kind to rise was coming, the time when dragons would sway the balance of power in the world. She had to be ready. Zollin would be waiting for her, and she refused to let him down.

We hope you have enjoyed
Crying Havoc

The adventure continues in
Fierce Loyalty
Five Kingdoms Book Five

Learn more about Toby and his
books at
www.TobyNeighbors.com

30670496R00274